PHANTASM

PHANTASM

— Book I —

CHRISTOPHER HALL
AKA MAXLEX

Podium

To my readers on Royal Road,
who started all this

Published in 2023 by Podium Publishing, ULC
www.podiumaudio.com

Podium

PHANTASM

CHARACTER GENERATION

I didn't experience the transition, or maybe I just don't remember it. I was at my computer watching YouTube, and then . . . I was lying on the ground. Naked.

What the fuck?

I sat up and looked around frantically. It was dark, but I could make out shapes. Before I could identify anything, though, glowing letters appeared in front of my eyes. I jerked my head back and then tried to dodge as the letters followed me. I fell over before working out what was going on, and calmed down enough to read them.

[Body Development] Level 1 awarded (free skill).
For gaining a skill level, you have been awarded 1 XP.
[Stamina Development] Level 1 awarded (free skill).
For gaining a skill level, you have been awarded 1 XP.

I stared at the notifications, not really grasping what was going on as they scrolled by.

[Female] trait awarded. +1 bonus to Charisma.
[Worldwalker] trait awarded. Level prerequisites for professions are overridden. +1 bonus to all stats.
[Gift of Tongues] trait awarded. All languages are understood.

I stared at the writing until it went away. Then I noticed that there were more words at the bottom of my vision.

> [Unspent Ability Points] : 240
> [Unspent Skill Points] : 15
> [Unspent Development Points] : 48

I closed my eyes and the words were still there. I put my hands to my face, but I couldn't feel any goggles or even anything hidden under my skin.

What the fuck?

I don't like to repeat myself, but I think the situation deserved it. I think I would have kept repeating that thought another fifty times, but I was suddenly reminded that I was naked in a strange room. By the sound of heavy breathing.

OK! Panic time! My eyes snapped open, and I peered around frantically, trying to find the source. Another notification popped up—

> [Perception] skill unlocked.

—but I didn't let that distract me from identifying my surroundings. It was pretty dark, but there was enough light to tell that . . .

I'm in a barn?

I really was. Packed earth floor, straw everywhere, tools and stalls for animals. The breathing sound was coming from what looked like horses sleeping in one of the stalls.

> [Identify] skill unlocked.

Sleeping, because it was night. What light there was seemed to be coming from outside, probably moonlight. Aside from them, and maybe some other animals farther down, I was entirely alone.

What the— No. Focus. I needed clothes, a weapon . . . I got up as quietly as I could and checked out the rest of the barn. I confirmed the presence of sheep and cows, all of them asleep or keeping quiet. I stayed well away from them in case they made a noise when woken up. I glanced over at the assortment of farming implements. There was an axe that would make for a nice weapon, but I just noted it for now. I didn't have anything to use it on, and I needed my hands free. I didn't see any clothes but there were some . . . blankets in the corner. Probably for the horses. They were smelly and itchy, but I wrapped one around me. It wasn't freezing in here, but it was colder than I wanted it to be. Now "dressed," I investigated the double door that was my exit.

It was locked, sort of. There was a couple of centimeters' gap between the doors and I could see that a thick bar had been placed on the other side, securing the doors in place. I could probably get a tool through and lift it, but it would make a lot of noise falling down.

It was at this point that I noticed the walls of the barn were made of stone, which I thought odd. Whenever I'd seen a barn in a movie, it had been a big old wooden structure. *Eh, it's not like I know anything about farming*, I thought. Looking higher, I saw that the upper level *was* made of wood, and had some big openings that were letting the moonlight in. And the warmth out, I supposed.

This . . . doesn't seem like a kidnapping. It was a stupid thought, but that had been my initial assumption. I'd been drugged and dragged out to this rural location, stripped and . . . left here? It didn't make sense. I didn't feel any soreness or . . . stickiness, so I probably hadn't been abused. I wasn't sure I'd be able to tell, but I felt . . . pretty great, actually. No hangover from whatever drug had been used. And of course there were the notifications. Now that I'd checked out my immediate surroundings, I returned my attention to the writing.

[Unspent Ability Points] : 240 **[Unspent Skill Points] : 15** **[Unspent Development Points] : 48**

It was only natural that I thought about spending Ability points while looking at the first line, and when I did a new notification popped up.

Ability	Actual	Base	Cost
[Strength]	2	1	1
[Agility]	2	1	1
[Finesse]	2	1	1
[Soul]	2	1	1
[Intelligence]	2	1	1
[Charisma]	3	1	1
Unspent Ability Points	240		

This is a role-playing game.

I thought really hard, but I didn't remember anything close to this sort of realism being available in VR. There was no way! We were decades away from this kind of realism! Could someone have kidnapped me to make me test their cutting-edge VR game? It . . . didn't seem likely. Had I died and been reincarnated in a video game? I didn't know how to start evaluating the likelihood of that. But . . .

QUIT.

EXIT.

END PROGRAM.

CTRL-C.

ESC.

I couldn't stop it. Unless I wanted to try dying, I was going to have to play the game.

So what commands did work?

Inventory. No result.

Character. No result.

[Status]. Just thinking *[Status].* Just thinking the word felt different, and there was a result.

Name	Kandis Hammond		
Level	1	[Unspent Ability Points]	240
Age	24	[Unspent Skill Points]	15
Abilities		[Unspent Development Points]	48
[Strength]	2		
[Agility]	2	[HP]	20
[Finesse]	2	[Stamina]	20
[Soul]	2		
[Intelligence]	2		
[Charisma]	3		

Skills			
[Body Development]	1		
[Stamina Development]	1		
Unlocked Skills			
[Perception] [Identify]			
Traits			
[Worldwalker]		Level prerequisites for professions are overridden. +1 bonus to all stats.	
[Gift of Tongues]		All languages are understood.	
[Female]		+1 bonus to Charisma.	

Oh, nice. I bet the [Male] trait gets extra strength. Again, just thinking about the Male trait felt different, and sure enough some text appeared.

> [Male] +1 bonus to Strength (0 points, overwrites [Female]).

Way to stereotype, game designers. It looked like the text in square brackets could be . . . clicked on, for want of a better word. To test it, I looked at something I didn't understand.

> [Body Development] : This skill determines your health and how much damage you can take.

That sounded important. Did that mean it determined HP?

> [HP] : When you run out of Health Points, you die. Determined by [Strength] x [Body Development] x 10.

Yeah, important. Wait, that meant if I didn't have Body Development, I'd have zero HP? I guess that's why I got it for free at the start then. Stamina would be something similar then . . .

[Stamina] : When you run out of Stamina, you fall unconscious. Determined by [Strength] x [Stamina Development] x 10.

Yeah. I started going through all the entries on the status page. I'd played RPGs before, so none of this was completely alien. Most games had just one value that covered all aspects of a character's nimbleness, so splitting them up into a whole-body Agility and hand-to-eye Finesse was a bit different, but I could see how it would work. Soul was a little unfamiliar but it turned out to be pretty much what some games called Wisdom or Willpower. Maybe it was time to look at spending some points.

[Ability Points], I thought and brought up the notification.

Ability	Actual	Base	Cost
[Strength]	2	1	1
[Agility]	2	1	1
[Finesse]	2	1	1
[Soul]	2	1	1
[Intelligence]	2	1	1
[Charisma]	3	1	1
Unspent Ability Points	240		

Now what Ability am I definitely going to need? They all looked important. Intelligence was probably up there; it seemed important for magic. This game, or whatever it was, better have magic. But the only thing I really knew it had at the moment was people. People skills were always useful . . . I added one to Charisma.

Ability	Actual	Base	Cost
[Strength]	2	1	2
[Agility]	2	1	2
[Finesse]	2	1	2
[Soul]	2	1	2

[Intelligence]	2	1	2
[Charisma]	4	2	9
Unspent Ability Points	**239**		

Whoa! Everything went up! That must mean—I did a little math. It must be that the cost of each Ability was the sum of all the Abilities . . . multiplied by the current level of that Ability? That didn't exactly match up, but—aha—a constant scaling factor to take the first level's cost down to one. That was . . . nasty. 240 points didn't look like as much as it did before, and there was something else to consider.

The order you buy stats in matters . . . For the most effective spend, I should buy the Ability I wanted to get highest, then buy the next highest stat and so on. Anything else would waste points . . . which meant I needed to calculate my entire stat buy before I went any further. Maybe leave this to later.

[Skill Points].

> [Unspent Skill Points]: 15
> Unlocked skills available:
> [Perception] [+] : detect hidden, concealed or obscured things.
> [Identify] [+] : gain information about target object or creature.

I couldn't spend Skill points on existing skills? Both those skills sounded really useful, though. I purchased both of them.

> [Perception] Level 1 purchased.
> For gaining a skill level, you have been awarded 1 XP.
> [Identify] Level 1 purchased.
> For gaining a skill level, you have been awarded 1 XP.

Huh. It did get a bit brighter in here. Not much, but . . . noticeable. I looked over at the horse in his stall. *[Identify].*

> Identification failed.

I tried again.

> **Identification failed.**

And again.

> **[Identification] : Horse (Female) – Threat Level: 2**

Of course I got the sex wrong. Well, it wasn't much, but perhaps it would get better when the level improved. I looked around the barn, Identifying everything in sight. It seemed to work about one time in five, and I didn't get any improvements. Onwards.

[Development Points].

> **[Professions] : Each profession, when taken, replaces any existing profession. Skill bonuses are replaced; skill unlocks remain.**
>
> **[Social] : Denotes membership of organizations, ownership of property, and titles. They can be acquired without Development points.**
>
> **[Innate] : Denotes inherent abilities that are not covered by a skill.**

Options, huh. [Professions].

A long list of professions scrolled by. I saw some that looked like wizards, but there were too many and they flowed by too fast to really see. At the end, though, was a note:

> **Query by: [Name], [Type], [Level Requisite], [Ability Requisite], [Skill Unlocks], [Skill Requirement], [Skill Bonus].**

Well, I'm trapped in this barn until daybreak; might as well get some reading done.

I learned a lot, but some things remained a mystery. For example, nothing I found described how skills worked, only which professions got what. Professions had requirements, mostly Level, Abilities, and a Skill. They unlocked some skill and gave bonuses to other skills. The higher the prerequisites, the better the bonuses. I didn't have to worry about the level requirements, but I did still need the abilities and skills.

I didn't want to waste my Ability points, so I looked to see if there were magic professions with a high Charisma requirement. There were:

[Beguiler] : Req: Level 3 – Charisma 6 – Mana Sense
[Illusionist] : Req: Level 3 – Charisma 6 – Mana Sense
[Mind Arcanist] : Req: Level 7 – Charisma 7 – Soul 4 – Mind Magic
[Phantasmal Artificer] : Req: Level 7 – Charisma 7 – Intelligence 4 –
Illusion Magic
[Bard] : Req: Level 3 – Charisma 6 – Play Instrument
[High Priest] : Level 7 – Soul 7 – Charisma 4 – Divine Magic

Looking at the prerequisites, Mind Arcanist and Phantasmal Artificer were upgrades of the Beguiler and Illusionist classes, so there were really only two choices there. High Priest and Bard weren't really choices. I didn't want to play music for a living, and I didn't even know what gods got worshipped here. *[Beguiler]*.

Profession: Beguiler
Development Cost: 10
Description: The Beguiler lures both men and monsters to their doom with enchanting magic through the medium of their voice.
Prerequisites: Level 3 – Charisma 6 – Sing
Skill Unlocks: [Mind Magic], [Mana Sense], [Mana Development]
Skill Bonuses: [Sing], [Mind Magic], [Mana Development] , [Weapon Mastery – Dagger], [Persuade]
Extra: 15 Spell Levels for each level of [Mind Magic]

I started calling up the Help for spells in the Mind Magic category. They were . . . pretty nasty. Sleep was as nice as it got; the rest were various forms of mind control and inflicting agonizing pain and disability. I supposed it wasn't as bad as throwing fireballs at people, but still. *[Illusionist]*.

Profession: Illusionist
Development Cost: 10
Description: The Illusionist tricks and deceives, leading others astray, and turns their own strength against them.
Prerequisites: Level 3 – Charisma 6 – Mana Sense
Skill Unlocks: [Illusion Magic], [Creativity], [Disguise]

> **Skill Bonuses:** [Illusion Magic] +2 , [Deceive], [Mana Development] ,
> **[Weapon Mastery – Dagger]**
> **Extra: 15 Spell Levels for each level of** [Illusion Magic]

Now, Illusion Magic was much nicer. Not completely without combat potential, Blind and Invisibility for example. And illusions were cheap. Invisibility was only fifteen spell levels to Fireball's fifty.

OK, so let's see if we can get the stats for Illusionist, or maybe the upgrade. I started working it out. It was a pain to calculate. I had to work out the costs for each level, while keeping track of the points I'd spent . . .Why was I doing this in my head? I found a knife amongst the tools and started scratching numbers into the dirt to keep track of where I was.

> **Competency displayed with [Scribe], Level 1 awarded.**
> **For gaining a skill level, you have been awarded 1 XP.**
> **Competency displayed with [Calculate], Level 1 awarded.**
> **For gaining a skill level, you have been awarded 1 XP.**

Huh, that was a full skill level, not just an unlock. I checked and my unspent Skill points remained the same. *Free skills, nice.* And now I could . . . bemusedly, I let my hand scratch out ten symbols that I'd never seen before. One through ten in the numeric system of this world. Somehow, I knew that it was like Roman numerals, but with a different symbol for each number up to ten. Plus fifty, 100, 500, and 1,000. *Another world that needs to be introduced to proper Arabic notation,* I thought to myself.

Continuing on, I worked out the numbers and then bought the stats. When I was done, the block looked like this:

Ability	Actual	Base	Cost
[Strength]	3	2	31
[Agility]	3	2	31
[Finesse]	3	2	31
[Soul]	3	2	31
[Intelligence]	4	3	49
[Charisma]	9	7	121

Unspent Ability Points	14

Maybe I went a little overboard on Charisma? Not sure if I'll get more Ability points again . . . The next step was to get Mana Sense, but I'd already found the obvious profession for this. I purchased the Apprentice profession and looked at my status again.

Name	Kandis Hammond	Profession	Apprentice
Level	1	[Unspent Ability Points]	14
Age	24	[Unspent Skill Points]	13
Abilities		[Unspent Development Points]	43
[Strength]	3		
[Agility]	3	[HP]	30
[Finesse]	3	[Stamina]	30
[Soul]	3		
[Intelligence]	4		
[Charisma]	9		
Skills			
[Body Development]	1		
[Stamina Development]	1		
[Perception]	1		
[Identify]	1		
[Scribe]	1		
[Calculate]	1		
[Dodge]	0 (1)		

[Persuade]	0 (1)		
Unlocked Skills			
[Mana Sense] [Mana Development]			
Traits			
[Worldwalker]		**Level prerequisites for professions are overridden. +1 bonus to all stats.**	
[Gift of Tongues]		**All languages are understood.**	
[Female]		**+1 bonus to Charisma.**	

Dodge and Persuade were on the list because of Apprentice bonuses, I supposed. Could I use a skill even if it wasn't unlocked? It was hard to tell, as I didn't have anyone to Dodge or Persuade. I guess most people would have unlocked the skills before they became an Apprentice. That put me in a bit of a dilemma. Those skill bonuses would probably help me "Demonstrate Competence" and get me the skill for free. But those bonuses would go away when I moved on to my next profession. I didn't want to lose two Skill points, but I really didn't want to face possibly hostile farmers without Illusion magic. So I moved on to the next stage. Oh, but wait! I had Identify at 2 now.

I went around and Identified everything again. Sure enough, this time it worked pretty much every time. No extra information, though. OK, moving on.

Wait.

I'd gotten so worked up on Professions that I'd forgotten the other tabs, Social and Innate. Checking them out, it seemed that Social was a bunch of traits relating to ownership of things and membership of groups. Some of them . . . no, all of them really, were kinda weird. Take Family, for instance.

[Family]: **You have a family that loves and protects you (10 points).**

If I bought that, would my family appear here as well? Would the system create a bunch of people that would be my family members? Or would a random bunch of people suddenly think I was related to them? Some of the others were less problematic, but I had similar questions. If I purchased Homeowner, was a new house created? Someone evicted? The description didn't say. I decided to steer clear of that section for now.

Innate had its own problematic options. These options were things about you that you could purchase, including your race. I looked down at myself. *Do I want to be an elf?* I still felt like myself; would that change if my body changed? Actually, had it changed? It seemed pretty much the same. I resolved to check more thoroughly the first chance I got. *No racial changes.*

Some of the other options were less concerning. They were abilities that didn't seem to fit into the skill system, like Night Vision.

[Night Vision]: **Allows you to see more clearly in darkness (5 points).**

There was some meta-magic stuff, like [Multi-cast] which let you cast two of the same spell at once. Two of them looked important for an Illusionist.

[Silent Casting]: **Allows you to cast spells without a chant (10 points).**
[Subtle Casting]: **Allows you to cast spells without gestures (5 points).**

So spells needed chanting and gestures, apparently. Well, not for me! At least if I could afford this . . . I went back and checked. Yes! Time to proceed.

I purchased Silent Casting, Subtle Casting, Mana Sense, and Mana Development, and then Illusionist. Then I purchased Illusion Magic.

[Status].

Name	Kandis Hammond	Profession	Illusionist
Level	1	[Unspent Ability Points]	14
Age	24	[Unspent Skill Points]	11
Abilities		[Unspent Development Points]	18
[Strength]	3	[Unspent Spell Levels]	15
[Agility]	3	[HP]	30
[Finesse]	3	[Stamina]	30
[Soul]	3	[Mana]	60
[Intelligence]	4		
[Charisma]	9		
Skills			
[Body Development]	1		
[Stamina Development]	1		
[Perception]	1		
[Identify]	1		
[Scribe]	1		
[Calculate]	1		
[Mana Sense]	1		
[Mana Development]	1 (2)		
[Illusion Magic]	1 (3)		
[Deceive]	0 (1)		
[WM: Dagger]	0 (1)		

Unlocked Skills		
[Creativity] [Disguise]		
Traits		
[Worldwalker]	Level prerequisites for professions are overridden. +1 bonus to all stats,	
[Gift of Tongues]	All languages are understood.	
[Female]	+1 bonus to Charisma.	
[Silent Casting]	Allows you to cast spells without a chant.	
[Subtle Casting]	Allows you to cast spells without gestures.	

So many new things. I should start with the basic spells; I'd have more points for advanced spells later. I purchased Static Illusion, Unseen Sound, and Light for five levels each. Two of those spells were out right now, as they might attract attention, but . . . somehow I knew the right chant and the gestures I needed to cast Static Illusion. My first magic spell!

The illusion of a single, unmoving object took form in front of me. The object I'd chosen was . . . a mirror. Yes, a full-length, freestanding mirror. Look, it's not that I'm vain—I'd just appeared in another world, and I needed to know if I was still me or not. There was no one to see, so I dropped the blanket and took a good look.

My first reaction was relief. *I'm still me!* Then, doubt. Was that really me? That looked like my face, but was I ever that good-looking before? And my body . . . I'd never been entirely happy with my body; what woman is? But looking at the me in the mirror . . . my breasts were maybe a bit bigger, a bit differently shaped? My hips a little wider, my waist a little thinner . . . small changes but they added up to . . . *Damn, girl, you are gorgeous!*

I was dirty, but that just made me look achingly vulnerable. My hair was a mess, but somehow it just looked "artfully tousled." I wasn't gay, but looking at myself, I was having second thoughts. If this was nine Charisma, then this world couldn't be all bad.

OK, focus. You've still got points to spend. I pulled the blanket up again. I had two more bonuses for skills I didn't have. I wanted to try turning them into free skills, but there wasn't anyone to deceive. I had a knife, but . . . *If I'm going to "demonstrate competence," I'll probably have to stab someone—or something.* I looked at the sheep. *Nope, not going to do it, let's move on.* I'd probably have to stab something at some point, but I wasn't going to risk angering the farmers by stabbing their animals.

I had more spells to cast. Looking into the mirror, I tried holding my head still and overlaying it with a static image of another face. If you must know, it was of a certain pop star that I'd had on my wall for years. I was pretty familiar with that face. Being in the image blocked out sight, which was a surprise, but I kept myself in place, giving the trick a minute to work.

Only it didn't. *Maybe illusions are cheating?* Disguise seemed like a useful skill to have, though, so I bought it.

> **[Disguise] Level 1 purchased.**
> **For gaining a skill level, you have been awarded 1 XP.**

I canceled both of the illusions. There was a small Mana cost to sustain them—cheaper than casting them, but I didn't feel the need to pay it. Looking at the wall, I tried to remember a painting I'd seen and reproduce it on the wall. One spell later, and a decent reproduction of Munch's *The Scream* was hanging on the wall. I'm no art historian, but that was the one that came to mind.

It's possible I wasn't dealing with being transported to another world as well as my calm experimentation would suggest.

> **Competency displayed with [Creativity], Level 1 awarded.**
> **For gaining a skill level, you have been awarded 1 XP.**

Clearly the System wasn't familiar with Earth art, but it knew what it liked. Time for the upgrade. I purchased Phantasmal Artificer.

[Status].

Name	Kandis Hammond	Profession	Phantasmal Artificer
Level	1	[Unspent Ability Points]	14
Age	24	[Unspent Skill Points]	10
Abilities		[Unspent Development Points]	3
[Strength]	3	[Unspent Spell Levels]	30
[Agility]	3	[HP]	30
[Finesse]	3	[Stamina]	28/30
[Soul]	3	[Mana]	50/60
[Intelligence]	4		
[Charisma]	9		
Skills			
[Body Development]	1		
[Stamina Development]	1		
[Perception]	1		
[Identify]	1		
[Scribe]	1		
[Calculate]	1		
[Mana Sense]	1		
[Mana Development]	1 (2)		
[Illusion Magic]	1 (4)		

[Creativity]	1		
[Disguise]	1		
[Deceive]	0 (2)		
[WM: Dagger]	0 (1)		
[Charm]	0 (1)		
[Conversation]	0 (1)		
Unlocked Skills			
[Enchanting] [Intrigue] [Memorize] [Research] [Teach]			
Traits			
[Worldwalker]		Level prerequisites for professions are overridden. +1 bonus to all stats.	
[Gift of Tongues]		All languages are understood.	
[Female]		+1 bonus to Charisma.	
[Silent Casting]		Allows you to cast spells without a chant.	
[Subtle Casting]		Allows you to cast spells without gestures.	
Spells			**Mana**
[Static Image]	Creates an unmoving image of a single object not more than 1 cubic meter in volume (upkeep 1/hour).		5
[Light]	Creates a light that can be moved, brightened, or dimmed (upkeep 1/hour).		5
[Unseen Sound]	Creates a sound from a source you designate (upkeep 1/hour).		5

Watch out, world! A level seven profession and I'm only level one! I now had spell points to spend, so I picked one that looked immediately relevant to my survival.

[**Simple Invisibility**]: **People and creatures are unable to see you (15 points).**

Blind was also fifteen points, but I didn't want to neglect the social side.

[**Disguise**]: **Modify your appearance and clothing as required (15 points).**

Then I took a look at the unlocked skills.

[**Enchanting**]: **Using runes, create permanent spell effects.**
[**Intrigue**]: **Safely negotiate the treacherous ground of politics and the Court.**
[**Memorize**]: **Perfectly recall details of what you have witnessed.**
[**Research**]: **Glean hidden knowledge from books. Allows training in skills from manuals.**
[**Teach**]: **Allows you to train others in academic or magical skills.**

Hmm . . . None of these looked bad, but they seemed more like skills I'd want after I established myself. I was going to stick with Phantasmal Artificer for a while, so I decided to wait before spending Skill points on them. I still had four skills on my list that I would need to buy if I couldn't demonstrate competence. What was left? Just three Development points. There wasn't much I could buy for that. I could leave them and hope that I got more later, or . . . maybe I needed to take a look at the Social traits again.

[**Modest Means**]: **You possess enough coin to support you for two weeks (2 points).**

It wasn't much, but it didn't seem like it was risking anything other than the two points. *Fuck it.*

I made the purchase.

One of my hands got suddenly heavier, and when I looked, I was holding a small leather pouch. *What the fuck?* I poured the contents out on my palm. There were fourteen coins in it, ten copper and four silver, all shiny new like they'd just been minted. The copper coins were stamped with a picture of a small bird, maybe a sparrow, while the silver coins had a bigger bird. Both of them had a picture of a tree on the other side.

> **[Identification] : Copper sparrows – 10**
> **[Identification] : Silver hawks – 4**

Oh, thank you, Identification skill, I might have never worked that out. I'm not sure why, but seeing these physical objects appear out of nowhere struck me pretty hard. I'd felt myself getting stronger and smarter when I bought stats, I'd actually cast a magic spell, but somehow the cold metal in my hands made it all seem real. I stared at them for a long time, but I had to move on.

What's next? Um . . . Nothing? I guess the next step was to wait until daylight and see what the farmers were like. I could try breaking out, but that would leave me naked and alone at night trespassing on someone's property, with nowhere to go. Better to see if they took pity on the strange girl. I could always break out the Invisibility spell if I needed to.

Waiting, though, that had its own problems. I thought about trying to get some sleep, but the floor was hard, the straw was scratchy, and so was this blanket. Plus, I was way too keyed up from . . . everything. I started practicing spellcasting to occupy time. I wasn't sure how to get my skills up, but this seemed like a likely method. Static Image took one Stamina and five Mana to cast, and I got six Mana back every hour. I could cast it once every hour without depleting myself, so I just sat back against a wall and waited for my Mana to return. Cast and wait . . . cast and . . .

Oh, I guess I can fall asleep after all, I thought, waking up. Pre-dawn light was coming through the upper windows, but it was the sound of the bar being lifted off the door that had woken me. I drew my blanket around me and prepared to face my destiny.

DEVELOPMENT

"W ho you and what do you be doing in my barn!" A large man had entered and was shouting at me. Despite this being pretty much exactly what I expected, I panicked.

"I-I don't know! I just appeared here, and it was night and I don't have any clothes . . ." Somehow just relating the events of last night made all the terror that I'd been suppressing come back to the fore. "I . . . just want to go home," I managed to get out before breaking down into sobs.

"Ack—Milly!" the man called. Dealing with crying girls was apparently not in his skill set. Milly arrived a few moments later.

"What's going on? My—" She broke off as she took in the scene. "Ah, lass, there's no need for crying . . ." She came in and put her arms around me for a hug. I held on to her and bawled like a baby. It was embarrassing, but I just couldn't stop.

[Charm] skill unlocked.

A short while later, I had clothes and was being fed breakfast, while wondering about that skill unlock. Had I suddenly started crying because that was the "charming" thing to do? Or was crying the right thing to do in this situation and it triggered the unlock? My breakdown had *felt* real, but it did just come out of nowhere.

At least I felt better now. I'd told Milly and Angus what had happened to me, about the status and the points options. I thought about hiding things, but they seemed really nice, and I really needed information about this world. Holding back secrets just made it harder to ask about stuff.

"Worldwalker?" said Angus. He was a large older man, about fifty-ish. His beard and hair were still mostly brownish-red, going on gray, and his face was tanned and weathered by a long time outdoors. "Well, that'd explain things well enough."

"Not to me."

He sighed, and looked away. "We've—our world—has had a few cases of people that come from another world. Not often—the last bunch was near two hundred years ago. But they left an impression."

"They say Worldwalkers are touched by Fate," said Milly. She looked worried. "Whenever they come, it means the world is going to change."

"But I'm just a . . . just a graduate investment analyst. I don't want to change the world."

"You may not have that option, dear. You should keep what you are secret, until you're ready. There are those who would use—twist—the fate of a Worldwalker to their own ends." Milly patted my hand reassuringly. "You might have made the right decision with your class, though. There isn't much better for hiding than an Illusionist."

"I'm only level one, though."

"That's a feat in itself!" Angus laughed. "Don't worry, though; we'll have you up to level two in no time."

"Um, what level are you guys?"

"I'm level four, Milly's at three," said Angus.

"Um . . . is that a lot?" I asked.

Angus shrugged. "It's about average if you're not hunting monsters all the time. Most people get to level two before they're fifteen years old, but it's hard to get to level three just with skill upgrades."

"So how do you get there?"

"Fighting." Angus said, looking a bit grim. "'Gainst humans or monsters, fighting to kill or defeat."

I gulped. "I've never really fought anything before."

He nodded, "Don't worry, we won't send you out into the world before you can handle yourself. At least as well as a teenager."

[Conversation] skill unlocked.

With that reminder of social skills, I purchased both Conversation and Charm.

> [Conversation] Level 1 purchased.
>
> For gaining a skill level, you have been awarded 1 XP.
>
> [Charm] Level 1 purchased.
>
> For gaining a skill level, you have been awarded 1 XP.

"So I'm going to learn to fight with an axe?" I asked uncertainly.

"Well, maybe." Angus grinned. "There's three things we're trying to do here."

He set out a quarter-log of firewood ready for chopping. I'd seen people chop wood before, of course, so I knew what we were doing. He showed me where to put my hands to hold the axe, and smoothly bisected the log. He then handed me the axe and rebalanced one of the pieces on the stump.

"First thing is, we get you a skill unlock for Axe Weapon." He gestured for me to proceed, so I took a swing. The axe glanced off the stick and embedded itself in the stump, while the stick went flying. Angus went and fetched it, while I struggled to free the axe.

"Second thing is, you need to get your Stamina development up." He replaced the stick and I took another swing. Looking at my Stamina, I could see that each swipe was taking me five points. I got three points back every minute, much faster than Mana, but I was running though it fairly quickly. This swing went much the same as the last one, but he didn't look discouraged.

"How long do I do this for?" I asked.

"Ah, I reckon two more swings before taking a rest," Angus said. "As for after that, you'll know when you've done enough."

It ended up taking another twenty minutes, during which I had to switch to the other half of Angus's cut stick, as the first half had been battered beyond standing up. After missing countless times, I finally landed a clean blow, though, and was rewarded with

> [Weapon Mastery: Axe] skill unlocked.

While I was recovering after that achievement, I got another:

> [Stamina Development] Level 2 acquired through use.
>
> For gaining a skill level, you have been awarded 1 XP.

"Whoa! That doubled my Stamina points," I exclaimed.

"Aye, it makes a big difference. You use Stamina for just about every-thing, so it goes up faster than most skills. It'll take a while to get level three, though, so let's move on."

The next step in "Combat Training for Toddlers" was the dodge skill. Angus took me outside the compound. His farm was set on a gentle hill, and he took me through his fields, toward a lone tree standing at their edge.

"Are we going to fight?" I asked.

"Ach. Normally, kids would get their skills fighting each other, but I'm a mite worried that I take a swing at you, you'll die in one hit."

"So . . ."

"So we'll improvise." Arriving at the tree, he examined the branches above. Then without warning, he jumped up into the lower branches, pulling himself up by one hand. *What the? Did he just jump higher than his own head?* As I stared flabbergasted, he rummaged through the upper branches and casually snapped off a branch before jumping down again. He raised his eyebrows at my stare.

"Don't worry, we'll work on jumping next," he said, stripping leaves and branches off his prize, leaving him with a flexible pole about six feet long. He gave it a few practice swings. "Hmm, not thin enough." He pulled out a belt knife and sliced into the broken end. It sank in like a knife through butter and he was able to just slice the whole branch in half, leav-ing him with something that he seemed pleased with. "Should do." He gave me look. "Sorry 'bout this, but it's for your benefit." Then he lashed out and hit me with it!

"Ow!" The switch had flicked around and thwacked me on the thigh. Even through the dress, it was painful.

"Did ya lose body?" the monster said, pretending to be concerned. I checked.

"No, but I did lose a point of Stamina, you bastard. What was that for?"

"Good," said Angus. "I was pretty sure it wouldn't count as a weapon." He grinned an evil grin. "You're going to want to dodge, though."

Thwack! "Ow!"

Thus did my torture begin. It went on for longer than my axe training, because once I'd unlocked the Dodge skill, Angus had me buy it and then "trained" me to level two.

> [Dodge] Level 2 acquired through use.
> For gaining a skill level, you have been awarded 1 XP.

"Ow! Ow! It levelled!" I called, and Angus finally stopped his relentless assault. Even though he "wasn't really trying," and even with the level one skill, I'd been only dodging maybe forty percent of his swipes. They hurt! He stopped to let me recover my Stamina, and I watched in amazement as the welts that had formed on my skin from each blow quickly faded as the Stamina returned.

"Are we going to train Body Development next?" I asked apprehensively.

"Nay, though you need it." He looked a little uneasy at the prospect. "Hopefully getting you to level two will give you enough HP to take a hit and live to heal it. Now, have you got the Jump skill?"

"No," I said doubtfully, "But I can jump . . . just not like you did, before."

"Give it a go, then. Give us a baby jump, as high as you can."

I focused for a second, then leaped as high as I could.

> Competency demonstrated with [Jump], Level 1 awarded.
> For gaining a skill level, you have been awarded 1 XP.

"It worked, I got the skill!" I tried jumping again; it seemed . . . much the same. Maybe easier somehow?

"Ah, well, the bar's pretty low for Jump; most kids get it, after all. Climb's next." He gestured at the tree he'd just climbed.

"The first branch is pretty high; can I get a boost?" I was actually pretty confident about this one. I'd climbed trees as a kid, and with three Strength, I think I was stronger than I was on Earth. Angus shrugged and lifted me by the waist. Before I had time to squeal, he'd lifted me about five feet and the first branch was in reach. I grabbed it to distract myself from screaming. Once again, Angus was *strong*.

But so was I. With a bit of struggle, I managed to pull myself up onto the branch and reach for the next. This was the first time I'd really had a chance to see how my strength had changed. A bit more effort and I was halfway up the tree, which prompted the notice

> Competency displayed with [Climb], Level 1 awarded.
> For gaining a skill level, you have been awarded 1 XP.

"I got it!" I called down. Level one Climb, again, didn't seem that much different from my natural ability. Since I wasn't here to climb trees, I went back down for my next task.

"Now, run back to the farmhouse, as fast and long as you can," Angus said once I was down again. "It's just about time for lunch."

I did as he asked, trying to remember how I was taught to run back in high school athletics. Pump the arms, elbows in.

> **Competency displayed with [Run], Level 1 awarded.**
> **For gaining a skill level, you have been awarded 1 XP.**

Evidently the System approved. Angus was less impressed, matching my run with an easy jog. As we headed back to the house, I noticed for the first time that it was more of a farm compound. All the buildings were behind that high stone wall I'd noticed before, and the house was also stone, with a . . . slate roof? It was big, too, way too big for just the two people. I resolved to ask about it over lunch.

First, though, my Mana had recovered, so it was time to cast more spells. It seemed a little unfair. I could dodge thirty times in a minute before my Stamina ran out and do the same again ten minutes later. With spells, I could exhaust my Mana with as little as four spells, and then it would take ten hours before I could do the same again. It made it a lot harder to practice. Still, I cast Unseen Sound a few times, testing an idea. With no chanting, I could make my voice whisper in someone's ear, which seemed useful for secret communication. It wasn't quite as versatile as Secret Whisper—I had to cast it each time instead of the way Whisper set up a moving communication link, but the second spell cost ten points . . .

Anyway, I asked why their house was so big and fortress-like, and they explained that this area *had* been pretty dangerous, eighty years or so ago. Back then, it had been settled by adventurers—heroes by the sound of it, who'd distinguished themselves in the formation of the Kingdom and had been rewarded with land. Milly's grandfather had tamed the land and built the place up. That had "settled the mana flows," whatever that meant. Milly tried to explain, but they didn't understand it well themselves. Just that the land affected the mana flows and the mana affected what spawns occurred.

Spawns were . . . well, apparently, animals just popped out of nowhere, when there were no people around. Normal feral creatures in places like this, monstrous versions in places where mana was "twisted." I expressed incredulity.

"So animals don't breed? They just pop up?"

"Aye, they breed, if enough of them pop in the same area," Angus explained. "There's a copse down the hill away that's always popping foxes. If I leave them be too long, they'll breed a litter and then they'll be after me chickens. That's where we're headed next."

"You're not going to have her fight foxes already?" Milly exclaimed. "She's still level one!"

"She'll be fine; she got her magic, ain't she?"

I looked at both of them. "Wait, I'm going to be killing something?"

"Aye, it's the quickest way for you to get level two." He detached his knife from his belt and put it in front of me. What had looked like a small knife in his hands looked very much bigger when I thought about using it. "You said you had skill bonus from that profession, right? That'll be enough to get the unlock on your first strike, if it's not expecting you."

I gulped. *I'm going to have to sneak up on an animal and stab it?* I reached out my hand and took the knife. It was time to start playing this game.

Some little time later (not nearly long enough), I was alone in the copse, invisible, looking for a fox. Actually, I was looking for everything.

Identification failed.
[Identification] : Eyilm Tree
Identification failed.
Identification failed.
[Identification] : Mavenbush
Identification failed.
[Identification] : Arbengrass
[Identification] : Salleberry

Without my bonus, I was back to failing about half the time, but I persevered. According to Angus, the key to levelling up Identification was to Identify new things . . . and there were a lot of new things in these woods.

[Stealth] skill unlocked.

I froze. That would only happen if the fox was near enough for me to have avoided detection.

> **[Stealth] Level 1 purchased.**
> **For gaining a skill level, you have been awarded 1 XP.**

It only made sense to buy it, given what I was doing. I looked around carefully. There it was! Digging under some roots. It hadn't noticed me.

> **[Identification] : Fox (Male) – Threat Level: 2**
> **[Identify] Level 2 acquired through use.**
> **For gaining a skill level, you have been awarded 1 XP.**

Angus had said that skill use under stress was worth more for levelling the skill, so it wasn't surprising that this had kicked me over the limit. My heart was hammering, both at the thought that the fox would notice me, and because of what I would have to do if it didn't. I crept forward.

> **[Weapon Mastery: Small Bladed] skill unlocked.**
> **You have inflicted 19 damage!**

My strike had plunged into the fox's side, drawing blood. So much blood! The fox made a weird kind of scream and twisted off my blade, which I somehow managed to not drop. I thought it would run, but it stood its ground, looking around for what had hurt it. I was still invisible, so it was confused, but it seemed to detect me somehow, hissing in my general direction.

Oh, shit!

> **[Weapon Mastery: Small Bladed] Level 1 purchased.**
> **For gaining a skill level, you have been awarded 1 XP.**

It came at me, but Dodge moved me to the side. I struck again!

> **You have inflicted 22 damage!**
> **For killing a Fox, you have earned 40 XP.**

I just stood there with the knife pointing at the corpse, breathing heavily. It was really dead—I'd gotten the XP notification. I called out: "Angus, I killed it." A few moments later, I heard him moving through the bushes. Stealth wasn't one of his skills, which is why he'd stayed back.

"Aye, well done, lass. Now let me show you how to dress it." He took the knife off me and moved over to the corpse. As soon as he started, I turned around and threw up.

I did not get my Hunting unlock. Angus was disappointed, but understanding. I still didn't have level two, but I should be close. We continued searching for a bit, but all we got for it was a level in my Perception skill. Angus took that to mean that I'd successfully perceived that there was nothing to find.

On the way back to the house, Angus was struck by a thought. "Lass, you were asking about how Mana worked before?"

"Aye—I mean, yes."

"You've got a Mage class, right? That'd include the Sense Mana skill—have you tried it yet?"

"Um, no . . ."

[Sense Mana].

Everything became . . . blurry? Cloudy? Angus became enveloped in a pale green mist, and there was a much brighter yellow mist all around me. Looking down, I could see it pouring off my body and evaporating when it got more than a foot away from me.

"Oh . . . this is weird," I said. I looked back at Angus, but he just pointed up. I looked.

Whoa.

There was a structure in the sky. Or more like the entire sky was made of it. It was like clockwork made of clouds. Streams of mist plunged down into the earth and stretched up as far as I could see. I couldn't make out anything clearly, but the clouds were moving, clearly to some purpose.

"What am I looking at Angus?" I asked wonderingly.

"Mana, I guess," said Angus. "What we were trying to explain before, but you can probably see better than we can explain."

"Mana . . . we don't have anything like it on Earth," I said. "Wait, if I use mana to cast spells . . ."

I cast an illusion of a sword in my hand. As I did so, my aura brightened and some of it flowed into where I wanted the sword to be. It took the shape of the image, an outline in golden light, and then it vanished and was replaced by the image.

"Well, great. So any mage is going to be able to see when I'm casting illusions? Plus . . ." I looked back at Angus. His aura was definitely dimmer than mine. "They're going to be able to tell I'm a mage as well, right?"

Angus shrugged. "I dunno what to tell you. I've heard that mages can tell another mage, but I've also heard stories where a fellow concealed that fact. There's probably something you can do."

It occurred to me that I'd seen something relevant in my spell list that I hadn't understood at the time.

> **[Conceal Mana]: Hides a caster's mana from others (10 points).**

OK, put that one on the priority list.

With that, we were pretty much done with skills for today. I was running out of Skill points anyway, though Angus told me that I'd get two more each time I gained a level. That was good, because I had more unlocked skills than points.

Back at the house, I asked Milly about how skills worked.

"I don't know about the numbers; 'higher is better' is as far as I know," she told me. "But you've got Calculate, right? Maybe you can work out something from your logs?"

"Logs?" I asked, but even as she answered, I knew what she had to mean.

[Log].

> **[Combat Log] [Skill Log] [Development Log]**

"Oh, you figured it out?" Milly asked. I suppose my suddenly glazed look gave it away.

"Uh, yeah. Let me take a look here . . ."

Development Log was most of the notifications that I'd already seen, to do with gaining skills and XP. Skill Log was the rest of them, entries for every time I used a skill. I'd gotten notifications for *some* of these, but this seemed to have entries for *every* time. I guess I would have gone mad if I'd gotten text every time I swung an axe, so there must have been some sort of priority rating. Wait, not every time. There were no entries for perception attempts. I guess getting a message could be used to get information even if you failed, so it must be redacted.

The other thing that these entries had was something called an "effect level." At least the successful attempts did; failures just said "failed." But the fact that there weren't any successes below ten made me suspect that I needed to get an effect of ten to succeed. *One in ten chance to succeed when I don't have the skill . . . could it be that simple?* It was hard to tell with most of my attempts, with failures cutting off the low end, but my Illusion magic had really high levels, ranging from 37 to 46—all successes, of course.

So a random factor from one to ten, added to . . . 36 is four times nine, which is my Illusion Magic times my Charisma. I looked at some more entries, and the same basic pattern applied. *OK then, now I know.* I didn't imagine it was any great secret amongst the numerate, but it was still good to know how things worked. I tried explaining it to Milly, but the idea of multiplication went over her head.

I quickly looked at the Combat Log and it was much the same. It stated the effect level and the damage, but for my two hits, damage was the same as the effect level plus ten. The dagger probably did ten damage. I thought that it might not always be like that, though, because for both of those hits, it stated that the strike was "Unopposed." That made sense for the first hit, but I wasn't sure why it was true for the second. The fox had been trying to dodge that time.

The conversation moved on to my getting level two. Angus thought that I'd only need to kill one more fox to get there, but he was doubtful that one would appear within a week.

"I'm sorry to be asking after you've done so much for me already, but can I not wait for a week to pass?" I asked.

Milly smiled sadly and patted my hand. "Oh, child, we'd love to have you stay longer, but you need to go."

"Uh, why?"

"Worldwalkers . . . we told you there are stories, going back a long time. Worldwalkers are—you are—always tasked with a grand destiny. Preventing great cataclysms, the fall of empires, that sort of thing."

"If you say so, but I don't really want to do any of that."

She nodded. "You haven't found your purpose yet, but it will come. Which is why you need to start growing as soon as possible." She paused, marshalling her thoughts. "First of all, whatever the destiny you bring, the grand scope of it is too much for Angus and me. You will bring trouble to nations, and if it starts here, our little farmhouse would be sure to be swept away."

I felt a bit guilty. I hadn't considered that these two might not want to be swept up by Fate. It's not like I was ready to be. But Milly continued.

"Second, the learned and the powerful have ways of telling when a Worldwalker has arrived. They will seek you out, to aid or hinder you according to their own purposes. At the least, you want to be established when they find you, better still for you to be long gone. Finally, in the stories, some of the disasters that were prevented could have been solved much more easily if the hero had shown up a few days earlier. Wasting a week may not seem like much now, but it could be that a year from now, you'll be cursing that delay."

"Wow, that's . . . comprehensive. I don't know what to say."

Milly smiled again and hugged me. "I know you'll do well for the world," she said. "Get yourself into town and join the Adventurers Guild and get yourself another level. Try not to stay for more than a month. And if a large caravan of important people show up, be very careful."

"This feels a little weird. I just killed my first fox today and I'm supposed to be considering the fate of nations? It's crazy."

"It is crazy," agreed Milly. "Come find us again when it's over, if the Kingdom still stands, and tell us all about it."

EMPLOYMENT

I was on the road to Oakway, the local town. Angus was taking me in the cart, since the trip was not safe for a level one, which gave me a chance to practice both Disguise and Sense Mana. The maintenance cost for the spell was less than my Mana regeneration, which meant I could hold it indefinitely. Not while sleeping, though. I'd workshopped a new appearance with Angus and Milly last night, trying to find a look that was both different from me and fairly unobtrusive. The last part was the hard part, because my Charisma kept shining through, making even the blandest appearance notable. We'd settled on blond hair and blue eyes with pale skin to go with a new name and a cover story of growing up in a very sheltered environment. I'd bought Memorize in the hope that it would help me keep the details straight. It was kind of helping at this point.

Oh, and Mana Development had gone up while I was asleep, so that was nice. Angus had threatened to make me run alongside the cart to build up Stamina, but I convinced him that Mana Sense would be more useful. So I was maintaining my disguise, while staring up at the sky.

It kept flickering out, when my skill failed, which was annoying, and I still couldn't make out any details, but the endless turning of the great mana structure was endlessly fascinating to me. Above and below, wheels turned, while I accumulated skills.

[Mana Sense] Level 2 acquired through use.
For gaining a skill level, you have been awarded 1 XP.
[Illusion Magic] Level 2 acquired through use.
For gaining a skill level, you have been awarded 1 XP.

Mana Sense at 2 meant that it hardly ever failed, which was nice. Illusion magic at 2 made a big theoretical difference to my effect level, but I couldn't see any different between the approximately forty it had been before and the around fifty it was now. Oh wait, a new skill level meant new spells!

I'd already decided that Conceal Mana was a necessity, so I got that, and cast it immediately. It felt as if I could choose between making my mana seem like a normal person's or hiding it entirely, but I had to decide when I cast the spell. I realize that's a little specific for a "feeling," but that's how these skills worked. It was like the System was interacting with my mind and muscle memory to move me in the right manner or prompt me for the required decisions. Creepy, but convenient? It wasn't like I could do anything about it. I opted for "regular human" and proceeded to maintain it for the rest of the journey.

Which wasn't to be long, because I could already see the town walls in the distance.

Angus left me at the gate, with a bag of food, a dagger, and some instructions. It cost a copper to go through the gate (and another for the cart), so he said his goodbyes and left me to enter the town on my own. Oakway hadn't looked like much when we were approaching, but now that I was closer, the walls looked a lot more imposing. They must have been six meters tall, with an overhang and some wicked-looking iron spikes pointing downward.

There were two bored looking guards at the gate, and a younger man not in uniform. "Name?" asked one of the guards.

"Katherine Meland," I said.

[Deceive] skill unlocked.
[Deceive] Level 1 purchased.
For gaining a skill level, you have been awarded 1 XP.

The younger man wrote down my answer in a book.

"Purpose of entry?" the guard asked.

"Seeking employment." Angus had told me how to answer the guards, but it wasn't exactly hard to get in. The scribe wrote this answer down as well.

"Entry charge is one copper," said the guard. I handed over the coin. He looked at it and then dropped it through a slot in a locked box. "Paid in full," he said to the scribe, who made a note. "Go on through," he said to me.

"Thank you. Could you direct me to the Green Tanner Inn, please?" I smiled at him and he blushed. *OK, maybe turn down the Charm a tad.*

"Ah . . . down the main street until the square, then turn . . . right. You can't miss it," he stammered.

"Thank you again." Charm seemed to want me to do a curtsy, so I let it take me through the motion. I moved gracefully, as I'd done it a thousand times before, even though I'd only seen people curtsying in movies. Maneuver completed, I moved on.

Oakway was a small but bustling town that boasted no less than four inns—five if you counted the Adventurers Guild, which had rooms available for members. The Green Tanner was a "locals" inn, where the outlying farmers tended to stay when they came in to sell goods. Angus said it was honest and clean, and a good place to stay, as long as I had an income, which he assumed I would from adventuring.

I indeed could not miss the inn. If I hadn't been able to read the sign, the depiction of a pair of bright green pants would have been a clue. Entering, I found myself in the common room, with tables and a bar. It *was* clean, at least by medieval standards—the sawdust on the floor was fresh and unstained. The room was about half full with patrons, eating lunch. I made my way over the bar, where an older man seemed to be in charge.

"Harold Riley?" I asked.

He looked back at me. "I am. And who might you be?"

I curtsied, almost taking myself by surprise. "My name is Katherine Meland," I said. "I was hoping you might have work available."

At this, a few of the nearby patrons perked up, and I could feel them checking out the upcoming "talent." *I really need to work on that blending in disguise.* Harold was also looking me over. "I can write and do sums," I volunteered, looking back at him. It seemed to me that those would be useful skills. It seemed to surprise him.

"Aye, you're—" He cut himself off and looked away, embarrassed. He picked up a tankard and started polishing it, apparently so he could focus on that and not me. "Well, I've got the work right enough. Just one thing, though," he said before pausing. "If you're . . . A lot of pretty girls working in a tavern are looking to make a little extra money on the side. Upstairs." He glanced at me, and I tried to keep my expression in check. Angus hadn't mentioned this. Was I expected to . . .

"Not in my establishment, though. If that's what you're looking for, you want the Horse and Spider across town."

I sighed in relief. "I wouldn't expect anything less from an establishment recommended by Angus and Milly."

"You know them?" he asked. "Well, ah, good. Glad we got that sorted out."

"Does that mean I can expect not to be harassed by the patrons?" I asked. He scowled and glared around the room.

"*Most* of my regulars know how to behave in public, but there's always a few. If you need to dump a tankard on someone, the first one of the night is free, after which you'll have to pay for them."

"Understood."

"The shift is from sunset till second bell; pay is four copper a night, unless you want room and board, in which case it's two."

"I'll take the room, please."

He nodded. "Ellie will show you where . . . you don't have any things?"

"I'm afraid not," I said, ignoring the obvious question. "If it's all right, I'll come back later? I need to pick up some necessaries from the market."

"Aye, that's fine. Just be ready by sunset." I nodded and took my leave.

I was still planning on joining the Adventurers Guild, but I wanted something more stable to fall back on. Angus had said that adventurers made good money, but I didn't want to burn my savings waiting on money from killing random monsters. What if nothing spawned this week? Also, I can't say I was confident on a new career based on killing monsters when I'd killed my first fox only yesterday. Still, stable income established, it was time to investigate the Guild.

The Guild was on the other side of town, only two doors down from the Horse and Spider, which I now knew to avoid. As I approached, I saw a few men enter and one man leave. They all looked . . . rough. *I guess that's the adventurer look*, I thought to myself. *They're only one step above hired killers, after all. Do I really want to join them?* Steeling myself, I pushed open the door and entered.

Inside was a large open area. There was a raised area around the entrance, so I could pause and get a good look at the place. The majority of the area was given over to tables, much like the Green Tanner, but the bar was over to one side. There were fewer people in here right now, probably because they didn't serve food. At the back of the room were doors leading farther back and stairs going up. The patrons were mostly, but not entirely, male. All of them looked . . . disreputable. They were dressed in mismatched armor, and all of them had weapons. Some of them had noticed me and were openly staring.

Opposite the bar was another raised area, separated from the main room by a railing. It contained a large notice board and a woman behind a counter. That was probably where I had to go.

"Hello, and welcome to the Adventurers Guild!" she said as I approached. She was blonde and older than me, but not by much. Her smile wasn't exactly fake, but it was professional.

"Um, hello," I said. "My name is Katherine, and I'm interested in joining the Guild, but I wanted to know what was involved."

"Of course," she replied. "As a starting adventurer, a bronze plate is just five copper, with an upkeep of two copper every year. There's no qualification required, aside from level two, and it entitles you to discounts for rooms here, free entry to the town, and access to bronze-rated jobs on the job board." She gestured to the notice board that I'd seen before. "You also get access to the local Dungeon—access to any Dungeon in the Kingdom is for Guild members only, according to the King's decree. You also get access to the bar, but I don't think that's going to be a big selling point for you."

"Heh, yeah." I looked over at the ruffians below. "You're not surprised I'm interested? I'm not exactly . . ."

"Like those guys?" she asked. "Those guys are the dregs of the Adventurers Guild." She had raised her voice for the last sentence, making sure they heard. She got a few jibes and cheers in response, but none of them seemed truly insulted. "Spending the afternoon drinking instead of doing jobs." She looked back at me. "I assure you, the Guild accepts all kinds, but the more professional types are going to be underrepresented in the Guild bar."

"I see."

"Don't worry, your safety is guaranteed within the building." She pointed to a pair of serious looking men wearing chain mail. I hadn't noticed them before; they were discretely standing at the edge of the room. "We operate under the King's charter, you know, so we have to take action if our members become unruly . . . or unlawful."

"Huh."

"Actually, I should have mentioned that criminals aren't allowed to join. You need to swear on the Truthstone that you haven't committed any crimes."

"Truthstone?"

"Yes. You do the whole induction while touching it so the information collected for the King is accurate. It's just name, level, and profession. And the crimes thing." She did something with a lever behind the counter, and a crystal ball came up through a hatch. I stared. It looked . . . well, kinda tacky. A glass ball sitting in a frame of . . . copper and brass? I could see runes on the metal, though, so I suspected that this was the first magical item I'd seen.

The woman put her hand on the ball. "My name is Paige," she said, and the globe glowed blue. "I have two noses," she said, and it turned red. "Want to try?" she asked me.

My mind was racing as I put my hand to the globe. I needed to beat this if I wanted to conceal my Worldwalker status. There was just no way for someone to be a level one Phantasmal Artificer without that trait. An obvious solution occurred, but surely they'd thought of it already? Maybe I could test it and write it off as a joke or an error or something if it failed.

[Static Image].

"I come from a land where everyone walks around upside down all the time."

Paige giggled. The ball turned red, as far as anyone could see, but I could see through my own illusions and knew it had turned blue. Interesting. No one else seemed to react, so it seemed like this would work. Also interesting that it registered what I said as being true. It wasn't *literally* true that people walked upside down in Australia, or maybe it was from a northern perspective, but the ball had known what I meant.

"Did you have any other questions? Or would you like to sign up?"

"Can I take a look at the jobs first?"

"Of course. Can you read?" she asked, and I nodded. "Great, so the format is like this." She pulled out a piece of paper from under the counter. "The first row of stars is the ranking—one star is bronze, which are the only jobs you'll be able to apply for. The second row is the risk—how dangerous the job is. The final row is the reward. Generally you shouldn't expect more than one difference between the ratings, but sometimes you get a three-star risk that's too low paying for the silvers to touch. Or an easy, high paying job—but those get snatched up pretty quickly. Under that is who lodged the job and a description of what the job is, and also if it's been attempted before. Go and take a look at the board."

I did as she suggested and took a look. There were several bronze jobs posted, and they all looked menial. Killing rats in the sewers, fetching this plant or this animal part . . . The pay was better than I was getting, though.

Even the one-star jobs looked like they'd pay fifteen copper for just one day's work—assuming I could find enough of the requested materials. I looked at the silver ranked jobs, and they paid in silver. The gold jobs . . . did not pay in gold, just more silver, for the most part. I went back to the desk.

"How do I qualify for the silver jobs?" I asked.

"A silver plate is one silver, with an upkeep of five coppers per year. You need to be level three and have completed ten jobs successfully. Ready to sign up?"

"I guess so, I—" I stopped, looking behind me. One of the thugs that had been sitting at the bar had wandered up and joined us.

"Ah," said Paige. "I should introduce you. This disreputable fellow is Raynard, the deputy Guild Master. Unlike all the other sots here, it's actually his job to be in the Guild Hall when the Master is unavailable." She gave him a dirty look. "Though *most* would say his job also involves not drinking during the day."

Reynard seemed unaffected by Paige's scorn. "Indeed. And as a Guild official, if you've got any queries or problems, you can come to me to resolve them." He smiled, or maybe it was a leer.

Great. "I'll be sure to keep that in mind," I said, thanking Conversation for keeping my words polite and my expression in check.

"So, let's sign you up before Reynard says something to change your mind." She glared at Reynard a bit more. He just laughed and backed off a few feet. "Now, name?"

[Static Image].

"Katherine Meland," I said, and she wrote it down on what looked like a standardized form.

"Profession?"

"Apprentice."

"Level?"

"Two."

"Have you committed, or are you wanted for any crime in the Kingdom of Latora?

"No."

"All right then." She took a small bronze plate and placed it on the form she'd filled out. "If you could place your hand on the plate, please?" I did so, and she placed her hand on mine and concentrated. I could feel magic going through me, and I activated Sense Mana in time to see a swirling pattern of mana coalesce under my hand where I couldn't see it.

"There you go!" Paige said, releasing my hand. I raised my hand to see that the bronze plate was now engraved with the details I'd given her. "This plate serves as your identification as a Guild member. It's locked to your mana, so if someone else holds it . . ." She demonstrated by picking it up and handing it to me. As soon as she did, the shiny metal turned black, only to revert once it was in my hand.

"That will be five coppers, please, and welcome to the Guild."

"Will you be taking rooms here?" asked Reynard, with what I'm sure was an ulterior motive.

"No, I've got accommodation elsewhere." I handed Paige her coppers, and she made some more notes in a ledger.

"Well, you're now an accredited member in good standing of the Oakway Guild Hall!" said Paige brightly. "Please remember that your behavior will reflect on the Guild, and on the King."

"Right. I've got to go now and do some shopping. I'll be back tomorrow." I thought about curtsying again, but this didn't seem like the place for it, so I just turned and left.

Exhausted and defeated, I fell back on my new bed. I'd thought the Adventures Guild would be the hard part of my day, but I'd reckoned without the market. What a nightmare! The crowds, the stink, the dust, but worst of all . . . the haggling! Nothing had a price listed, everything was negotiable, and I didn't have a Bargain skill! Well, now I had one. But before I'd gotten a skill unlock, I'd stammered my way through about eight transactions, each of which I'd either paid too much for or gotten run off for insulting the vendor's mother. It was uncanny how as soon as I switched to trying to buy something, my (now) normal eloquence abandoned me and I became a blithering idiot. A couple of times I even slipped back into speaking English—which was crazy, because normally I wasn't even aware that I was speaking a different language.

Anyway, eventually I got Bargain and then things went much more smoothly. I had gotten most of what I wanted. I looked at my worldly possessions laid out on the small table in my room. A large knife (a gift from Angus), a second dress and underclothes, a hairbrush, paper and ink, a canvas satchel with multiple pockets. Oh, and three copper, which was all that was left from my Modest Means.

I contemplated my Status.

Name	Kandis Hammond	Profession	Phantasmal Artificer
Level	1	[Unspent Ability Points]	14
Age	24	[Unspent Skill Points]	1
Abilities		[Unspent Development Points]	3
[Strength]	3	[Unspent Spell Levels]	20
[Agility]	3	[HP]	30/30
[Finesse]	3	[Stamina]	60/60
[Soul]	3	[Mana]	98/120
[Intelligence]	4		
[Charisma]	9		
Skills			
[Body Development]	1	[WM: Dagger]	1 (2)
[Stamina Development]	2	[Deceive]	1 (2)
[Perception]	2	[Charm]	1 (2)
[Identify]	2	[Conversation]	1 (2)
[Scribe]	1	[Dodge]	2
[Calculate]	1	[Jump]	1
[Mana Sense]	2	[Climb]	1
[Mana Development]	1 (2)	[Run]	1
[Illusion Magic]	2 (5)	[Stealth]	1
[Creativity]	1	[Memorize]	1
[Disguise]	1	[Bargain]	1
Unlocked Skills			

[Enchanting] [Intrigue] [Research] [Teach] [WM: Axe]		
Traits		
[Worldwalker]	Level prerequisites for professions are overridden. +1 bonus to all stats.	
[Gift of Tongues]	All languages are understood.	
[Female]	+1 bonus to Charisma.	
[Silent Casting]	Allows you to cast spells without a chant.	
[Subtle Casting]	Allows you to cast spells without gestures.	
Spells		Mana
[Static Image]	Creates an unmoving image of a single object not more than 1 cubic meter in volume (upkeep 1/hour).	5
[Light]	Creates a light that can be moved, brightened, or dimmed (upkeep 1/hour).	5
[Unseen Sound]	Creates a sound from a source you designate (upkeep 1/hour).	5
[Simple Invisibility]	People and creatures are unable to see you (upkeep 3/hour).	15
[Disguise]	Modify your appearance and clothing as required (upkeep 3/hour).	15
[Conceal Mana]	Hides a caster's mana from others (upkeep 2/hour).	10

Tomorrow I'd find a job to do at the Guild, get a level, and improve some skills. But right now, it was time for my first shift.

I'm going to die. Or get fired. Wait, which is worse?

> [Stamina Development] Level 3 acquired through use.
> **For gaining a skill level, you have been awarded 1 XP.**
> [Charm] Level 2 acquired through use.
> **For gaining a skill level, you have been awarded 1 XP.**
> [Disguise] Level 2 acquired through use.
> **For gaining a skill level, you have been awarded 1 XP.**
> [Calculate] Level 2 acquired through use.
> **For gaining a skill level, you have been awarded 1 XP.**

Work had been hell. I had so much less Stamina than the other girls! Harold had thought I was shirking at first, so I had to run my Stamina down to where I got dizzy. The only thing that saved me is that once I'd proved I could calculate, he let me rest while counting the takings and managing the tabs. But those breaks had been oh so short. The work itself wasn't so hard, at least. I gather some people had trouble memorizing who ordered what, but that wasn't a problem for me. Once the shift was done, I staggered up to my room and fell unconscious. Now it was . . . late morning or early afternoon, and it was time for me to get up, but my body did not want to move.

Come on, move! How are you going to eat if you don't go downstairs?

With that logic, hunger moved me out of my room. Fortunately, I remembered to recast my Disguise spell. And my Conceal Mana spell just in case.

The Green Tanner didn't do a special breakfast, which was just as well, as I'd have missed it. The food available was bread and cheese, with stew being available in a few hours. I elected not to wait, on account of me being starving. Harold gave me a stern look, but nodded to me.

"Not bad for the first night. Work on that Stamina, though."

"Yes, sir." I winced. "My Development already went up one last night." It felt weird to be talking about my own stats with another person, but that seemed to be how it worked in this world.

"I heard you made quite a spectacle of yourself at the market," he said. I blushed. Word traveled fast!

"Yes?"

"If you need someone to bargain for you, ask Cerys." Cerys was his wife, currently busy in the kitchen. I'd met her last night, along with the other serving girls, Charlotte and Eve.

"I . . . needed to get the skill unlock." Was that giving too much away? It must be kind of weird picking up a basic skill like that at my age, right? But Harold just nodded.

"It's a good skill to have."

I just nodded and took my leave. I wanted to find the Dungeon today and get my second level.

At the Guild, Paige gave me directions to the Dungeon and some basic guidance as to what would be found there. Apparently the first level was mostly lizards, and their main value was in their hides. Since I didn't have the skill to skin them, I'd have to bring back the bodies, which would sell for a lesser price *and* I wouldn't be able to carry as many. Paige let me know which lizards were worth money and cautioned me about going deeper.

"The next level down is guarded by about five of the threat three lizards and the boss. They don't come out of the cave, so unless you're good at close combat in the dark, it's a nasty fight."

I thanked her for the warning and headed out. The Dungeon was about half an hour out of town, and there was a well-traveled dirt path leading to it. The entrance didn't look like much, just a cave entrance in a hill, but they'd built a low stone wall around the area to keep kids out. Apparently if you built over a Dungeon in a way that blocked the flows of mana, either the Dungeon died or the building would fall apart.

I'd passed a few early birds coming back from the Dungeon, but there wasn't anyone about right now. I cast Invisibility and stepped into the cave.

DUNGEON

I took a few steps into the darkness, and then I was bathed in light.

What? How? Even though I'd been warned, it still took me by surprise. I was in a large open area, much larger than the hill the cave had gone into. There was a sky, or a reasonable facsimile of one. It was impossible, but apparently normal for this world.

Looking around, the area was like a big bowl, with a river in sight running from my left down the center to the right. Behind me, the rock wall rose steeply, curving over slightly. I'd been told that the sky was fake, and if I managed to climb the walls, I'd reach where they became colored blue. I'd pass—a lot of effort for no reward. The river was where the most valuable creatures of this level were found—the tiny Galcan newts. They had sounded like a pain to catch, though, and with less XP, which was my main goal today. That meant I should be scouring the brush for Yonen skinks and Idnul lizards.

The vegetation in here was totally different from outside, which was good news for my Identify skill. I'd picked up the names of six new random plants before I saw it, sunning itself on a flat rock.

[Identification] : Yonen Skink (Male) – Threat Level: 2

It hadn't seen me. I started sneaking toward it and was soon in range.

You have inflicted 20 damage!

The monster twisted wildly, snapping in all directions. Somehow it managed to latch on to my arm and bit down painfully.

> **You have taken 5 damage!**

"Aaaaggggghh!" I screamed. Fortunately it hadn't grabbed my weapon arm, so I stabbed it again.

> **Attack failed.**

Continuing to hold on to my arm, it brought its body around and tried to do more damage with its claws. However, my frantic movements dislodged its grip and it went flying, twisting like a cat to land with its feet on the ground. It hissed at me. I was still invisible, but it could probably smell my blood.

I moved forward for another attack. Weapon Mastery guided my arm as I struck.

> **You have inflicted 29 damage!**
> **For killing a Yonen Skink, you have earned 40 XP.**
> **You have gained a level!**
> **You have been awarded 25 Ability Points.**
> **You have been awarded 5 Development Points.**
> **You have been awarded 2 Skill Points.**

Yes! Finally! Wait, don't get cocky; that's how they get you. Heeding my own advice, I checked carefully around to see if anything had been attracted by my scream. Then I took the lizard corpse and hung it from a branch to bleed out. I still wasn't certain if I was going to take these things back. If they bled out into my satchel, it'd be ruined and soon too stinky (*skinky*) to carry. Maybe I should have gotten a cheaper sack that I could throw away after each trip. For now, though, I put my back to a rock and contemplated my Status.

Name	Kandis Hammond	Profession	Phantasmal Artificer
Level	2	[Unspent Ability Points]	39
Age	24	[Unspent Skill Points]	3

Abilities		[Unspent Development Points]	8
[Strength]	3	[Unspent Spell Levels]	20
[Agility]	3	[HP]	60/60
[Finesse]	3	[Stamina]	180/180
[Soul]	3	[Mana]	240/240
[Intelligence]	4		
[Charisma]	9		
Skills			
[Body Development]	1	[WM: Dagger]	1 (2)
[Stamina Development]	3	[Deceive]	1 (3)
[Perception]	2	[Charm]	2 (3)
[Identify]	2	[Conversation]	1 (2)
[Scribe]	1	[Dodge]	2
[Calculate]	2	[Jump]	1
[Mana Sense]	2	[Climb]	1
[Mana Development]	2 (3)	[Run]	1
[Illusion Magic]	2 (5)	[Stealth]	1
[Creativity]	1	[Memorize]	1
[Disguise]	2	[Bargain]	1
Unlocked Skills			
[Enchanting] [Intrigue] [Research] [Teach] [WM: Axe]			
Traits			
[Worldwalker]		Level prerequisites for professions are overridden. +1 bonus to all stats.	

[Gift of Tongues]		All languages are understood.
[Female]		+1 bonus to Charisma.
[Silent Casting]		Allows you to cast spells without a chant.
[Subtle Casting]		Allows you to cast spells without gestures.
Spells		**Mana**
[Static Image]	Creates an unmoving image of a single object not more than 1 cubic meter in volume (upkeep 1/hour).	5
[Light]	Creates a light that can be moved, brightened, or dimmed (upkeep 1/hour).	5
[Unseen Sound]	Creates a sound from a source you designate (upkeep 1/hour).	5
[Simple Invisibility]	People and creatures are unable to see you (upkeep 3/hour).	15
[Disguise]	Modify your appearance and clothing as required (upkeep 3/hour).	15
[Conceal Mana]	Hides a caster's mana from others (upkeep 2/hour).	10

Okay . . . gaining a level restored everything to maximum? I looked at my arm and saw the wound was completely gone. My HP, Stamina, and MP pools had all doubled, which probably meant that they were multiplied by my level. I wonder if it affected skills the same way? I identified the nearby lizard corpse.

[Identification] : Yonen Skink corpse – Quality: Mediocre

Quality? I hadn't seen that before. I checked my logs, and I'd managed an effect level of 22, which was significantly higher than I'd ever managed before. I tried again on my dagger and got a 17 and no extra information, then tried again, and got a 23. This time the extra information was there.

[Identification] : Steel Knife – Quality: Average

Huh. I wondered if there was additional information at the thirty or forty levels. The only other skills I was getting above twenty were Charm and Illusion Magic and they didn't give me notifications of additional bonuses. I got the impression that higher effect levels made Illusion Magic more difficult to see through, but that was just speculation.

I turned my attention to my new points. I now had 38 Ability points, which was enough to put one of my lowest skills up to four. That wasn't bad . . . but I wanted to put my Intelligence up next. Or even my Charisma. I resolved to try and find out how often I was likely to get more points before I spent them.

Development points . . . were much the same. There were a lot of things I wanted to buy with them, but I might need the points to change professions, or face some specialized need where they would come in handy. They could wait. Skill points also. I was definitely looking to buy Enchanting, Intrigue, and maybe Research, but I kept coming across skills like Bargain which were a sudden necessity.

Next order of business . . . the lizard corpse.

Ugh.

Next order of business, get some more lizards while I wait for that to drain.

Now that I was level two, everything became much easier. I could move more easily through the bushes without making noise, I no longer missed with my dagger strikes, and I could even find the lizards more easily. The downside was that I now got twenty XP per kill instead of forty. Every time I killed a lizard, I brought it back to that first clearing to drain, and it wasn't long before I had six corpses hanging there. Two of them were of Average quality, and one was Poor. The couple of hours I had spent had been enough to level both my Stealth and Weapon Mastery: Small Bladed, which were now both at two.

It was time to decide what to do with the corpses. Most of them had stopped dripping now, at least, and I'd had an idea that might help with the mess. I'd found some wide leaves that seemed to be pretty absorbent and half-filled my satchel with them. I placed the drier corpses in, and covered them with more leaves. I now had a stuffed full backpack containing half as many skinks as it should, but hopefully I'd still have a backpack at the end of this.

As I prepared to leave, I heard voices coming up from the river. *Another adventuring party? What do I do? I should probably . . . introduce myself?* I thought about it, and it seemed like the right course of action. I hadn't been warned about adventurers poaching on other people's kills, and if I hid and got found, it would look suspicious. Speaking of suspicious, I was still invisible and needed to reset my disguise. I took care of that and moved back toward the Dungeon entrance.

I saw them first—they weren't showing any concern for the dangers of this level of the Dungeon. Which was unprofessional, but probably OK. From what I'd seen, the lizards didn't go out of their way to attack people. *Oh, wow. My first non-humans.*

It had been only humans in the Guild and around town, but this group was a mixture of races. There was one human, in metal armor and armed with swords. He had a medium one strapped to his back, and two shorter ones at his sides. I don't know swords, so that's all I could tell. There was some sort of Beast-person, with blond fur all over him and big pointed ears. A cat-man? Wolf-man? He was in leather armor and carried a bow. The third one had to be a dwarf. He was short and stocky and had a red beard and hair. He carried a lot of knives. The final one was something I didn't recognize. She had gray skin and black hair, and some sort of black speckles on her skin which I couldn't make out. She was wearing normal clothes, though she did have some sort of leather armor strapped to her arms and legs.

"So that's when I—Oh, hello, are you new?" It was the human that was talking and now looking at me.

"Yes, I'm a new adventurer at Oakway Guild. My name's Katherine, pleased to meet you." I approached with a smile on my face, hiding my nervousness. I'm not sure if it was my Charisma or Charm, but somehow the words flowed out of my mouth as if it were the most natural thing in the world. It was like being drunk, without the mental impairment. Not that I was normally shy, but these people were heavily armed, and gave off a . . . dangerous vibe that I hadn't seen before. Not the sleazy "probably a criminal" vibe that I'd felt at the Guild, just . . . dangerous.

"Well, then, fellow Guild member, let us introduce ourselves," said the human. "I'm Sean; this is Eric, Edvard, and Nina." He pointed at the beast-kin, the dwarf, and the gray woman in turn. "We're all silver rank, just coming back from a trip to the third level. And you?"

"Bronze, and I've just been killing lizards." I held up my bag.

"It's how we all got started," he said, reassuringly. "Well, except for Nina—she started with giant cockroaches." He held his hands about a foot apart to indicate what "giant" meant. "Really nasty."

"That does . . . sound really nasty," I said uncertainly. I looked over at Nina, who was rolling her eyes at her companion's antics.

"Would you like to accompany us back to the Guild?" Sean said. "I can regale you with the tale of how Nina got started as an adventurer."

"Sure, that would be fine, I guess."

"I warn you, it's not a tale for the faint of heart. Lots of tiny insect parts and ichor."

"Shouldn't Nina tell the story, since it's hers?"

"She doesn't tell it right, not nearly enough embellishment."

As we headed back into town, I found myself in an extraordinary contest with Sean. I wanted to ask about them, about higher-level adventuring and the next level of the Dungeon. I didn't want to pester them with questions, especially ones that might give away my lack of knowledge about this world, so I was letting Conversation do the work. Sean wanted to tell stories of excitement, adventure, and really gross things and seemed to have a Conversation skill higher than mine. Not high enough that I *couldn't* win, but he won more often than not.

We fought furiously for control of the conversation, while at the same time keeping the mood light. Sometimes it was like chess, laying conversational traps to be triggered later. Sometimes it was more directly brutal, a quick joke or insult to incapacitate the other long enough to get a word in edgewise. The others participated in the conversation, but not the conflict. I don't know if they were even aware of what was going on.

I did manage to learn that Nina was an oread and Eric was cat-kin, that all four of them were level four, and that they weren't locals, but were passing through to challenge the Oakway Dungeon. Reynard had a requirement that you be gold rank before fighting the final boss on the third level, so they were grinding missions for the Guild to get there. Sean told a number of extremely gross and disgusting stories, but the less said about them the better.

I'd planned on asking the Guild where I could sell my corpses, but they took me right to the skinner's stall and left me to haggle.

"It was a pleasure jousting with you, Katherine," Eric said. The others looked confused. "I look forward to the rematch."

"Me too," I said, and it wasn't a lie. There was a certain kind of pleasure in having to exert my skill to the utmost that my regular conversations just hadn't had. The ebb and flow of our contest, the jokes and teasing comments. *Wait a minute. Have I been flirting with Sean?* I blushed, the realization coming not late enough that Sean didn't catch my flush on the way out. He gave me a wink, the bastard. I took a deep breath and turned to the skinner to sell my wares. I got three copper for the pair of Mediocre corpses and five for the Average ones. After I emptied out the leaves, the backpack was still useable. The skinner pointed out a tool that most collectors used—it was a long stick with some small nooses along half of it. You could string up eight lizards and sling it over your shoulder. It was gross, but better than ruining a bag. I told him I'd think about it and headed back to the inn. I wanted to get a meal before sunset, and my next shift.

I was feeling really good for my second shift. At level two, I could keep up with the other girls, turning a nightmare march into . . . a fairly easy night's work. The difference between a child and an adult. The mood of the room was good, and the ale flowed freely. Harold seemed happy, and even smiled at me occasionally.

I wasn't even worried when some adventurers showed up—Reynard and a couple of his buddies. They didn't fit into the crowd, but found a table in the corner and kept to themselves. No one seemed shocked. I guess it wouldn't be unusual for adventurers to occasionally switch taverns, but I had my suspicions as to why they were here. Suspicions that were confirmed when Eve came up to me.

"He wants you to take his order," she said, gesturing. I looked over and Reynard was looking at us both with a satisfied smile. *Ugh.*

"That's fine," I said and collected a pair of tankards before I went over. "These might be on me, boss," I told Harold. He scowled and scanned around the room.

"Trouble?" he asked, his gaze fixing on the adventurer's corner. It really was ridiculous how much they stood out from the rest of the townsfolk.

"Nothing I can't handle," I said with a smile. I headed over to their table. Wanting to get it over with, I went over to Reynard first.

"What would you like to drink, sir?" I asked, with a reasonable amount of politeness.

"Giving up on adventuring already, Katherine?" He grinned.

Oh great, he remembers my name. "Not at all, I just like to hedge my bets," I said.

"I bet you do." He leaned forward and beckoned me closer. I obliged, to an extent. This dress had a pretty high neckline, so I wasn't worried about giving him a show or anything; I just didn't want to get too close. I wasn't close enough for him to whisper, but he spoke softly. Over the noise of the tavern, I doubt his friends could hear.

"I know you lied under the Truthstone, girl. Saw your illusion."

Deceive took over, locking my face into an unworried and unamused expression. "I don't know what you're talking about."

His grin got wider. "You've got some front, I'll give you that. And it was a good, solid image. But I'm a level five Ranger, darling; you can't deceive my eyes."

Fuck. My illusion had been around effect level . . . 53, Memorize helpfully provided. If he was level five, and had, say, five intelligence and only three perception, that would be five times five times three . . . 75.

"If that was the case, then you would have spoken up at the time," I said calmly. Deceive was still trying to cover my ass.

"Let's just say, I saw an opportunity—for you to have your secret kept and me to get . . . a little favor."

I didn't like that idea, and I let it show on my face. He just laughed.

"Don't worry, nothing you haven't done already. It will take me a while to set up, so I'll get back to you with what I need." He got up and turned to leave, his friends tagging along. "Just make sure you stick around town— I'd hate to have to send hunters after you in the King's name."

I watched him go, and headed back to the bar. This wasn't a problem I could solve by dumping a tankard on their heads. Harold looked at me, somewhat pleased. At least he was getting his beer back.

"You got rid of them—good."

"You're not concerned about losing customers?" I asked. He shrugged.

"Their money is good, and they didn't cause any trouble, but . . . I don't like their type."

"Adventurers?" I hadn't actually mentioned joining the Guild, but it wasn't something that would stay secret long.

"Nay, layabouts. The money's good from delving, so a lot of that sort just do enough to pay for their daily ale, and not a jot more." He scowled. "Pisses me off that those doing honest work do a full day all week, while they work two days, if that."

"Not everyone does that?" It was true that I'd made more this afternoon than I would working for a week at the tavern.

"Equipment's expensive. If you want to progress, you need to upgrade, get potions and such. So you need to bring back more to afford it, go deeper to get better loot. Which wears out your gear."

"It's a cycle . . ." I said, considering. "They keep going round, selling goods, gaining levels, spending money in town."

"Aye, that sort's good for all sort of commerce, whereas the other lot is only good for buying ale."

"Which you do . . . but your customers are the townsfolk, who buy ales when business is good for them."

He nodded. "You've put it in a nutshell. Now go take Ridiley's mead out to him."

I woke the next day in a far better state than last time. *I love being level two!* With all this extra energy, I considered starting a morning exercise routine. What would help? I could do jumping jacks to work on Jump, but doing it in here would make a hell of a racket. I could jog when I was heading out to the Dungeon, as I planned on making that a regular thing. Climbing . . . there were rock walls in the Dungeon, but I didn't think that would be very safe. Nor did I want people around town seeing me climb walls or trees . . . I had my dignity to maintain, after all. I resolved to think on it further.

I took a trip around the market, looking at the more expensive items this time. There was a bookseller, which interested me, but when I asked about prices, the man told me they started at five silver. Bargain told me I could probably get him down to two or three, but that was still out of my price range. For now.

There was a wide variety of weapons and armor, and Identify told me various items were of Average, Good, or Excellent quality. Most of the armor was leather, with lots of types. Most off it was made from lizard skin; the vendors were quick to tell me that it was made from local Dungeon lizard. Some of it was basically heavy clothing, and some of it had tiny plates of hard leather sewn all over it. There were heavy gauntlets, and hard pieces you could strap on to various body parts. I learned that they all had different names, like "vambrace" and "bracer." I was going to have to get some advice about armor, so I put it on the list of things to ask Sean's team.

There was even more variety in weapons. Most of them were made of ordinary steel, but some of the more expensive ones were of "darksteel" and "silversteel." Aside from the obvious difference in look, it wasn't clear to me what they were good for. More questions for some experienced adventurers.

Heading back to the Guild, I got into a conversation with Paige—she told me Sean's team had already gone back into the Dungeon. I mentioned

I'd been looking at books, and she told me that the Guild had a small library if I was interested.

"It's just a few books on adventuring-related subjects," she said.

"That's just what I'm interested in. Can I see?" I asked.

She lit a lamp and took me through the door at the back into the Guild offices. There was a small windowless room, with a table and chairs and bookshelf.

"I'm afraid you can't take anything out; you have to read in here," she said, leaving me with the lamp. It only took a moment for me to go over all the titles—there were only four books on the shelf. They were:

On Advancement

Bestiary of Latora

A Compendium of Dungeons of the South

Coleman's Herbarium

I started with *On Advancement*. My progress was slow, Scribe kept cutting out on me, but I persevered. This book contained a lot of details about the System that I'd missed so far. Ability points, for example. Apparently people got ten Ability points every year until they were 25. Yes, from age one. There was a lot of talk about how important it was to stop kids from spending their points until they were old enough, but I couldn't see that working. Skill points were much the same, one each year until age fifteen. Development points were two each year until age 25, but the book talked about "inherited situations" which caused Development points to be pre-spent. For example, if you were born into a family, you didn't get any points until the development cost for that had been paid.

It seemed a little unfair. If you were adopted by a family later on, you didn't have to pay the points. It looked like I was really fortunate, to just appear in this world with all my accrued points at once.

Moving on to levels, level two happened at 100 experience points, which I knew, and level three happened at 1,000 XP? That was a big gap. Level four was even worse at 10,000 XP, and level five was "speculated" to happen at 100,000 experience points. Given that the System didn't display your experience, I guess it was hard to get people to add up their logs to 100,000, but the pattern was pretty clear.

Every level got you an additional five Development points and two Skill points. Extra Ability points were more complicated. I'd gotten 25 points when I got my level, and according to this, I'd get another 25 each year from now on, for the next ten years. If I got to level three, I'd get fifty points every year for five years. Fourth level was 125 points for two years, and fifth was a once off 250 points. Why they made it that complicated instead of giving you 250 points every level, I don't know. The book had no answers there.

I was skimming through the advice on purchasing Abilities when the door opened and a teenaged girl walked in.

"Hello, do you mind if I join you? My name's Felicia."

FELÍCÍA

I stood up, pushing the chair back and covering my startled movement with a curtsy.

"Of course, please come in. My name's Katherine." Felicia returned my curtsy and moved over to the bookshelf.

"Paige said I should meet you to show that not all adventurers are villainous cutthroats," she said. "But I really just wanted some time to study the *Herbarium*."

"You're an adventurer?" I asked. Of course she was; this library was for members. She didn't look like one, though; she was dressed in a simple dress . . . like me. *OK, brain, feel free to turn on any time now.*

"Yes, I'm just starting out as a Witch," she replied. "Paige said you were an apprentice, but you must be almost ready to move to your level three profession? Have you decided what you're going to be?"

Why would she think that? Oh, right, because I'm older than her. "I, uh, haven't decided yet. Some sort of mage?" We both sat down at the table with our books. "What are you hoping to be?"

"Oh, a Healer," she said.

"Right . . . so what does a Witch do, as an adventurer?" I asked. Like me, she didn't seem the type to wander around killing monsters.

"Witches don't have a particular role in a party, if that's what you're asking," she said. "I have some useful skills like poultice making, but I don't have the equipment yet to make herbal brews." I nodded like I knew what she was talking about.

"So are you going into the Dungeon?"

"Sometimes, but not on my own. I've a friend, Kyle, who's a Warrior that comes with me. Most of the time I do Gather requests in the nearby woods. It's much safer, as long as you're not out after dark."

I made a face. "I don't have the Gather skill; it seemed like a requirement for those quests."

"Pretty much," she said, nodding. "You can find the right herbs with Identify, but it's much faster with Gather. It's an easy skill to unlock, though; you just need to pick plants until you get it."

"I'm short on Skill points, though; I mean, I *have* the points, but there are some skills I'm saving them for. I'm not sure if Gather or Hunt will be as useful once I'm a mage."

"I know what you mean. There's a few Witch skill unlocks that I haven't purchased. Like S-Singing." She blushed for some reason. "It would be really nice to be able to sing, but there are so many important skills to get first."

"Singing is a skill?" I blurted. *Of course singing is a skill; why wouldn't it be?*

"Of course," she said, looking a little puzzled. "It's useful for Bards, but for anyone else it's just for fun."

"Right. Of course," I said, trying to make as if I'd just forgotten something obvious. Deceive and Conversation can't save me when I insist on asking stupid questions . . .

"So, what are you doing for adventure work?" Felicia asked.

"I've been going to the Dungeon for lizards," I said with a grimace.

"On your own? That's dangerous!" she said.

I shrugged. "I'm just going a little way in."

"That's not a guarantee of safety, you know. The Ilan lizards hang out in the rock walls, but if you leave enough corpses around, they'll come out to eat them."

"That's . . . good to know, but I didn't have any problems with them last time." I considered. I *thought* I could take an Ilan lizard. They weren't supposed to be that bad a threat. They were good for XP, but bad for cash rewards, so I hadn't looked for them before. Now that I was looking at a thousand XP for the next level, I thought they might be worth another look.

"Is that the difference that having all your Ability points makes?" she asked. What was she . . . oh. She must think that I've had level two for ten years now, and have actually got the full 250 points for second level.

"I guess? I don't think my stats are that much higher than yours, though. I'm just impatient." I thought for a moment. *How to put this . . .* "I . . . had a sheltered existence until recently, and never got the chance to gain XP. Now that I do, I'm willing to take some risks to get to where I want."

"I see," Felicia said, nodding. "That's very . . . determined."

"That's—I don't think it's that special," I said. "I'm sure lots of adventurers are willing to take risks."

"Maybe, but I haven't been," she sighed. "Would you be willing to team up with me?"

"To go into the Dungeon?" I asked, and she nodded. "Um . . ." *If I take her, I can't go invisible . . .*

"Please?" she said. "I've got a bladed skill, and I do have Hunting. I can skin what we catch—"

I held up my hand. "OK—I mean, all right. Can we meet here tomorrow at . . ." *How did they refer to time again?* ". . . eighth bell? Tomorrow?"

"Sure thing!" Felicia grinned, excited.

"Well, I've got more reading to do before I get going, and you were here for that book, so . . ."

"Right! I'll leave you alone for now."

We both went back to reading. An hour went by before I got the notification that Scribe had gone up, at which point I took my leave and told Felicia that I'd see her tomorrow.

Right, time to start my exercise plan. It wasn't going to be much of a long-term plan; I had to get as much done today before Felicia started hanging out with me to see me act like an idiot. First thing was to jog to the Dungeon. That went pretty well. The path was empty again, and even with a Run skill of only one, jogging was far easier than I remembered it being.

On entering the Dungeon, I saw smoke rising up to the fake ceiling. Someone else must be in here? They were on the other side of the river, though, so I didn't change my plans. Turning invisible again, I turned right and made my way along the cliff that marked the edge of the room. There were supposed to be caves here, with the bigger types of lizard. Despite that, the first lizard I saw was another skink. I was an old hand at killing these by now, though I hadn't managed to kill one in a single hit yet.

This time, though, instead of draining the corpse, I threw it closer to the wall. It was a good throw, too, landing near some dark openings that I thought were caves.

[Thrown] skill unlocked.

Oh, what, on the first try?

I didn't have Hunting, but the idea behind baiting animals to come out wasn't complex. I felt like I should be hiding the bushes, but instead I just stood quietly nearby, invisible. *How long am I going to have to stand here, though*, I wondered.

Not too long, as it turned out. A bigger lizard poked his head out of a cave and looked around carefully. He was about a meter long, gray-brown and mean looking.

Identification: Ilan Lizard (Male) – Threat Level: 3

As I held my breath, he slowly crept out of the cave, seized the bait . . . and started dragging it back to the cave. Wait, that didn't work for me. *You can't eat outdoors?* Thinking quickly, I cast a quick static image of a bigger lizard between him and his hole. It can't have been terribly convincing, what with it not moving and having no smell, but it startled my victim, who dropped his meal and jumped back. Right into the real threat.

You have inflicted 32 damage!

He thrashed around under my blade, his tail smashing against my side.

You have taken 5 damage!

He was strong! Stronger than me, I think, but I had a knife. I stabbed down again.

You have inflicted 34 damage!

He still wasn't dead! He'd gotten turned around so he could bite me now, but he missed, jaws snapping too close to me for comfort. I swung again.

You have inflicted 37 damage!
For killing an Ilan Lizard, you have earned 60 XP.

Yes! Ow! Ow ow ow! This time, I didn't get my damage healed by my level going up. It hurt! I didn't seem to be bleeding, but still. I stared at the corpse, trying to decide what to do next. Ilan skin wasn't worth much, apparently, and this corpse was much bigger than a skink's. Should I just leave it here? I heard a noise.

Two noises. I looked to one side and saw another lizard crawling into the open.

Identification: Idnul Lizard (Male) – Threat Level: 2

On my other side was . . . another lizard.

Identification: Idnul Lizard (Male) – Threat Level: 2

Idnuls were smaller and redder than Ilan lizards, which was as far as my zoology went. More concerning was that I was sort of trapped between them. I still had the option of fleeing into the brush, or closer to the Ilan caves, but that wasn't appealing. They weren't as big a threat as an Ilan lizard, but there were two of them, and I was injured already.

They approached slowly, and I took a step toward the caves. Both of them reacted, moving their heads around warily. *Can they see me? Smell me?* Maybe it was the blood on the knife they could smell—Ilan lizards had much more blood than a skink, and it seemed to stink more, too.

If I was going to fight, I wanted to do it one on one . . . thinking quickly, I cast Unseen Sound, making a dog's growl come from behind the second lizard. When its head whipped around looking for the threat, I lunged at the first.

It sensed me coming somehow, but not enough to evade me.

You have inflicted 38 damage!

Like the others, it twisted around, trying to bite the unseen thing stabbing it, but I backed off in time to avoid it. Time for another stab!

You have inflicted 38 damage!
For killing an Idnul Lizard, you have earned 20 XP.
You have taken 17 damage!

Argh! The other lizard had come up and bitten me while I was distracted. I stabbed down at it, slashing it as it tried to get away.

> **You have inflicted 32 damage!**

We both backed away. This time I was bleeding; I could feel the blood going down my leg. The lizard was casting about, trying to find me, but it seemed to be narrowing down my position. I moved in, ready to finish this fight. It sensed me coming, but it couldn't dodge in time.

> **You have inflicted 29 damage!**
> **For killing an Idnul Lizard, you have earned 20 XP.**
> **[Weapon Mastery: Small Bladed] Level 3 acquired through use.**
> **For gaining a skill level, you have been awarded 1 XP.**

Forget profiting from these corpses; I had to get out of here. I headed back toward the entrance. Once I had gotten a little distance, I made a makeshift bandage from a strip of my petticoat and bandaged my wound, but after that I didn't stop moving until I was out of the Dungeon.

Once I was out, I stopped for a rest, and to take a look at my wound. It didn't look . . . *too* bad? It seemed deep, but it wasn't bleeding too badly. I should get someone to look at it. Would it get infected? Probably; it was an animal bite, after all. Recalling an option from my first night, I brought up the Development menu.

> **[Disease Resistant]: You are more resistant to disease of all types (4 points) (upgradeable).**

Well, thanks, helpful help files. How much more resistant? And what does upgradeable mean? There was another option:

> **[Immunity to Disease]: You are immune to all diseases (12 points).**

I only had eight points to spend. Still, it seemed like a good idea. Diseases could get pretty terrible. I bought Disease Resistant and watched as the cost of Immunity to Disease went to eight points. *So that's what it meant.* I dismissed the menu and started limping back to town.

I ran into Felicia at the Guild, and she offered to treat my wounds. I gratefully accepted and we went back to my room, as I'd have to take my dress off for her to look at my side.

"How much do I owe you for this?" I asked as she looked at my injury.

"Don't be silly!" she said. "We're party members now, aren't we?"

"I guess so, thanks."

Felicia mixed up two different poultices and applied one to each wound. "These should make it heal up twice as fast as normal. It'd be three times if you rested up properly, but you're working tonight, aren't you?"

"Yeah."

Felicia nodded. "I don't recommend it, but adventurers often have to keep going when they're injured, so it's good practice? I put something in the leg poultice that should help with the pain."

"Thanks again," I said gratefully. I had not been looking forward to tonight.

"Do you . . . do you still want to go out tomorrow?" Felicia asked hesitantly. "Or did you want to heal first?"

"I'm not going to let this stop me," I said confidently. "Today was a good reminder of how dangerous delving solo is, but tomorrow we'll be a team."

Felicia smiled, relieved. "I'm glad you said that," she said. "What you said before, about how impatient you were . . . well, it was inspiring."

"Oh come on," I said, embarrassed. "It wasn't anything special."

"It was," she insisted. "I want to follow your example, become high-levelled and become a great Healer."

"I'm sure you will," I reassured her. "And as to that . . . there's something I should have mentioned."

"What?"

"Just before I got these, I levelled. You're partnered with an Illusionist now."

"What? Wow, congratulations!" Felicia seemed beside herself. "Why an Illusionist?"

"I'm not sure . . . partly because it's Charisma based? Also I like the idea of tricking monsters more than burning them to death."

Felicia made a face. "Yeah, I've never seen a fireball in action, but I hear it can get pretty ugly. You've still gotta kill the monsters, though."

"A knife is cleaner," I said, and to my surprise I meant it. Maybe it was the skill, but I was finding it surprisingly easy to stick a knife in monsters.

"I guess? Oh, that would pair well with Kyle . . . when he gets back."

"Where is he?" I asked.

"Oh, that idiot," she said with an exasperated grimace. "We were gathering Galcan newts in the river . . . were you warned about the iridescent ones?"

"Yeah, they're poison—I mean venomous."

"Poisonous, too, if you were tempted to have a snack." She smiled. "Well, we had antidotes, but Kyle got bitten and didn't tell me."

"Why not?"

"Because. He's. An. Idiot," Felicia said through pursed lips. "He wanted to prove his strength or some . . . stupid. . . boy . . . thing."

I laughed. "He's all right, though?"

She sighed. "Luckily, we were almost back to the entrance when he collapsed. I gave him the antidote at once, of course, but a lot of damage had been done. We barely made it back to my Master's house."

"Master?"

"Master Oliver, the town Healer," she said. "He's been training me up until now. Kyle needs special care, so he's going to be there for another week." Suddenly, she grinned. "I made Master promise to give Kyle the worst tasting potion every day and tell him it was required for healing."

I laughed again. "I'd better remember to stay on your good side!"

"It was for his own good!" Felicia protested. "He needs to learn not to do that again!"

Felicia didn't stay much longer. I promised her I'd rest until sunset and that I'd see her tomorrow, and then she left. It was a relief to know I wouldn't have to hide my illusions from her anymore. *Just some of them.* At level three, it made sense for me to be an ordinary Illusionist, but not the advanced type. Of course, I wasn't level three yet, but that would come. How much I could tell the Guild was still up in the air, though. If they knew I could cast illusions, they might start looking out for them.

Time for some skill training. Two nights ago, I'd gotten Calculate from scratching some numbers in the dirt, but I knew a lot more mathematics than that. Calculate was really useful, allowing me to perform arithmetic much more quickly and easily than I could before, but at level two it only worked on numbers up to four digits. With my quill and ink from yesterday, I took two random nine-digit numbers and added them together, making sure to write them out in the Latorran notation first. I got the notification when I wrote out the answer in Latorran.

**Competency displayed with [Calculate], Level 4 awarded.
For gaining a skill level, you have been awarded 2 XP.**

Nice, but I'm not done yet.

I wrote out some power series, demonstrating how to raise two to the second power and third and so on. I wrote out Pythagoras's theorem, and then worked an example. I wrote down a set of numbers in Latorran, then calculated the average, then the variance of the set. I moved on to trigonometry, Memorize helping me with remembering the formulas from high school. Calculus, at least some simple examples. It took all afternoon, but eventually the System relented.

> **Competency displayed with [Advanced Mathematics], Level 2 awarded.**
> **For gaining a skill level, you have been awarded 2 XP.**

I grinned in triumph. I'm not sure why it was important to me to have my skills recognized, but it definitely was. And now I could calculate the cosine for any angle in my head. I'm not sure if that would come in useful anytime soon, but it was a nice skill. A good way to spend an afternoon. There was still some time before I had to go to work, so I thought about spells.

Today had shown me that Simple Invisibility wasn't completely effective against animals, as they could still smell me. There were a couple of options for dealing with that. First off, there was a variant of Invisibility that worked only on scent. Only ten points. I could get that, and cast both it and Simple Invisibility. And the mana one. That meant casting three spells, and an upkeep of seven an hour. That was still less than my regeneration, and it wasn't like I was going to be casting this in combat.

Another option was Improved Invisibility for twenty points. That covered both scent and sound. Yes, there was Silence spell, but it was fifteen points. Adding that to option one would take the upkeep to ten points versus four for Improved Invisibility.

There was also an Invisibility spell I could cast on others for twenty points, but that didn't help with my immediate problem as it just provided coverage for sight. If I was willing to wait until the next skill level, though, I could get Greater Invisibility for thirty points, which could be cast on a group and covered all the senses, including mana. Did I want to wait for the better spell? It seemed like a good idea—I'd have to hide the other Invisibility spells from Felicia anyway. Which did beg the question of why I was teaming up with her. The answer was that soloing was better for levelling, but teaming up was better for money, and I needed both. Also allies.

I'll wait, I decided, and headed out for work.

Working that night, I picked up skill levels in Conversation, Memorize, and Run. The last was a surprise, but I guess I was running back and forth between tables. In the morning I got another notification:

> **You have healed 6 points of HP.**
> **[Body Development] Level 2 acquired through use.**
> **For gaining a skill level, you have been awarded 1 XP.**

All right! Even ignoring the healing, I'd gained more HP than I'd lost yesterday, so overall I was still up. I washed, put on my Disguise, and headed out. I was meeting Felicia at the Guild, and she hadn't arrived when I got there. Paige was busy, so I examined the jobs board, and pointedly ignored Reynard. *What am I going to do about him?* It was tempting to just comply with his demands, whatever they were, but I was sure that wasn't going to be the end of it. Committing some sort of crime on his behalf would just give him more of a hold on me.

Wait a minute. This was an intrigue, wasn't it? I'd been thinking that unlocking Intrigue would come in later, when I was rich and powerful and dealing with nobility all day. But here I was, still dirt poor, and some guy was trying to blackmail me. I almost bought the skill right then, but a thought stopped me. *Would a skill make a difference?* He was level five, doubtless with much higher stats than me. If he had . . . five Charisma and just one Intrigue, he'd have a 25 skill total, totally overwhelming my level two and nine Charisma. And that was just the minimum, if he'd just bought the skill. If he'd been using it for any amount of time, he'd have level two . . .

But did he have it? He had more Skill points than me, but he would have bought a lot of weapon skills . . . and hunting and other outdoor skills. Would he even have had a chance to unlock it? It certainly wouldn't be on the Ranger skill list. Without it, his level would mean nothing, multiplied by zero. It was worth a shot.

> **[Intrigue] Level 1 purchased.**
> **For gaining a skill level, you have been awarded 1 XP.**

Everything became clear.

Reynard didn't have Intrigue. If he had, he wouldn't have approached me at the Green Tanner. Too many witnesses, and he was clearly acting out of character. That mistake might cost the both of us dearly. It would have been better to take me aside when I was at the Guild. That he hadn't suggested he was mainly worried about witnesses *in* the Guild. Paired with his remark about "nothing I hadn't done already," he was definitely going to ask me to cover up lying on the Truthstone. I'd have to ask Paige about what they used the Truthstone for, since I doubted he wanted to lie about his registration. In the meantime . . .

I glanced over the tables below, and I could identify Reynard's clique. They'd all looked like bandits before . . . and they still looked that way. But now I could see how they related, how Reynard was the central figure down there. There were a few disinterested drinkers, but just about everyone was either hoping to gain favor, was out of favor, or had rejected Reynard's overtures.

So Reynard has a posse. That wasn't a surprise; he'd brought two of them the other night. I didn't see either of them drinking right now, though . . . which meant they were somewhere else. Working?

I kept watching, teasing out the finer details of the group. I was looking for someone who was in Reynard's group but wasn't being well treated. Someone out of favor . . . there were a few candidates, but just then Felicia walked in the door.

"Ready to go, partner?" she asked. For a second, I just blinked at her.

Whoa. That had been a rush. Intrigue had just . . . taken over my thinking there for a bit. Recovering, I smiled and joined Felicia in heading out, but in the back of my mind, Intrigue was still racing. That had been a crazy risk, cheating the Truthstone like that. They had to have Illusionist protocols; it had just been blind luck that they didn't use them in my case. I should have—

OK, OK, shut up, Intrigue. Doing other stuff now. I managed to focus on what Felicia was saying.

"Were there any supplies you wanted to pick up before we left?"

"Probably? I don't have much in the way of supplies." I glanced enviously at her satchel. It was packed with stuff. She wouldn't be carrying any lizards home in that. Instead she had some sacks tied to the outside, like some kind of organized person.

"What do you have?"

"I've got this satchel, and . . . this knife."

Felicia sighed. "You really have led a sheltered life haven't you? Come on."

She took me to the market. I got a canteen made of hardened (boiled?) lizard leather, a first aid kit ("for when I'm not around"), and something called a mess kit, which was a cup and bowl combination that fit into each other, with some space to hold some collapsible cutlery. There was some "utility rope," which was a three-meter length of rope with an eyelet at one end and a hook on the other. It was used a lot by adventurers for various purposes. The hook fit through the eyelet, so you could feed it through for a lariat, or hook it on to the eyelet for a fixed loop. Or if you had two, you could connect them. I picked up two sacks and some leather strings to tie them to my satchel with. Along with a few extra strings, because they seemed like they'd come in handy.

Seeing as it was just a day trip, we didn't get a lantern or a bedroll. But I did get a flint and steel—Felicia promised to show me how to use it. It wasn't actually included in any skill, apparently. That pretty much took care of my funds. I did manage to Bargain effectively, which impressed Felicia and made me feel a little better about being educated by a teenager. We also got some lunch—bread and cheese and a hard-boiled egg. *I should use Memorize on every cooking show I've ever watched. I'd make a fortune selling Gordon Ramsay's recipes in this world!* I put it on my to-do list.

Shopping complete, we headed off to the Dungeon, and to adventure!

SAGE ADVICE

Felicia wanted to show me how to hunt for newts, so we headed down to the river.

"You can find newts anywhere along the river, but there's a couple of deeper pools that they like to gather in," she said. She pointed ahead of us, and I could see where the stream got deeper. The water was pretty clear; it looked about a meter deep here. I could make out darting movement along the bank and, more clearly, the brightly colored forms of the iridescent newts. It looked as if I could reach in and grab some, but I had the feeling that it wouldn't be that easy.

Felicia took out some sort of fine net. She needed to assemble it, attaching the conical net to a flexible wooden hoop that she'd been carrying in a more tightly curled configuration.

"Here's how this works." She tied her skirt up, leaving her lower legs bare. "One of us goes upstream and makes a lot of splashing and noise. The other stands downstream with the net. The lizards flee the noise and run into the net."

"Sounds simple," I said. "I take it Kyle normally did the splashing?"

She nodded. "It's not quite like fishing; the newts can go on land to escape, so some of them do. There's also a risk of getting bitten—the splashing role is more dangerous in that regard, but you only need to worry about the poison bites, and we have the antidote."

"It seems less dangerous than Idnuls," I agreed. "I think I've got some ideas about how to flush them out, so how about you manage the net?"

"Great! Just let me get set up." Felicia moved downstream a few meters and then waded in, carefully bracing the net in the water. "Go ahead!"

I carefully contemplated the deeper section, planning the spacing. I cast a Static Image on either side of the stream, of an Idnul Lizard, half in the water. They looked a little odd with the way the water flowed through them, but it seemed to have an effect. There was a change in how the newts darted about, but they didn't make a run for it yet. Then I put another Static Image in the water upstream, of the bigger Ilan lizard.

That got a reaction. A good number of newts dashed downstream, with none of them making for the bank, my other illusions proving enough of a deterrent. The whole flock moved downstream at speed.

Felicia shrieked, scooping up the net and dashing toward the bank, laughing.

"That was scary! There were so many!" she exclaimed. She held the net upright, full of small struggling forms. "Can you hold this?"

I did so, and she brought out a small club. I held the net against a rock, and she carefully clubbed each one to death.

> **Your party has killed 11 Lesser Galcan Newts.**
> **Your share of the XP is 22 XP.**
> **Your party has killed 2 Iridescent Galcan Newts.**
> **Your share of the XP is 60 XP.**

"That's about twice as good as our normal haul!" she exclaimed. "That illusion technique is great!" She turned the net inside out and delicately removed the corpses from the netting. "The lesser lizards are worth two copper each, but the iridescent ones are worth a silver."

"Wow, that's a lot of silver for not much effort."

"I know! I think we've fished out this pond, though; we should move on to the next chamber."

"Sure."

We packed up our haul and headed downstream. Felicia explained that there were five chambers to the first level, and four of them were arranged in a circle with the stream flowing through each one. There was some kind of spatial magic that made the stream flow around in a loop, always going down. You could go around either way, but down was easier. The final chamber was reached from the furthest chamber from the entrance. The passageway to each chamber was guarded by an Ilan lizard.

"The guardians spawn whenever the group that kills it goes down to level two," Felicia said, "which makes it a bit of a gamble as to whether they're there or not. That level four group went through this morning, but I'm pretty sure they went down already."

"So it should be guarded?"

"Probably, unless some other adventurers are messing around on this level. Do you think we can take it?"

"I guess?" I'd fought an Ilan on my own, but that was while invisible. Still, there were two of us and my blade skill had gone up. "I'll try a different trick this time—I'll put something over their head so they can't see. When that happens, we rush it!"

"Sounds good." Felicia grinned.

It wasn't long before we reached the passage. It was guarded, a big lizard standing right in our way. It saw us coming and hissed like a steam kettle.

"Ready?" I said, and cast my spell. *[Static Image].*

The Ilan's hissing turned into a startled raspy shriek as we ran forward to attack. Unlike what I could do with Blind, I couldn't make the darkness follow the movement of the target, so it was only a matter of time before it moved out of it. Before it could, though, we attacked.

> **You have inflicted 26 damage!**

The lizard thrashed around, but all it accomplished was to get out of the darkness. Felicia and I struck again.

> **You have inflicted 25 damage!**

Finally able to see us, the Ilan struck back, biting at me, but I twisted away. Felicia stabbed him again, and I managed the finishing blow.

> **You have inflicted 19 damage!**
> **For killing an Ilan Lizard, you have earned 30 XP.**

We stood triumphant over the corpse, grinning at each other.

"Kyle never let me fight these," she confessed. "It's exciting!"

"Yeah," I said. *This is the first time I've fought one when I was visible. Scary. Hang on, though . . .* As the adrenaline faded, something started bugging me about my combat notifications. *Shouldn't I be doing more damage now? My Dagger skill went up . . .*

Looking at my logs, I could see that my effect totals had gone up, but my damage . . . had gone down, if anything. *I must be getting some bonus when my target can't see me. That would make sense.*

"Katherine?" I heard Felicia say, and I realized I had zoned out for a bit.

"Sorry, I was just checking my logs for something," I said. "Shall we move on?"

We repeated our fishing trick, this time netting five silver between us and 140 XP each. Fighting the next chamber guardian went just as easy, and I gained a point of Dodge and Illusion Magic from it. A Dodge of three took my base effect level to eighteen, and I was pretty sure that meant that a lizard probably *couldn't* hit me anymore. Feeling confident, I proposed that we keep doing this around the ring and then call it a day.

It proved a good decision, as our catches on the next two caves were even higher. We caught six iridescent newts at the next cave, and five at the one after that. We were raking in both XP and money. Felicia hit level three after the third cave, and I reached it after the fourth. Of course, we only celebrated Felicia's level, but I felt relief that reality had caught up with my lie.

We talked about Ability development on the way back. Felicia was disappointed that she didn't have enough for another point of Intelligence. Since she didn't have Calculate, she couldn't really tell how the cost system worked, just that it cost X points, and she didn't have that many. After getting her numbers from her, I was able to reassure her that after she got her next block of Ability points from her two previous levels, she'd have enough. I also warned her that if she bought one of her cheaper stats, she wouldn't have enough until next year. An Intelligence of six was a requirement for Healer, so she decided to wait.

As for me, I also wanted to wait. Maybe it was vanity, but I wanted Charisma at ten. More importantly, I had to decide on spells. Greater Invisibility was now available, which meant that I didn't have to worry about the lesser versions any more. Blind seemed like a useful combat spell I could cast when fighting in a group, but since I had more points, I went for Improved Blind, which covered hearing and smell as well.

I brought up my full Status again.

Name	Kandis Hammond	Profession	Phantasmal Artificer
Level	3	[Unspent Ability Points]	88
Age	24	[Unspent Skill Points]	4
Abilities		[Unspent Development Points]	9
[Strength]	3	[Unspent Spell Levels]	0
[Agility]	3	[HP]	180/180
[Finesse]	3	[Stamina]	240/240
[Soul]	3	[Mana]	360/360
[Intelligence]	4		
[Charisma]	9		
Skills			
[Body Development]	2	[WM: Dagger]	3 (4)
[Stamina Development]	3	[Deceive]	2 (4)
[Perception]	2	[Charm]	2 (3)
[Identify]	2	[Conversation]	2 (3)
[Scribe]	2	[Dodge]	3
[Calculate]	4	[Jump]	1
[Mana Sense]	2	[Climb]	1
[Mana Development]	2 (3)	[Run]	2
[Illusion Magic]	3 (6)	[Stealth]	2
[Creativity]	1	[Memorize]	2
[Disguise]	2	[Bargain]	1
[Intrigue]	1	[Advanced Mathematics]	2

Unlocked Skills		
[Enchanting] [Research] [Teach] [WM: Axe] [Thrown]		
Traits		
[Worldwalker]		Level prerequisites for professions are overridden. +1 bonus to all stats.
[Gift of Tongues]		All languages are understood.
[Female]		+1 bonus to Charisma.
[Silent Casting]		Allows you to cast spells without a chant.
[Subtle Casting]		Allows you to cast spells without gestures.
[Disease Resistance]		You are more resistant to disease of all types (upgradeable).
Spells		Mana
[Static Image]	Creates an unmoving image of a single object not more than 1 cubic meter in volume (upkeep 1/hour).	5
[Light]	Creates a light that can be moved, brightened, or dimmed (upkeep 1/hour).	5
[Unseen Sound]	Creates a sound from a source you designate (upkeep 1/hour).	5
[Simple Invisibility]	People and creatures are unable to see you (upkeep 3/hour).	15
[Disguise]	Modify your appearance and clothing as required (upkeep 3/hour).	15
[Conceal Mana]	Hides a caster's mana from others (upkeep 2/hour).	10
[Greater Invisibility]	Invisible to all senses, can be cast on others (upkeep 6/hour).	

[Improved Blind]	Blocks sight, sound, and smell from reaching one target (upkeep 4/hour).	

Looking good, at least for a start. I still wasn't in a position to take on Reynard, but there was a decent chance my illusions would fool him now. I really needed to think about spending those Development points. The problem was that there were so many things to spend them on. I probably wasn't going to take another profession at this point, but there were spellcasting traits, extra spells, skill bonuses, physical traits . . . so many choices.

Getting back into town, I persuaded Felicia to let me take care of selling our harvest. She was reluctant as she'd been the one to do this before, but I pointed out that I had Bargain.

Competency in [Persuasion] demonstrated, Level 1 awarded.

Was that really the first time I had persuaded someone since coming here? Oh well, no complaints. Selling the lizards went well. I didn't have the Bargain skill to overwhelm the experienced merchants, but just having the skill made a big difference. I got a 50% price increase on our Average quality corpses, which was most of them, thanks to Felicia's careful clubbing technique. Calculation came in handy, too . . . it must be incredibly annoying dealing in multiple small items with people who can't multiply.

"Oh, you have Calculate?" the man said, after I added up how much he owed us. "That makes things easier." His face relaxed somewhat from the pained look he'd gotten when he realized he wasn't going to get the same prices as before. "And Bargain as well; are you a merchant yourself?" He made a complicated shape with one hand, bending his middle fingers over his thumb with the palm up.

"No, but I have a background in . . . something similar." I glanced down at his hand. "Is that the sign of your secret society?"

He flushed. "Ah, no, no, just a Guild recognition sign. Here's your money. Thirty silver and six copper, as agreed."

"Pleasure doing business," I said. I quickly arranged the coins into four piles, fifteen silver and three copper twice so that Felicia could easily see, then handed her her share. She had the presence of mind to squeal *after* we left the store.

"This is more than Kyle and I made working together!"

"This is just the start," I said. "Now we can start planning for the next Dungeon level."

"What, really?" Felicia asked, shocked. "But they say the boss is really dangerous . . ."

"Not right away," I reassured her. "We'll get more information first. But the first level isn't a challenge anymore—I don't think even the Ilan lizards can hit us."

"I guess . . ."

"And did you notice how the XP went down when you hit level three?"

"I hadn't."

I sighed. "I've got to teach you how to calculate."

"I've got the skill unlocked, but I'm saving my points."

I considered. "I've got something I can try. Don't know if it will work, but it won't cost you Skill points. Anyway, the thing is, we need to go after higher threat level monsters if we want to keep gaining levels."

"I suppose . . . it's scary, though."

"That's why we've got to prepare," I told her. "Get some armor, maybe some better weapons . . . Let's head back to the Guild for now."

Felicia followed me back to the Guild. Looking over the tables, I saw what I'd hoped to see, and dragged Felicia over to Sean's table.

"Hi, guys," I said. "Are you busy? We were hoping to get some advice."

All four of them were at the table, Nina and Edvard on one side, and Sean and Eric on the other. Nina smiled at me, but it was Sean who spoke first.

"Of course, we've always got time to guide pretty young adventurers like yourselves. Take a seat!"

They shifted a bit closer and we each took a seat on one of the benches. Felicia sat next to Nina, and I was next to Eric.

"Everyone, this is Felicia; Felicia this is Nina, Edvard, Sean, and Eric," I said, pointing to each in turn. "Sean, don't bother; she's got a boyfriend."

"I—what, I never said—" Felicia spluttered.

"Oh, great, this is starting again, and I'm in the middle," said Eric with a chuckle.

"I don't even want to know what you think you're implying," I said, loftily. "We're here on serious business. We're thinking of attempting the first level boss."

That sobered them up. This was a group that took adventuring seriously.

"I can't really recommend that," Edvard said. "It's way too early at level two."

"We're level three!" Felicia interrupted.

"Oh, congratulations. Hmm, that's better . . ." Edvard paused, thinking it through.

"Not in a combat class, though," said Nina. "Casters?"

"Illusionist," I said, keeping my grimace to myself.

"And Healer!" said Felicia. "Well, I'm not a Healer yet, just a Witch until I get my Intelligence up."

"Oho," Sean said. "Those are rare classes in a Dungeon."

"*Support* classes," Edvard stressed. "Don't get me wrong; they're great to have in a party, but—"

"You need to have a fighter of some sort to support," Nina finished.

"Oh, we will!" said Felicia. "Kyle's a fighter; he'll be part of the group."

"Huh, then maybe . . ." Edvard ran his fingers through his beard. "Maybe it's doable. You'd need—"

"Advice about what arms and armor to get?" I interrupted.

"What?"

"Look," I said, "I get that we're just starting out. But first level isn't a challenge anymore, so while we've started making silver, we're not getting the XP we need to grow. We need to start investing in gear before we get to the next level, and I'd like some advice on what to get. There are so many options, I don't know where to start."

Eric laughed. "I guess we're not your mothers after all. What did you want to know?"

"Well to start with . . . we're both dagger users. What should we be looking at for more damage?"

"A bigger weapon?" suggested Sean. "I'm very fond of mine." I gave him a look, and he laughed. "But if you want to stick with knives, you need to ask the expert."

We all looked at Edvard. "Hmph. Daggers are all about skill, and speed—which is a skill. The weapon itself doesn't make such a difference like it does with a sword. Let me take a look."

We handed over our knives. "About what I expected. Average quality, no specializations. These are fine." He shrugged. "You can buy something like this for two silvers. Could pay a bit more for a slightly bigger weapon that would still fit into small bladed, something with a proper guard that would help you parry better. Maybe three silvers total, get you to plus-fifteen damage." He handed the weapons back. "Or you could pay more for a Good quality weapon—ten to fifteen silver. Good quality daggers run from about fifteen to 22 damage."

"So a fifty percent damage bonus?" I asked. Edvard hesitated, looking over to Nina, who nodded. Another person without Calculate! I should start a school.

"I guess so," Edvard continued. If you really want to spend the money, you can upgrade to silversteel. Generally you only find Good quality ones; they go for fifty silver and can do up to thirty damage. There's darksteel as well, but that isn't about damage."

"What is it about, then?"

"Darksteel is dark—it doesn't reflect light at all, nor does it make a sound. And it halves the value of steel armor it goes through."

"A metal for assassins, then?"

"Yeah, it's not any better against the monsters here. It's only so common here because it's dropped at the Oakway Dungeon. Anywhere else you could expect to pay a hundred silver for a darksteel dagger, but around here you can get it for the price of a silversteel one."

"Is that dropped locally as well?"

"No, but there's a bunch of Dungeons near the capital that drop it. Trade tends to be either toward or away from Dorsay, so it's traded in most places throughout the Kingdom. Other areas have their own local steels, but it's rare to find them outside of the capital or the local area."

"Huh." I kind of wanted to drill down into the trading details, but I had other priorities right now. "So if the bonus that quality or silversteel gets you is percentage based, that would explain why it's more useful for bigger weapons."

"Uh . . ." I'd lost Edvard at that point, and Felicia as well, but Nina was still with me.

"Yes." She turned to Felicia. "The bonus for a plus-ten dagger is only five, but the bonus for a plus-forty sword is twenty. That's a lot more."

"Indeed," said Edvard. "It is worth upgrading if you're a dagger user, but not that worthwhile. It's better to have a lot of cheap ones, at least for me."

"Why a lot?"

"Thrown weapons, for one. Also, my profession allows for dual wielding."

"And extra stabbing, don't forget that!" Sean chimed in.

"Yes, skills that allow for multiple attacks work best with small weapons."

"Multiple attacks . . ." I said. Thinking back, all my fights so far had been trading blow for blow. "How do you get those?"

"Profession, mostly," Edvard said. "There are some traits, but it's much cheaper to get the profession."

"Switch to Rogue after you get Invisibility, and you'd be practically an Assassin!" Eric said.

"I'm not going to be an Assassin!" I protested.

Edvard shrugged. "It's a valid build for Dungeon delving. Good for solo delves."

I made a face and protested some more, but I had to admit that was the path I was on. Although I wasn't planning on switching professions just to get better at stabbing.

"The thing is," said Edvard, "if you're attacking twice as fast, you wear out the dagger twice as fast as well."

"Weapons wear out?" I asked, surprised.

"Not quickly," Edvard replied, "But daggers wear out faster than most weapons, especially if you use them more."

"I guess it would be annoying to drop a large amount on a weapon, only to see it break."

"You can repair them, but you need a better smith than the one that forged it, or it will drop a quality level."

"So, moving on to armor," I asked.

"Ah, my time to shine," said Sean. "For armor, it depends on if you have the skill or not."

"There's a skill?"

"Armor Use." It reduces armor penalties and lets you parry with your armor."

"Wait, parry with armor? I thought that it took a weapon to parry. Not that I've been doing anything other than dodge. Is that another skill?"

"No it comes under Weapon Mastery," Edvard told me. "You'll want to keep dodging, at least while you're using a single dagger. With two daggers, you'll get a small bonus to parry, even if you can't attack with both."

"OK, so armor parry?"

"When you've got hard armor, you can use that to block a blow, just like you would with a sword." Sean gestured at Nina, who had hard leather armor strapped to her forearms. "It works best with gauntlets or armor on the arms, but you can do it with any armor in principle. The main advantage is that even if you fail the block, you get the full benefit of your armor. Oh, and Armor Use also makes it more likely that an attack will hit the armor, instead of a gap."

Now I was starting to get lost. "So everyone needs Armor Use?"

"No. Soft armor doesn't have much in the way of gaps, and doesn't have encumbrance until you get to chain mail, so Armor Use isn't going to do much for you if that's what you're wearing." He pointed to Eric, who was wearing what amounted to leather clothing. "I don't think Armor Use even unlocks for leather, does it, Eric?"

"Nope," Eric said. "I've got it unlocked, on account of having worn chain before, but I've never gotten it."

"Casters generally go for either no armor, relying on their team, or light soft armor, for a bit of extra protection." Sean continued. "Nina's a special case."

I looked at Nina, who explained: "I have tougher than normal skin, almost as good as leather, and I wear these vambraces"—she held up her arms—"to block more damaging attacks."

"Quality bonuses?" I asked.

Sean shrugged. "Generally not worth it for leather-crafting, hard or soft. Metal reinforced leather benefits from skilled crafting, and there are all sorts of things a skilled metalworker can do with armor. And before you ask, darksteel is popular for armor as it doesn't make any noise. It's not any more protective than steel, though it is immune to the darksteel armor piercing effect. Silversteel is as well, and it negates a lot of other metal qualities."

"Oh," Nina interjected. "Don't forget there are enchanted options for cloth and leather once you get rich. That's why casters don't often go for the Armor skill—they plan on getting enchanted robes."

"I think I'm almost as lost as I was before," I complained. "There are so many options."

Sean smiled. "For the boss, leather will be fine. If you don't want to get the skill, get some leggings, jacket, and gloves out of leather and you'll be fully protected. That should see you through the boss and the second level as well. Your current boots are workable, but you want to upgrade to a steel reinforced pair as soon as you can. They will stay with you unless you go full steel—as the smart people do." Sean was the only steel-armored person at the table, so this last bit was greeted with a round of jeers.

"That's going to set me back . . . fifty silver? I only have fifteen!"

"Then you need to just keep farming the first level," Sean said sympathetically. "Just be patient and don't take risks until you're fully prepared."

Felicia giggled, then blushed when everyone looked at her. She'd been pretty quiet so far, somewhat overawed by the level fours.

"What is it?" Sean asked.

"Oh, ah, it's just that you told Katherine to be patient," she said. "I don't think that's going to go down well."

FOOLISH ACTIONS

In the end, I bought a dagger. That might seem as if I was ignoring Sean's advice . . . OK, it totally was me ignoring him. Felicia had been right: being told to be patient just made me want to push myself more. That was why I was headed out to the Dungeon, alone, a few hours before dawn. I'd left after work, unable to sleep and itching to try out my new dagger.

It was a nice piece. It had the guard like Edvard had said, and was of Good quality. I'd haggled the price down to thirteen silver, which I considered a win. I still had my old knife, and I was planning to try some of that two-handed parrying that Edvard had mentioned.

The reason I was pulling an all-nighter (aside from the unreasonable amount of energy I had from my new level) was that the Dungeon reset at midnight, while the town gates opened at dawn, which would mean that I had the whole place to myself for a few hours. Also I was meeting Felicia in the morning, which meant that if I was going into the Dungeon before I saw her again, it had to be *now*. She'd want to come along, and there were still a few things that I didn't want to show her.

The town gates were closed, of course, but it was easy enough to get up on the wall and Jump down. There were stairs on the inside. There were guards as well, but they were easy to avoid with Greater Invisibility. It wasn't an easy jump down, but I managed to land without hurting myself. Getting back the same way would be impossible, of course, but the gates would open in a few hours.

I ran all the way there in the moonlight. It was crazy how much energy I had—level fives like Reynard must be super-humans walking amongst mortals. Coming up to the Dungeon, I found that my assumption of having the place to myself might not be accurate. There was a light being reflected, a little way off from the entrance. Puzzled, and feeling invulnerable from Greater Invisibility still being on, I casually made my way toward the light.

It turned out to be a campfire, with one man standing watch, and three or four bundled up forms of sleeping men.

What's going on here? I asked myself. I moved closer. I felt like an assassin in a video game, able to sneak around with impunity and dispatch my enemies with a quick head-jerk. *No assassination!* I reminded myself. Getting closer, I realized that I recognized the guard as one of Reynard's followers.

That's interesting, I thought. *Why does Reynard have people waiting outside the Dungeon?*

I turned Intrigue on the problem. A few things came out.

One, I knew that Reynard wanted me to enable him to lie to the Guild. So I knew that whatever fishy business he was up to, it was to do with the Guild. Two, the most important Guild business was the Dungeon, so it probably had *something* to do with the Dungeon. Now he had people . . . watching the entrance? They couldn't do that from where they were, but they probably didn't expect any traffic during the night. Looking around, I saw a nearby place where someone could keep an eye on the entrance while staying hidden. That must be their lookout, but they were off duty right now. So why did he care who went into the Dungeon?

Didn't Sean say something about restrictions on challenging the final boss? Hmm. But Sean also said that they were grinding through the requirements and would be able to do it soon . . . So Reynard was only delaying them. Delaying until he was ready for . . . whatever it was he wanted me to cover up? And it was down on the bottom level.

Which is out of reach . . . for the moment. From what others had said, level two would be quite nasty, and level three was a lava floor. I'd need more equipment before tackling that.

Anyway, the watchers weren't an impediment, so I made my way into the Dungeon. It was bright daylight inside—it always was, down here. I let my eyes adjust, and then headed for the passage to the next chamber.

This time around, I didn't have to worry about stealth. I only moved with enough caution to make sure I didn't trip over a lizard, moving quickly to where the guardian was . . . standing? Could you call that standing? Regardless, he was completely unaware of me, as I walked calmly up to him.

Let's see if we can do this in one hit, I thought to myself. Lining myself up, I braced and struck with all my power at the lizard's neck.

You have inflicted 62 damage!

Dammit, not enough! I thought as it staggered away from the wound. It seemed too stunned to even react, so I finished it off with another blow.

You have inflicted 59 damage!
For killing an Ilan Lizard, you have earned 30 XP.

I got more for the fox! Since I didn't feel like I was in much danger, this probably wasn't even doing my Dagger skill much good. I moved on to the next room guardian, with much the same result . . . I needed to take on the boss.

The final chamber was lacking the ecosystem shared by the first four, consisting only of an open area of rocky sand, surrounded by rock walls, with a single cave entrance. Adventurers who preferred ranged combat had tried luring or smoking the boss out here, but he stayed in the cave. I poked my head in and saw it was how it had been described. A main passageway headed straight on for about ten meters and then took a sudden turn. The boss chamber would be just past that. Before the turn, four other small passageways branched off. These were two small for me to easily crawl through, but they had been explored. They led to the boss chamber as well, each of them passing through an Ilan lizard's nest. The boss's minions could either come out to aid the boss, or appear in the passageway to cut off escape, or maul the backline.

Why am I doing this? some part of my brain asked. Was it because Milly had freaked me out with her talk of destiny and hunters? Back home, I'd dealt with risk every day, but it had been research. Quantifying and cataloging each aspect of risk, packaging it up and offsetting . . . until it wasn't risk any more but saleable product. Taking risks was for the boys on the floor, the traders and the hedge managers, swaggering about the place as they won or lost millions of the firm's or other people's money.

They looked down on us, I knew. Oh, they could be sweet enough when they smelled a bit of juicy info, a bit of an edge, or the chance to get in someone's pants. But we heard how they talked about us when they thought no one was listening. Mostly because they didn't seem to realize how loud they were talking. *No reward without risk*, they'd say. *I know what I'm doing*, I told myself, and stepped into the cave.

I did not know what I was doing, but I did have a plan. As soon as I got to the corner, I cast the brightest Light spell that I could, at what I estimated was the center of the room. It was painful to look at directly, but not debilitating. The boss was revealed in all his ugly animal glory.

> **[Identification] : Greater Ilan Lizard (Male) – Threat Level: 5 – Condition: Unhurt**

I decided to call him Gil. Gil raised himself up, looking for his opponent, but there wasn't anybody. I was actually moving back down the passage as he roared, summoning his minions.

Sean had warned me, when it looked like I might be going in without fully preparing, that Invisibility wasn't going to be the trump card that it normally was. I hadn't actually told them I had Invisibility, but it was a pretty obvious Illusionist spell.

"A lot of bosses have blind fighting," he told me. Well, us; Felicia was still there, but he was addressing me. "It allows them to fight in a melee without any senses. This guy is stuck in a dark cave, so he probably has it."

"You don't know?" I asked. "You've fought him, right?"

Sean shrugged. "He's a level one boss," he said. "We go in with torches, and I one-shot him while the others take out the minions."

So if I went into the chamber, the boss would engage me, and his minions would hamper my movement. They wouldn't be able to sense me, but if the boss got ahold of me, then I was sure to get swarmed. So step one was to take out the minions in the corridor.

> **You have inflicted 66 damage!**

I struck at one of them, then immediately moved away. My target started snapping randomly around him and lashing his tail, but I wasn't there to be hit. The outer corridor was actually a fairly spacious place to fight, and I could escape outside if I had to. With them not being able to sense me, it was easy to avoid them as long as I kept my distance. When they tired of snapping at air, I snuck in again.

> **You have inflicted 65 damage!**

Different lizard, so no kill, but boy were they angry now. Gil remained inside his cave, but I could hear him roaring. I wondered how much he was aware of what was going on. I let a few seconds go by, waiting for my chance.

> **You have inflicted 59 damage!**
> **For killing an Ilan Lizard, you have earned 30 XP.**

Now there were three. I backed off outside. I was worried about dripping blood from my blade giving me away, so I tried wiping it in the sand outside. It didn't clean it, but it got enough off so it didn't drip. Interestingly, the lizards seemed to smell the blood outside and came closer to the entrance. Not out of it, though; there appeared to be a rule. A rule that I could abuse, darting in and out again.

> **You have inflicted 64 damage!**
> **For killing an Ilan Lizard, you have earned 30 XP.**

Lucky! The two remaining backed away from the entrance, but it didn't make a difference. They couldn't see me coming, and it wasn't long before I had sixty more XP. Now the main show could begin.

I moved cautiously forward, and rounded the corner once more. Gil was pacing about, clearly agitated. He couldn't sense me, but that wouldn't matter when I got close.

"They can't see you, but they can dodge your attacks," Sean had said. "They can't sense you, but if you're in melee range, they can attack you."

My heart was thumping like crazy, but I moved in.

> **You have inflicted 39 damage!**
> **You have taken 8 damage!**

Blind fighting confirmed, I thought. *But I hurt it more!* I backed off, to give myself time to deal with the pain, but . . . it didn't hurt as much as before? *I have more HP now, so it's a relatively lighter wound?*

Gil had reacted to my backing away by charging for the exit, perhaps expecting to find me there. But I wasn't going to be so predictable. It cut me off from escape, but it meant that he was over on the other side of the chamber. I charged in again.

> **You have inflicted 47 damage!**
> **You have inflicted 36 damage!**
> **You have inflicted 42 damage!**
> **You have taken 8 damage!**

Ow! I thought, but I was grinning like a madwoman. It had taken him time to get turned around, and I'd easily dodged his awkward bites, but then he'd switched things up with a tail sweep. I backed away again, easily keeping away from him as he stalked around the chamber.

> **[Identification] : Greater Ilan Lizard (Male) – Threat Level: 5 – Condition: Bloody**

Bloody, all right. Even though I was injured, I felt powerful. They were only light wounds and Gil's blood was everywhere around the room. Even I could smell it. I was going to win this fight!

> **You have inflicted 33 damage!**
> **You have taken 5 damage!**
> **You have inflicted 32 damage!**
> **For killing a Greater Ilan Lizard, you have earned 150 XP.**
> **For clearing the first level of Oakdale Dungeon for the first time, you have earned 100 XP.**
> **For clearing the first level of Oakdale Dungeon, you have earned a reward.**
> **For clearing the first level of Oakdale Dungeon alone for the first time, you have earned 100 XP.**
> **For clearing the first level of Oakdale Dungeon alone, you have earned a reward.**

I stood in the cavern and laughed like I was crazy. I felt like I should be coming down from an adrenaline crash, but my body was ready for more. I still had 200 Endurance; I was barely even winded. *Is this what it feels like to win a million-dollar trade?* I wondered. *No, this is better.* Slowly, I calmed down. About the time I could no longer hear my heartbeat, I was reminded of my wounds.

Ow! This time they were all on my arms and legs, so they were easier to check. Cleaning them with water and wrapping them in cloth wasn't enough for a First Aid skill unlock, but they didn't hurt as much, and they stopped making a mess. Once that was taken care of, I could start paying attention to the changes in my environment.

Without me noticing exactly how, a new passageway had opened, headed into some lighted area. On either side, two small chests had appeared. They were only about twenty centimeters long and made of brass, or bronze, or something else that was yellowy, but wasn't gold. I tried picking one up, but it didn't move. Opening it, I found a small ingot of a black metal, a small medallion, and some silver coins.

> **[Identification] : Darksteel Ingot – Quality : Good – Properties: Silent, Steel-piercing**
> **[Identification] : Oakway Token – Properties: Key**
> **[Identification] : 20 Silver Hawks – Quality : Good – Properties: None**

And here's the reward to go with the risk! I scooped up the goods and opened the other chest. This held an identical ingot, and silver, but no medallion. My funds were now officially recovered. I turned my attention to the lighted passage. From what I'd heard, most of the gains from the second level required Hunt or Gather to collect, so there was little point in going through.

But it couldn't hurt to look, could it? I went through, and found myself in the jungle.

> **[Identification] : Denine Fern – Condition: Healthy**
> **[Identification] : Moinal Creeper Vine – Condition: Healthy**
> **[Identification] : Polenth Tree – Condition: Infested**
> **[Identification] : Undra Weevils – Threat Level: 0 – Condition: Healthy**
> **[Identification] : Wakas Finch – Threat Level: 0 – Condition: Healthy**
> **[Identification] : Yerper Beetle – Threat Level: 0 – Condition: Healthy**

The Identification notifications scrolled on, but I stopped paying attention to them. There was so much here! A wall of diverse plants and trees filled my field of view, starting two meters from the entrance, starting so suddenly, it looked as though the jungle had been sheared off with a knife. There were three paths leading off in different directions, but they twisted quickly and I couldn't see where they went from here. The noise was something else—birds, insects, unidentified screeches . . . This was the next level, all right.

Not today. This could wait until I got Felicia down here. I headed back. My mood picked up again as I passed the bodies of my defeated enemies. If I really wanted to maximize my gain, I should bring back the bodies . . . but I'd made a lot of profit already; no need to weigh myself down. I also didn't bother with the room guardians on my way out. Invisible, I could just walk around them. That reminded me that Greater Invisibility blocked sound as well—even if I was talking. For the first time in a while, I had privacy—and there was something I had to do.

"Weee are the champions, my friends,
And we'll keep on fighting til the end
We are the champions
We are the champions
No time for losers, 'cause we are the champions
of the wooooorrrrrrllld!"
Yeah, it was cheesy, but damn was it the right song for right now.

> **Competency displayed with [Sing], Level 1 awarded.**
> **For gaining a skill level, you have been awarded 1 XP.**

Ha! The perfect cap to a great . . . wait, this day had only just begun.

Getting past the watchers had been as easy as I anticipated. By the time I got back to town, dawn had arrived, and the guards were opening the main gate. I could have appeared and shown them my Guild plate, but it was easier to just stroll past and head back to the inn. Cerys was already up, getting the place ready to open. I'd ask how she managed on so little sleep, but I knew. The fact that just about *everyone* had one of these crazy level three bodies was something I was still getting used to. I'm amazed that everyone wasn't jumping through second-story windows and stuff.

I got washed up and changed and started on breakfast. As I was eating, Harold came up and sat down next to me.

"Sir?" I asked. That was . . . Charm, I think, having me say that. I'm not normally so respectful at the breakfast table.

Harold wasn't one to mince words, so he got right down to it. "Are you going to be staying with us long, Kathrine?"

"Huh?"

He gestured at my bandaged arm. "You've been going adventuring, and at night too, for reasons passing understanding."

"Oh, that was . . . I was just really full of energy last night and needed to burn it off—"

He waved away my explanation. "You don't need to explain why," he said. "As long as you show up to work, that's not my business. But." He looked at me. "Unless you're terrible at it, you made more last night than in all the time you've worked here so far. You don't need this job, so why are you still here?"

It was true; I'd made much more last night—this morning—than I ever had here. In fact, considering he paid us weekly, I had made infinitely more. The thing was, people had conversations in taverns, and being a waitress meant overhearing them. I was learning a lot about this world from overheard conversations—not secret things, but things that everyone knew about. I'd look pretty weird coming up to people and asking, "How does law enforcement work in this country?" Of course, for the same reason, I couldn't *say* that to Harold, but I could spin it slightly to something acceptable.

"It's not about the money, sir," I said. "It's true that I make more adventuring, and I'm not planning on staying in town for very long, but while I'm here I'd like to keep working at the Tanner. It . . . grounds me. Doing honest work for pay, having a place to stay that's stable, that I'm a part of. It's something I want more than adventuring."

He nodded slowly. "How long?"

"I'm not sure," I said. "It depends on . . . a lot of things. A month?"

He nodded again. "Make sure you show up at sunset. Your injuries aren't serious?"

I shook my head. "I'll be there."

"Wow, aren't you dressed . . . expensively?" Felicia said. We were meeting at the Guild, and she wasn't wrong. I'd made another trip to the market and was looking like a real adventurer now. Leather jacket, pants, and gauntlets had me almost entirely encased in leathery protection. Under all that were some new regular clothes—I wasn't yet ready to be a fetish model, and dresses were impractical anyway. I was still a long way from fitted clothes—they cost more than steel apparently, but everything fit . . . well enough.

"You went and did it, didn't you!" Felicia accused me. "And after everything they said!"

I wanted to put on a serious look, but thinking about that fight again put a grin on my face that I couldn't suppress. I didn't say anything, just showed her the medallion, about the only thing left from today's treasure haul.

"Is that the key to the second level? Can I see?"

"Nope!" I said, but handed it to her anyway. Or tried to. When she tried to take it, an invisible force prevented her fingers from closing. When I tried dropping it into her hand, it flew back into mine.

"Wow, it's real Dungeon magic," Felicia said wonderingly. "Wait, I'm still mad! You weren't supposed to go without us!"

"I really am sorry," I said. "I got Invisibility, and there were tricks I could try if I was on my own."

"Sean said Invisibility wouldn't work on the boss!" she protested.

"It didn't . . . not entirely anyway," I said. "It worked on his minions, though, so I could fight him alone. It was . . . amazing, Felicia. And the second level . . . you're going to love it."

She glared at me some more. "Master's told me about the second level," she said. "Most of his herbs come from there. I'm just worried that you're going to clear it before Kyle's ready to fight again."

"Oh, come on, he's going to be ready tomorrow, right? It's gonna take me at least a week to clear level two." I grinned.

"I know you're joking, but you probably will, won't you?"

"Who knows? I didn't actually enter the jungle; it looked like I'd get lost before I took three steps."

She nodded. "That's a danger. You need—wait, I'm not going to tell you now."

I laughed. "That's fine," I said. "What I had in mind for today was some skill training. For you." I held up the blank pages I had purchased that morning. "Let's go back to the library."

Some time later, we were approaching the moment of truth. Felicia could already count and write out numbers. The Roman-ish system of numbers they used sort of included the concept of adding. Fifteen was XV, which was X + V (different symbols, of course). I vaguely recalled that there was some trick like on-paper multiplication that worked for Roman numerals, but my plan was to get Felicia off them entirely. She quickly memorized the symbols—I suspect Scribe helped her with that. It took a while for her to grasp the position system for numbers higher than ten, but not too long. Addition was reviewed with the new system, and then we moved on to multiplication. I explained how it was repeated adding, and constructed a multiplication table for her going up to times ten.

"I'm not sure if you'll need to memorize this for it to work," I said, "but for now, just know that you can work out the multiple of any two digits with this." Felicia nodded, uncertain.

Now for the moment of truth. Just adding was enough to get a skill unlock, but she already had that. I moved on to teach her how to multiply longer numbers on paper. It was easy to explain a method that didn't require anything other than addition and the one-digit multiplication we'd already covered. But you could use it to multiply arbitrarily large numbers. I got her to multiply 322 by 21. I knew that with a four-digit result, you would normally need Calculation of two for the skill to work.

"6,762," she said, finishing the calculation. "Oh! I . . . got the skill! At two!"

I was a little distracted, because I was dealing with my own notification.

Competency displayed with [Teach], Level 2 awarded.
For gaining a skill level, you have been awarded 2 XP.

"Yes! Free skill!" I crowed. Felicia was looking at the notes. I assumed that she was redoing the calculation in her head, to see what it was like. But she wasn't.

"Katherine," she said slowly. "That 'sheltered background' of yours . . . where in Ryvue was it?" She looked at me. "What's 'English'?"

Oh shit. I looked at her notes.

[Identification] : Calculation Notes (English) – Quality: Good –
Properties: [Teach] Calculation

KYLE

Felicia, I— ” I said. Conversation couldn't help me when I didn't know what to say.

"I'm sorry!" Felicia exclaimed. "I shouldn't be prying, but—"

"No! No, you're right to wonder." I paused, my mind racing. "I'll tell you everything . . . when we get to level two."

"What? Why then? Does the Dungeon have something to do with . . ."

"Nothing like that," I assured her. "Just that I want to meet Kyle before I commit to anything. After all, I can hardly expect you to keep this from your boyfriend."

"Kyle isn't my boyfriend!" she blurted. "He's just—you're changing the subject again, aren't you?"

"Of course not. That was very convincing, by the way. I totally believed you."

"You—I'm—He's—" she spluttered. "When you meet him tomorrow, you are absolutely forbidden from saying anything embarrassing about boyfriends!"

"OK, OK," I said, holding up my hands in surrender. She glared at me.

"That had better mean 'yes' in that 'English' of yours," she said.

I spent the rest of the morning reading the book on Dungeons while Felicia played with her new Calculate skill. I told her she could get it higher quickly by using the paper method to multiply much larger numbers, but she didn't see the need. As it was, she could handle any calculation up to ten thousand, and she didn't see a need for more.

The Dungeon book was interesting. It listed details for twenty publicly available Dungeons—only about half of those that existed in the Kingdom of Latora, according to it. And it didn't include any of the "private" Dungeons that had been claimed by the nobility of the Kingdom for their own use. What was really interesting, though, was the introductory section on common knowledge about Dungeons. Apparently, Dungeons held a unique magic that was not even detectable by current magic skills. While they could produce regular enchanted items, things like my "key" were not magic, as it was understood, and could produce effects that regular types of magic could not.

Despite being naturally occurring, Dungeons seemed to have an intelligence involved, either behind the design, or in some cases, actively guiding the activities that went on inside. It was theorized that this was due to something called a Dungeon core, always located on the bottom level of a Dungeon. Removing the core resulted in the destruction of the Dungeon. This always affected the mana flows in the area, generally causing increased monster spawnings. In most cases, though, the conditions that formed the Dungeon in the first place were still there, so a new Dungeon would form again in the same place.

Due to the effects of Dungeon destruction, and because Dungeons were considered a resource for the Kingdom, it was illegal to remove a Dungeon core without official permission. However, the book noted, this was difficult to enforce due to a demand for cores from highly powerful mages. It didn't say what mages did with the cores. The other thing that made it hard to enforce, the book said, was that cores did not register as magical items, and could not be scryed on.

Maybe that's why wizards want them, I speculated. They want their privacy.

Nothing much of note happened for the rest of the day. I took a nap and worked the tavern. The next day was payday, and I tried to look suitably grateful for the few coins I received. No one was fooled, I think—while I didn't wear it to work, everyone knew I had twenty times as much as this invested in equipment. It wasn't about the money, though. I was wearing the armor when I collected my pay, but rather than being ostentatious, it seemed to be a mark in my favor. Harold had mentioned that the type of adventurer he disliked were the ones that earned just enough money to drink themselves under the table and never did any more. By sinking so much money into equipment, I seemed to have moved into the second category.

Today, I was meeting Felicia and Kyle, and heading down into the Dungeon as a group. We were meeting at the Town Healer's place, because

Felicia had said her Master wanted to meet me. I hadn't quite grasped the nature of the master-apprentice relationship here. It existed, I knew, but there was very little training involved, as that all tended to be done by the System. Instead, I think, it was an exchange of labor for resources. Felicia could find her own herbs, and knew how to prepare poultices, but she needed a mortar and pestle, containers, cauldrons, and other ingredients that couldn't be found in the forest. It was the same for other craftsmen; they needed raw materials to practice on before they could get good enough to sell them.

It seemed to me that another way to establish yourself would be to adventure for a year or two, get a few levels and money, and then take up a profession. The fact that Felicia was adventuring while serving as an apprentice would seem to contradict that theory, but maybe she was the exception that proved the rule.

As Town Healer, Felicia's Master (she always referred to him as "Master") was paid a retainer to make himself available to heal town officials (guards mostly) and aid the town during emergencies. When he wasn't required, he made extra income by selling healing potions. This was all information I'd gleaned from tavern conversations. Councillor Webster was always complaining about the extra expense of retaining a healer when no one needed healing. As a town employee, his shop wasn't located in the market, but off the main square. I had seen it on my first day, but I wasn't in a position to be buying potions then. Anyway, I found it without trouble and went inside. Felicia was staffing the counter.

"Katherine, good morning," Felicia greeted me brightly. She must be in customer service mode.

"Good morning to you, too," I replied. "Is everyone here?"

"Master! Katherine's here!" she called out. "Yes, just go through," she said, a trace of nervousness entering her voice. "Remember—you promised!"

I giggled and went on through to the back room. This was a workshop for processing herbs, at a guess. It looked like a cross between a chemistry lab and a florist. There was also a bed, but I think that was for clients rather than where the master slept. Occupying the room were two men. One was about forty and dressed in shirt and trousers and a leather apron. The other was a teenager, dressed in what looked to me to be ill-fitting metal armor.

Until now, Charm had been having me curtsy at every opportunity, and introductions were definitely one such. However, without a dress,

I couldn't curtsy properly, so Charm was telling me to just skip it and behave like the confident and assured adventurer that I was dressed as.

"Hello, I'm Katherine," I said. I stopped myself from giving a "how you doing" look at the young man who had to be Kyle. *What the hell, Charm?*

"Greetings," said the older man. "I am Oliver Heath, and this young man is Kyle Warner."

I shook Oliver's hand, and then carefully made sure that any seductive vibes I was sending out were turned off before turning to Kyle and shaking his. "I've heard a lot about you, Kyle." Kyle was a pretty tall kid, who'd probably be a pretty large man in a few years. He had blond hair and blue eyes and an eager look to him.

"Ah, really?" he said. I just grinned.

"Before anything else: Katherine, are you injured?" asked Oliver.

"Just some scratches," I said.

"Allow me," Oliver said, holding out his hand. Confused, I took it. His hand glowed, and I instinctively opened my Mana Sense. I could now see tendrils of mana reaching out from his hand and touching each of my wounds. I felt a warmth and a pleasurable feeling as my wounds closed.

"Oh, thank you, that feels really good!" I exclaimed.

"You're welcome," Oliver said. "I have a limited number of points I can use to heal each day, but they go to waste if they don't get used."

"Do I owe you . . ." I reached for my pouch, but Oliver waved me away.

"Please, it's the least I can do for how you've helped Felicia." He gave me a warm smile.

"Well, thanks again. Felicia said you wanted to meet me before we went into the Dungeon again?"

He nodded. "Please, sit." he gestured for me to use the only chair, Kyle sat on the bed, and Oliver pulled a stool out from under a workbench. "I did want to see what sort of person I'd be putting my apprentice in the care of."

"Well, here I am," I said, "Though I don't know about taking care of Felicia; she may be younger, but she's actually a bit more experienced at this than I am."

"Hmmm," he said, leaning forward. "If that's true, then you've got it extremely early."

"Got what?" I asked, puzzled.

"The adventurers call it Dungeon fever," he said. "You've got it, don't you? That urge to plunge deeper down the levels. To go faster, harder, than all the others."

"I've got . . . reasons . . . to push myself," I said. I hesitated. "Sometimes I wonder if they're entirely rational."

"You have some self-awareness, at least. Listen to me. The easy levels are behind you now. Its going to be a long, hard slog to get to level four, and that's just the start of the journey you're contemplating. You're not going to kill a boss and get even halfway there."

"I'm aware," I said, somewhat embarrassed. "I'd need to fight a threat level of sixty for that amount of XP. I don't even know if that level exists."

"I'm a little worried that you focus on the *existence* of such creatures as the difficulty here. My point is, you need to pace yourself. Keep pushing, and you *will* get killed. Worse, you could take these two with you."

"I'd never put their lives at risk!" I protested. "Sure, I take risks—managed risks—but that's when I go alone. Going in a party—even if I was willing to risk their lives—would only be a third of the reward."

Oliver frowned. "How do you *manage* danger?" he asked.

I shrugged. "Assess the severity of the risk, based on likelihood and consequences, measure against the expected reward, take steps to mitigate either the likelihood or consequences—or both—depending on which would have the greater effect." I could rattle off this stuff in my sleep. It seemed to confuse Oliver, though.

"What does that even . . . does that make sense?" he said. "Is that a skill?"

"Katherine knows a lot of things that aren't skills," Felicia said. She'd come through from the front of the shop. "She knows a lot of things she hasn't told us. But I don't think she's going to get me killed."

She moved in front of me. "I can't say the same for yourself, though! Will you get it through your head that everyone's worried about you?"

I sighed. "I know what I'm doing, all right? If it makes you feel better, I can't really go off on my own anyway—at least for a while."

"And why is that?"

I counted off the points on my fingers. "I don't know my way around the second level; I'd get lost and die. I don't know how to find the valuable plants in that jungle. I can't collect the valuable bits from animals down there. I have thought about this. I need you to do things down there—and that means taking it slow and steady, with backup"—I pointed at Kyle—"and a plan."

Felicia looked at her Master. They seemed somewhat mollified.

"Besides, today we're just going to do level one until Kyle gets to level three, right? Should be a cakewalk."

"Don't say that!" exclaimed Felicia. "You don't want to tempt the gods."

I shrugged. I kinda did want to tempt them. "So, Kyle," I said, transparently changing the subject. "Nice armor. Family heirloom?"

"Uh, yes," he said, manifestly uncomfortable with being brought into the conversation. "I . . ." He looked to Felicia for help, but I interrupted instead.

"I'm no expert, but I went looking at a lot of armor yesterday. That suit looks like it's supposed to be worn over some leather under . . . armor?" My technical vocabulary had been exhausted, alas.

"That's right!" Kyle was evidently a lot happier with technical conversations. "It's supposed to be attached directly, but it needs a specially crafted tunic with the fastenings on it. When Da retired, he put the metal away carefully, but he kept wearing the leather."

"Adventurer family, then?" He nodded in response. "Is that the one that I heard is the closest thing to nobility that this area has?" While everyone in the area had started out with equal grants of land, some families had prospered, while some hadn't. Farms had been purchased or inherited, and now there was a wide variety of landowners. From what I'd heard, the Warners were the biggest of them.

"That's us," he said, reluctantly. "But, uh, my family isn't one of the important branches. Oh, and don't let the rest of the clan hear you compare us to nobles."

"Why not?" I asked.

"Great-grandfather hated the nobility, made his sons swear to never become them, or like them. There are a few families like that around, which is why the nobles have stayed away."

"Huh." Interesting. I'd heard that Oakway was fairly unusual in not coming under a feudal lord. That the *town* was free wasn't that unusual—it seemed like fifty-fifty odds—but generally the nobles owned all the land around the town, giving them—at the least—an outsized say in the town's business.

"So you'd be looking to get that under-armor then?" I asked. Kyle perked up, much happier to be talking about armor than his family.

"Yeah, I ordered it, and I've paid a deposit already. It should be ready as soon as I've got the thirty silver. As it is, the armor isn't too bad, though. The gaps are high, but my skill is enough to cover them."

He had a sword as well; it also looked to be an heirloom, from the quality of it.

> **[Identification] : Longsword – Quality: Good – Damage: +60.**

"Well, I'm reassured," I said. "You look to be just the kind of protector two casters should have. Are you all right with working with me?"

"You're asking me?" he asked, startled. "Well, yes, of course Felicia said you were . . ." He straightened. "Yes, I'm happy to be working with you."

"Great," I said.

"And . . . about the danger." He hesitated and I made an encouraging face. "Well, it's just that Da always said—pushing yourself to the limits is just what an adventurer does. You've just got to be sure you know what those limits are."

I grinned. "Thanks for that. I couldn't agree more."

Before we left, I made sure to buy a healing potion.

"You still have injuries?" asked Felicia. "Master, can you—"

"Master Heath already took care of it," I interjected. "This is for insurance."

"I wouldn't let Felicia go without one of her own, but she's to use it only for emergencies," Oliver said.

"That's good to know, but it's always better to have more—just in case," I said.

"Fine," Oliver said. He took a small vial off the shelf. "Five silver, should heal twenty HP."

> **[Identification] : Lesser Healing Potion – Quality: Great – Heal +20**

"Thanks," I said, handing over the coin. "Here's hoping I can build up a collection."

Since the day was about getting Kyle up to level three, I proposed a division of labor. Kyle was perfectly capable of killing an Ilan lizard on his own. If he did it on his own, he'd get sixty XP, whereas if we were involved he'd net only ten. Felicia could concentrate on skinning the lizards he killed, so we made money, and I would guard Felicia and kill any lizards that came after us.

It all worked perfectly well. So much so, my biggest problem was keeping myself entertained. A few lizards showed up where we were, but they were quickly dispatched and added to the "to be skinned" pile. Since Felicia knew about English, I started practicing my Sing skill, treating her to the works of Taylor Swift and other classics. At first they were *a cappella*, but then it occurred to me to use Memorize and Unseen Sound to give myself musical accompaniment. That was probably unwise, but . . . even though it hadn't been a week, I missed music something fierce.

Kyle protested that I would draw lizards to my location, but I pointed out that just meant more skins. And hearing my voice meant that he could keep track of us while hunting. He didn't look convinced, but . . .

[Persuade] Level 2 acquired through use.
For gaining a skill level, you have been awarded 1 XP.

It took most of the day, but we ended up with ten Ilan skins and four Idnul skins. Most of them managed to give us an Average quality hide.

"That should come to . . . 94 copper, all up?" Felicia said, a bit disappointed. "We got more from the newts."

"I think we should keep Kyle away from the newts for a while," I said. Kyle grimaced. "The important thing is that we're all level three now. Who's ready to take on the next level?"

"The boss is sure to have been killed by now," Felicia said. "He won't be back until midnight, unless the group that killed him went to level three."

"Is that likely?" I asked.

"Maybe. The level two shaman drops a fetish that lets you teleport straight to level three from the entrance, so you don't *need* to. But"—she looked over my shiny new armor—"I hear it's a pretty rich reward, so it might be worth the time to take the long route. Of course, it's late enough that they've probably come *back* and killed it again."

"There's no booking system for the boss?" I asked hopefully.

"No, the first one there gets the benefit."

"Boo. Well, we could just head down to the second level, take a look round?"

"But we didn't pick up any second level jobs—we wouldn't know what's needed for collection!"

"I'm sure we could pick up something valuable. But if you're fine waiting another day for that conversation . . ." I trailed off.

Felicia narrowed her eyes. "I *am* fine with that, because we are going to do this *properly,* and not hare off on a whim!"

"Fine, fine. Tomorrow then. How early do you think we'll need to be to catch the boss?"

"Pretty early," she said doubtfully "If someone's going after it, they'll leave as soon as the gates open at dawn."

"Um," said Kyle, "I live outside of town, so I don't have to worry about the gate. I can get there earlier."

"But we can't have you going alone," I said with a sly grin. "I hear that's dangerous." Felicia huffed at me, but I continued. "What we should do is have Felicia stay at your place overnight."

"What!" both of them exclaimed in unison, before diverging into different incoherent stammers. Undaunted, I continued on.

"Yes, that's clearly the best plan. I can slip out of the town before dawn, and meet you at the entrance at dawn. Felicia will have to get permission from her Master, of course, but I'm sure, Kyle, that your mother would be happy to offer her hospitality?"

"Well, we-we have a spare bed, so I guess it would be fine."

"Then it's settled. Let's head back and pick up some Guild quests."

On the way out, I thought to check on the watchers. Telling the others to go on and I'd join them later, I turned invisible before leaving the Dungeon and went to take a look. Oddly, there was no one keeping watch, and the camp was abandoned. Odd. I quickly rejoined the others, deflecting their queries with speculation about Felicia meeting Kyle's mother. Just bringing up the topic was enough to fluster them into not asking further questions.

Back in town, I was able to net a little more for our skins. We ended up with 47 copper each, but I handed my share to Kyle, on the grounds that he did most of my work, *and* he needed to get that under-armor. I wasn't hurting for cash at the moment, so I was tempted to give him another ten silver to get him there sooner, but I knew he wouldn't accept pure charity.

At the Guild, Felicia spent some time poring over the job requests, evaluating them on some criteria that I wasn't aware of, while I talked to Paige.

"Do people register parties at the Guild?" I asked.

"Why, yes," she replied. "It will be good to have a third official party in the guild."

"You only have two?" I asked. I'd never seen less than twenty people in the Guild Hall, so this seemed low.

"I think I already saw you talking with the Delvers, and there's a local group called the Oakway Raiders. They're mostly level three. Reynard has his crew, but they're not an official team. And there's almost a dozen loners who just go down to the first two levels enough to make a living." Sean's group were called the Delvers? It sounded a little embarrassing, which was maybe why they hadn't mentioned it. Although now that I thought about it, could you have a team name that wasn't embarrassing? It was like a brand—you needed to grow into it, get people to attach positive feelings toward it. We weren't going to do that killing lizards in a jungle. *We need to save a town from something. Milly said something like that was in my likely future, though.*

"So is there a benefit to being in a party?"

"Being registered? Well, any Guild points that the party earns are also awarded to the members, so it makes it easier to climb up the Guild rankings. Higher Guild ranking is required for the more dangerous jobs."

"Oh, like having to be Gold rank to face the final boss of the Dungeon."

"That's not a requirement," Paige said, puzzled. "Did you hear that somewhere?"

"I'm not sure . . ."

"Well, the other thing with registration is in case of a death. No one wants to talk about it, but arranging for next-of-kin or survivor benefits is easier if you're in the same team."

"Ah. I take it the standard arrangement is for the surviving team members to split the . . . inherited assets?"

"You can specify something different if you want . . . It's awkward to talk about, but it's a lot worse after an . . . incident."

Felicia came up at this point. "We'd like to register for these jobs, please?" she said, holding three job listings. I called Kyle over, and we started taking care of the paperwork.

"What do you want to call yourselves?" Paige asked, pen over the registration book. *Too much pressure!*

"Do you guys have any ideas?" Blank looks and shaking heads. *Hey, can Creativity help with this?* I focused and something came up.

"How about Eureka Company?" Puzzled looks this time.

"Eureka? What's that?" asked Felicia.

"It's . . . something you say when you find what you've been looking for," I said.

"I've never heard of it," said Paige, "But it's just a name; you can put whatever you like."

"I like it," said Kyle. Felicia nodded agreement.

"Let's go with that then," I said.

* * *

Early morning found me outside the Oakway Dungeon. I hadn't pulled an all-nighter this time—I was due the occasional night off, and I'd sweetened the deal by offering to help with the setup for the early morning baking. I slipped over the walls in the darkness, as before, but predawn was lighting the countryside by the time I got to the entrance. I'd wanted to get here a bit early, to see if the watchers were back, and where they went during the day.

Sure enough, it seemed as if they had spent the night here again. They were stamping out the campfire and packing up their gear when I arrived. I didn't make my presence known, just watched and followed as they headed into the Dungeon. As soon as they entered, one of them pulled out a red gem the size of my fist, and they all grabbed ahold. Without any ceremony or ritual, they simply disappeared.

I canceled my spell and made my way back outside. I pondered the added data but didn't come to any conclusions before my team arrived.

R A P T O R

I t's just a pair of kids and their mother!" the man snorted derisively to his companions.

Felicia and Kyle looked uneasily at each other, as more adventurers filed into the room. We were in the level one boss cavern, cleaning up after finishing the boss. Felicia hadn't wanted to leave any money "lying around on the ground," so we'd stopped to process the corpses, while I filled them in on my story. We'd almost finished, when we were interrupted by voices approaching.

"Can we help you with something?" I asked. We'd moved to the side of the cave to process our hides, so we weren't in the way if they wanted to proceed to level two. The man spat at my feet.

"We came here for the boss loot, girlie. How'd you get here quicker than us?"

I smiled thinly. "Not everyone hides behind the town wall until dawn. If you're out already, you don't have to wait for the guards to let you out."

"Bullshit," he snarled. "It ain't safe outside at night. Couple of kids wouldn't have made it."

Did he really believe that? It was true that monsters tended to spawn outside at night, but from what I'd heard from Angus, this Dungeon was the most dangerous area in twenty miles. Kyle certainly hadn't had any problems walking here before dawn. *Sleeping* would have been unwise, but Reynard's friends had been fine just posting a watch.

I shrugged. "We didn't have any problems. Now, as you can see, there's nothing for you here, so if you'd like to head back"—I pointed at the jungle passage—"or move on, that would be great."

"Bullshit," he growled again, but weaker this time. He glanced at his buddies for support and tried again. "We came here for the coin. The way

I see it, that's still here for the taking." He took a step forward. My heart started beating frantically. Is this Intimidate? The sudden ramp up in the threat level had me worried, but I'd dealt with bullies in my previous life, before I had magic even.

> **Competency displayed with [Intimidate], Level 1 awarded.**
> **For gaining a skill level, you have been awarded 1 XP.**

As soon as the notice came up, the fear eased. "Felicia," I called out, not taking my eyes off the man. "What are the Guild rules about attacking other members?"

"Uh, well, if there is a complaint, it goes before the Guild master, who adjudicates. The guilty party is generally thrown out of the Guild and handed over to the town authorities."

"And the guilty party is the one who strikes the first blow?"

"I think so?"

"Well then." I gave my opponent a shit eating grin. "Care to start something?"

"We aren't afraid of you," he growled. It was true, I hadn't used [Intimidate] yet. That was about to change.

"Maybe not," I said. "But I know you're afraid of the dark." I cut my Light spell.

I'd lit the cave up for Kyle's fight with Gil—the ground was quite treacherous and was a significant hazard in the darkness—and kept it on to help Felicia with her skinning. With the exit open, it wasn't quite as dark as normal, but there was a moment of confusion before everyone's eyes started adjusting. I was as blind as anyone, but I didn't need to see to target myself. *[Simple Invisibility]. [Light].*

When the light returned, I was gone, at least as far as these rubes could tell. They gaped and looked around for where I might have run to, while I casually strolled around behind the group. Kyle and Felicia looked as worried as everyone else, but they kept up a good front, Felicia hiding behind Kyle.

[Intimidate].

"So tell me, Felicia," my disembodied voice coming from behind them now. "What happens if there's no one left to bring a complaint forward?"

They didn't wait for Felicia's answer; they knew it already, after all. They broke as one and started running back to the upper level.

"Wow," Felicia said. "That was amazing."

"Would they really have robbed us?" I asked.

"Maybe," Kyle said, with a rueful look on his face. "I couldn't have held off all five of them, and they'd have threatened to hurt Felicia if I said anything. So are we going to talk some more about the Worldwalker thing?"

"Maybe?" I said. "You probably know more about this than I do."

"Worldwalkers were a long time ago, though," Kyle said. "We don't know any more than the stories we were told as kids."

"That's more than I've got. Milly seemed to think that . . . I was in danger—either of failing what I needed to do, or death—if I didn't get to a high level quickly, and then disappear."

"That's why you were—wait, you're going to disappear?" Felicia asked.

"That was Milly's advice," I replied. "What's yours?"

"So there's a trick to not getting lost on the second level that Master taught me," Felicia said. She unrolled a parchment backed with leather and showed it to us. From what she said, I expected a map, but this didn't look like any map I'd seen before. It looked like a complicated Venn diagram, all overlapping circles.

"The paths all change when the Dungeon resets," she continued. "So they can be good for finding your way back, if you can remember them, but they can't help you find anything that's in here. You can do what most adventurers do and cut a path, but that will reset as well."

"This is a map, right?" I asked.

"Yes. This level doesn't have much in the way of geography, like rivers or rock walls—it's just one big open area. Though . . . I guess the Kobold holes could serve as landmarks, if you could easily find them. But what it does have is plants."

"Lots and lots of plants," I agreed. I made a note to come back to the Kobold holes later.

"Some plants, though, only grow in certain areas." She tapped her map. "So if you know which plants to look for, you can know where you are!"

"That . . . doesn't seem likely?" I said, looking around us. "I mean, it's just one big area with the same climate throughout. Surely plants would spread?"

"Normally, yes," Felicia said. "And some plants do spread, or get moved around. Just not these ones. It has to be a deliberate design feature that's maintained by the Dungeon magic itself!"

"Why would it do that, though? Help us find a way through?"

"Dungeons are weird," Kyle said, pausing when we looked at him. "Uh, I mean, it's something Da said a lot. Said that they had their own rules, and one of them was always you got to be able to go down all the way."

"So it wants to kill us, but it also wants us to be able to get down to the bottom level?"

"The biggest monsters are all on the lower levels," Felicia mused. "Maybe it can't put them higher up so it needs for us to go down to them?" She paused, then went back to her presentation. "So, anyway! If you take a look at the map, you'll see that Enos root is right next to the entrance." She pointed at a fairly unassuming shrub with yellowish flowers.

> **[Identification] : Enos Root – Condition: Healthy – Properties: None**

"Now, the three jobs that I picked are for items that are all up here." She pointed to a spot on the map that didn't look far from the entrance. "So all we have to do is find the Ross vines, then the Tasmor bushes, and when we find the Sayina flowers we'll know we're in the right area!"

"Huh," I said. I looked at Kyle; this was clearly news to him. "How many people know about this?"

"Not many, I think? It's local knowledge, handed down, so no one would tell most Guild members. The Oakway Raiders might know?"

"Nice." I looked at the map. I could just about make sense of it, and if I looked it over carefully enough, Memorize should retain all the details. The circles were the navigational plants, but there were also points marked for what must be various medicinal ingredients. As were the Kobold burrows. There were eight of them, spread widely across the map. None near where we were going, though.

"So do we need to worry about the burrows?" I asked.

"Not immediately; they tend to avoid humans in the jungle," Felicia said. "Wait—do you know what a Kobold is?"

"Nope. Something that burrows?" I replied.

She shook her head. "They're a tribe of small . . . lizard people, who live in burrows under the jungle floor. They're about three feet tall."

"Wait . . . an intelligent race?" I asked. "How does that work as a Dungeon monster?"

Kyle shrugged. "Just like anything else. Only difference is they use knives." He didn't seem to see the problem.

"But they're *intelligent*," I stressed. "It can't be OK to kill them." *Oh damn, I finally slipped up and said OK.*

Neither of them noticed my slip, but Felicia at least realized what my problem was and tried to explain: "Dungeon creatures—universally—harbor an endless hatred for non-Dungeon creatures. Intelligent or not, they'll always attack."

"But if they can speak . . . my Worldwalker trait should let me understand them. We could negotiate . . ."

"You can try; we won't stop you," Felicia said. "I'm not even worried about you talking to them and getting fooled into letting your defenses down. You might learn something about why they always attack—but they will attack no matter what you do."

"I can't even imagine Dungeons working any other way," Kyle said. "How do they work on your world?"

"We don't have them," I said, still thinking about the upcoming possibility of having to kill a sentient. "Or monsters. Or magic, for that matter."

Kyle and Felicia looked at each other, but neither said anything. Finally Felicia said, "It must be . . . very different?"

"You're not wrong." I sighed. "Well . . . let's get to looking for Ross vines. Kyle, if you take the lead, Felicia can stay behind you and point you in the right direction, and I'll take rearguard."

Three steps and we were in the jungle. Three more, and the vegetation closed around us so thoroughly, the edge was a distant memory. We kept to the paths, not wanting to waste Kyle's sword on tree branches. *Mental note: get machete.* Using the paths got us turned around, but there was almost always a path going in the direction we wanted. With Felicia's pathfinding, we (hopefully) didn't have to worry about getting lost.

Our first warning of an encounter was a clicky sounding purr from up ahead. Kyle stopped and held his hand up for Felicia to stay back. We froze in place, as the sound got louder. I couldn't see clearly past Kyle's bulk, but something moved through the jungle ahead. Suddenly, Kyle went down on one knee, crouching behind his shield, and I got a good look at our opponent.

Fuck me, it's a velociraptor. It was just like the ones in *Jurassic Park,* maybe a little smaller? Gray lizard skin—I'd heard that they were supposed to have feathers now, but maybe this Dungeon hadn't gotten its journal subscription yet.

"Blind!" I called out. I didn't have to, but it was part of keeping the others informed. That was why Kyle had dropped, to give me a clear shot, part of the simple team tactics that we'd worked out. When I Blinded a lizard, they all tended to do the same thing: thrash around, biting and slashing like a madman. After about ten seconds of that, assuming they didn't latch on to something, they'd freeze while they tried to work out what to do next. That was when we'd stab them, so I don't know if there was a third stage.

Our latest victim was exhibiting the same behavior, so Kyle was carefully keeping his distance as he waited for his shot. That was when the chills I was getting from seeing *Jurassic Park* come to life coalesced into a coherent thought, and I looked around wildly.

Velociraptors hunt in packs, was the thought. I have no idea if that was accurate paleontology, but it was certainly the case here. "Behind! Blind!" I screamed, bringing my daggers up to block another raptor that had snuck up behind us while we were distracted by the one in front. At the same time I cast Blind, but not on my attacker. On Felicia's. It went crazy—falling to the ground and lashing out with its claws at everything around. One of its attacks hit my guy, but despite hissing in pain, it kept its focus on me, biting at me with its enormous jaw. I almost kept it at bay with my knives, but it turned its head at the last minute and sank its teeth into my gauntlet.

> **You have taken 2 damage!**

Ouch! I thought, feeling the teeth scrape my skin, but the gauntlet had mostly done its job. *You know, as long as you're going just keep your head attached to my arm, I might as well . . .*

> **You have inflicted 49 damage!**

I'd decided that Blinding it might not have done much good if it knew where I was. As it was, being stabbed in the head made it let go to scream at me, so bonus there. Kyle had abandoned the front to push Felicia's attacker back into the jungle. He might have stabbed it again; I wasn't really paying attention.

> **You have taken 7 damage!**

A kick this time, or maybe a rake? Those legs were too low for me to block easily.

> **Your party has killed a Hunting Raptor – your experience share is 80 XP.**

"Blind!"

Like the others, he went crazy with the kicks and bites. I managed to Dodge back, and looked over the rest of the fight. Kyle had actually finished Felicia's one, and was checking my side out.

"I've got this," I said. "Felicia, keep an eye out for others?" She nodded.

After that, it became mechanical.

> **Your party has killed a Hunting Raptor – your experience share is 80 XP.**

I got in two more stabs, but Kyle actually finished off his and moved over to strike the final blow on mine.

> **Your party has killed a Hunting Raptor – your experience share is 80 XP.**

That sword did so much more damage than my knives, I was jealous. After it was over, we all just stood there—not back to back, but each of us scanning the jungle in a different direction—waiting as our breath came back.

"That was a little bit scary," I said. "Felicia, are you all right?"

"Yes, just a minor wound," she replied. "You?"

"Two scratches," I said. I tensed as I saw a leaf move, but it was just an insect.

"I'm fine as well," said Kyle.

"Yeah, armor is really nice to have . . . let's get Felicia some as soon as possible, shall we?"

"About that . . ." Felicia said hesitantly. "We want to get the skin and claws off these monsters."

After a bit of discussion, we decided to process the corpses where they fell. Felicia was of the opinion that the least likely place to find a monster was right here, where these guys had been hunting. And given how thick the jungle was with scents and foliage, it didn't seem that the corpses would attract scavengers quickly. We didn't feel safe with just one person watching, though, so Felicia did the work, while Kyle and I kept watch in different directions, weapons drawn. No scavengers appeared, only insects, which were enough of a problem, quite frankly. I put insect repellent on my list of adventuring gear.

We then continued on to our target area. Once again, we chose the safer but less efficient route of having Felicia look for our target plants, while Kyle and I kept watch. It didn't help. With no warning, a screeching mass of flying creatures descended on us, biting and scratching. I lashed out with my daggers, trying to keep them at bay, but . . .

You have taken 15 damage!
You have taken 13 damage!

[Greater Invisibility]. Having their target disappear on them confused them for a moment, and I was able to fend them off and back off enough to get a look at what we were fighting. Our attackers were birds? With teeth? *No, wait, these are proper dinosaurs.* I'd seen pictures of something that looked like this. How velociraptors were *supposed* to look, with feathers and sort-of wings. Felicia was being mauled by one; Kyle was successfully fending off *three*. I'd gotten away from mine, but that just meant that they were going to switch targets . . .

"Blind!" I called out the spell this time, forgetting that Greater Invisibility wouldn't let my party members hear me. The . . .

[Identification] : Flying Raptor – Threat Level: 8 – Condition: Blinded

---

. . . Flying Raptor—*yes, thank you*—that I'd targeted behaved a little differently from the other lizards I'd blinded. He just curled up his wings and lay still on the ground. *I guess when you fly, you don't want to move around when blind?* I thought. That was great, but I'd only taken care of one. The other moved to attack Felicia.

"Felicia!" Kyle called, panicked. He slashed one of his attackers, and it fell, but he still had two on him and wasn't able to help. Felicia was defending herself, but I saw slashes on her arms.

Your party has killed a Hunting Raptor – your experience share is 160 XP.

[Blind]. I cast again, giving her some respite. There was only one attacking her now, but it managed to land a deep bite.

[Blind]. And she was safe. I dropped Invisibility—it was getting in the way of party coordination, and the remaining raptors seemed focused on Kyle.

"Blind!" I waited to see which raptor Kyle was hitting, and then cast it on the other one. "How are you?" I asked Felicia. Behind her, Kyle finished off the last moving raptor.

Your party has killed a Hunting Raptor – your experience share is 160 XP.

"I'm . . . mostly fine." Felicia said, checking over her wounds.

"Do you want the potion?" I asked. Felicia's face wavered, and I could see she was struggling to say no. I shook my head and gave her the bottle.

"Are you sure?" she asked. "You paid for it, and I do have an emergency one that I can use."

"I bought it for the team, and I don't want to have to explain to your Master that we were in an emergency. Though . . ." I looked around at the still forms of the flying raptor. "We're not quite out of it yet."

Felicia looked over at Kyle, who had moved on to hacking off his blinded raptor's head. "If we touch them, they'll lash out," she said. "It might be better to wait for Kyle to finish."

Your party has killed a Hunting Raptor – your experience share is 160 XP.

I looked daggers at the still raptors. "It ought to be possible to take them out with one carefully placed stab . . ." I mused. I hadn't had much luck trying that with the lizards upstairs, though.

"You mean like Precision Damage?" asked Kyle, coming over. He lined up a swing on one of the raptors, and we both took a step back. "Assassins have that."

Not an Assassin! I protested in my head, but I consulted the help files. "[Precision Damage] is a pre-requisite for the Assassin Profession . . . but it is not a Skill, it is a Trait. 5 Development points."

"Look at the Rogue class," Felicia suggested.

"Rogue . . . gets it for free, and it only costs ten points for the entire profession!" They got other stuff as well, so it was a pretty good deal.

"It's always cheaper to get the relevant profession than to buy the skills or traits separately," Felicia said.

Rogue wasn't an option—I didn't have the Finesse requirements, and

I didn't want to give up my Illusion magic bonus anyway. Precision Damage, though . . . I looked it up while Kyle cleaned house.

> **[Precision Damage]: 2x damage total against unmoving or unaware targets when using [Small Bladed] weapons (5 points).**

Hmm. I'd already noticed that I did more damage when I was invisible. I think that's because their defenses were reduced or something like that. I'd been doing twenty-something damage to those Ilan lizards before, but more like fifty when I was invisible. Precision Damage would have taken that to 100 . . .

> **Your party has killed a Hunting Raptor – your experience share is 160 XP.**
> **Your party has killed a Hunting Raptor – your experience share is 160 XP.**

Hmmmmmmmmmm. But Kyle's sword did a *base* of sixty damage, plus whatever he hit by. He was taking out those Ilans in one shot. I was a lot better off blinding his opponents and letting him do the damage.

> **Your party has killed a Hunting Raptor – your experience share is 160 XP.**

Speaking of which . . .

"Oh, guys, I feel I should mention that I'm down to 48 mana points. That's two more Blind spells, and then I'm done casting until I rest."

We made it out alive. Felicia had almost finished her ingredient collection when we were attacked, so she hurriedly finished up while we gathered the bodies. We didn't want to stop and process them here, and they were a fair bit smaller than the hunting raptors, so we managed to stuff all six into sacks and have Kyle carry them. Then we headed back as quickly as we could while trying to keep an eye out for more ambushes.

We did run into a few more creatures—a large snake, boa constrictor sized, and a different type of raptor. The snake was slow enough that we could just avoid it, and the feathered raptor made the mistake of ambushing Kyle. Its green feathers camouflaged it really well, though—none of us saw it until it attacked. Identifying it was the final trigger for my skill going up.

We camped out on the first level to finish with the corpses. Anything we left behind would disappear at midnight in the Dungeon, so it was great for not leaving a mess. Kyle and Felicia did most of the work, though I ruined most of one carcass plucking enough feathers to unlock the Hunt skill. They didn't let me touch the claws, though, which were apparently the real prize. Felicia had cut off the feet when we were in the jungle, but now she carefully prized out the talons from each toe.

"Level two is infused with darksteel ore," Felicia said. "The Kobolds mine it, and a lot of the animals incorporate it in their bodies somehow. See?" She handed me talon. It was pretty dark, parts of it were pitch-black, but it had a varied pattern to it that I had to admit looked kind of pretty up close. "When it gets polished and carved up, it's one of Oakway's signature products."

"So . . . how much?" I asked. Felicia grinned at me.

"The big ones we can probably get five silver for, the little ones three silver. Even if they're damaged too badly for carving, you can melt the darksteel out of them, get a few coppers each depending on the weight."

Calculate did the heavy lifting for me. "That's 198 silver!"

"Plus eight pounds of feathers, all the skins, and the boss reward," Felicia added happily. "I think we can clear more than 300 silver for today!"

It ended up being much more than that, mostly because Felicia had forgotten about the quest rewards. They added up to 120 silver (we got docked ten silver from Felicia's hasty gathering at the end, but we didn't feel inclined to argue). And with my Bargaining, we managed to get about 25% more than Felicia had been expecting. When we finally split the profits, we were each holding sixteen gold and eight silver. We spent the remaining time in the market. Kyle and Felicia had their obvious armor purchases to make, but I hadn't made my decision when it was time to go to work.

Yes, work. It *was* starting to feel ridiculous, working for a few copper a week, when I had gold in my pocket. It was still the case, though, that I had a lot to learn about this world, and listening to random conversations *was* helping with that. Of course, now that I had come clean to Felicia and Kyle, I could just ask them about all this stuff, right? I think that if

I had been planning on staying, it would have been a good idea to buy a house and settle in. But I wasn't planning on staying, was I? Felicia hadn't looked happy when I told her I planned to disappear, but she hadn't had any advice of her own. She had told me she'd think about it. Maybe it was time to start thinking about my next destination . . .

Then I realized there was a situation I needed to deal with before I could leave—and that was because he walked in the door of the Green Tanner.

Reynard.

PLANNING

Reynard strolled in like he owned the place and took a seat at the edge of the room. He didn't bother catching my eye or anything; he knew I had to come to him. On one level it was my *job*, while on the other . . . *Ugh.*

"Are you going to order anything this time?" I asked. I kept it professional, but didn't try to hide my distaste. This wasn't a valued customer. He just looked at me for a second, then he laughed.

"Hard to believe you're still working here, kid," he said, shaking his head. "I saw you in the Guild wearing leathers that must cost ten times what you've earned here so far. You trying to blend in or something?"

God, he pissed me off. "Sure, I pulled down fifteen gold this morning . . . but that's gotta be chump change for the likes of you, right? So what are *you* doing here?" I glared at him and interrupted when he tried to give a smartass answer. "I mean here in this town. Shouldn't you be drinking fine wines and screwing high-class whores in the capital with all the other high-level assholes? Instead you're fucking around with me on some two-bit scam you've got going with the Guild."

That struck a nerve. "You know *nothing*," he snarled. "You think the Guild exists to help those with drive reach the top?"

"It doesn't?" I asked. I hadn't given the question much thought, actually, but Intrigue prompted me to keep him talking.

"The Guild exists to *control* adventures. Keep the powerful commoners in line, so they don't threaten the nobles. The higher you rise, the more oversight you get—oh, if you're a good little adventurer, you get to live in the pretty city, but step out of line . . . and they send you here."

"Not exactly a hellscape."

"It's a dead-end hole for someone like me, and even you know it," he said. "A dying three-level Dungeon, and a countryside with nothing of any threat. I could kill monsters for a decade and never gain another level."

"So you want to get out of here," I said thoughtfully.

"I am getting out of here. There's just one tiny problem that's cropped up, which you're going to help take care of for me. Next week, Guild Master Lyons is out of town—there'll be a hearing held just after he leaves."

"And I'll be attending?" I asked doubtfully.

He snorted. "An Illusionist like you, you've got an Invisibility spell, don't you?" I nodded. He'd called me an Illusionist. Did that mean he *didn't* know I was a Phantasmal Artificer? Or was he keeping that card hidden for now? "Right, then, you should have no trouble getting in. I'll give you a heads-up closer to the date. All you gotta do is keep that Truthstone glowing blue."

"Doesn't the Guild have some sort of check for Illusion magic?" I asked.

"Maybe if we thought we needed it," he said smugly. "But I'll be running this hearing. All the witnesses are arranged. We just need to make sure that no inconvenient lies are exposed. Easy as pie."

"Sure," I said, noncommittally.

"And if they were exposed," he said, leaning forward. "Well, depending on how it goes, I might be done with the Guild, done with restraints on my actions. I'd just cut my way out of there, and there'd be no one who could stop me. You might try to hide, but I've seen through your illusions once—would you care to gamble a second time?" He laughed at my blank stare, and then got up and left.

You have recovered 6 HP.
You have recovered 96 MP.
[Mana Development] Level 3 acquired through use.
For gaining a skill level, you have been awarded 1 XP.

My morning notification was welcome, but I still hadn't recovered all my mana from our last expedition. We had expected this and weren't planning on delving today. I needed to take my mind off Reynard, which meant I was going shopping.

I wasn't quite ready to throw out the equipment I bought yesterday, so I wasn't looking for upgrades. I did look for, but couldn't find, a magic weapons shop. There was an alchemist store, though, so I thought it might be worth a try. Upon entering, I found myself corralled on two sides by a waist-high railing as a loud bell announced my entrance. Directly in front of me was a counter with a man behind it. He looked up as I came in, frowning at what he saw.

"I'm afraid we don't stock any of the lesser herbal concoctions here, miss," he said. He gestured at the walls, which I now saw were lined with shelves of small bottles. Out of reach behind the rails and behind glass to boot. "These are Alchemical potions, and the least of them are sold for gold."

"I have gold," I said. He didn't look convinced. I hadn't dressed in armor to go shopping, so I was wearing a dress like any other town girl. More respectable, but poorer looking. Charm had reverted back to having me curtsy, but it was grudgingly allowing a little of the confidence I'd projected while wearing pants to show. I pulled out my nameplate. "I'm with the Guild."

"Ah. Well, then, welcome valued customer." A smile flickered across his face and left as quickly as it came, leaving his face . . . still in a scowl, though a lesser one. "You must be new."

"I guess so," I said brightly. Charm seemed to take his attitude as a challenge. "I have been down as far as level two, though!"

"Have you. I had noticed one of my jobs had been fulfilled. Did you bring back any Qua'rodu lily?"

"I think so? To be honest, one of my teammates was taking part of the collection part."

"How . . . organized." He mused, peering closely at me now. "And . . . you do not appear to be drunk. Well, I look forward to working with you in the future, Adventurer. I am Noah Herbert."

"Pleased to meet you, Mr. Herbert," I said. I'd wanted to go with Noah, but Charm insisted. "I'm Katherine Meland." I curtsied.

He nodded in acknowledgment, his expression easing into something that was almost pleased. "You should know that I maintain my own job list, similar to what the Guild holds."

"Is that allowed?" I asked.

"The Guild allows it, as long as some restrictions are met. I can only request for myself, and I can only offer store credit. If you were planning on spending money in my store, though, you'll find the rewards 50% greater than when the Guild takes their cut."

"That's a pretty good deal," I said. "I'll have to run them past Felicia, though—she takes the jobs based on what we'll find on our planned route."

"Planning?"

"Is that so surprising?" I asked, getting a little worried. I knew that adventurers as a group were not that impressive, but there were *some* good ones.

"Unusual, but perhaps not so surprising. This Felicia, would she happen to be Oliver Heath's apprentice?"

"You know her?"

"He has spoken of her . . . spoken well of her," he corrected himself. "Should I assume that the boy Kyle is in this team of yours?"

"It's a small town, isn't it?"

"Quite. Now, was there some business with me that you had in mind?"

"Well, it's my first time buying potions, so I'm hoping you could go over your range and give me some ideas for what would be useful for an adventurer."

"Hmm. I suppose I can spare the time. Let us start with healing. Are you familiar with Master Heath's work?"

"Yes, but those potions aren't alchemy?" As I spoke, Noah was going around selecting a few potions which he placed on the counter.

"Correct. I do stock a few that I've gained in trade,"—he waved to one corner of the room—"but healing potions utilize the unique Healing gift that belongs to Oliver's profession. The rest of his wares are not, strictly speaking, magical. Alchemy cannot replicate the way that they simply restore health in one hit. Instead, we have these."

He indicated three potions in blue colored bottles. "Enhancing natural healing. Three times, ten gold; five times for fifty gold; and ten times for 200 gold. The effects last for thirty days."

"That's . . ." I thought for a minute, letting Calculate do its work. "If your natural healing was high enough, that's much cheaper than the regular potions."

"It depends heavily on circumstances," he said. "On your natural healing rate, on when the wounds are taken, and on one other thing." He grimaced slightly. "A person can only be affected by one alchemy potion at a time. When a person takes a second one, the one with the longer remaining duration is canceled out."

I tried to game out situations in my head. "It seems like, in *most* cases, it would be easier to just take a healing potion."

"Probably," Noah agreed. "Its main use is for high-level individuals who have taken large amounts of damage and want to heal over thirty days."

"Right. What else have you got? Anything to restore mana?"

"Potions, no, *restore*, no. However . . ." He reached under the table and produced a softly glowing blue gem. "Mana crystals are a natural product, but alchemy can be useful in merging smaller or damaged stones into a larger, healthy crystal."

"How do they work?" I asked.

"You can put mana into them, and take it out at a later date," he replied.

"Ah, so it doesn't restore mana, it lets you save it."

"Exactly," he said. "Cost averages about two gold for each mana point of capacity. This one is 200 gold, 100 mana capacity. You can expect them to become costlier when the size increases above 250, 500, or 1,000 mana, due to the rarity."

"That's a little out of my price range," I said wryly. "Moving on?"

"Of course." He indicated three more bottles, then paused. "Oh, one thing I should have mentioned. My prices are fixed; there will be no haggling. My prices are set as low as is possible while still allowing me to profit. As a local producer, you should find my product priced cheaper than most of the market stalls will haggle down to. They have significant shipping costs, after all."

"That sounds like a relief, actually."

"Excellent. Now, as I was saying, these four are especially popular with adventurers. Heat Resistance, Cold Resistance, Water Breathing, and Dark Vision. Heat Resistance is five gold, the others are three. Duration is four hours."

"Why does Heat Resistance cost extra?" I asked.

"It's practically a necessity on the third level," he said. "It's tunnels with lava, after all. This will protect you almost completely from that type of heat. If you should touch lava, you would find it very painful, but you would be unharmed. I don't recommend you do, however, as your armor would certainly start to melt or burn, whichever is appropriate."

"It doesn't protect my gear, then?"

"It does not. Most arms and armor are capable of withstanding the heat levels there, as long as you avoid the lava. They get painfully hot of, course, but that isn't a problem as long as you are under the effect of the potion."

"Have you got anything useful for the second level?"

"Ah . . . Dark Vision is useful in the tunnels on the second level, but otherwise . . . insects are a common complaint, yes?" I nodded, shuddering. "I have a few options there, but they all have limitations." He pulled out a small, sealed pot. "First, insect repellent. This isn't a potion that affects you; it's an ointment which causes insects to flee. For best effect, smear it on exposed skin. It's pungent, but not noxious to humans."

"What's the limitation?"

"It is pungent, and while not especially attractive to beasts, it does attract their notice if in range. The next two are potions—one changes your smell so that it does not attract insects. This keeps you from attracting them, but it does nothing for the ones that are already there—perhaps attracted by a fresh kill. Still, you will be less bothered by them."

"And the final one?"

"It changes your skin's oils to become violently toxic to insects. Any insect that touches your skin or hair will die within a second."

"That sounds tempting, but . . . ultimately useless?"

"There is no XP, and the creatures will reset at midnight regardless, but some people gain satisfaction from it." He shrugged and pulled out some more containers. "These are not potions, but they have particular alchemical effects that you might find useful. Glue trap. Smoker. Firetrap. Steel Eater."

"Steel Eater is some kind of acid?" I asked. The other concoctions seemed fairly self-explanatory.

"You're familiar with such? Interesting. Not exactly, though. Steel Eater can be thought of as an *ideal* acid, which only eats steel. Even darksteel and silversteel are unaffected. It and the Firetrap are ten gold; the others are two."

I guess anything's possible with magic, I thought. Noah moved on.

"And finally, these three. Improved Strength, Agility, and Finesse," he stated, pointing to each one in turn. "Plus-one to the aforementioned Ability for six hours. Ten gold."

Oh, that would be handy. "Only one at a time though?" I asked plaintively.

"I'm afraid so," he said, sadly. "Now, that is the basic outline of what I have available that would be useful to delvers. There are variants to these, extra duration for the most part, but they are probably prohibitively expensive for you at this time. As for other possibilities, if you have specific needs in mind, I might be able to suggest something?"

"I can't think of anything," I confessed. "That's a lot to take in." I thought for a moment. "I think I'll take a Darkvision, though, and the Insect Repel."

"Excellent choice," he said, making the other bottles disappear.

"Oh, can I ask another question? It's not potion related, but I think you might know the answer."

"Ask away." He shrugged.

"Is Oakway Dungeon dying?" I guess I hadn't managed to distract myself from Reynard after all. Maybe I needed *clothes* shopping.

"Hmmm." He paused, considering. "It is commonly speculated that it is, but there has been no sign of degradation so far."

"Then why do people think it is?"

"Because there has been no sign of growth, either—there hasn't been a new level in twenty years. Common received wisdom states that Dungeons are either growing or dying; if it is not growing, then it must be dying. However . . ." He paused again. "Oakway Dungeon, despite being on the smaller side, has always struck me as being more ambitious than most. Each of its levels is significantly larger than the last, and the ramp-up of threats is much higher than you'd find in a typical Dungeon. It's possible that it has spent these twenty years building an even more ambitious level and simply hasn't finished yet."

"So there's no way to know until something happens?" I asked.

"Exactly right. Here are your purchases; have a nice day," he said.

There were no enchanting shops in this town. I knew there was such a thing as enchanting—it was one of my unlocked skills, after all. And there were a few enchanted weapons for sale, but no shop. After scouring the town, I decided to find someone who might know something.

"No, there are no Enchanters in Oakway," Paige said.

"Then where do enchanted weapons come from?" I asked with some exasperation.

"Elsewhere," she replied unhelpfully. "Adventurers bring them in for the most part. The ones you see in the shops would be sold by them. You'll mostly find Enchanters closer to the capital, where the money is, or out by the frontier where there's demand and cheap materials."

"Well, that's just not fair," I said, sulking.

"If it's that urgent, I can put out a request for information on the nearest Enchanter for one gold?" she suggested. "Or maybe your out-of-town friends know someone?" She pointed to where Sean and the others were chatting at one of the tables.

"I guess it can't hurt to ask," I said, and headed over.

"Enchanting?" Eric asked incredulously. "You must be getting gold to spare from level two, if you're thinking about that already."

"Maybe," I said. "You guys are doing level three, right? Are you using potions for the heat?"

"I have a spell for that," Nina said. "I use it on Eric as well, but the others have enchanted protection."

I turned to the others. "Can I see? And how much did it cost?" I asked.

Sean rolled his eyes. "I found mine, which was lucky, because it's much better than Edvard's." He pulled out something like an army dog tag—a small plate of metal attached to a chain around his neck. He didn't take it off but invited me to come close to look at it.

> **[Identification] : Silversteel Amulet – Quality: Great – Properties: Enchantment (Temperature Control)**

Looking at it, I could see seven glittering runes inscribed in different colors arrayed around what looked like a much smaller mana crystal than what Noah had shown me. "How does it work?"

"You need to charge it with your mana," Sean said. "Takes ten mana, which lasts for two hours."

In the meantime, Edvard had taken his necklace off, and held it out for my inspection. It did seem cruder than Sean's, and was made of a green-yellow metal which I couldn't identify.

> **[Identification] : Brazen Jade Amulet – Quality: Good – Properties: Enchantment (Cool)**

OK, I guess I can *identify it.* This amulet only had three runes and no mana crystal.

"Brazen jade?"

"It's another magic metal found in a Dungeon up north," Edvard said. "I'm not sure of its properties; I think it makes poor weapons, but good armor. Not that it matters for an amulet. This one cost me 100 gold, and it works all the time, without charging."

"Is that because it's simpler? And do runes have to go on magical metal?"

"Probably, and I think so. I've been told that if you don't, it degrades the steel in a week or so."

Ah, fuck it, I thought to myself. There wasn't any point to delaying getting the skill, was there?

[Enchanting] Level 1 purchased.
For gaining a skill level, you have been awarded 1 XP.
You have 3 unspent Rune points.

Then I looked at the amulet again.

[Identification] : Brazen Jade Amulet – Quality: Good – Properties:
Enchantment (Cool)
[Identification] : Rune [Constant Effect] – Quality: Good
[Identification] : Rune [Cool] – Quality: Good
[Identification] : Rune [Touch Effect] – Quality: Good

Huh. "Can I look at yours again?" I asked Sean. He allowed it and I saw that his had the same three runes, plus Sense (Temperature), Trigger, Warm, and Accept Energy.

"Why all the interest?" Sean asked. "Don't tell me you're thinking of taking it up yourself?" The others laughed.

"Maybe," I hedged, unwilling to reveal that I'd bought it just now.

"Oh, come on, there's planning, but planning ahead for a level seven skill? Keep your eyes in front of you, girl!" Sean chuckled, shaking his head. "I mean, even getting ready for the next level of the Dungeon is premature—you're not ready to take on the Kobold nest."

"It's supposed to be quite difficult?" I said idly. "Lots of cramped dark tunnels and traps?"

"And lots of Kobolds. Ten tunnels full of them." Sean got a dark look on his face. "We only went through there once to get the key, and it was a trial."

"Did you really have to k- . . . clear out all the tunnels to face the boss?" I asked. "And aren't there only eight entrances to the system?"

"The more you clear out, the easier it is," Edvard said calmly, unaffected by Sean's emoting. "When you face the Kobold Chief, he summons every surviving Kobold to help him fight. Then he tanks your attacks, while his shaman casts spells. Even if you clear all eight entrances, there are two warrens that can only be accessed from the Chief's room. So you're guaranteed to have a whole lot of minions getting underfoot . . . it was a decent fight."

"The tunnels are all right to move through, but they're too cramped to swing a longsword. Had to do everything with my spare weapon." Sean was still reliving the fight.

"Well, at least that won't be a concern for me."

"Will be for your teammate, you know, the one that does all the damage," Eric pointed out. "You can see how it affected our fighter. Edvard was fine, but I was pretty much useless until the final fight."

I shrugged. "I heard that Kobolds have low threat levels, though."

"That's only the half of it," Edvard said. "Nina, you can tell her how it works."

"Kobolds have skills," Nina explained. "So their effect level isn't simply Threat times Ability; they are also multiplied by their skill. Like us."

"It's that 'like us' that actually worries me," I said. "I don't want to kill humans, and they seem a bit too close to human for me to feel good about killing them."

The others exchanged a look, one that made me think that they might not have the same problem. *Have they killed humans?* I wondered. The adventurer's life was a dangerous one, but even so . . . *They seem too nice to be killers, but if someone attacked them outside a town, what else could happen?*

"Unrelenting hostility," Nina said, breaking me out of my reverie. "Focus on that. Kobolds will never be anything other than the enemies of humans. You'll see soon enough."

"Why is that, though?" I asked. "Why would Dungeons make them like that?"

"Well, they say that Dungeons were the creation of the God of Destruction. That he sought to put an end to the races by creating an endless supply of monsters seeking the death of all civilizations."

"That's . . . not what Dungeons do, though?" I said.

"No," Nina continued. "The other gods opposed him and set limits on the Dungeons. Naldyna blocked them from coming into this world, and Fyskel is said to have made them drop treasure, so that adventurers would come and be killed, partially appeasing Ashmor. Phadan made them expose their cores, enabling them to be killed. I don't remember the rest of the story, but they were all supposed to have a hand in it."

"Huh," was all I could say. I'd heard most of those names in the tavern, enough to know that Naldyna was the Goddess of Nature and Phadan was the God of the Dead. Was the story true? I suppose there was no way to know. I let the conversation move on, taking a less active part. I wanted to get back to enchanting.

Runes were like spells, in that there was now a list that I could purchase them from. They cost less, but I had fewer points to spend. I'd probably get more if I raised the skill, but . . . I had a feeling that I could get spells, and now runes, from finding a spell book, if I had the Research skill. Now here were some runes, laid out in front of me. Was it worth seeing if I could learn them? I would want it anyway when I found a spell book, and that was a fairly high priority . . .

> [Research] Level 1 purchased.
> For gaining a skill level, you have been awarded 1 XP.

I stared at Edvard's amulet, trying to activate Research. I got the sense that it was working, but would need more time. Then I looked away, and tried concentrating on Memorize's relocation of it. I got the same sensation. Excusing myself from the group, I retired to my room.

> You have learned the Rune: [Cool].
> You have learned the Rune: [Heat].
> You have learned the Rune: [Effect: Touch].
> You have learned the Rune: [Constant Effect].
> You have learned the Rune: [Sense (Temperature)].
> [Research] Level 2 acquired through use.
> For gaining a skill level, you have been awarded 1 XP.
> You have learned the Rune: [Trigger].
> You have learned the Rune: [Accept Energy].

It took almost an hour to learn each one, so that was how I spent the rest of the day. And that was how I learned enchanting.

KOBOLDS

I think I know how to beat the second level, but I'm not sure if I should," I said to Felicia as we moved through the jungle of the second level.

"And since I know you, I know it's not because of the danger; it's because you think the Kobolds can be reasoned with," she retorted. She was wearing her new armor—she'd gone with a stiff leather skirt and high boots to cover her lower half and a jacket similar to mine.

"Guilty," I admitted. We were trying a different tactic this trip. Last time, we had exhausted my mana casting Blind so many times, so this time we were trying Greater Invisibility. If I had been alone, I would have just cast it on myself and slipped through the jungle like a deadly ghost, but there were logistical issues with casting it on all of us.

I could still see those targeted by Greater Invisibility, but they couldn't see me, or each other, and I couldn't hear them either. We couldn't act as a group, not even to the extent of keeping together. So instead, we were trying something else.

I'd made *Kyle* invisible. He was "taking point," as they said in the movies, moving ahead to try and spot any potential danger, then coming back to make sure he was moving in the right direction. He could see us, so he could stay nearby, and I could see *him*, and so would know if something happened to him.

We were still dependent on Felicia for directions. While I had memorized the map and could find the plants using Identify, Felicia's Gather skill let her pick up wanted plants just by glancing over an expanse of jungle. Trying to emulate her had eventually unlocked Gather for me, but with only one skill point left I was holding out for a better skill.

Kyle, on the other hand, was a complete monster when his opponent couldn't see him. Most of our encounters now, we'd just hear a scream, and then move forward to see the corpse, or Kyle fighting a second monster. The few times something got by Kyle, I'd blind it and we'd call for support.

All up, it seemed a much more efficient method of moving through the jungle. We'd decided to focus on listed jobs this trip, so weren't spending too much time harvesting creatures—the exception being darksteel talons, as we could quickly cut off the feet. We were also collecting the bodies of the flying raptors that attacked us, with the aim of collecting their feathers later.

It was all going well, so naturally my thoughts had turned to the next stage.

"I know everyone you've spoken to has confirmed it," Felicia said, continuing the conversation. "So what will it take to convince you?"

"I'm sorry to be so stubborn," I said. "But there's a lot of incidents in my world's history where everyone was completely certain about something—and completely wrong. Like when they proved the Earth wasn't flat."

"Wait. The world's not flat? What is it then?" Felicia asked quickly.

"One world-shattering revelation at a time," I said wryly. I paused, considering my words. "I don't know if Ryvue is the same as Earth, but Earth is a round ball of rock, about eight-and-a-half thousand miles across." Latoran miles were a little shorter than Earth miles, but Calculate gave me effortless conversion regardless.

Felicia boggled for a second at the thought of such a thing, but quickly rallied. "But if *we* could be wrong, that means you could be wrong just as easily."

"Yeah," I said. "So to figure out who's right, we'll have to do an experiment."

Some time later, I was staring at a fairly well-concealed hole in the ground. Felicia and Kyle had gone back out to process and sell our goods, but I'd had her lead me here, to one of the entrances to the Kobold lair. Hopefully, I'd be able to find my way back.

The lair entrances were always guarded, so I knew there was a warrior hidden in there. If I hadn't been invisible, he'd have spotted me by now, and either raised the alarm or attacked me. I wanted to lure him out, so I used Unseen Sound to mimic the sound of a crying child coming from just out of sight of the hole.

Sure enough, after a few seconds, an ugly lizard face popped out and started creeping toward the sound. He got confused for a second as he tried to identify where it was coming from, and I chose that moment to make my approach.

"I just want to talk," I said in Kobold. My process was a little awkward. I had to say what I wanted to the Kobold, to let my Gift of Tongues provide a translation, and then mimic the result with Unseen Sound, as he couldn't hear through Greater Invisibility.

"Where human! Show yourself!"

"I need you to promise not to attack me," I said, carefully gauging the effects of my words on the little savage.

"Yes! Promise!"

Not fully trusting his eager acceptance, I made a shadow appear behind a bush using Static Image. With a cry of triumph, the Kobold launched himself toward it.

"Yes! Kill!" He crashed into the bush, but found no prey. "Tricked! Tricked!" he cried.

It went on like that for a little while. I really didn't want to believe in this "unrelenting hostility" thing, but I was convinced of it by the end. The little brute wouldn't stop, attacking anything he thought was me, no matter what I tried to offer, or threaten him with. It was time to move on to phase two. I hadn't actually run this phase past Felicia, as there was no way she would have helped me get here if she'd known.

"Going to see your Chief now!" I said, making the voice come from the hole. The Kobold shrieked and dived inside. I swallowed my Dark Vision potion and carefully followed him.

The Kobold tunnels were clearly not dug by Kobolds, despite the fact that they were miners. The tunnels were simply too tall to be there for anything other than adventurer convenience. Though narrow and twisting, the rocky ceiling was never less than eight feet high. There were tunnels that looked made by Kobolds, small offshoots too small for a human to fit down. But the way to the Kobold Chieftain was made for humans to use.

My unwilling guide hurried down the main tunnel, cursing, as he chased after my fictional intruder. Some other Kobolds stuck their heads out of the side tunnels, but he told them to get weapons and guard the entrance.

At one point, he stopped and looked confused. Catching up with him, I saw that he was inspecting the gravel on the ground. *Surprised that a trap wasn't triggered?* I thought. He turned back, perhaps suspecting that his prey had taken another tunnel, so I made mocking laughter come from further down. He cursed again, and took a running jump over the suspicious gravel.

Then we came to a more open area, which the Kobolds had been using for primitive smelting. Darksteel ore was lying about everywhere and a number of Kobolds were industriously tending to a forge.

"Where intruder?" he yelled. Naturally, they professed no knowledge, which enraged him somewhat. "Go search! I warn Chief!" he ordered. About half of those in the room did what he said; the others made rude gestures. In the larger room, I had no trouble avoiding the obedient ones, as they rushed toward every exit but one. The one my guide headed for. The tunnel that led to the Chief.

Two more traps needed to be avoided, but I got plenty of warning when my guide took a large leap. With Dark vision, I could probably identify the pit traps without a guide, but it was useful to have him point them out to me.

Finally, we made it to the Chieftain's quarters. To my surprise, they were blocked off from the tunnel by a proper door. My guide opened it hastily and called out as he entered.

"Boss! Boss! We got intruders!" He looked around wildly, perhaps expecting his mysterious enemy to be waiting for him. Instead, the room contained only the Chieftain and the Shaman, looking at him with dumb expressions. His enemy casually strolled in behind him.

"Where!" the Chieftain demanded, but he never got an answer. Instead, both he and my guide stared dumbfounded at the empty space where the Shaman used to be.

The Shaman was still there, of course, somewhat confused as to what the others were going on about. He soon found out, though.

[Greater Invisibility].

This time, I targeted the Chieftain, and it was the turn of the Shaman to be surprised.

[Greater Invisibility].

Casting it on the guard Kobold might have been overkill, but I wanted the others not to realize what was going on for as long as I could.

You have inflicted 57 damage!

My guide just looked at his wound in surprise. It seemed greater intelligence wasn't always helpful, as his incomprehension delayed his return attack.

You have inflicted 55 damage!
For killing a Kobold, you have earned 80 XP.

He fell to the floor, and I canceled the Greater Invisibility spell. Now the Kobolds realized they were under attack. The Shaman cast his spells, and the Chieftain drew his sword and called for reinforcements. Neither of those actions worked when you couldn't make a sound, though.

You have inflicted 59 damage!

The Shaman could only swing widely with his staff; he wasn't combat trained. I easily avoided his strike, and went for the kill.

You have inflicted 62 damage!
For killing a Kobold Shaman, you have earned 150 XP.

That just left the Chief. He had moved over his man and was wildly swinging his sword. I took a few steps to one side and canceled the Shaman's invisibility. As expected, he rushed over, leaving himself wide open.

You have inflicted 50 damage!

At the moment he felt my dagger, he twisted, turning for a strike of his own. I barely parried it with my other blade. Then, as I tried to strike again with my main blade, he somehow managed to disengage and parry me.

Shit. I backed off. *He's this good when he can't see me?* I wasn't sure if it was blind fighting or his skill, but he definitely couldn't see me. When I backed off, he stayed in place, moving his sword around, as if to block possible strikes. I started to wonder if I hadn't been too hasty. Maybe I could have worked out how to get Kyle into these tunnels?

Still, I was committed now. No sense in holding back.

[Blind].

I wasn't sure if it would make a difference, but it couldn't hurt to try. He didn't panic, but his movements became more uncertain. I moved in behind him and tried another strike. He spun and parried me at the last minute, and once again, I barely managed to parry his return strike. He looked a little unsteady after spinning, though, which gave me an idea.

Moving over to the Shaman's corpse, I sheathed my parrying dagger and grabbed the corpse. Kobolds are pretty small, and I was easily able to toss it one-handed, not at him, but at his feet. He must have felt something—air from the fall perhaps, because he whirled to face that direction.

I was already redrawing my blade and moving around again. Even as he was trying to figure out what was going on, I was rushing in from behind again. I'd noticed that his parry and return strike involved a backward step, so this should . . .

You have taken 12 damage!

Ow! But he was down, having been tripped by the corpse. Open again! I jumped on top of him, letting my blade lead.

You have inflicted 53 damage!
You have taken 37 damage!

He couldn't bring his sword to bear, but he could still bite and kick, and now he knew where I was. We struggled furiously on the ground, and I stabbed him as quickly as I could.

You have inflicted 51 damage!
You have taken 29 damage!
You have inflicted 58 damage!
For killing a Kobold Chieftain, you have earned 280 XP.
For clearing the second level of Oakdale Dungeon for the first time, you have earned 500 XP.
For clearing the second level of Oakdale Dungeon, you have earned a reward.
For clearing the second level of Oakdale Dungeon alone for the first time, you have earned 500 XP and a reward.

I made myself crawl a few feet away from the bodies, before letting myself slump to the ground. 102/180 HP. *Time to try that healing potion.* I'd bought two healing potions of the next grade from Oliver for five gold.

Taking one out and drinking it, I felt the exquisite feeling of my wounds closing. It healed me fifty points, almost back to full. It seemed a waste to take the other one, so I just let myself rest.

After a minute, I raised my head to look around. There was a new tunnel and two silver chests. Bigger ones than last time. Energized again by the thought of rewards, I went and opened them.

One contained twenty gold coins, and a weird looking doll. The other contained twenty gold coins and . . . an exact copy of my new dagger, only made in darksteel? I identified the items.

> [Identification] : Darksteel Dagger – Quality: Great – Properties: Silent, Steel-piercing
> [Identification] : Oakway Token – Properties: Teleport

Ah, I'd heard of this token, but no one had mentioned it looking like *that*. And the dagger was nice? Customized to me, I guess?

It occurred to me that my victims might also have items, so I went and searched the bodies. I was getting quite inured to corpses by now, though I still hadn't seen a human body. The Chieftain had a Mediocre quality darksteel sword, which was worth taking for the metal if nothing else. The Shaman's staff was also Mediocre, but it did have a mana crystal about one centimeter across tied to the end of it. I was a little leery about disassembling it, but it didn't look like anything special to Mana Sense, so I took my knife to the string and removed the crystal.

> [Identification] : Mana Crystal – 20/45 capacity

Nice. From what Noah had said, this should be worth ninety gold on its own, but I had other plans for it. There wasn't really anything of note. I took a dagger and spearhead since they were made of darksteel, but left the Shaman's collection of fetishes and herbs. I couldn't tell if they were worth anything and they smelled really bad. Then it was time to face the music.

I channeled mana into the doll, and the world disappeared, getting replaced a second later with the entrance to the first level. I sighed, and started heading down. I'd agreed to meet Felicia outside the first boss's chambers. Since I was still invisible, it was no real effort to get down to where she was.

"What happened to you?" was the first question she asked, her tone halfway to a scream.

"It's fine, really," I said, waving away her concern. It was mostly true. Being thirty HP down would have crippled me at level one, but now I just had some deep scratches and bruising. Painful, but even that had faded. I sat down on the ground and slowly fell over.

"Katherine!" Felicia rushed over.

"Sorry, don't worry," I said. "I guess I ran out of adrenaline."

"What's that?" she asked, checking over my partially healed wounds.

"Hmm? Oh . . . it's a drug your body makes for stressful moments. Makes the heart beat faster, increases blood flow . . . makes you fight or run. I'm sure you've felt it a few times in the last few days." I laughed, but Felicia's hands faltered as she went over my wounds.

"The body . . . makes drugs?"

"Yeah, lots of different drugs for every occasion. That's how the stuff you do with Herbalism works. It just mimics the drugs that the body uses to have the same effects."

Felicia was silent as she finished checking me. Eventually, she sighed and sat back. "You're fine," she conceded.

"Told you. And . . ." I pulled out the Dungeon token. "I beat the Kobold Chieftain!"

"You . . ." She looked exasperated. I heard a snort from over where Kyle was. "That was way too dangerous!"

"There's no way you killed all those Kobolds, though," Kyle said. "You'd have run out of Endurance."

"Ah, but they can't summon their minions if they're invisible." I smirked. It took Kyle a second to get it, but then he laughed.

"You turned them invisible?"

"Yep! The Chief was a pretty hard fight, but other than that it went pretty well."

"Don't encourage her, Kyle," Felicia scolded, but her heart wasn't in it. "She was still taking crazy risks."

"Yeah, it was crazy," he agreed. "But she didn't put yo- . . . us at risk. So she kept her promise." He gave me a direct look, and I nodded.

"Incidentally, there's a special reward for completing it solo," I said, taking out my new dagger.

"Did it turn your dagger into darksteel?" Felicia asked incredulously.

"No, this is a new one. Just the same, but better quality," I replied.

"Perfect for your new assassin profession," Kyle joked.

"Don't even," I said with a scowl. "But, seeing as it's a magical material, it will be the first thing I enchant properly."

"So you say, but I have a hard time believing you can enchant things," Kyle said doubtfully.

"Well, I *can't* yet," I said. "It's very frustrating. Also, I don't really want anyone knowing that I've got the skill, so . . . that's another difficulty. But I have a plan."

Felicia and Kyle groaned.

That afternoon, a man emerged from between two buildings off the main square. He was dressed in a black hooded cloak, subtly embroidered with mystic symbols that glinted darkly silver. He didn't look around, but headed straight toward the only jeweller that this town possessed.

"Hello . . ." said the shopkeeper, his voice trailing off as he beheld his mysterious visitor. "Sir?"

"You are a goldsmith, are you not?" I said. Disguise didn't actually cover my voice, so I was forced to use Unseen Sound to project a male voice. My face was obscured by the shadows of the hood, so he couldn't quite see that my mouth wasn't moving . . . but he must have suspected something was off, because he looked quite shaken from the simple question.

"Uh, yes? Sir?"

"I require an enchanting scribe. I understand its manufacture is the provenance of goldsmiths."

"Why do you want an enchanting scribe?" he asked, before thinking. I didn't answer, figuring the answer was obvious, and the silence would be more intimidating. I watched his face as he thought it through. If I wanted a scribe, then I wanted to do enchanting, and if I had the Enchanting skill, then that meant . . . he was standing in front of a level seven wizard. The blood drained from his face.

"Uh, yes, yes, that item does come within my skill. Requirements are . . ." he blanched further. "Sir, that item requires a mana crystal—I don't normally stock such—"

I interrupted him by placing the Shaman's stone on the counter. "Will that suffice?" I asked. He stared at it, skill clicking to life behind his frightened eyes.

"Yes, that will. I can have it ready in two days, for five gold."

I wanted to Bargain, but that didn't seem in character for Mysterious Wizard, so I just put five gold down on the counter.

"I will also require gemstones. Diamond, sapphire and tourmaline. Your lowest grades will do."

"Yes, of course." He quickly headed to the back, leaving the gold on the counter. He came back with two trays of gemstones for my inspection. I just put fifteen gold on the table.

"Diamond," I said. He dutifully started placing the smallest diamonds on the counter. He stopped when there were about twelve in the pile. They were the tiniest things. I cleared my throat, and he put another two on the pile.

"That's all I can do, sir; there's no local source for these!" I looked at him. Was that going to be enough? I didn't actually know. My rune list just said diamond dust, not how much. *If it isn't enough, I'll just have to spend more*, I thought. I put ten more coins on the table.

"Sapphire," I made myself say, and the man started adding blue gems in a separate pile. Some of these were larger, almost half a centimeter across, but it still made for a pitifully small pile. Five more gold coins. "Tourmaline," I said. My cash reserves were running out as quickly as they had arrived. I still had the money from our latest expedition, but I still had more purchases to make.

The tourmalines were the largest yet, three murky green stones about a centimeter across. I got the impression they weren't of great quality, but they still cost five gold. I just nodded, and the merchant sighed in relief. He brought out three small ceramic containers and put each pile in one. Then he tied lids to each small pot, one green, one blue, and one unglazed. I gathered all three pots, then turned to leave. "I shall return in two days for the scriber."

Walking across the town square, I could see that I'd attracted some attention, but no one came near. I did look over my shoulder to see someone slip into the jeweller's store, but I didn't let that distract me. I headed over to Noah's alchemy store.

"I require enchanting dust." Noah responded better than the jeweller had to my demands; perhaps alchemists dealt with the higher levelled more often.

"Of course, sir," he said, examining me closely. "I'm afraid I don't stock any, but if you have the raw materials, I could produce some in a day?"

I nodded. I'd expected this—why would he stock the stuff when there were no Enchanters around? I put the cups down on the counter, and he opened them up and examined the contents.

"I see," he said. He brought out a small balance scale and carefully weighed the contents of each pot, noting down the measured weights.

"Three gold to powderize each sample . . . I presume you will want them combined with purified gold dust at the usual ratio?"

I nodded. *Wait, gold dust now?* There hadn't been a mention of it in my so-called help file, but at least this meant my dust would go further. Noah continued:

"Then an additional six gold to cover costs and to purify down to a suitable grade."

I managed to maintain my composure as I casually handed over almost all of my gold. *Just one coin left*, I berated myself. *This had better be worth it!*

"I will return in two days," I said.

That night, the talk of the tavern was all about the mysterious Enchanter who had visited. I was learning a lot, as speculation about who he was covered various mages from the capital and the frontier, as well as rumors from the other nations. All of it way off base, of course. They were all confused by the fact that he'd "only" picked up thirty gold worth of gems. They seemed to think that an Enchanter would have cleaned out Ethan's (that was the goldsmith's name) shop entirely.

Ethan was actually in the tavern that night, enjoying free drinks from the other townsfolk pumping him for every word that the stranger had said. Some speculated that the stranger was scouting out the town, preparing for an eventual takeover. Others said that this was a distraction, a way to start rumors of a top-tier mage in Oakway to attract other forces, diverting them from his true purpose.

Others said that he was here to steal the Dungeon core. That was always a concern with mages, apparently, but most folk thought that if that was what he was here for, he was pretty stupid to be wandering around town letting everyone see him. Just go in and take it was what he should do.

The debate raged, and I served drinks while noting potentially useful names and locations, while trying to keep the smirk off my face.

SPECULATION

So what do you think?" Felicia asked. She was referring to my new workshop. It wasn't much, just a narrow two-room shed, really. The previous tenant had moved to a place with a shopfront, and this place was now mine for a month for the low cost of fifteen silver. It had come with a workbench that had been left behind, and I'd bought a stool. At some point I'd look at getting a bed, but for now I was still sleeping at the Green Tanner.

"It seems secure," I said, and it was true. I'd spent my last gold on a Good quality lock to go with the door. Tomorrow, I'd collect my enchanting equipment and start practicing, but for now there wasn't much to be done.

"Got any money left?" she asked, lightly.

"Nope. Well, some copper and a few silver. Another Dungeon run tomorrow?" I said, knowing the answer.

"Sure," she said. I don't think she was anywhere near as hard up for cash as I was. I'd spent all my extra reward on tools, while she didn't have anywhere near my expenses, unless she'd splurged on potions. "But level two, right?"

"Right, right," I said. There were a few good reasons I hadn't gone to level three yet. First of all, I wanted to try making my own runic protection from the heat rather than spend money on potions. I know, I'd already spent more than I would have for a set, but that spend was an investment in the future. Potions would just be drinking my money away.

The second reason was that the third floor, apparently, was a complicated maze of tunnels, and we wouldn't get far without a map. Which was available, from the Guild, but only to silver members. Getting silver rank was a matter of completing quests, which brought us to the third reason: most of the Guild quests were for the second level.

It's not that the drops on the third level weren't valuable, but they weren't as specific as the plant and monster parts of the second level. Third level was mostly inorganic rewards, and smiths just paid for what people brought in, avoiding the Guild cut.

Potions, though, had specific recipes. More than one, according to Felicia, so each potion maker would change the mix according to what ingredients were cheaper. A glut of Sayina flowers could increase demand for Baneld orchids, for example. Specific quests were how the Guild and the potion makers responded to the needs of the market.

All that wasn't any of my concern at the moment. There was something I wanted to ask my friends now that we had a certain amount of privacy.

"Guys," I said, looking over to make sure that I had Kyle's attention. "Does the third level have a key like the second level?"

"I don't think so, no," Kyle said. "The key is to get you past the boss, so you don't have to fight him each time you go down and up again."

"There's nothing past the third boss, so there's no reason for it, right?" I asked thoughtfully. This had actually been mentioned in the quick Dungeon primer I'd been given by Paige on my first day, but I wanted to check with the others.

"Katherine, I can't believe you're already thinking about the third level boss," Felicia interrupted. I held up my hand to stop her.

"It's not that," I said. "That first time we went down in the early morning, I saw something before you arrived. A bunch of Reynard's lackeys entered the Dungeon, took out a red gem, and disappeared."

"That sounds like they used the second level key, except . . ." Felicia looked at the doll I'd taken out.

"Exactly. The key is themed to the level right?"

"Bloodstones are a pretty common drop for the third level, right?" Kyle asked. "If the key was one of those, it would be on theme."

"But if the third floor has a key . . ." Felicia's voice trailed off.

"Then it must mean that there's a fourth floor, that only Reynard and his goons know about," I finished her thought.

"Oakway Raiders don't go for the boss, that I've heard," Kyle said thoughtfully. "But aren't the Delvers pushing to get there? If they beat the boss, the secret will be out."

"If Reynard wanted to still keep the secret," I said slowly, "he'd have to kill them either before or just after they killed the boss. Would the death of an adventuring party in the Dungeon be a reason to hold a hearing?" I asked.

Kyle and Felicia looked at each other. "Yeah, I think it would be required," Kyle said.

"So," I said. "Reynard wants me to cover up the murder of the Delvers." I waited for one of them to disagree with me, but there was only a troubled silence. "Is . . . there anyone that we can go to with this?" I asked. I wasn't entirely sure how law enforcement worked. There *was* a Sheriff on the town council, appointed by the King and responsible for enforcing the King's Law, but . . .

"Guild members are supposed to be regulated by the Guild," Felicia said slowly. "Guild Master Albrecht would be the one . . ."

"Reynard told me the Master would be away—do you know if he's already left?"

"I don't know . . ." Felicia replied. "But even if he isn't, what are we going to tell him? This is all speculation . . ."

I thought for a minute. "If our suspicion is true, then there will be a passage after the boss—so all we have to do is get the Guild Master down there and kill it? Can Albrecht do that?"

"He may be old," Kyle said, "but he's level six. He can kill it, and make sure Reynard doesn't try anything, as long as he believes us." He got a thoughtful look for a moment, but I was tired of talking.

"OK, let's go find him now."

"How did you know the Master was going on a trip?" Paige asked. "And yes, he's already left. Did you want to speak with Reynard?"

"Um, no thanks," I said. Deceive kept an unworried smile on my face. "We'll just wait until he gets back." I rejoined my companions with the slightest shake of my head.

"What now?" asked Felicia once we were back in the shack. "We could warn the Delvers?"

"They'd probably believe us, at least," I mused, thinking it through. "But without proof, all they could do is confront Reynard, same as us. Could the Sheriff do anything?"

"Maybe," said Kyle, "But he wouldn't want to go against a level five on some story, and he wouldn't want to go down to check it himself. He's only level four, after all."

"How do you know that?" I asked, curious. "Do you use Identify on the townsfolk?"

Felicia looked at me like I was odd. "Identify doesn't work on people, Katherine."

"Oh, really?" I said, embarrassed. "All this time I've been thinking the only reason I haven't been exposed is because using it was rude or something." Relieved, I tried it on Felicia, just to be sure.

[Identify].

There was no result. *Well, that's one less thing to worry about.* Back to the main concern.

"If we secretly accompanied the Delvers to fight the boss, could we make a difference?" I wondered.

"Do all your plans have to involve you going deeper into the Dungeon?" Felicia asked wryly. "I don't think Kyle and I would make much difference. Reynard will have his crew as well, and some of them are level four. Maybe your invisibility might help?"

"Reynard has seen through my illusions before," I said. "But that was a few levels ago. If I figure him for five points in Intelligence, Perception, and Level, he'll have a base of 125. I've got . . . 162 base, so they might work?"

"That's insane, being able to overpower a level five like that," Felicia said. She considered some more. "Reynard might have six skill . . . maybe even seven? He *is* a Ranger, after all."

I groaned. "And there's no way Reynard isn't keeping a watch on the Delvers. He needs to know when they make their move. If Albrecht is away, Reynard might be ready to make his move the next time they go down." I knew that the Delvers were on the same 'every second day' schedule that we were on—taking the extra time to heal and recover mana. Today was an off day, since I'd seen them in the tavern, so they could be murdered as soon as tomorrow. Without a better idea, we decided that I'd secretly contact them on their way to the Dungeon and join their team.

"You'll need a potion," Felicia said. "I'll get one for you."

I wanted to say no, but we really did need to do this. "I'll owe you," I insisted. She shrugged.

"I just wish we could be more help down there."

I nodded.

I had a lot on my mind while serving drinks that night, so I didn't immediately notice when the old man entered the tavern. However, it was hard to miss the silence that spread as the other regulars noticed him and stopped whatever it was that they happened to be doing.

To my eye, the most unusual thing about him was how he was dressed. Wait, wasn't there a special word for it when you were dressed in armor? He was wearing matte black chain mail, with matching black metal armor pieces covering his arms and legs. Was that darksteel? I wondered. If so, he was a walking pile of gold. The axe on his back might have discouraged muggers, though. It was made of some kind of . . . wait. *[Identify]*.

[Identification] : **Blood Moon Axe – Quality: Perfect – Properties: Runed, Blood Rage – Damage: 180**

I still wasn't used to being able to analyze things I didn't actually know about. Wow, that was some weapon. While I was staring, goggle-eyed like everyone else, he walked straight up to the bar, and to Harold.

"Harold," he said, with a nod. "Need your girl Katherine for a bit." Harold stared at him, then almost involuntarily looked at me. That was enough for the old man, who walked over to me. "Need some space," he said to the nearest table. The men sitting down scrambled over themselves to take their drinks to another table.

He gestured for me to sit. All around, the noise of conversation suddenly returned as people started talking, about anything, just to avoid the impression that they were listening in on the old man's business.

"Who are you?" I asked wonderingly.

"I'm Liam Warner. Kyle's my grandnephew," he said, sitting down. "I hear you've got a story to tell."

"Kyle's—he asked you to help us?"

"No. He knows better than that," the old man said. "I'm retired. The problems of the Guild are none of mine."

"But people are going to die . . ." I trailed off as he just shook his head.

"Anyone who goes into a Dungeon knows they're risking death. Monsters or humans, it makes no difference and is none of my concern."

"Then why are you here?" I asked with anger in my voice.

"To hear your story, girl," he said grimly. "Let's hear it."

So I told him how I'd lied to the Guild, and how Reynard was blackmailing me. What I'd seen at the entrance to the Dungeon. My speculation about what was going on. When I'd finished, Liam looked at me for a bit, his face unreadable.

"Thin," he finally said. "Nothing like evidence."

"Unless the fourth level is there—that should prove everything. Or if the Delvers die in the next few days."

"True enough. You up for a trip?" he asked.

"What, now?" I asked, startled. He nodded.

"It's past midnight; that wyrm should be up again," he said casually. "I don't plan on putting this armor on any more times than I have to, I'll tell you that much."

"Um, I'll have to get changed . . . will you wait for me?" He nodded again, and I rushed upstairs. I met Harold's eye as I went up. He shrugged, apparently resigned to whatever the whims of the Warner patriarch were.

"Why are you doing this?" I asked. By this time, we'd avoided the guards on the gate and were walking to the Dungeon. "If this is no business of yours, why confirm my suspicions?"

Liam snorted. "If Reynard's pulling a load of treasure out of the Dungeon, where's it going?"

"I . . . don't know?" I said, confused.

"If he'd been selling loot in town, his secret wouldn't stay that way for long." Liam lectured. "And it's not like he's been displaying a whole lot of suddenly gained wealth, right?"

"He said . . . there was someone who could get him out of this posting." I thought back to our earlier conversation. "That must be where the wealth is going?"

"Right. And that person's gotta be either a corrupt guild official, or a noble." He thought for a moment. "Probably both; where there's the one, there's the other."

"I see . . ." I said, but I wasn't any clearer.

"*That's* my business," Liam said darkly. "Keeping the nobility out of Oakway."

"Oh." It was more clear now. "Did I mention that Reynard had people watching the entrance?"

"Yeah," he said and then paused. "Ah, I suppose it would be better if word didn't get back to him. Do your Invisibility, then turn it off once we're inside."

I complied. I wondered if he had some power to stop spells working on him, but if so, he had turned it off, and I was able to render him Invisible without problems. He continued walking toward the entrance, and I followed the outline of his form. *Had he been planning to just kill the people at the entrance?* I shivered at the thought. Adventurers in this world became way too causal about death. I'd felt it myself—skills made it just so easy to kill, and I had to kill so many things to progress. *Will I be the same way when I'm high level?*

Once inside, he waited for us both to appear again and then asked, "You've got a key to the third level, right?" When I nodded, he continued. "Take us down, then."

"Don't you have your own?" I asked, taking out my key.

"Ah. Lost it years ago," he said, with a grimace that might have been embarrassment.

Is that even possible? I wondered. Mine returned to me whenever I tried to drop it. I didn't ask any more questions, though, just concentrated on the token for a moment, taking us down to the third level.

Darkness. Heat. After the bright light of the first level, the sudden transition made me freeze. As my eyes adjusted, I could see that there *was* light, just not much. A ruddy glow ran down on a few spots on the walls of the large cave we found ourselves in. It took me a moment to realize they were also the source of the oppressive heat, as they were rivulets of lava flowing down to somewhere underneath.

They provided just enough light to see by, but I wanted better. *[Light].* The spell revealed the cave in more detail, but there wasn't much to see. Just five exits and my companion, who'd also been waiting for his eyes to adjust.

"Good. Useful spell," he said, and started off.

"Wait!" I exclaimed and started digging for my Resist Heat potion. I drank it and sighed with relief as the heat faded to a comfortable coolness.

"Don't you need one of these as well?" I asked. Liam shook his head.

"Nah." He tapped one hand on his black armor. "Darksteel's good for more than light and sound. Absorbs heat as well. Makes it a bugger to forge, though."

Your party has killed a Hatap Wyrm – your experience share is 46 XP.
Your party has killed a Tonasnys Creeper – your experience share is 120 XP.
Your party has killed a Elm'vor Lizard – your experience share is 20 XP.
Your party has killed a Elm'vor Lizard – your experience share is 20 XP.
Your party has killed a Eona Giant Beetle – your experience share is 80 XP.
Your party has killed a Eona Giant Beetle – your experience share is 80 XP.
Your party has killed a Eona Giant Beetle – your experience share is 80 XP.
Your party has killed a Rogue Saycha Ant – your experience share is 46 XP.

Truth be told, I was expecting my first trip to level three to be more exciting than this. Liam stalked through the tunnels ahead of me—most of the time, I didn't even get a chance to react before he slew whatever monster came out of the darkness.

"How does it know?" I wondered aloud. "That we're a party, I mean. It's not like I'm contributing here."

"Dunno," Liam grunted. "Just does. It's pretty smart about it, too—they say if your XP is more than it should be, it's because you have a traitor in your group."

That level of omniscience is a bit terrifying, I thought. But maybe it made sense. The way that skills inferred what you wanted, like they were reading your mind . . . it was clear that the System was capable of understanding much more complicated things than social dynamics.

"Right. Another question . . . could you explain more about the nobles trying to take over the Dungeon? I'm not from around here."

"Kyle said something about that," Liam said. "Let's see. So Dungeons are a big source of wealth—which is power, see? And ownership—no—controlling access to Dungeons is the King's gift, right?"

"Right."

"So the King puts out about half the Dungeons as available to the people, controlled by the Guild, and the rest are divvied up by the noble houses. But the thing is, Dungeons aren't equal."

"Some have more levels, or have better drops," I say. "So everyone wants the *best* Dungeons."

"Everyone wants, not everyone gets," he agreed. "Guild gets the dregs, so we only get a good Dungeon when some noble's left with a choice of it going to a rival instead."

We paused our conversation to let Liam slay another two . . .

Your party has killed a Hatap Wyrm – your experience share is 46 XP.

Your party has killed a Hatap Wyrm – your experience share is 46 XP.

. . . of those. We weren't stopping to pick up loot. Liam had told me that the most of the monsters down here had small mana crystals in their heads, but that he "didn't have the time, nor the inclination, to go rooting around their brains for them." Using Mana Sense, I could see a concentration of mana in a number of heads, but I wasn't prepared to let Liam go on ahead without me.

"So if Reynard is working with a noble, then that guy has advanced knowledge that Oakway is a better Dungeon than most people think."

"Aye, so he can lay the groundwork in advance to get his dud Dungeon swapped for this one."

"And he gets whatever profits Reynard can extract from having exclusive access." A thought struck me. "Does the Guild actually get much profit out of Oakway?"

"Not much. They take a cut from the quests," Liam said dismissively. "Other places, they have different rules—like charging for access. Oakway's always had a tradition of free access, and it's not much of a Dungeon, so they've never bothered exploiting it too much. Might change if there's a fourth level."

We walked on in silence for a bit, when Liam stopped in a section of straight tunnel. He looked at me.

"Time for a little local lore," he said. "Worth remembering that no matter what the guild tells you, the locals will always know more of a Dungeon's secrets than they do."

"So what's the secret?" I asked. Looking around, this tunnel was one of the more boring ones. It didn't have any of the lava alcoves that apparently held blood crystals—yet another treasure that Liam didn't have time for.

"Ever wonder how the Guild can sell maps that don't give away the boss's lair?" Liam asked.

"I haven't seen them yet, but I presume they don't show all the tunnels?"

"That'd be a bit of a giveaway, wouldn't it?" he said, grinning. "All you'd have to do is find a tunnel that wasn't on the map. Though you're right, they don't show all the tunnels." With a grin, he lashed out at the wall with his gauntleted fist. With a shattering crash, the wall exploded under his blow.

I was sort of used to superhuman feats from these people—and from myself—from time to time. But I wasn't expecting the whole wall to shatter like glass! Liam laughed at my shock.

"It's a secret door," he said. "There's a mechanism . . . somewhere, but this is faster than finding it."

"Is that allowed? I thought there was some rule about a clear path to follow."

"Seems so." Liam shrugged, not caring. "Let's get going."

> **Your party has killed a Giant Unt'acka Centipede – your experience share is 80 XP.**
> **Your party has killed a Giant Unt'acka Centipede – your experience share is 80 XP.**
> **Your party has killed a Giant Unt'acka Centipede – your experience share is 80 XP.**

In this section, the monsters seemed to come in greater numbers. Twice, Liam stopped and had us turn into a side tunnel, based on something he could hear.

"Swarm snakes," he said the second time, after the threat had apparently passed. "Probably too many for me to keep you safe."

"Thanks for the consideration, but I could go invisible, if it would help?" *I'm not just baggage here!* is what I wanted to insist, but I wasn't sure it was true.

"Nah, we're almost there. Just one more door."

Sure enough, it wasn't long before he'd punched his way into another chamber.

"Stay just inside the door," he said, striding forward. The chamber we'd entered was large, too large to be fully lit by the thin streams of lava that flowed down the walls and converged into a central pool. The pool occupied about half of the cave, leaving a ring about five meters wide of rough, rocky cave floor, broken up by thin channels for the lava to flow.

Liam walked straight up to the pool, letting his axe ring out against the rocky outcroppings in his path. It looked as if he fully expected to see the monstrous head that rose out of the lava pool.

> **[Identification] : Greater Lava Wyrm – Threat Level: 10 – Condition: Healthy – Qualities: Immune to Fire**

"Wakey, wakey, little wormy!" Liam called.

He's crazy. That thing was anything but little. A somewhat lizard-like head attached to either a thick neck or a long body rose up about two meters out of the lava, looking down on the old man as he taunted it. For about a second, before it attacked!

Liam jumped back and to the side as the head came for him. It flew past, bringing the rest of its body with it. *OK, it's like a snake, then.* I could now see the rest of the body as it came out of the pool, twisting around to get another strike at its tormentor. Who . . . jumped over it? Eschewing his axe, Liam just jumped over the wyrm, forcing it to twist around further in a complete loop. Not that it had any problem with this, turning and striking with the speed of . . . a snake, even as its tail whipped around to try and bash Liam from behind.

Liam dodged both blows with the same movement, moving calmly to his side, farther away from the pool. Undaunted, the snake turned to strike once more, but this time Liam seemed done with dodging. Instead, his axe swung, right in the path of that incoming mouth.

> **Your party has killed a Greater Lava Wyrm – your experience share is 166 XP.**
> **For clearing the third level of Oakdale Dungeon for the first time, you have earned 333 XP.**
> **For clearing the third level of Oakdale Dungeon, you have earned a reward.**

When I blinked the notification away, I saw that the lava had stopped flowing and the pool had started draining away somewhere. As the lava level dropped, it revealed a raised central section with a familiar looking chest sitting on it.

"Looks like you were right, girl," Liam said grimly. He pointed to where the pool was disappearing. "Used to be, the lava didn't go down all the way."

Below the level of where the lava had been, there was a bridge, clearly intended to allow access to the central platform. Now I saw that a staircase extended down from one side of that bridge, spiralling down around the platform.

"Get the reward," Liam said, his guard still up. I didn't hesitate, jumping down to the bridge and going over to the chest. Inside were fifty gold coins and two red jewels. One was glowing brightly; the other looked just like the one I'd seen Reynard's cronies using.

> **[Identification] : Fire Crystal – Charge: 500 – Qualities: Fire Mana**
> **[Identification] : Oakway Token – Properties: Teleport**

"This is it," I said, holding out the token. "This is what I saw those guys using."

"All right. Grab the treasure," Liam said. "Might as well see what all the fuss has been about."

We headed down the stairway and along the passageway it led to. It wasn't long before we saw light ahead and entered the fourth level.

"Gods above," Liam swore as we took in the view.

"Quite a view, isn't it?" said a familiar voice. We quickly turned to see Reynard and some others, about fifteen meters away, slowly getting up. "Took you long enough."

BOSS FİGHT

If we're going to die here, at least our last sight will be this fantastic view. It really was amazing. The second level had been a vast expanse, but it was hidden behind the ever present jungle and misty ceiling. I had no idea how big the third level was, but even knowing where to go, we had been walking through twisting tunnels for hours. The fourth level, though, was all spread out below us.

It was a vast bowl, the sides steeply sloping at the edges and gradually levelling toward the center. At the center, there rose a massive mountain. There was no way it could be as tall as it looked—I think the layout of this place was deliberately arranged to play tricks with perspective. It looked like it was fifty kilometers away and a towering 2,000 meters high, but I think it might have been much closer, and shorter.

The rest of the bowl was divided into triangular sections, like a pie, each with a different terrain type. I could see Arctic wastelands, a forest of tall trees, a swamp, and open water. Past the water, I could see what looked like a sandy desert, but the final terrain was hidden behind the mountain.

Carved into the edge of the bowl were sloping paths that led around the edge and toward the nearer terrains. They all converged on a flat ledge about twenty meters wide outside of the entrance. That was where we all were. Liam and I, facing Reynard, and seven other men. They were split up on either side of us, blocking the paths down.

Liam didn't seem too worried. "I thought we avoided your guys upstairs?" he said casually.

"You did," Reynard stated. He pointed at me. "But I had men watching this one—they came and got me as soon as they saw the Warner patriarch walking out the door with her."

"Ah. Never was good at this subterfuge stuff," Liam said. "So all I need from you is the name of whoever is behind all this."

Reynard laughed. "What good would a name do for a dead man?"

"You think you can kill me?" Liam actually sounded surprised. "You're going to attack the Bloody Moon?"

"Empty words, old man. You haven't worn that armor in ten years."

"Fifteen, but so what? The numbers don't go down." Liam's axe, which had remained in his hands the whole time, started to glow. It hadn't done that in the caves, and now it was glowing bright enough in the near daylight of this level. Reynard tried to hide it, but that glow worried him, I could tell.

Liam looked back at me. "Girl, use the token and get back to town. I'll deal with the rest myself."

"Right," I said, gulping. I took out the token, but I didn't use it. Instead, I cast Greater Invisibility on myself. Then I took a few steps back into the shelter of the entrance. I had a feeling things were going to get dangerous out here.

Reynard didn't make a move to stop me. He watched me disappear and then returned his attention to Liam. "My men outside will take care of her."

"Reckon she might be a bit more slippery then you're counting on," Liam said. "Well, shall we get started then?" He was swinging his axe before he was even finished speaking. Two quick swipes sent two arcs of that red light toward the group behind him.

> **Your party has killed Samuel Henderson – Your share is 53 XP.**
> **Your party has killed Declan Joyce – Your share is 53 XP.**
> **Your party has killed Owen Cooke – Your share is 53 XP.**
> **Your party has killed Luke Hunt – Your share is 53 XP.**

Just like that, it had begun. Reynard looked shocked, but the bodies hadn't even finished falling before he was barking orders. "Fall back! Follow the plan!" he called out, even as he jumped backward. I mean *jumped*. Thirty meters backward, landing unerringly. His surviving men also jumped back, but not as far, or as adroitly. It didn't seem to make a difference to Liam, who simply swung his still glowing axe again. With this third stroke, as the red light flew off, the red glow faded and the axe looked as it did before. The red arc was just as strong as the others, though, and had no problems reaching even Reynard. He managed to get his sword in front of it, though, which absorbed some of the damage.

His men had mixed fortunes. One was actually still in the air as the arc flew out, avoiding being cut entirely. The other two staggered as they were hit full on, blood flying out. They were still able to run, though, and they did, fleeing as if a demon was after them.

Maybe one was. Liam seemed pissed that his quarry was getting away and took off after them. Literally—he jumped as well. *Does everyone with high Strength move this way?* I wondered. I watched him follow the others off the path and jump their way into the forest. Within moments, they were out of sight. A few moments more, and a tree started falling. *Well, they should be easy to track?* First, though, looting the bodies.

I felt a bit sick as I approached the bisected guild members. I'd grown used to some bloody sights from skinning lizards, but it was a bit different when the corpses were humans. I debated what to take off them. The armor was out; it would take too long to remove and be too bulky to carry. It was a shame, though; even torn up as each suit was, they were still the most valuable equipment they had. Their swords were much the same. Identify labeled them as Good or Great quality, which meant I could probably get some gold for them, but they were just too big to easily fit in my backpack. I resolved to limit myself to their money and any small hidden items.

> **Your party has killed a Raging Boar – Your share is 167 XP.**
> **Your party has killed a Raging Boar – Your share is 167 XP.**

What was that? Had Liam gotten diverted into hunting boar? Whatever, I needed to focus. One of the dead guys had a small leather bag hidden in his shirt. When I opened it, I found something surprising. Gems! Not many, but bigger than the ones I'd spent all my money on yesterday. Suspicions aroused, I looked more carefully, and all of the corpses had at least one gem concealed about their person. When I finished, I had ten gems of various colors.

Maybe this level drops gemstones? I wondered, but I didn't have time to spend thinking on it. I dumped all the gems in one bag, and all the gold in another, larger, bag. Then I headed off after Liam.

> **Your party has killed a Davalik Bear – Your share is 120 XP.**
> **Your party has killed Logan Hughes – Your share is 53 XP.**

I headed off at a run. I was still slower than Liam, but he had to keep pausing to fight—and to rearrange the landscape. I passed trees sheared in half, shattered rocks . . . and corpses. After every fight, the trail changed direction, but it was always headed in the general direction of the central mountain.

Your party has killed a Faris Wolf – Your share is 80 XP.
Your party has killed a Faris Wolf – Your share is 80 XP.
Your party has killed a Faris Wolf – Your share is 80 XP.
Your party has killed a Faris Wolf – Your share is 80 XP.
Your party has killed a Faris Wolf – Your share is 80 XP.

Damn, Liam, are you going to carry me all the way to level four? I caught up with the remains of what must be Logan Hughes, and stopped to loot. Like the others, he had a few gems and plenty of gold. I spared a glance for the dead bear that was also in the clearing. I noticed that there were a lot of arrows scattered around, but none in the bear. Were they using the local monsters as traps for Liam? Didn't seem to be slowing him down any. I started running again.

I must have run five kilometers before I caught up with them. That was approximately five kilometers more than I could run before coming here, but I wasn't even puffed. I got a skill level even, so I was running faster at the end than I was at the start.

I heard them before I saw them, so I slowed as I reached the edge of the forest. I don't think the cover of the trees made much difference, but I was hesitant to approach. Ahead of me, jagged rock rose up steeply—the foot of the central mountain. It rose above, and as I thought, it was "only" about four or five hundred meters high. About fifty meters up, Liam was fighting a dragon.

[Identify] : Lesser Wyvern – Threat Level: 13 – Condition: Injured –
Qualities: Fire Resistance, Flying, Armored Skin
[Identify] Level 4 acquired through use.
For gaining a skill level, you have been awarded 1 XP.

I don't care what you say, Identify, I know a dragon when I see one. Maybe that's what you call the small ones? I wouldn't call it small, though; it must have been . . . ten meters long? It was clinging to the slope with its four legs, wings flapping for balance while it tried taking bites out of Liam.

Giving them plenty of distance were Reynard and his men. Separated from each other and standing well away from the main fight, they'd found stable perches from which to launch pot-shots at Liam. There were five others, so he must have had more men hidden in the forest?

Liam . . . wasn't looking good. He was dodging and parrying the dragon all right, but there were three arrows sticking in him and even from here, he looked covered in blood. What worried me, though, was that he was screaming in incoherent rage as he fought, seemingly unaware of the other combatants.

Was this what the "blood rage" I'd seen on his weapon was? Well, whatever, I needed to do something to help, and I only had two tricks.

[Greater Invisibility]. Nothing happened. No mana was spent, even. Did my spell have a range? I'd have to get closer. Even as I started moving, though, the fight took a new turn.

Liam got in a good strike, and the dragon shrieked in rage and took to the air. It shot up and away from the mountain, but stopped at about twenty meters. I knew that wasn't a safe distance, but safety wasn't what it had in mind. As soon as it had achieved some distance, it unleashed a torrent of flame at its tormentor.

Two doubts of mine were dispelled in an instant. One, that was obviously a dragon, whatever Identify said. And two, Liam was definitely in berserker mode, because he leapt directly *into* the flame.

As I stared in horror at Liam getting engulfed in fire, everything slowed down. I remembered that his armor absorbed heat, so maybe it wasn't as stupid as it looked? Certainly the dragon hadn't expected it.

Your party has killed a Lesser Wyvern – Your share is 346 XP.
For clearing the fourth level of Oakdale Dungeon for the first time, you have earned 500 XP.
For clearing the fourth level of Oakdale Dungeon, you have earned a reward.

It was still stupid, though, because once the dragon was dead, there wasn't anything holding either of them up. They fell down the mountain, onto the rocky lower slope. The dragon was on top.

After the bellowing roars from before, the silence that fell was uncanny. None of Reynard's men said anything. They just stayed where they were, arrows trained on the corpse. After about thirty seconds, Reynard started heading carefully down. Before he'd moved far, though, the dragon started moving, and he halted. We all waited in tense silence.

With a furious grunt, Liam pulled himself out from under the dragon's corpse. His axe was still in his hand, and he started looking around for more people to kill. In the next instant, five arrows sprouted in his chest. He looked down at them, then took another step. Five more arrows. Very slowly, he toppled over.

Your party member, Liam Warner, has died.

There were scattered cheers from above, as they got their own notifications. They all started making their way down the mountain—the ground must have been too treacherous for their mountain goat leaping method.

"Should we go up and collect the reward?" one of them asked.

"No," Reynard answered. "The chests will only open for a party member. Strip him of his gear; it's worth more in any case. Then we'll head up and see if those losers managed to catch the girl."

It took a few minutes for them to go through all of Liam's pouches and strip him of his armor. Reynard took his axe, and looked at it reverently. "The Bloody Moon. It's got some history behind it. Maybe it will be enough to get the Lady Rankin to overlook this debacle." Then he took out a red gem and teleported them all away.

Well, this is a mess and a half. What were my options? I could teleport up to the entrance, but that was currently filled with people who wanted to kill me. I might be able to avoid them, but it would probably be a good idea to give them time to disperse. In the meantime, I'd just heard that there was a treasure up there with my name on it.

[Climbing] Level 2 acquired through use.
For gaining a skill level, you have been awarded 1 XP.

OK, now I was tired. And dirty. At least my scratches were just Stamina damage, and started fading even as I watched. But I'd made it. Not to the top, thank God. *Should I start saying thank the gods?* The wyvern made its nest in a fairly expansive cave about three quarters of the way up. I suppose that if you could make your way up here without attacking its attention, this would be a much better ground to fight it on.

The chest this time was made of . . . jade? Intricately carved green stone . . . Identify didn't work on it. Inside was . . . *Wow*. Gems. A pile of gems that put my current horde to shame. All different colors . . . I gathered up my riches and put them in my gem bag. *I have a gemstone bag.* Between this and the gold I'd gathered, I was rich, wasn't I? But that didn't help me with my immediate problems.

As I pondered my next move, a small passageway caught my eye. Curious, and looking for a distraction from my problems, I investigated. It was short, making one turn before opening out into a small cave. In the center of the cave was a pedestal with a large, spherical, glowing crystal. I stared at it for a bit. This must be the Dungeon core, and as per the rules, now that its final guardian was dead, it was there for the taking.

If I took it, I'd be in more trouble. Breaking the King's Law and all that. A new Dungeon would probably grow back eventually, so long term, nothing would change for Oakway. But in the short term, Oakway would no longer be attractive to Reynard's boss, the Lady Rankin. And it would piss off Reynard something fierce.

That was reason enough to do it, in my opinion. But I needed more than that. I needed a plan for what to do next . . . well, I had a few ideas. Milly said I would be bringing trouble to nations, and I guess this would be the start of that.

I reached out to grasp the stone. To my surprise, there was a barrier in the way, but it wasn't strong. Maybe the old me couldn't have pushed through it, but I had no trouble now. As my hands touched it, I was struck by a sudden thought, and used Mana Sense. I really needed to get in the habit of using that. In my new vision, the smoky crystal somehow faded away, and I could see the immensely complicated mana working inside. Imagine the most intricate, complicated clockwork device, and then superimpose a half-dozen more on top of it. More than a thousand wheels and spirals of mana, some interacting with each other, some sliding through . . . I still couldn't see half of the detail.

> **Do you wish to assume control of the Dungeon? Corporeal form will be abandoned. [Y] / [N]**

What? *[No].* I hadn't heard of that being an option, but I wasn't ready to abandon my body. With a simple tug, the stone came free.

> **Dungeon core has been removed from external mana construct. Five minutes before external construct unravels.**

As the message popped up, the stone in my hands started to shrink. With my mana vision, I could see that the outer layers of mana machinery were now outside of the globe, and had slowly started to disintegrate. It was fascinating to watch, but I did not have time.

I could hold the globe in one hand now, which was nice. I grabbed my token in my other hand, and teleported to the entrance. Empty. Well, it had been a few hours. I guess Reynard figured I'd slipped through his cordon and he was better off searching for me in town. I headed out carefully (and still invisible, just in case), but there wasn't even anyone on watch outside.

Running short on minions, Reynard? I thought to myself. This might work out well; it might be a little while before anyone noticed the Dungeon was gone. I tucked the Dungeon core away in my satchel—it had stopped glowing, which was nice. Time for my next move.

I knew roughly where it was, and it wasn't difficult to find. I suspect any of the large houses in this area would have done, but I wanted the house where I had an in, so to speak. I'd canceled Greater Invisibility a while ago, but I was still in Disguise as I knocked on the door. It was opened by an older woman with a familiar look to her, which made me think I was in the right place.

"Mrs. Warner?" I said. She nodded warily. "My name is Katherine. I'm a friend of Kyle. I'm afraid I've got some bad news about your family."

Lewis Shaw was having a bad day. As the town Reeve, responsible for administering the King's justice, he was charged with some troubling responsibilities, but seldom did they weigh so heavily. When half the Warner clan descended on the town, demanding the head of the one who killed their patriarch, he had kept some hope that he could keep things civil.

The problem was that the King's justice—or at least Lewis's administration of it—didn't extend into Dungeons. That was the responsibility of the Guild Master for the town. With Guild Master Albrecht out of town, and the villain in question being his deputy, people turned to the Reeve to do something. Normally, he wouldn't have dared.

Quite aside from the legal aspects, Reynard was a dangerous man, and Lewis Shaw did not like to cross dangerous men. However, the Warner clan boasted a fair number of current and former adventurers, and some of them were quite dangerous as well. They normally kept to their estates outside of town, but now they were here, filling up the Green Tanner Inn, and making demands.

At their insistence, he'd had Reynard's home and Guild office searched. It went beyond his authority, and likely Reynard would have put up more of a fuss were it not for the presence of angry Warner mid-levelers. They'd found a large number of gems, which was suspicious, but not necessarily incriminating, and Liam Warner's possessions, which definitely was.

Now that the girl's story had been proven, the Warners were even more fired up. But he managed to calm them somewhat, leaning on their loyalty to the crown, promising them a trial once there was someone with the authority to hold it. He'd sent messages to Albrecht, and to the Court, desperately pleading for someone to come and take this problem off his hands.

Then came the news that the Dungeon had been killed. The Warners were incensed, accusing Reynard of doing it to destroy the evidence of his crimes. Reynard blamed the girl, of all things, claiming the level three adventurer was some sort of master criminal. Lewis was inclined to side with the Warners on this one. Of the crimes that Reynard was accused of, concealing an extra level of the Dungeon was the one most likely to stick. Without a Dungeon to examine, all his accusers had was a suspicious number of gems and opposing statements.

But that was assuming that it was either of them. An Enchanter had been seen in town, and everyone knew that high-level mages were prone to stealing Dungeon cores. Lewis was still waiting for *that* shoe to drop. There was no way a master mage had come to Oakway just to make some piddly little purchase.

Now there was this little wrinkle.

"Gone? What do you mean she's gone?" he asked incredulously.

"I mean that rat bastard guilder has kidnapped her!" Luca shouted. He was the latest Warner to force his way into Lewis's official chambers.

"How is that even possible? You Warners are all over the inn she was staying at."

"I don't know." Distraught, the man sat down uninvited. The Reeve looked at him sourly, but didn't say anything. The man could probably beat him to death with his bare hands. "It was noisy last night; the innkeeper told us that she was just gone the next morning."

Noisy was one word for it. Lewis had heard that while the Warners spent the day harassing him and the Guild, they spent their nights trying to empty the Green Tanner's cellar. Lewis himself had avoided the place since they showed up—he got enough of them during the day.

"Are you sure she hasn't just skipped town?" he asked. "She's an adventurer, after all; they're not known for . . . sticking around."

"She cared about justice for Sir Liam as much as anyone!" the annoying man declaimed. "And . . . the window latch was broken, and there was blood on the bed!"

"Well, that's something we can investigate," the Reeve said, heading toward the door. "I'll put my best men on it." As he'd hoped, Luca got up and followed him out of his office. "Abbott! Take this man back to his inn and look into this missing girl case."

"Sir!" Abbott led the man away, which was job done as far as Lewis was concerned. Who cared what happened to Katherine Meland?

The best inn in Oakway was one that Kandis had not even visited, the Blue Girdle. It set its prices high to deter adventurers, who had money, but were famously averse to spending it. A lack of adventurers meant it was a safe haven for merchants passing through town. They were not put off by high prices, but they did require a certain level of luxury that the Blue Girdle was happy to provide.

The man that had taken rooms yesterday did not fit in with the other guests. His lean figure made for a stern contrast with his plumper fellow travelers. Unlike the other merchants, he didn't mingle. He sought no new contacts, looked for no fresh deals. Instead, he disappeared into town on his own business.

Today, he had returned to his room after breakfast. In the privacy of his room, he set up a runic apparatus and placed a clear crystal in the center of it. He waited a moment for the magic to activate, and was rewarded with a blue glow from the crystal, and then an illusion of his master's face appeared.

"The girl is gone, there may be another mage, and the Dungeon is dead," he said. His master did not care for pleasantries.

"Fled?" the image said, focusing on the most important issue.

"Unknown," the man said carefully. His master did not like incomplete reports, but he did not tolerate inaccurate ones. "There are reports that she was taken but . . . the signs could have been easily faked. A splash of blood and a broken latch. People are talking about an Enchanter being seen in the town, so there could be another player."

"Description?"

"Black robes, hooded face. He cast some sort of . . . portal spell to escape from further attention."

"A *temporary* portal?"

"They described it as a golden doorway that he stepped through and disappeared."

His master was silent as he contemplated this. He didn't enlighten his servant, but the man already knew—that did not match the description of any spell known.

"A description of the girl?" his master finally asked.

"Yes, but she registered as an Illusionist with the Guild."

His master cursed, a rare exception to his control. "Yes, no need to bother with the details then. We won't be able to trust any account of events. Is there anything else you can say for certain?"

The man thought for a minute. "Lady Rankin's cat's-paw has been severely compromised. Even if he doesn't get arrested or thrown out of the Guild, she will likely cut him off. Also, she will not be getting any further jewel shipments."

"Trivialities. Very well, take a week and see if you can determine what actually happened here. I'll go over your report when it's written and see if there's anything I can use."

"You don't want me to try pursuing? She can't be more than two days away."

"No, this is a wild goose chase. We've been set up to fail." Anger filled his master's voice, and the man was glad it wasn't directed at him.

"The Oracle lied? Is that possible?" he asked nervously.

"No, they just gave me the information too late to do anything with it. Even gave a warning about how slippery this one would be. We'll keep an eye out for when she surfaces again, but I'm not going to waste any more resources on this one. I'll see you when you get back, Parkes."

The man bowed, but the image had already disappeared.

In the same moment that Kandis Hammond appeared in a barn in rural Latora, six others appeared in the world. Their locations were widely dispersed, but no less carefully chosen. One such person, a male, appeared in an austere room. As he looked around, he quickly became aware of the other person in the room, an older man dressed in gray robes with silver embroidery.

"Rejoice, mortal, for you have been chosen as champion by Rakaro. Here, clothe yourself." He handed the naked stranger a white tunic.

"What? How am I understanding you? What's going on?"

"All will be explained," the man said. "First clothes. Do *not* spend your Ability or Development points."

"You know about the messages?"

"Dress." The man complied. "Good. Come with me." He led the man to the next room, which contained a single chair, and a desk with a book on it.

"My name is Anril," said the man in gray. "What is yours?"

"Borys," said the Worldwalker.

"Sit then, Borys. Rakaro, in his wisdom, has decreed that you will choose the Development path that is right for you. However, the Status will not tell you everything you need to know to make an informed choice.

The book before you outlines the proper methods to develop yourself. Read—and then choose."

"But this book isn't even in Polish . . ." Borys looked at the book and was surprised to see that he could read the cover. He opened the book and started to read.

"I will return in an hour," Anril said, and left the room. When he returned, Borys was still going over the material.

"Have you chosen?" Anril asked.

"I have questions—"

"I do not have answers for you. I do not know where you came from, or how you got here. I only know that you are to serve Rakaro's will."

"What if . . . I don't *want* to serve?" Borys asked cautiously.

"Obedience is one of the things you will learn here," Anril said grimly. "Do not think yourself capable of escape. Even with your points spent, you will still be level one."

"What the fuck is this . . ." Borys muttered to himself. He glared at his captor. "Fine. Guess I'll choose the path of the warrior."

"Leading to the Sword-saint?" Anril said. He smiled slightly, apparently happy with Borys's choice.

"Yeah, sure."

"Then you should know what to do. You will not have enough points to meet the requirements until level four, but that should not be a problem. Focus on Finesse and put the remaining points in Strength. Have you chosen an intermediate profession?"

"Weaponmaster?"

"Suitable. That has skill requirements, which we can see to shortly. Save Development points for that, but spend the rest. You will earn enough Development points through levelling to afford your final profession by the time you meet the prerequisites."

"Fine." Borys stared at the air for a short time, before announcing he was done. Anril then led him to the next room which was set up something like a gym, albeit with some unfamiliar looking equipment.

"Run," Anril said, pointing to a side of the room that had been kept clear. "Back and forth, until you run out of Stamina."

"Won't that knock me unconscious? And what's that thing over there?" Borys said, pointing at something that looked a lot like a medieval rack.

"That is none of your concern." Anril withdrew a coiled up whip from his robe. "You can lose consciousness from running, or you can lose it from pain."

"What the—arrgh!" Anril was done talking. His whip lashed out and struck Borys on the arm that he'd instinctively raised to protect his face.

"You fuck!" Borys screamed, and rushed at Anril with his fists clenched. Anril calmly caught Borys's first strike in one hand. As Borys froze in shock at having his blow stopped, Anril twisted the captured limb. Suddenly Borys was kneeling on the ground, crying out in pain.

"Run," Anril repeated, letting go of his victim. Borys swore some more, but got up and started running, one arm hanging limply by his side. Anril watched his charge carefully, noting the moment when the Run skill was awarded. Every time Borys started to slow down, Anril "encouraged" him to keep going with a lash of his whip. After about ten minutes, Borys fell to the ground, unresponsive even as Anril lashed him a few times to make sure.

Putting away his whip, Anril easily picked up the fallen man and carried him over to the device Borys had noticed before. He started fastening Borys into the device, manacling his arms and legs with heavy steel shackles.

Borys came to as Anril was carefully positioning a very dubious looking device over Borys helpless body.

"What are . . . you doing? You . . . bastard," Borys said weakly. He pulled at his shackles but to no avail. Crafting skill times levels trumped his mere Strength.

"Good, you're awake," Anril said, repressing his emotion. The next part was going to be quite difficult. "You should have thirty Hit points, correct?"

Borys swore, and screamed, but when Anril reached for his whip again, he nodded. "Thirty, yeah."

Anril nodded back. "This will be quite painful, but it is necessary. The device allows us to generate precise amounts of damage, so we don't have to risk killing you."

"Damage? *Killing* me?! Wait!" Borys screamed, but Anril had already triggered the device. Three slim blades sunk into Borys flesh, and he screamed some more. They quickly retracted and Borys was left gasping under Anril's emotionless gaze.

"That should have done fifteen points of damage, correct?" When Borys didn't immediately reply—aside from curses—Anril made an irritated noise and produced a small healing potion. Borys was so shocked by the sensation of his wounds closing, he forgot to curse for a moment.

"Fifteen points?" Anril repeated, remorseless. Borys nodded, defeated. "Your Body Development should increase in the next round," Anril continued. "The more damage we can do each round, the less rounds we need to do."

"You sick fuck! I'll kill you when I get out of this!" Borys raged impotently. Anril looked on calmly.

"You are quite unable to do that at the moment. If it helps, after you have been recognized as Rakaro's Champion, you will outrank me in the Church hierarchy. My fate will be for you to decide." He paused to let that fact sink in, before giving his charge the bad news. "Our target for today is 1,200 damage."

Woken by the crack of thunder, Farzin Zolfali knew that the gods were feuding again. Another man might have dismissed it, but Fazin was a man who had been directly touched by the Gods actions twice, and he knew that this would be his third time. The stars stared down at him from a clear sky, as he looked all around the dark waters that surrounded his boat. A second bolt of lightning struck, hitting . . . something dark a few miles away. Downwind, of course. His presence had been planned.

His course of action obvious, Farzin raised sail and headed toward the dark shape, now dimly visible as flames took hold. He sighed. You could try and avoid the gods' plans, but it was far easier to go with the flow.

By the time he reached the vessel, it had almost burned down to the waterline. He wondered at that. Were there no sailors to fight the fire? Or had those lightning bolts been carefully aimed? He did not worry about a third bolt. The gods got to have their little tantrums, but as soon as they did, the rest banded against them, forcing them out for a while.

There! In the water! Clinging to a barrel, a single figure drifted. Farzin adjusted his course to take him next to the castaway.

"Ho, there! Can you grab a rope?" The man—for now he was closer, he could tell that much—weakly shook his head. Farzin shrugged, and threw a rope ladder over the side. Then he lashed a line to the mast and jumped over with it.

In short order, he had the man aboard, as well as the barrel—you never knew when a bit of salvage would be profitable—and they were both drying themselves off with blankets that Farzin had dug out of stores.

"Rough night?" Farzin asked, which provoked a bout of choking laughter. "Once you've dried off a bit, I'll see if I can find you some clothes."

"Thanks," the man said. "You saved my life."

"It was nothing," Farzin demurred. He was still waiting to see just what sort of trouble the gods had seen fit to dump in his lap, but there was no point in being rude about it. "My name's Farzin Zolfali, a humble deepwater fisherman. What's your name, and where were you headed?"

"The name's Wilson Tylar. I wasn't headed anywhere; one moment I was home, and the next I was on a boat . . . that was on fire." Wilson hesitated and then continued. "Does the word 'Worldwalker' mean anything to you?"

Ah. There it was.

On Latora, zombie infestations were a rare but well-known fact of life. Zombies themselves were not any great threat—even the strongest of them could be defeated by a level four. Every now and then, though, the zombies got lucky. An isolated village without a healer, a lack of guards on walls, a victim too drunk to wake up screaming. It took a number of chance events for a zombie spawning to get out of hand. As it had in the village of Burves. Now, it lay deserted. With nothing living in the town, the zombie villagers had left in search of fresh kills. Only those zombies too damaged to walk were left, and without prey, those few had gone into torpor.

Eventually, the roaming zombies would encounter civilization. Exterminators would come, the area would be cleansed, and life would return to Burves. That would take some time, though. Burves was isolated and saw few visitors. For now, the streets were silent. Nothing moved in the darkness.

Until it did. New life was detected in the heart of the village. Slowly, the remaining zombies woke from torpor. Slowly, they aligned themselves in the direction of the new life. Slowly, they started crawling toward it.

The only thing that could be stranger than suddenly appearing in a different world, Isidre found, was appearing in a home that was fully furnished, but completely empty. She was able to find her way around, thanks to a glowing gem that served as a light source. Clothes were a priority, and she managed to find some that fit in the rooms upstairs. She'd found a weapon as well—a heavy walking stick that doubled nicely as a club.

She had just started puzzling over her Status screens, when she heard a noise from downstairs.

"Hello?" she called, but there was no reply. The scraping noise came again. Gathering her courage, her weapon and her light source, she cautiously headed down the stairs.

There was a corpse crawling through the door.

For far too long a time, she just stared, frozen by the impossibility of what she was seeing. Then she realized it was headed straight for her and she screamed and fled back to the master bedroom. Slamming the door shut, she pressed her back against it.

This isn't going to work, she thought. *This never works in movies. Think, Isidre. There are zombies, you have a stick and . . . the professions. They're all fantasy professions . . . there has to be a profession that works against zombies.* She started browsing through the list, frantically searching for one that sounded like it would work. She could hear that the zombie had reached the stairs, so there wasn't much time. Finally, she found it. Paladin.

The zombie was pushing against the door by the time she was ready, but it was much easier to hold with her new strength. She took a deep breath, and then opened the door.

"*[Holy Light]*!"

She cast as soon as she had eyes on her target. She was surprised and relieved when it worked, a golden light streaming out and evaporating the crawling corpse.

"*[Divine Weapon]*!"

Her stick started to glow with a golden light. Emboldened by her victory, she started heading out, only to see another corpse creeping up. It took three blows from her stick to finish the zombie off, but only because the first one missed.

By the time dawn broke, she had finished off every crawler in the village. She spent the day going through houses, finding the occasional trapped zombie, but also acquiring food, better weapons, clothes and armor. She spent the night barricaded in the sturdiest house, but there were no further attacks.

In the morning, she headed out along the only road, looking for civilization. It would be three more days before she learned that this was a minor incident, that she hadn't been transported into the zombie apocalypse. In a way, it made for a nice distraction from the fact that she'd been kidnapped into another world.

In one moment, Washiyama Kaito had been rearranging his figure collection. In the next, he was standing, naked, in a strange room. It took a moment for him to realize this, however, because in the room was the most beautiful woman he had ever seen.

"Kyaaaa . . . are you a real cat-girl?" he asked in wonderment. The vision giggled.

"No, silly, I'm a fox-kin! Can't you tell?" She struck a pose, showing off her fluffy tail. Like her ears and hair, it was a silvery white color, darkening to black at the tip. "Did you want some clothes?" she said.

Kaito now realized that he was naked. "I'm very sorry!" he apologized, covering himself and bowing deeply. The girl just giggled, and handed him some clothes.

"They said you might be a little strange. You're pretty funny!"

Kaito tried to respond while dressing and simultaneously keeping himself covered, but it was all too much for him. He wanted to ask for some privacy, but he was too embarrassed. The girl herself showed no signs of embarrassment, seemingly more interested in entertaining herself at his expense. Kaito wanted to resent her, but couldn't hold a grudge against this goddess.

Eventually, he managed to get the clothes on. "Please excuse me," he said again. "My name is Washiyama Kaito."

"Pleased to meet you, Washiyama Kaito! I'm Ettalle!"

Is that a first name or a surname? Kaito wondered. "Please, call me Kaito!"

"Sure thing, Kaito!" Ettalle said. "I guess I should explain about what you're doing here, right?"

"If that's all right?" Kaito didn't want to seem demanding. Ettalle giggled again. *Such a lovely sound*, Kaito thought. Pointing at some cushions, she indicated that he should sit.

"So. You've been summoned by Naldyna, the Goddess of Nature, to be her Champion."

I've been isekaied? But I didn't get hit by a truck . . . Kaito thought to himself. He waited for Ettalle to continue.

"Um, that's it. That's all I know," Ettalle said. "Oh, wait, you might not know about the Status thing? You buy Abilities and stuff through it. You should have a bunch of points to start with, but you'll get more as you level."

"Ah, but if I've been summoned, then I've been summoned for a reason, yes? Is there some great danger I'm supposed to save everyone from?"

"Oh! Well, probably, that does sound right." Ettalle said airily. "But I don't know what that is. I'm not aware of any particular huge danger. Latora can be a pretty dangerous place sometimes, though."

"Is there someone I can talk to who would know?" Kaito was starting to suspect that his goddess, while *lovely*, was not the best person to be getting information from.

"Well, Lady Naldyna would know what she summoned you for, of course, but she, um, makes her own appointments." Ettalle looked a bit awkward. "She'll probably tell you what she needs when you've gotten a few levels? You won't be good for much until you do."

"Ah . . . and you're here to help me get some levels?"

"Yep!" Ettalle said, bouncing up and down. "It'll be fun. But first, you should spend your points."

"Right . . ." Kaito started going through the screens. There was a lot of information there, even if it was annoyingly concise. Eventually something jumped out at him. "Wait . . . I can change my race?"

"Is that option there?" Ettalle asked. "We don't get it because we're born with it already taken. But if it's there, you can take it. You can probably only take it once, though. I'll bet the other options disappear once you take one. Gender should be the same."

Kaito shivered as a cool wash of clarity swept through him. All his life, he'd been preparing for this moment, and he'd never known.

I . . . I . . . I could be a cat-girl?

On the Run

You have defeated Reynard Moore in an Intrigue. You have earned 125 XP.

[Intrigue] Level 2 acquired through use.

For gaining a skill level, you have been awarded 1 XP.

I looked at the notification for a long time before dismissing it. *Interesting.* No one had mentioned that Intrigues were a thing. From the looks of it, it was half of the points that I would have gotten from killing him. Not a bad deal—I could theoretically Intrigue him multiple times, while I could only kill him once. Of course, it had taken quite a while to complete this one, while it only took two minutes to shank a monster.

I was sitting in a carriage, making small talk with the other passengers as we made our way slowly from Aldwich to Anchorbury. In a weird reversal from what I knew about the history of my world, carriages were one of the slowest ways to travel. The fastest way available to most people was running. That was how I'd gotten from Oakway to Aldwich—carrying my possessions on my back.

But that was how the poor, and adventurers, traveled. When I left Aldwich, I was a merchant, and comfortably well-off. After arriving in the city, slipping invisibly through the gates, I'd shed my disguise, and purchased clothing suitable to my new station. Then I found out that Aldwich was of sufficient size to boast a salon that offered bathing and beauty treatments. Heaven!

Anyone looking for the desperate adventurer Katherine Meland would never connect her with the merchant's daughter, Kandis, of the Hammond Trading Company. After that, there was the matter of my next destination.

Everyone had told me that my choices were between the capital, where the wealth and power was, and the border, where the opportunity and experience were. North and west of Oakway, the settled farmland slowly changed into less settled farmland, and then forests and hills. There were a few outposts of civilization out there, but they were embattled forts holding back the monsters and trying to carve out new settled lands. Dorsay, the capital of the kingdom, was actually quite close—only three days by carriage southeast from Aldwich.

I'd decided to take neither of those options. Instead, I'd opted to travel west from Aldwich into the neighboring province, which put me in an entirely different duchy, that of Bargougne. I hoped my destination—Anchorbury—would be enough of a city that I could find books, Alchemists, and Enchanters to help me develop my less stabby skills. Felicia didn't know my plans—so she couldn't be forced to betray them—but I'd promised to write in a few months, once I'd gotten myself established.

In the meantime, I had this journey. Four days was a long time to be cooped up and jostled around with the same people, but at least it was a chance to practice my social skills. And there was something else to occupy my time.

I couldn't examine it in the carriage, of course, but that night, in the privacy of my room at the inn, I took out the Dungeon core and examined it with both my eyes and with Mana Sense. It had shrunk to about ten centimeters across, but it was still filled with complicated mana machinery, all whirling away. As an experiment, I pushed mana into it, as I would a mana gem.

Everything went white.

Then, some things appeared. A modern looking desk, with a glass surface and a couple of fancy office chairs. A man was standing on the other side of the desk. He was wearing a business suit—I couldn't see his face, as he was looking away, but the big pointed ears poking up on the top of his head marked him as a beast-kin of some sort. He turned around.

"Oh, hello!" he said. "You're the one who took the core!"

I looked around. At him, at the nothingness, at the desk. None of this made sense. "I'm Kandis," I said. "Who are you?"

"I, ah . . . don't actually have a name," he said brightly. "I'm a fox!"

"A fox?" I repeated. "Not a fox-kin?"

The man looked down at himself, and then put his hands against his face, feeling what was there. "Ahaha . . . that feels weird," he said. "Yes, a fox. A long time ago, I was the first being to find the Oakway Dungeon core after it had formed. I tried to take it back to my den, and somehow became the Dungeon Keeper."

He paused, as if reminiscing. "There have been a few upgrades since then. Not least this one! I've never had a humanoid body before!" He grinned at me, apparently delighted with these events.

I needed to sit down, so I did. The chair was soft and comfortable. As I sat down, words lit up on the desk's glass surface.

Insufficient Mana for Dungeon Construction

The fox watched me closely as I sat, then looked at the other chair. He very carefully moved over to it, and then, just as carefully, sat down. He looked very happy with the result.

"First time sitting down?" I asked. He nodded happily. I sighed—this was all too weird. Acting on some strange impulse, I said, "You can also do this," and spun my chair around.

"Whooooo!" he cried, spinning around.

"Don't do it too much," I cautioned. "It will make you sick." I didn't stop him continuing, though, which he did until he fell off the chair. It took him a bit to figure out how to get up, but he eventually got his feet under him.

"I'm OK!" he cried. My eyelid twitched. I'd just realized we were both speaking English, not Latorran. I wanted to ask, but I knew the answer already. He'd been upgraded with my language, along with the body and the suit.

"OK . . . first thing, you need a name."

"A name? Oh good! What name shall I have?"

"Do you have any preferences?"

"I get to choose? I thought people got named by someone else?"

"Where'd you pick that up?" I asked. It was a weird detail for him to know when he didn't even have a name.

"People in the Dungeon would say stuff occasionally to each other. 'Blame my parents for my name,' that sort of stuff. Oh, and sometimes someone would do something notable that would cause their party members to give them a name."

"Well, it's true, but that's because most people get named when they're babies, before they can speak. You're . . . able to speak, so you should choose your own name." I was going to put "an adult" in that sentence, but I couldn't bring myself to say it.

"Are you sure? You're kind of like my mother, when you think about it . . ."

"No. No to that, and no to being your mother. I'll veto anything you come up with that sounds stupid." He pouted, but seemed to think seriously about the question.

"Should I pick a name that I heard in the Dungeon, or something that I never heard?"

"Either is good," I said. "Names are supposed to be somewhat unique, but there's a lot of repetition. Each culture has its own rules for names, but you're not part of any of those societies, so I don't think you need to be bound by them."

"I see," he said. After a pause, he continued. "How does Rhis sound?"

"It's fine," I assured him. "Short, unique, and easy to say."

"Then . . . my name is Rhis," he said, getting a feel for it.

"Well then, Rhis, what can you tell me about why I'm here? What is this place?"

"This place . . ." Rhis's voice trailed off as he considered. "I think it's the same place I was in before, only changed because of you. It's where you control the Dungeon from."

"Where I would control the Dungeon from . . ." I echoed, ". . . if I were to take your place."

"And if there was enough mana to run it, which there isn't," Rhis agreed.

"What would happen to you, if I did that?" I asked.

"I think . . . that I would stop existing?" Rhis said, uncertainly. "Or maybe I could take over your body, since you wouldn't be using it. I'd definitely give that a go."

"Lovely. Well, I already refused to take the position, so I guess this remains all yours." I gestured to the emptiness. "What do you do when I'm not here?"

"Haven't you always been?" Rhis asked, looking puzzled. "You only just took the core, after all."

I stared at him. "It's been four days since I took the core."

He looked a little shocked. "Then . . . I guess time doesn't pass for me when you're not using the core? I guess I won't have to worry about getting bored?"

"Wait, so if you need mana to exist, then . . ." I focused on my own mana store. Sure enough, I was spending mana. Slowly, at slightly less than my replenishment rate, but I was definitely supplying the mana to run this . . . whatever it was.

"One more question. Do you have any idea what a mage might want with a Dungeon core?"

"The only use for cores that I know of is to build Dungeons." Rhis shrugged. "Maybe they want to build Dungeons?"

"Maybe."

"Do you want to build a Dungeon?" Rhis asked hopefully. "I could run it for you, if you don't have anyone better."

"I don't know what my plans are, Rhis." I smiled at him. "But I can't think of anyone better to run a Dungeon for me."

"Why, thanks!" Rhis said, pleased. I smiled again, and cut the connection.

OK, that was weird, I thought to myself, safely back in my room. *So I'm now responsible for an uplifted fox?* The thing was, I *did* feel responsible. I'd taken the core for my own reasons, but I hadn't thought there was someone in there I could talk to. Whatever I ended up doing with the core, it would have to be something that took Rhis into account.

A problem for another day . . . or another year. For now, I concentrated on practicing Illusion, spamming Static Image to put paintings on the walls and fancy carpet on the floor. I didn't manage to improve Illusion Magic, but there was one benefit.

[Creativity] Level 2 acquired through use.
For gaining a skill level, you have been awarded 1 XP.

The system was still mistaking my memories of art for original works. I wasn't sure what use Creativity was going to be for me, but I'd take it. I could recover around 120 points of mana overnight, so once I'd spent that much, I allowed the illusions to fade and went to bed.

Four days later, and Anchorbury was distantly visible if you leaned out the carriage window. I still hadn't levelled up Illusion Magic. Level four was really hard to reach! Maybe the lack of stress had something to do with it. Or maybe I needed new spells to cast. Of course, to get new spells, I needed to improve my skill, so . . . it just went around in circles.

I decided to focus on whether I should set up shop in Anchorbury. I had been quizzing my travelling companions for details of our destination, and I had a pretty good idea of what was ahead. One thing that made me pause was that Anchorbury wasn't a free town like Oakway, but ruled by a noble family.

Exactly what that meant in practice, I would have to find out, but I could already see one difference, namely the massive fortress that squatted on that side of the city. The walls that surrounded the city had been extended to link with the outer wall of the fortress, but it was completely separate from the larger city. The city itself was much larger than Oakway, with tall walls running around the entire perimeter, leaving only a few gaps for gates and for the river that ran through the town. I wondered how they dealt with water-based monsters . . . perhaps there was a grating?

As we entered the town, there was the usual inspection and queries as to who we were and what we were doing. It was a bit more thorough than at Oakway, but I was quite capable of lying through the bits that I needed to. I didn't show them my Adventurers Guild plate, as I'd thrown that away some time ago. Apparently at the border or the capital, I'd need to show papers of some sort, but this was still the lackadaisical hinterlands.

We disembarked at the travel company's office off of the main square, and I arranged for my luggage to be held in their storage until I worked out where I would be staying. I would have actually been able to carry the large trunk where all my dresses and adventurer's gear were stored—my mere three Strength was enough for that level of superhuman feat—but it would have been awkward to tote the thing around town.

I'd just started to head off exploring, when someone stepped into my way.

"My my, what a delight we have here!" the man said. He was fairly young, younger than me, but obviously old enough to be called a man. The most obvious thing about him was that he was richly dressed, but had terrible taste. I mean, jewels sewn into a waistcoat? Also obvious was why he was accosting me in the street like this. You see, I'd learned some things about Charisma, and how it was perceived in this world.

Charisma wasn't *just* about looks. Being beautiful was definitely a part of it—as I was reminded every time I looked in the mirror—but it was also about force of personality. And there was considerable variation in how those aspects were applied. A person with six Charisma might have a six in looks and the same in personality, but they might instead have only a four in looks and a much stronger personality. And, of course, it went the other way around as well.

So when arseholes like this saw a beautiful woman, they tended to think—or at least hope—that her beauty was a sign of a weak personality.

The sort of person who might be bullied into some kind of compromising position. Whoever was responsible for this world had somehow made it worse for women than mine. Of course, *my* looks were the real deal.

"I'm sorry, did you address me, or did you just pass wind particularly violently?" I asked loudly, and then watched as he froze in shock. Charm didn't want me to act rudely, but I was in charge, so the skill dutifully provided me with the *best* way to act rudely. The exact dismissive tone and sneering face to best discommode this noble in front of his friends. Because *of course* he'd brought backup along when he went out to harass women.

Charm also gave me the timing to interrupt him just as he was managing to get a retort out.

"I'm sorry, I don't have the time to wait for you to figure out how to talk. Why don't you write it down and have your father pass it on when I meet with him tomorrow?"

"My father? You—"

"Count Lowell. You are Aubert Duvost, yes?" I interrupted again. Invoking his father had put him off guard. Normally, *he* would have been the one to do that. "He mentioned he had a wastrel son in his correspondence, and you certainly meet his description." From the way his face went red, and his hand went to his sword, I was pretty sure I'd guessed right as to who this was. He wanted to kill me . . . and he probably could have, legally. This was his family's town, after all. What stopped him was the thought that I had some business with his father, business that he didn't know about—and that he would be punished if he interfered with it.

Under the circumstances, my rudeness was transformed into confidence. Confidence that my business with his father was so important his father would see him shamed and humiliated rather than offend me. He still hadn't broken off, though, so I increased the pressure.

"Let's see, how did that description go?" I idly wondered aloud, as he struggled to control himself. "Foolish, check." He flinched.

"Rude. Check." His friends were laughing at him now. I could tell that he noticed.

"And terrible taste in fashion." I paused, letting my gaze run over him. "Definite check."

> **You have defeated Aubert Duvost in a Tier 3 Social Contest! You have earned 20 XP.**

What? What was that?

Aubert seemed to get a similar message, as he slumped, losing his arrogant bearing.

"I-I shall inform Father that you have arrived in town," he managed to get out. He turned to leave, and his coterie went with him, half of them looking abashed, while the others were still giggling.

"I hope you know what you're doing," said a voice from behind me. I turned to see that it was one of my travelling companions speaking. "Your business with the Count may well be affected by his son's account of you."

"I don't have any business with the Count, Master Brooks," I replied lightly. "I only knew his name because you were so kind as to warn me about his son on the way here."

Master Brooks's eyes widened at my audacity, and he let out a choked laugh. "Then I hope even more that you know what you're doing. The lordling won't be back until tomorrow, but if the Count finds out that you've humiliated his son . . ."

"It shouldn't be a problem," I said airily. "I'm just passing through and won't be here by the time he finds out." That was another lie, though. I was pretty sure that Aubert wouldn't want his father finding out—and I wasn't here to do business, so the Count had limited recourse to interfere with me. I might end up running, but the time to do that was when it was necessary. Still, it couldn't hurt to leave a rumor that I was leaving town . . .

Master Brooks shook his head, but he gave me a small bow of respect as he turned away. It was time to check out the city!

One day later, I was moving into my own modest dwelling. Like my last place, I'd rented it for a month, but hopefully I'd get to use it for the entire lease this time. Meant for a crafter, it had stone walls for the workshop area, with a second story made of wood for living quarters. It was perfect as a private space for me to study and to practice rune-crafting.

Both those pursuits required money, though. I had a fair bit, but it wasn't going to last forever—or long at all, if I had to start buying more enchanting dust. So I'd checked out the local Dungeon as a way to make money—and gain XP. Results were mixed.

This Dungeon was owned by the local lords, the Duvost family, but it was open to the public. For a price. There was a charge to get in, and all the loot had to be sold to the Duvost company store. That meant there was no Guild presence, which I wasn't sure if I liked or not. I was on the run, after all, so if I signed up I'd have to lie again. On the other hand, with certain notable exceptions, the Guild had maintained a certain amount of control over its members, which I thought was lacking in this town.

From what I'd seen, the delvers (they weren't Guild members, so they couldn't call themselves "adventurers") were a rougher bunch than even Reynard's crew. More desperate, too—Reynard may have complained about Oakway's low level, but it was fairly easy to make a living there. Here, with the Duvosts skimming as much as they could off the top, it seemed like it would be harder.

Still, they did seem to manage a living, so the next morning, I went to try it for myself. In my Disguise as a man, I'd booked—you had to book— a slot for the second level, which meant starting at second bell. At the appointed time, I showed my token to the gate guard, and they let me in.

I was only allowed as deep as the second level, though I wasn't clear on how they'd check for that. I was allowed to kill anything I liked on the first level, but if someone booked that level, they were allowed in about half an hour before me, allowing them first chance. However, when I'd booked, the first three levels for the next week were all untaken, making me believe I'd have free rein of the first two levels.

Of course, that meant that most people thought the first three levels weren't worth their time. But it was only one gold—the same price as a map of a single level—so I'd see for myself.

God, that was excruciating, I thought to myself when I got home. The Dungeon was undead themed, which on the first level meant lots and lots of zombies. They were only threat level one, so they were easy to kill, but I only got three XP for each one. I must have killed twenty before I found my way to the second level, only to find . . . more zombies. These were called ghouls, and were a bit more animated . . . and were threat level two. I had an easier time finding my way on this level, as the next group had passed me while I was exploring, and they left a trail of ghoul parts that led right to the next level. It also meant that I missed out on the second level boss fight, though.

The worst part was that undead apparently have a "detect life" ability which my Greater Invisibility didn't work on. That wasn't a problem with low level creatures like that, but it was probably also true for the higher level undead further down. The monsters were too stupid to fool with regular illusions as well, which was saying something since they'd worked with lizards. Basically, my magic was useless there, and I was just a level three with a nice knife. Oh, and let's not forget how . . . messy killing zombies is. I needed a bath. No, I needed to wash, and *then* have a bath.

Fortunately, that was one amenity I could manage. Water was easy—there was a public well that you could take from, but even easier was to get a large barrel delivered. My crafting area had both a large double door for such deliveries, and a drain that led to a bona fide sewer. Not all Latorran cities had a sewer, but Anchorbury had been built by the Empire long ago. I still hadn't read the history of how (and why) the last lot of Worldwalkers took down the Empire, but if they had sewers, they couldn't be all bad.

I got out of my armor and then scrubbed it clean of zombie bits, then let it dry and filled a bathtub with fresh water. Hot water was no problem, thanks to the fire crystal I'd picked up in the Oakway Dungeon. I'd learned one of the things you could do with it, which was make heat. I activated it and dropped it in the tub to do its thing. It wasn't long before I had a tub full of steaming water, and I could finally take my bath.

Soaking in the hot water, I contemplated my situation. I hadn't been keeping track, but I thought I was very close to level four. Liam's rampage had netted me at least 4,000 XP, and my solo adventures had been pretty rewarding as well. I had to be on at least 9,000 XP, which meant a few more zombie runs would put me over. The low-level delves were tiring, and disgusting, but they were pretty easy. And they did net me a slight profit—copper coins and as many rusty weapons as I could carry.

So it was *probably* worth doing another run, at least until I hit level four. For now, though, I resolved to focus on study and enchanting.

ᴇпᴄнᴀпᴛɪпɢ

Name	Kandis Hammond	Profession	Phantasmal Artificer
Level	4	[Unspent Ability Points]	88
Age	24	[Unspent Skill Points]	1
Abilities		[Unspent Development Points]	9
[Strength]	3	[Unspent Spell Levels]	0
[Agility]	3	[Unspent Rune Levels]	3
[Finesse]	3	[HP]	180/180
[Soul]	3	[Stamina]	360/360
[Intelligence]	4	[Mana]	480/480
[Charisma]	9		
Skills			
[Body Dev.]	2	[WM: Dagger]	3 (4)
[Stamina Dev.]	4	[Deceive]	2 (4)
[Perception]	2	[Charm]	3 (4)
[Identify]	4	[Conversation]	3 (4)

[Scribe]	2	[Dodge]	3
[Calculate]	4	[Jump]	1
[Mana Sense]	2	[Climb]	2
[Mana Dev.]	3 (4)	[Run]	3
[Illusion Magic]	3 (6)	[Stealth]	3
[Creativity]	2	[Memorize]	2
[Disguise]	2	[Bargain]	2
[Intrigue]	2	[Advanced Mathematics]	2
[Persuasion]	3	[Sing]	2
[Teach]	2	[Intimidate]	1
[Enchanting]	1	[Research]	2
Unlocked Skills			
[WM: Axe] [Thrown] [Hunt] [Gather]			
Traits			
[Worldwalker]		Level prerequisites for professions are overridden. +1 bonus to all stats.	
[Gift of Tongues]		All languages are understood.	
[Female]		+1 bonus to Charisma.	
[Silent Casting]		Allows you to cast spells without a chant.	
[Subtle Casting]		Allows you to cast spells without gestures.	
[Disease Resistance]		You are more resistant to disease of all types (upgradeable).	
Spells			Mana
[Static Image]	Creates an unmoving image of a single object, not more than 1 cubic meter in volume (upkeep 1/hour).		5

[Light]	Creates a light that can be moved, brightened, or dimmed (upkeep 1/hour).	5
[Unseen Sound]	Creates a sound from a source you designate (upkeep 1/hour).	5
[Simple Invisibility]	People and creatures are unable to see you (upkeep 3/hour).	15
[Disguise]	Modify your appearance and clothing as required (upkeep 3/hour).	15
[Conceal Mana]	Hides a caster's mana from others (upkeep 2/hour).	10
[Greater Invisibility]	Invisible to all senses, can be cast on others (upkeep 6/hour).	30
[Improved Blind]	Blocks sight, sound, and smell from reaching one target (upkeep 4/hour).	20
Runes		
	[Cool], [Heat], [Effect: Touch], [Constant Effect], [Accept Energy], [Sense (Temperature)], [Trigger]	

On the bench in front of me was a small flat disk of ordinary steel, a mana scribe, and three types of powdered gemstone. That should be all I required to craft my first enchantment. I took up the scribe and started filling it with diamond powder. The scribe was something like a fountain pen, except with diamond dust instead of ink. The other difference was that the tip was made of a mana crystal with a hole drilled through it for the dust to flow.

Under the influence of my Enchanting skill, the dust was currently held in place, as I hadn't started crafting yet. As I brought the tool down to the plate, I felt that change, as my will forced the dust, infused by my mana, into the silversteel. I etched the Constant Effect rune, and I felt something intangible stir at the edges of my skill. There was nothing I could identify, though, so I finished the rune, and started cleaning out the tool.

Which took longer than etching the rune! I had to empty the chamber, and then charge the tool in the air to clean out every last particle of diamond. I made a mental note that multiple scribes would be a good investment.

When I started carving my second rune—Target (Touch), in tourmaline—I felt the intangible stirrings take a more perceptible form. I had the option, which I took, to link this rune to the previous one. I could also define the target of the rune more precisely than just "touch." I wanted the rune to affect anyone who held or wore the amulet, so that was how I defined it.

Finally, after another long cleaning process, I started on my third rune. Again, I felt the opportunity to more clearly define the spell. I wanted the user to be cooled to a comfortable temperature, perhaps around 25 degrees Celsius. My skill seemed to understand that, or at least it set a temperature. It felt like I had the option of setting any temperature above freezing. I'm not sure of the utility of cooling an object to 400 degrees, but it seemed possible with this rune. Finally, I also linked it to the other runes. I linked it to the second rune first, and then completed the circle to the first rune. As soon as I did, I felt a surge of mana go into the amulet.

> **You have crafted an Amulet of Cooling – Quality: Mediocre. You earned 15 XP.**

It worked! And I got XP! Picking up the amulet, I did feel a cooling sensation. Since it wasn't magical steel, it would decay in about a week. Probably wouldn't get a chance to use it before it did. But a Mediocre enchantment would decay anyway, so it wasn't worth wasting magical metal until I got my skill up.

I took another look at my stocks of gem dust and figured that I had enough for three more attempts. Since my first priority was raising my skill, I should work on that before anything else. But I didn't really need three decaying amulets . . . thinking about it, I decided to take a break and do a bit of shopping.

Once again, I sat down to enchant. This time I set the temperature to three degrees, and the Target (Touch) to the contents of the container the amulet was attached to.

> **You have crafted a Cooling Element – Quality: Mediocre. You earned 15 XP.**
> **[Enchanting] Level 2 acquired through use.**
> **For gaining a skill level, you have been awarded 1 XP.**

Interesting that the name changed. I hadn't thought about the name, but it matched my intent. When I picked up the plate, it didn't feel cool to the touch, indicating that my desired target was working. I then glued the plate to the bottom of my freshly purchased water jug, filled it, and awaited results.

It worked! It took a little while to cool, but now I had cold fresh water for about a week until the plate decayed. For my next trick, I used a small barrel. Since it was designed to hold liquids, I thought it the most likely to resist warping from the cold. In the future, I might look at getting a fridge carved out of stone, but this was a temporary prototype anyway.

> **You have crafted a Cooling Element – Quality: Average. You earned 45 XP.**

Improvements already! It would be interesting to see how much longer this one lasted than the others, but hopefully it would be an academic question. I was already good enough to avoid Mediocre enchantments; by the time these ones gave out, I should be crafting Good, or even Great ones.

What next? Now that I was thinking about kitchen equipment, I wanted to make myself a hot plate. It occurred to me that I hadn't actually cooked myself a meal since I arrived in this world. There was probably a skill to be had. Problem was, the Heat rune required ruby dust and I didn't have any of that. I had rubies, though, so that wasn't an insurmountable obstacle.

If I was going to buy rubies, though, I'd want to buy other gems . . . but which ones? My so-called help system didn't tell me the gems required until I had acquired the actual rune. My Enchanting skill had gone up, so I should think about buying other runes. Before that, though, I should look in the shops and see what other runes I could copy. Shopping then, for runes and books.

Anchorbury didn't have a resident Enchanter, at least not one that anyone knew about. It was a bit of a sore point from the people I asked, apparently. Anchorbury was big enough a city to rate having an Enchanter, but was being shunned unfairly. Even so, they did have a few enchanted items for sale, some of which they let me examine.

> [Identification] : Rune [Sharpness] – **Quality: Good**
> [Identification] : Rune [Target (Self)] – **Quality: Good**
> [Identification] : Rune [Trigger] – **Quality: Good**
> [Identification] : Rune [Generate (Fire)] – **Quality: Good**
> [Identification] : Rune [Target (Cone Projection)] – **Quality: Good**
> [Identification] : Rune [Undead Bane] – **Quality: Great**

Undead Bane was quite popular, given the nature of the local Dungeon. I asked the shopkeeper about it, and he said that it doubled the damage to that type of creature. So biased against daggers again. Still . . . if I was going to stay here a while, it would be a nice spell to enchant my dagger with. I could sell it when I left, as I wouldn't get as good a price anywhere else.

I felt a pang at the thought of selling that dagger, though. It had been custom created for me by Rhis. Well, I didn't have to sell it, or enchant it with Undead Bane, for that matter.

On to books. No Enchanters in the city meant no books geared toward enchanting, it seemed. And books that could be used to learn magic were rare as hen's teeth. There were some spell books, but until I learned a magic skill, they were useless to me. A few vendors promised to keep an eye for anything, and one offered to send to the capital for something. The cost was eye-watering, but I could afford it. I gave him the ten gold as a deposit.

I did find some useful books on more mundane topics. Geography, History, Heraldry. I checked, and confirmed that if I read a book and didn't need it anymore, I could sell it back for a reasonable fraction of the cost. Memorize couldn't be a very common skill here. One book that I made sure to buy was *Thoughts of the God-Chosen*. It was a collection of writings of previous Worldwalkers, and was sure to have some good advice.

I ended up taking three books home with me. I could have bought more, but I wasn't sure how long it would take me to read them. I was pondering whether I should get some ruby powder now, or wait until I knew what other gems I needed, when I heard a familiar voice cry out.

"You! Woman!"

I turned to see Aubert Duvost running toward me. *Ugh. He hasn't even learned my name. How am I going to deal with this?* The first thing that came to mind was that whatever I pulled, I didn't want witnesses, so I ducked into a nearby alley. Normally I wouldn't consider this a good idea, but he wouldn't be deterred by any commoner witnesses, while there were a lot of things that I didn't want people talking about.

It would have been great if I could have used the alley to lose him, but he was right behind me as I entered. As soon as I'd broken line of sight with the main street, I turned and confronted him.

"What?" I said with irritation. He seemed somewhat put off, but he didn't let it stop him.

"You lied to me! You weren't going to meet my father!" he accused.

I laughed. "Did you just work that out?" I asked. "Or did it take you this long to work up the courage to ask him about it?"

"I, it wasn't . . ." he spluttered. "It took a while to find you!"

"Sure it did," I said sarcastically. "And the first thing you did is rush into a blind alley after me." As an accusation, it didn't make much sense, but it kept him confused.

"What does that have to do with . . ." he trailed off. "If you think I have improper intentions—"

"Not you," I interrupted, and pointed behind him. "Them."

There was nothing there, but he was dumb enough to look. When he turned back, there was nothing in front of him either, as I'd cast Greater Invisibility and taken few steps backward.

"What! Where did you go?" he yelled, as if I was going to answer him. After a quick glance at where I might be hiding, he surprised me by jumping straight up two stories to the roof of the nearby building.

Oh yeah, people can do that. I guess it made more sense to check for stealthy jumping than invisibility. Too bad for him, though. Maintaining my invisibility, I headed back home. *Looks like I'm going to have to do something about him, though.*

You have learned the Rune: [Sharpness].
You have learned the Rune: [Target (Self)].
You have learned the Rune: [Trigger].
You have learned the Rune: [Generate (Fire)].
[Memorize] Level 3 acquired through use.
For gaining a skill level, you have been awarded 1 XP.
You have learned the Rune: [Target (Cone Projection)].
You have learned the Rune: [Undead Bane].

Not a bad evening's work, even including a break for dinner. I'd continued my eavesdropping habit in the tavern, and yes, they were talking about his lordship running around town looking for a beautiful woman.

It didn't sound as if he was well liked, though, so hopefully the townsfolk wouldn't be helping him.

I started thinking about tomorrow. Should I work on my skill, or on my level? It was tempting to hole up and work on temporary home enchantments, but improving my level would improve my Enchanting total, and help with . . . everything else as well. Which meant . . . *ugh. Zombies.*

Turns out, third floor was skeletons. I'd headed over to the Dungeon early enough that they let me take the third level slot on the same day. This time, I headed straight for the third level, killing only the zombies and ghouls that got in my way. Skeletons were still pretty easy, and much less gross than zombies. I killed a few, then waited for the next party to come through. Sure enough, they beat a path straight to the exit, letting me know where it was.

They also inadvertently showed me the traps that needed to be avoided or disarmed. At this level, traps were more of an annoyance, but I didn't have a good way to deal with them. *I need a party . . .*

I let them go on their way and stayed back to kill skeletons.

You have inflicted 54 damage!
You have inflicted 55 damage!
You have inflicted 54 damage!
You have inflicted 51 damage!
For killing a Skeleton, you have earned 30 XP.

Damn things took too many hits. They did each contain a small mana crystal, though. Most Dungeon monsters did, apparently, but at least with the skeletons, it was just rattling around in the skull. I wasn't going to go digging in the brains of a ghoul.

You have inflicted 57 damage!
You have inflicted 55 damage!
You have inflicted 54 damage!
You have inflicted 53 damage!
For killing a Skeleton, you have earned 30 XP.
You have gained a Level!
You have been awarded 125 Ability Points.
You have been awarded 5 Development Points.
You have been awarded 2 Skill Points.

Finally. I headed back. I was disappointed to learn that the Dungeon shop would only give me six silver for my skeleton mana crystals. *And* they wouldn't let me keep them. I would have argued about it, but I didn't really need such small crystals. If I went down again, I'd make sure to conceal a few to keep.

After all that, I made more of a profit than I had from the first two levels. After the entry cost, I was up 88 silver, which was a decent amount. It wasn't anything compared to level three of Oakway, though, and I resolved to congratulate Rhis on making a much better Dungeon than whoever was responsible for this one.

Once I was home, it was time to spend Ability points! After all those . . . days saving them, I was looking forward to improvements. I brought up the Ability screen again.

Ability	Actual	Base	Cost
[Strength]	3	2	31
[Agility]	3	2	31
[Finesse]	3	2	31
[Soul]	3	2	31
[Intelligence]	4	3	49
[Charisma]	9	7	121

I had 213 points now, so I definitely had enough for another point of Charisma. I'm not sure why I wanted ten Charisma, but could I . . . Yes. I would still have enough points. I put one point in Charisma, one in Intelligence, and one in Finesse—it would help with both Enchanting and dagger work.

Now my screen looked like this:

Ability	Actual	Base	Cost
[Strength]	3	2	37
[Agility]	3	2	37
[Finesse]	4	3	58
[Soul]	3	2	37
[Intelligence]	5	4	79
[Charisma]	10	8	163

I didn't get a special notification for Charisma ten, nor did it cut me off. I could buy more! I probably . . . wouldn't, though. Level five was a long way away.

It was also time to stop holding off on Development points. There were just so many options to choose from, but I think that I'd narrowed it down to a few.

> **[Socialite]** : +1 Bonus to all social skills (6 points).
> **[Wizard Born]** : +1 Bonus to all magical skills (8 points).
> **[Extra Spells]** : 15 more spell levels per Casting Skill Level (8 points).
> **[Precision Damage]** : 50% extra damage if conditions are met (5 points).
> **[Combat Reflexes]** : Increases speed of combat actions (8 points).

Once again, the help system was being super helpful. Social skills weren't listed, but I could guess, and I had most of them. Wizard Born would only help with two, maybe three of my skills for now. But I definitely wanted to get more magical skills.

Extra Spells was also something I needed, as I still hadn't gotten Illusion Magic four. I'd done pretty well with the spells I had, but the only actual illusion spells I had were pretty basic. Precision Damage continued to tempt me—it wasn't clear what "conditions" needed to be met, but I was pretty sure that backstabbing someone while invisible would count. But, I kept reminding myself, I wasn't an assassin.

Combat Reflexes was another one with a vague description, but faster in combat was always better, right?

After a certain amount of agonizing, I decided to go with Socialite and Extra Spells. *Focus on my strengths*, I thought.

Of course, that meant I had to pick some more spells . . . *OK, if I eliminate the ones I have, and the rest of the Invisibility ones, what have I got?*

> **[Sourceless Scent]:** Creates a scent from a source you designate (5 points).
> **[Phantom Touch]:** Causes target to feel a physical sensation as you designate (5 points).
> **[Intangible Taste]:** Causes target to taste the designated sensation (5 points).

[Moving Image]: Creates an image of an object that can move and make sound (10 points).

[Display Image]: Defines an area no more than 4 meters cubed in which images can be displayed (10 points).

[Phantom Pain]: Causes target to feel intense pain, causing 15 points Stamina loss (10 points).

[Displaced Self]: Moves image of the caster up to 3 meters in any direction (10 points).

[Heavenly Indulgence]: Creates an illusory meal that can be eaten and tasted (15 points).

[False Spellcasting]: Reproduces the effects of a spell that the caster is familiar with, as an illusion with sight and sound (15 points).

[False Life]: Creates an image of a living thing that can move and act as directed (15 points).

[Silence]: Can be cast on a target or area. Prevents sound from being made by the target or in the area (15 points).

[Conceal Object]: Causes an object to look like another object of no more than twice the size (15 points).

[Dispel Image]: Destroys an existing illusion if caster's effect level is higher than the target's (20 points).

[Improved False Spellcasting]: As [False Spellcasting], but can include smell, taste and physical sensation (20 points).

[False Emissary]: Creates a false image of the caster that they can see and hear through (20 points).

[Improved False Life]: As [False Life] but includes smell (20 points).

[Privacy Ward]: Defines a volume no more than 27 cubic meters in size from which sight and sound cannot enter or leave (20 points).

[Darkness]: Creates a volume of complete darkness no more than 27 cubic meters in size (20 points).

[Illusory Room]: Creates a complex image no more than 27 cubic meters in size (25 points).

[Phantom World]: Cast on a single target, generates an entire illusory sensorium. Only target can perceive vision (30 points).

[Phantasmal Object]: Creates an illusory object not more than 1 cubic meter in volume (15 points).

> [Phantasmal Entity]: Creates an illusory creature or person that can move or act as the caster directs (25 points).
>
> [Phantasmal Emissary]: Creates an illusory version of the caster that can interact with others (30 points).
>
> [Phantasmal Structure]: Creates an illusory structure no more than (5 x [Illusion Magic]) ^ 2 meters cubed (40 points).
>
> [Phantasmal Terrain]: Creates illusory structures or terrain within a limit defined when the spell is cast (50 points).

I frowned. Were those Phantasmal spells there before? I hadn't looked at the full list since the first day. Did they show up when I took the Phantasmal Artificer profession? It was right there in the name, after all. And what did they do? Phantasmal Object created an "illusory object," while Moving Image created an "image of an object." Was there really a difference between them? It cost more, so it should be better . . . well, the only way was to get it and see.

It looked like there were Phantasmal versions of most of the spells, so I should probably hold off on getting them until I knew what the difference was. That left Silence, but I'd worked out that Greater Invisibility worked for that. Actually, Improved Blind should do the trick as well, at least for silencing spellcasting.

False Spellcasting didn't really appeal, but Phantom World sounded useful. I could do something to Aubert with that. I decided to check out the Phantasmal Object, and then see. If it wasn't amazing, I'd get Phantom World.

[Phantasmal Object].

Just as I'd expected, a copy of the ceramic jug I'd bought yesterday appeared on the bench. *How is this different from an image?* I wondered. *Test the senses?* I reached out and gave it a poke, to see if I felt it when my finger went through.

The jug fell over with a slight "dink." *Wait, what?* I picked the jug up. Moving Image would let me move the image around, but this was real. Wasn't it? I looked up the spell—it should have a little more information, now that I'd bought it.

> [Phantasmal Object]: Creates an illusory object not more than 1 cubic meter in volume (upkeep 3/day).

So there was an upkeep per day? I released the spell, and nothing happened. Confused, I realized that just relaxing the mana flow didn't end the spell. I had to sever it before it would end. When I did, the jug disappeared.

So this spell would probably continue when I was asleep. I cast the spell again, creating a jug. I scooped some water out of the water barrel and drank it. *How is this not real?* I poured some of the water on the floor, then made the jug disappear. The remaining water in the jug fell to the floor, joining the small spill I'd deliberately left.

I made a dagger, and tried to scratch the bench with it. I couldn't. Nor could I hurt myself with it. It dented the skin, but couldn't penetrate it. I used a two-handed grip and struck down on the bench with all my strength, but the dagger just disappeared.

This is crazy, I thought. *Is this more useful than a normal illusion?* I had to think so. If nothing else, it was more convincing. I wondered if people could still see through the illusion. Given I was looking at a 240 effect total, I doubted I'd find someone who could test that.

Anyway, the question at hand was what spell I should purchase with my remaining points. I had thirty left, which meant I could get Phantasmal Entity, Phantasmal Emissary, or Phantom World. I decided to stick with my original choice. The phantasmal spells were interesting, but they could wait for a little bit. I had to find a way to dissuade Aubert from harassing me, and that spell had more immediate combat potential.

Choice made, my thoughts turned to my Aubert problem. What I needed were allies . . .

ΠΕGOΤΙΑΤΙΟΠS

Name	Kandis Hammond	Profession	Phantasmal Artificer
Level	4	[Unspent Ability Points]	5
Age	24	[Unspent Skill Points]	3
Abilities		[Unspent Development Points]	0
[Strength]	3	[Unspent Spell Levels]	0
[Agility]	3	[Unspent Rune Levels	6
[Finesse]	4	[HP]	240/240
[Soul]	3	[Stamina]	480/480
[Intelligence]	5	[Mana]	800/800
[Charisma]	10		
Skills			
[Body Dev.]	2	[WM: Dagger]	3 (4)
[Stamina Dev.]	4	[Deceive]	2 (5)
[Perception]	2	[Charm]	3 (5)
[Identify]	4	[Conversation]	3 (5)

[Scribe]	2	[Dodge]	3
[Calculate]	4	[Jump]	1
[Mana Sense]	2	[Climb]	2
[Mana Dev.]	3 (4)	[Run]	3
[Illusion Magic]	3 (6)	[Stealth]	3
[Creativity]	2	[Memorize]	3
[Disguise]	2	[Bargain]	2 (3)
[Intrigue]	2 (3)	[Advanced Mathematics]	2
[Persuasion]	3 (4)	[Sing]	2
[Teach]	2	[Intimidate]	1 (2)
Enchanting	3	[Research]	2
Unlocked Skills			
[WM: Axe] [Thrown] [Hunt] [Gather]			
Traits			
[Worldwalker]		Level prerequisites for professions are overridden. +1 bonus to all stats.	
[Gift of Tongues]		All languages are understood.	
[Female]		+1 bonus to Charisma.	
[Silent Casting]		Allows you to cast spells without a chant.	
[Subtle Casting]		Allows you to cast spells without gestures.	
[Disease Resistance]		You are more resistant to disease of all types (upgradeable).	
[Extra Spells]		15 more spell levels per Casting Skill Level.	
[Socialite]		+1 Bonus to all social skills.	
Spells			Mana

[Static Image]	Creates an unmoving image of a single object not more than 1 cubic meter in volume (upkeep 1/hour).	5
[Light]	Creates a light that can be moved, brightened, or dimmed (upkeep 1/hour).	5
[Unseen Sound]	Creates a sound from a source you designate (upkeep 1/hour).	5
[Simple Invisibility]	People and creatures are unable to see you (upkeep 3/hour).	15
[Disguise]	Modify your appearance and clothing as required (upkeep 3/hour).	15
[Conceal Mana]	Hides a caster's mana from others (upkeep 2/hour).	10
[Greater Invisibility]	Invisible to all senses, can be cast on others (upkeep 6/hour).	30
[Improved Blind]	Blocks sight, sound, and smell from reaching one target (upkeep 4/hour).	20
[Phantasmal Object]	Creates an illusory object not more than 1 cubic meter in volume (upkeep 3/day).	15
[Phantom World]	Cast on a single target, generates an entire illusory sensorium. Only target can perceive vision (upkeep 6/hour).	30
Runes		
	[Cool], [Heat], [Effect: Touch], [Constant Effect], [Sense (Temperature)], [Trigger], [Accept Energy], [Sharpness], [Target (Self)], [Trigger], [Generate (Fire)], [Target (Cone Projection)], [Undead Bane]	

Gustave Langelier, the Guild Master of the Ironworkers Guild, took his time, carefully examining the sword in front of him. I knew what he was seeing, but I couldn't help taking another look for myself.

> **[Identification] : Holy Avenger – Quality: Good – Damage: 80 – Properties: Enchantment (Undead Bane)**

He looked up, and at the man beside me. "This is your work, Marsilius?"

"The sword, yes," Marsilius said nervously. "I sold it to the lady two days ago. For fifty gold."

"And bought it back again now. For how much?"

"400 gold, Guild Master. And . . . this meeting."

"Well." The Guild Master turned to me. "It's quite flattering to think my time must be worth upward of 100 gold. What can I do for you, Madam Hammond?"

I leaned back into my comfy chair. The Guild Master lived well. "I heard that Anchorbury does not have a resident Enchanter," I said.

"Indeed, that is true," Gustave agreed. "Shall I assume that you are one, and that this is an example of your work?"

"Yes," I said. There was a pause as Gustave considered his next question. Despite common belief, there was a way to get the Enchanting skill without being a level seven mage. If a mage had both Teaching and Enchanting, he could quite easily teach others the skill, in theory. In practice, no one ever did it.

Exactly *why* that was hadn't been spelled out to me. I thought at least part of it was that Enchanting used up gemstones at a prodigious rate. Having another Enchanter around meant more competition for resources.

"Can I ask where you learned the skill?" Gustave finally asked. Of course he would ask that; an endless source of Enchanters was worth much more to him than a single one.

"Unfortunately, I'm not at liberty to disclose that," I said, with a sympathetic smile. He grimaced, but that answer can't have been unexpected.

"What, then, brings you to us?" he asked. "Enchanting is not under any Guild regulation, so you don't need our permission to operate." That was true. Enchanting wasn't regulated, because no one regulated a high-level mage. They did whatever they wanted.

"Rather than operate independently, I was thinking my needs might be better served by working in partnership with the Guild."

"And what would those needs be?" he asked, but I could see his eyes glaze over as he started thinking of the benefits the Guild could get from having their own source of enchanted goods.

"Oh, you know, items to enchant, materials, and tools. A secure workspace. The security that comes from being a part of a larger organization," I said, watching him trying to control his greed. "If I could have access to enchanted items to study, that would benefit us both as well."

"With such an arrangement, would enchantments to order be possible?" he asked.

"Of course, as long as I have knowledge of the runes and the materials are available."

"Of course . . . well, we'd have to work out the details of such an arrangement—"

"There's just one problem," I interrupted. "A small detail that might prevent me from setting up shop in your lovely city."

"Do tell," Gustave said, keeping the smile on his face with an effort. He was experienced enough to know he'd taken the bait, and was now going to feel the hook.

"I've been having a certain amount of trouble from a certain lordling . . ." I hinted.

"Lord Aubert," he groaned, and I nodded in response. "He has a certain . . . reputation, it's true. He's never actually *forced* a woman, but there have been some . . . complaints."

"I have to say that even his current harassment would be too upsetting for me to stay in this city, if it continues."

"Of course, I understand," he assured me. "It's difficult, though. Really the only one who can restrain him is his father, and he hasn't shown any inclination to do so."

"Is the Count a reasonable man? Someone who understands the business requirements of his people?"

"In most cases . . . perhaps . . ." Gustave trailed off, clearly thinking furiously. He had clearly had an idea and was thinking it through. A moment passed, and he addressed me again. "In truth, madam, we would rather the situation with Lord Aubert was dealt with. We've had to deal with a number of . . . distressing situations for daughters of our members."

"How terrible." I felt bad that he was going to do something for *me*, when he hadn't for *them*, but there wasn't much I could do about that.

"In those cases, the women involved didn't want to raise a formal complaint about his lordship. Since it would be adjudicated by his father, they felt . . ."

"It would be a lot of distress for them, and would just get swept under the rug." With only a token support from the Guild no doubt.

"Yes." He had the grace to look embarrassed. "But this time, we have an unusual confluence of factors. You have a very forceful personality, and a noble bearing. If you were to lodge a formal complaint, with the Guild's full support—"

"Including legal representation?" I interjected.

"If it comes to that, which it won't," he declared confidently. "Count Lowell will definitely want this to be settled before it comes to open court. Transcripts are sent to the capital, after all—he'd be a laughingstock. No, he'll put pressure on you to drop the complaint—maybe even try to buy you off. But if we were to impress on him how important you were to the future of the city . . . he'd be forced to negotiate in good faith."

"So in the end, it would come down to me."

"I'm afraid so. The Count will be able to put pressure on whichever link he feels to be weakest. That will be you—but I suspect he will find he's wrong. After that, he may try to pressure us, but anything he brings to bear on us is going to impact his own revenues. In theory, he has ultimate power over us, but so far he has kept to much more reasonable limits."

"All right," I said reluctantly. He smiled.

"Then let us discuss much more pleasant matters, like our future profitable relationship. Marsilius, can you fetch Ancelote and Calandre from downstairs? Oh, here." He passed my sword back to its owner. "You'll be wanting this."

The next day, I walked into the courthouse. There were no signs, but I'd received directions.

"Is this where I file a formal complaint?" I asked the young clerk, who quickly straightened up as I approached him.

"Ah. Yes?" he said, somewhat awestruck. "Yes. This is where you file complaints," he said, pulling himself together.

"Here you are, then," I said, handing over the first document. I had to admit, handwritten legal documents looked very impressive. The clerk glanced at it, then did a double take. "Um, ma'am?" he said, quickly trying to read the entire document as quickly as possible. "Are you sure you want to . . ."

"Here," I said. "This letter is for the Count." I handed over the Guild's declaration of support. The clerk looked at the seal and swallowed. "I'll see that it gets to him, ma'am."

"You do that," I said, and left.

The next day, a soldier knocked on my door, hand delivering a letter inviting me to the Count's residence . . . for a chat.

I sure am regretting not taking the Phantasmal Emissary spell now, I thought as I approached the entrance to the Count's fortress. That said, I had no idea if the range of that spell would have been sufficient. I approached the fortress from the inner gate that connected the town to its rulers. I had brought my letter as an introduction, but it wasn't necessary. A man wearing indigo and blue—the Count's colors—was waiting for me.

"Miss Hammond?" he said briskly. "Come with me," he continued, not even waiting for confirmation. He led me past the outer walls and into the building. Taking me through a bewildering array of corridors and rooms, all of which were richly furnished, he led me deeper inside. I would have been quickly lost without Memorize. Finally, we came to a small room set out with a low table and two comfortable chairs.

"Please wait here, and do make yourself comfortable." He gestured to the fresh fruits displayed on the table. "The Count will be with you shortly."

"Thank you—" I said, but he was already gone. I took a seat, and a slice of orange, and waited.

It was not, in fact, very long before Lord Duvost made an appearance. He swept into the room unannounced and took the seat opposite mine without ceremony. I had jumped up and somehow managed a quick and graceful curtsy. Charm had somehow improved its game with my Charisma increase—I could swear that I'd started moving before he'd entered the room. Since he hadn't said anything, Charm told me that it was OK for me to sit, but that I should sit composedly until he decided to speak.

Lord Duvost was tall, but even sitting down, he exuded power. He looked about fifty, his hair just starting to go gray, but his beard was still brown. He stared at me with an expression that was difficult for me to read.

"I've spoken with my son on this matter," he said suddenly. When he spoke, it felt as though waves of pressure were coming off him. "Even assuming everything he said was true, the insult that he claims is not worth pursuing. I've instructed him to leave you alone, and you will drop this complaint."

"Thank you for your consideration, my lord," I said, bowing my head. I couldn't say the words I wanted to say.

> **You have been defeated in a Tier 3 Social Contest.**
> **You may not act against the winner for one day.**

I guess this is the power of the nobility, I thought. I wanted to protest. Yes, this was what I wanted, but it wasn't enough!

"May I ask a question, my lord?" I managed to say. It wasn't acting against him I told myself, or maybe the unseen force that was holding me back.

He looked surprised, but nodded permission.

"The Guild told me that you were a reasonable man," I said. It was a struggle for me to even speak at all, but thanks to Charm, my voice was calm and unwavering. "So why do you permit your son to act the way he does toward women?"

Duvost frowned, and I felt the pressure come back with full force. "My son's behavior has been exemplary, this isolated incident notwithstanding. There have been no other complaints like yours."

"Are you really so naive—" I had to stop for a second, due to the pressure at the insult. *This is helping him, not hurting him,* I thought to myself, focusing on that. "—to think that a commoner girl would come to you with such a complaint? Have you thought about *inquiring* as to what the townsfolk think of your son?"

"And what is it that you think I would find?" At his words, the pressure lifted, as I was answering a direct question.

"I was warned of your son on the carriage ride into town," I said bitterly, "The Ironworkers Guild contains only a small fraction of your townsfolk, but its Master knew exactly who and what I was talking about. He has had to help daughters of his members in the past recover from your son's attention."

Suddenly the pressure was gone entirely. Duvost had a stricken look on his face. "There have been rumors," he admitted. "But the girls denied it when my people asked about it, or were gone . . ."

"No one wants to admit to being used," I said. Reluctantly, I added, "And no one wants to think ill of their children."

There was a long silence then. Duvost was lost in thought, and I had nothing more to say. I would have liked to get up and go, but Charm informed me that the audience was not yet over, so I watched as his face went from shocked, to something more calculating.

"You are an unusual woman," he finally said. "Capable, strong-minded, and charismatic. The Guild's letter didn't say why they stood by your claim."

Something they didn't do for their own members. I felt the question there. Apparently not being able to act against also meant not keeping information from. Despite my reluctance, I was compelled to answer.

"I've entered into a joint venture with them, to provide Enchanting services."

His eyebrows rose. "So young? What level are you?"

"Level four," I said. These questions were becoming dangerous.

"Ah. A patron, then." That was not a question, so I could stay carefully still. "So quiet all of a sudden? Oh, of course."

> **Your social penalty has been rescinded!**

"Thank you," I said, somewhat shocked. I really needed to learn more about social combat. He waved off my thanks.

"I have no need of help from the Status," he said. "I'd like to know more about your patron, but I will not compel you."

"I'm grateful for your consideration, but I'm afraid I'm not able to tell you anything about my patron," I said, *on account of him not existing.*

"That you didn't call on *his* support on this matter is interesting, but is headed away from the matter at hand. I'd like to engage you as my son's tutor."

"What?"

"My son needs educating, and I'm simply not in a position to do it. You strike me as the ideal candidate."

"Why should I educate your son? I want nothing to do with him!" I objected.

"For one, I'd be paying you," Duvost said calmly. "For another, if not you, then who?"

"Anybody?" I suggested.

"I'm afraid not. There are very few people in this town who will stand up to my son. Even without my support, they know he will be the Lord someday, and they don't want him to bear a grudge."

"Even so, there must be—"

"There are a few that I could name," he conceded. "But they don't fear him because they have important positions in my administration, or they are mercenaries who plan on leaving before the transition. I can't spare any of my officials, and the mercenaries that I know of weren't hired for their social skills. And then there is you."

"I can't control your son," I protested.

"You have been dealing with him well so far. He seemed quite upset with you."

"I came to you because I couldn't deal with him!"

"You were concerned, because eventually he would resort to violence and you would have no legal recourse, correct?" he asked, and I nodded. "That will not be a problem anymore. I will inform him that he now answers to you, and you may command him as you wish."

"That's . . . not going to just work like that."

"True, he will no doubt try to intimidate you into leaving him alone. He may still resort to force, but if he does, the Law will be on your side— and he will know that. He fears my word enough to keep it a social contest, and you will win that, I have no doubt."

"I can't . . . I don't know how to teach someone that. I can't sit him at a desk and have him write 'treat women with respect'—that's not going to work."

Duvost smiled, no doubt because he was winning. His Persuasion was just too high! "I suspect that—for a start—it will be enough for him to keep company with a woman that will stand up to him. Formal lessons do seem unwise." He thought for a moment. "You are an adventurer, are you not?"

"I dabble," I said cautiously.

"You've no doubt noticed that there is no Adventurers Guild in Anchorbury. Jobs that they would normally handle are taken care of by either my household guard or mercenary teams funded by me. I propose that I fund another such team, with you as the leader. You'll take on jobs I assign you for rewards similar to the Adventurers Guild, and when there are no jobs, you can raid the Dungeon."

"My skill set isn't great for your Dungeon," I admitted.

"All the more reason to have a team," he countered. "You should have no problem attracting members when there is a retainer of one gold a day."

"Seriously? You'd pay that much?" That sort of money was nothing to me with my Enchanting gig, but it seemed a lot compared to what the townsfolk made.

"That's about standard for these mercenary groups," Duvost said. "It's little enough, compared to what they could be earning in a Dungeon. I'd need to pay more if I wanted you to stand ready at all times, but as an incentive to keep the team together, it suffices."

"So we'd—*they'd* make most of their money from delves and quest rewards."

"Yes. Incidentally, with Aubert in your party, you would get to use the Dungeon free of charge." The Count smiled; he'd noticed my slip and could tell I was seriously considering the job.

"*And* keep stuff we find?" I asked. Damn, but that was a nice incentive. The deeper levels of the Dungeon were expensive.

"Of course."

I groaned, but only in my mind. Charm kept me from making such an undignified noise. Was it the arguments, or his Persuasion? Whichever it was, I knew he'd be getting his way. Again.

"Fine, I'll do it." I sighed.

You have been defeated in a Tier 3 Social Contest.
You may not act against the winner for one day.
You have defeated Aubert Duvost in an Intrigue. You have earned 80 XP.
Your social penalty has been rescinded!

"Excellent. Do you want to come with me while I inform my son of the new arrangement?"

"Gods, no!" I exclaimed, somehow remembering to use the plural. "Though he would have gotten a notification about losing an Intrigue, so he will be thinking something's up."

"He should be in a fine mood, then," Duvost said, unconcerned. Well, it wasn't like he had anything to fear from his own son.

"Have him come to my house at . . . tenth bell. We can discuss the team then . . ." I trailed off, a bit uncertain.

"You will have full discretion as to the team composition. I recommend not more than five in total. Aubert may have some suggestions as to who to hire, but the final decision is yours."

"Then, if that's all, my lord . . ." Charm once again providing me with the proper form.

"Yes, you'll need some paperwork once you've decided on your hires, but Aubert can bring it to my Seneschal."

"Then I shall take my leave," I said, curtsying.

There was another servant waiting to lead me out, so I didn't need to test Memorize. About halfway out of the building, I thought I heard an outraged shout, loud enough to be heard through all the doors and corridors in the way.

"Father!"

The next morning, just as the bells were ringing, there came a knock on my door. When I opened it, Aubert Duvost was standing there, resplendent in an outfit that glittered with bad fashion decisions.

"Good morning, Aubey, why don't you come on in?" I said brightly. I'd spent last night thinking about how to greet him, including his new nickname. He loved it, I could tell from the way his face went red. I didn't give him time to complain, though, just left the door open and went back into my house.

It took him a moment to compose himself, but he eventually came in to find me standing by my workbench, which held my travelling trunk containing most of my worldly goods.

"Rule One," I said sternly. "Never let me see you wearing something like that again. Dress like a normal person."

"This is normal," he said, frowning. "And you can't tell me how to dress."

"I can't?" I asked. "Didn't your father tell you to obey my instructions?"

"Yes, but—"

"Was there some exception, like 'all her instructions except on how to dress?'"

"No, but—"

"So if you're unable to follow my *simple* instruction, then go back to your father and tell him that."

He glared at me in silence, but there was only one way it could end. He wasn't going to defy his father on this.

"I-I understand," he said.

> **You have defeated Aubert Duvost in a Tier 3 Social Contest! You have earned 20 XP.**

"Do you?" I asked. "Because if you don't understand how to dress like a normal person, I can take you to the nearest tailor and have them dress you in a craftsman's outfit."

"I can dress more plainly," he said, and took a deep breath. "Did you want me to go back and change?"

"No, let's not waste time; we've got a lot to do today." I tapped my trunk. "Take this, and follow me."

"I thought we were going to be discussing a mercenary team?" he asked, confused. When I narrowed my eyes at him, he quickly moved to take the trunk.

"And we will," I said. "But first, I'm going to have you help me move house." I picked up my three books, which were my contribution to this effort, and then, as if it was the most normal thing in the world, headed out, leaving him to follow me.

"Manual labor?" he said, his voice in a higher pitch. I ignored him, leaving him no choice but to follow.

"That's right," I said once we were outdoors. After easing my trunk through the door, he hefted it with one hand and balanced it on his shoulder. "Best you get used to following my orders now, with easy stuff, before we move on to life-and-death matters."

He wanted to dispute that, I could tell, but he couldn't really. It was quite a good rationale, if I said so myself. I didn't want to leave it there, though.

"Besides," I said brightly. "You'll be saving me as much as one silver, working for free."

TEAM-BUILDING

Yes, I had a new house now, courtesy of the Ironworkers Guild. Negotiating my contract with the Guild had been exhausting, but I think we were both happy with the outcome. Of course, Master Gustave's Bargain and Level skills had been higher than mine, so he probably got the better end of the deal, but from my perspective, it was quite satisfactory.

Gustave had mainly been concerned with getting as much money as possible out of the deal, and while I did want the money, I had been more concerned with maintaining my freedom. Both to act, and to leave when it was time to move on. Fortunately, Gustave had no intention of turning me into an Enchanting factory. Because my raw materials were so expensive, and the market so rarefied, putting massive numbers of enchanted goods on the market would raise costs and drop prices.

So I was contracted to produce six items a week according to the Guild specifications, for which they would provide all the raw materials. I'd get twenty percent of the profits of the sale. That wasn't much—that had been the number Gustave was most eager to bargain down in return for concessions, but when you considered that the average profit on a Good enchanted item was around 300 gold, I'd be making 360 gold per week, for about one day's worth of work.

For any other enchantment I wanted to make, they would provide materials at cost—which was a substantial discount for ironworking, and a smaller discount for the gems. They had first offer rights if I wanted to sell them, but I could sell elsewhere if they couldn't meet my price.

My main concern had been making sure I wasn't locked in. They'd put in a provision that I couldn't leave to work with other guilds in this city, but otherwise I was able to exit the contract with no penalty. I wasn't sure if they'd keep to those provisions, but I had an ace up my sleeve there. I hadn't told them I had Teach, which would let me create a replacement, which should ease the pain of my leaving. I hadn't told them about it because I didn't want them pressuring me to Teach them.

The house had been a perk—we had both agreed that I needed a more secure work area. They'd managed to find me a place on Smithy Street—it was occupied only by Guild members. Of which I was one now—I had been awarded the rank of Senior Member, which was as high as I could go without having duties as an official. The house was a considerable upgrade from my old place, with more rooms and thicker walls. There was space for working, dining, a library, even a room for my maid.

Oh . . . yeah. I was getting a maid. It felt ostentatious, but Gustave had insisted that I needed one for both companionship, to keep me fed, and to keep me from "bringing disgrace to the Guild." Which I took to mean that as a Senior Guild member, I needed to dress well and keep my hair in some sort of elaborate style. Honestly, I wasn't sure if he was just saying all that so that he could have someone keeping an eye on me, but it didn't matter. It wasn't like a spy could learn Enchanting from observing me, and I wasn't planning on betraying the Guild, so it didn't matter. It would be nice to have someone to do the cleaning and such. I'd task Aubey with cleaning, but he'd be rubbish at it.

Speaking of Aubert, he was just now coming back from his final trip. Most of my belongings had been packed into my trunk, but there were a few larger items that needed separate transportation. I'd feel bad about making him carry them, but it really wasn't a problem for him to lift a one-ton barrel of water. I'd unpacked while he was doing that, so once he'd placed it correctly, we were ready to start with what he'd *thought* he'd come here for.

"So, a mercenary team," I said briskly, sitting down at my new table and gesturing for him to take a seat. "Should I presume that your talents lie with the sword?"

He looked at me suspiciously before taking the seat. "Yes," he said. "I've achieved level six with Bladed Weapons. I'm also proficient with bows, and I can wear heavy armor. May I ask what your talents are?"

I grimaced, both because of what I was about to reveal, and the fact that I was going to reveal it. "Enchanting and Illusions." I felt the need to demonstrate, so I gestured and made an apple appear on the table.

"Neither of which will be of any use in this Dungeon," Aubert sneered.

"You are correct," I sighed. "But the Dungeon is only to be our sideline. I don't believe the jobs your father has for us lie in there."

"I don't know anything about that. He hasn't said."

"Well, we'll need to get a team together first," I said. "To my mind, we have the support and tank roles covered. We need fire support and a Rogue type to take care of traps and scouting. We also need healing, but we can cover that with potions."

"I can work at range as well," he reminded me, "but it would be good to have a fire mage. Working with a Rogue, though," he sniffed. "They are beneath me."

I raised an eyebrow. I could do that before, but now I could indicate five degrees of disbelief. "It's my understanding that Rogues aren't actually criminals."

"Too many of them are," he sniffed again. "And all of them . . . they fight dishonorably, in the shadows with knives and stabs in the back. With commoner weapons."

I rolled my eyes. "Weapons like this?" I asked, pulling my dagger out of a slit in the side of my skirt. I used Unseen Sound to make my voice come from behind him. "With tricks?"

He quickly whirled around, knocking over the chair in his haste. When he saw nothing behind him, he glared at me.

"I think there's a fair amount of synergy between a Rogue's tactics and my own," I continued. "How do you deal with traps without a Rogue?"

Aubert carefully restored his chair to the upright position and took his seat once more. "Poorly," he admitted. "A Ranger or some class with good Perception can often spot them, but the only option for disarming it to trigger them at a distance."

"Rogue and fire mage, on the list," I said firmly. "That's four; do we want more?"

"A Healer would be useful . . ." he said. "And with two—or three—backline roles, it would be good to have another . . . Protector role in the team."

I drummed my fingers against the table as I thought about it. "I do know a Healer, who comes with a fighter-type. She's not in town, though."

"Do you want to write to her, and save her a place? Healers that go into combat are rare."

"Yes, I'll write and see if she's interested. We can work on filling the other two spots for now. Do you know anyone suitable?"

"There is a fire mage not currently in a team," he said. "But she won't work with me."

"I like her already. Tell me more."

"Yeah, I don't want to say that guy's right about anything, but he's right about that. There's no way I'm working for him." Janie leaned back in her chair, already on the defensive. She was one of the rougher-looking denizens of the delvers bar that I'd found her in. Tattoos on her neck and wrist, piercings in five places that I could see—but it was her armor that had made her easy to pick out. Leather, and dyed bright red, it stood out, which had to have been her intention.

"You wouldn't be working for him," I said calmly. "You'd both be working under me."

Janie froze, then very deliberately sniffed at her drink. "I thought I was hallucinating when someone like you walked in here, now I know I am."

"Someone like me?" I was not wearing my ladies dress for this outing; I'd reverted to my leather armor. While still new, it had enough faint bloodstains to fit in here.

"You think you can hide quality looks like yours just by putting on a suit?" she replied. "Plus you're just now telling me that Aubert the Shit is working for you—are you a princess or something?"

"I'm not any kind of noble," I said. "I've a contract with his father that puts me in a . . . supervisory role over his son."

"He must fucking love that," Janie said, grinning. "Almost worth signing up to see that in action."

"You know . . ." I said. "I told Aubey not to bother telling me exactly how he incurred your enmity, but now that I've met you, you don't seem like his type."

"Are you calling me ugly?" Janie's eyes narrowed.

"Strong," I replied. "And obviously the type that won't be browbeaten into anything."

Janie scowled. "I'd have to take ugly, if it came from you. But yeah, it wasn't me he was latching on to, it was a friend of mine."

"Is she all right?"

"Yeah, she's fine. It wasn't like he'd dragged her out to a back alley or something. Just wouldn't take no for an answer. Things got ugly, least until his burn scars healed." She smiled at the memory.

"You got away with burning him?"

"Ah, it was just a little bit. He didn't want to admit he lost, so he didn't take it further. Officially. He put a surcharge on my Dungeon entries; that fucked things up for my team, so I had to leave it. Since then, I've been barely scraping by."

"Why not leave? Join the Adventurers Guild?"

"I've got family here, you know?" She looked a little embarrassed at the admission. "Makes it hard."

"It seems to me," I said carefully, "that this is an opportunity to have the Duvost family make up for what they've cost you."

"The money is good," she said wistfully.

"If you can manage to avoid setting Aubey on fire, I'll make sure to keep him under control. That's what I promised his father, anyway."

"Can I call him that?"

"Absolutely."

You have defeated Janie Baker in a Tier 3 Social Contest! You have earned 20 XP.

Social penalty rescinded.

When we got to the bar, Janie pointed out Cloridan. He was sprawled out behind a table, sitting beside an unconscious man. He perked up as we approached.

"I'm in!" he said. He looked pretty tall from what I could see. His eyes were green and his blond hair was long for a man. He had a thin braid which ran behind one ear.

"We haven't even told you what we're here for," Janie said, a wry smirk on her face.

"I thought you said this guy was reliable?" I asked Janie.

"Reliably sober on the job, reliably drunk off it," she replied.

"Indeed, ma'am, she speaks the truth," Cloridan said, only slurring his words a little. "And while I'll happily comply if you need something right away, I would be re-rem- . . . foolish, if I didn't warn you that I won't be at my best for the next eight hours."

"It's a long-term job, with a retainer's fee," I said. "I can't have you being drunk every night."

"That's fine," he said, making an expansive gesture. "The company of a woman as beautiful as yourself is like fine wine to me. I can stay sober for as long as you need, knowing that I will be fulfilling your desire."

I looked over at Janie. "Are you sure . . ."

"He won't try anything," she said firmly. "He won't *shut up*, but he's not the type to make unwelcome advances. I wouldn't be on a team with him if he was." She gave me a significant look back. *Touché*. I took a seat opposite the Rogue.

"The job's long-term, with a retainer of one gold per day. Missions from the Count, pay dependent on the job. In our downtime, we get free access to the Dungeon."

"Free access? The Count?" Cloridan's eyes narrowed for a moment, but then he shook his head. "I'm too drunk to think about this . . . Janie, is this job all right?"

"It's legit," she said. "There's a shit-shaped twist to it that she hasn't told you about, but it's a twist, not a stinger."

"Good enough!" he exclaimed. "I'll have more questions tomorrow, but I'll do it. I take it Janie vouched for my skills?"

"Yeah. I'm not going to ask you to demonstrate anything drunk. Janie, can you get him to my place tomorrow afternoon?"

"Sure thing . . . boss," she said, trying the word out.

"I'll get the details sent to the Count. He might have something for us already. If he doesn't, we'll work on our tactics and try out a Dungeon level or three.

"We'll be there."

"Brace!" Janie yelled, and our front line responded by ducking back behind their shields. A streak of fire flashed past the two boys and exploded into an inferno that engulfed the room. The screams from the tentacled horrors were terrifying, but mercifully brief.

> **Your party has killed a Octopoid Abomination – your experience share is 135 XP.**
> **Your party has killed a Octopoid Abomination – your experience share is 175 XP.**
> **Your party has killed a Octopoid Abomination – your experience share is 135 XP.**
> **Your party has killed a Octopoid Abomination – your experience share is 135 XP.**
> **Your party has killed a Octopoid Abomination – your experience share is 175 XP.**

With no monsters immediately threatening, Cloridan dropped his shield and carefully moved into the room. Aubert presented his shield to me, and I drenched it in water, doing the same for the other shield. The boiled leather facing wouldn't catch fire *easily*, but if we didn't keep it wet, it would burn eventually.

"Are you sure this is still an undead Dungeon?" I asked. "It seems more Cthulhu horror to me."

"I don't know what that is," Aubert said, turning back to face the room. "But this is what you get when a Necromancer has a bunch of leftover flesh from making skeletons."

> **Your party has killed a Octopoid Abomination – your experience share is 175 XP.**

I looked over to see that Cloridan had finished off one of the still-twitching abominations.

"Wait, is that actually how these were created?"

"No," Aubert said. "But once they were created, they became available to spawn in Dungeons." He paused in thought. "The boss does have Necromancy, though, he can raise any delvers that die in his room."

Cloridan gave us the all-clear, so we moved into the room. We each had a job to do. Cloridan and Aubert covered the exits, while Janie stood ready to torch any entrance that looked to start spewing abominations. We weren't actually expecting trouble. Janie's strategy had been to have our fighters hold off the horrors for long enough for them to all gather in the one place. Then she could take them out with one big spell.

They should be all gone, but they moved—slid—entirely soundlessly, so we were keeping an eye out for any stragglers. Well, except for me. As the baggage, with low defenses and little damage potential, my job was to collect the treasure.

Ugh. At least the Undead Bane runes on my knife meant it cut through the flesh like butter. I had to slice through the main body to get the mana crystal at its core. These were ten of mana capacity, probably the minimum for me to use in enchantments. Twenty gold per monster, which was actually low for a level this deep, but all the good loot was with the Master, apparently.

Eventually I was done, and we moved on. Aubert pointed out the entrance to take, and I lit it up. Lighting spells were my main spell contribution so far. Octopoids didn't even *have* regular senses. I wasn't being much of a leader here. Aubert was the one with prior knowledge, Cloridan led the way, and Janie provided our strategy.

Cloridan had stopped up ahead.

"Trap," he said when we'd caught up. He pointed up at the ceiling. "Corpse rats dropping down."

Ouch. Corpse rats weren't much of a threat—if you saw them coming. Dropped on top of you, spread out amongst the party . . . nasty. We'd seen this sort of thing already, though, and Janie had a response ready. She cast a spell and a flamethrower-like jet of flame washed out and covered the ceiling. Hardly any of it found its way through the stone, of course, but Cloridan then triggered the trap.

With another horrible shriek, rats fell into the flames. There were hundreds, but none of them was much tougher than a normal rat. They were charred before they hit the ground.

Your party has killed a Corpse Rat Mass – your experience share is 175 XP.

Corpse rats were just one monster, with lots of little bodies that all worked together. Each rat killed was just some HP lost. We all paused for a moment, thinking about what that would have been like without warning.

"Do you see the stone?" Janie asked me. With Mana Sense, it was easy to make out the central rat that held it. I retrieved it, and we continued on our way.

Things continued in much the same way for a few more rooms. Finally, we came to the end of the level.

"Your chance to shine," Janie said.

"Pretty sure this is the opposite of shining," I said, casting Greater Invisibility on Cloridan. "But it's nice to be finally useful."

"Your lighting spells have been useful," she objected. "Believe me, it's a real pain having to fight carrying your light source."

"Doesn't Fire Magic have a light spell?" I asked. Cloridan handed me his shield, and I hefted it experimentally.

"There's a continual flame spell, but the upkeep is ridiculously expensive unless you give it a fuel source . . . like a torch," she said, grimacing. "I normally carry a torch, drop it during the fight, and then relight it when the fight's done. Everybody ready?"

I raised my shield and nodded. Aubert did the same, and we moved forward in a line, first Aubert, then myself, and finally Janie. We moved briskly into the chamber.

The boss of this level was a vampire, threat level thirteen. He was waiting for us on top of a dais that held his sarcophagus. He contemptuously bellowed out a challenge in what I'd been told was a long forgotten language, but I could understand it.

"Foolish mortals! You dare trespass on my domain? I will teach you the pleasures of death's sweet embrace!"

Little clichéd, I thought as we ran toward him. Aubert took the lead, hoping to close the distance and engage in melee, while we casters hung back. The vampire released his magic, shadows radiating out in all directions and threatening to engulf us.

The room was thrown into darkness as the shadows swarmed toward us, my light spells obscured. Then Janie lit up the room.

A pillar of fire extended from her hands as she cast Torrent of Flame. It punched through the shadows surrounding us and cleared them away from Aubert—possibly going a little too close for comfort—before finally striking the vampire. He screamed, but this wasn't enough to take him down. He shouted something about raising us as his undead consorts and unleashed more shadows.

The boss and Janie started trading spells, fire for shadow. My job was to try and block the shadow fragments that didn't get burned up by Janie's spells. I wasn't great at, though I did unlock Weapon Mastery: Shield. I thought that we were getting the better of the exchange, especially once Aubert managed to make it up the dais and land a few blows. All of this was a distraction, though.

Cut off in mid-insult, the vampire looked down. As his shadows evaporated away, we could all see an empty hole, perhaps an inch across in his chest. We watched as he slowly crumbled into ashes.

> **Your party has killed a Necromancer Vampire – your experience share is 325 XP.**
> **For clearing the 10th level of the Crypt of Ineris, you have earned 250 XP.**

"Nice work, Cloridan!" I called, canceling the spell. Cloridan appeared holding the wooden spear that he'd stabbed the Vampire's heart with.

"I've done this before, but invisibility makes it easy," he said.

We all gathered on the dais. The chest for this level was actually the vampire's sarcophagus. We heaved off the lid and took a look inside. The others had seen it before, but no one ever got tired of looking at gold.

[Identification] : 1000 Gold Eagles – Quality: Great
[Identification] : Crypt of Ineris Token, Level 10

Everyone looked at me, the pack mule. "Yeah, yeah," I said, as I started shoveling gold into a leather sack. This beat taking crystals out of dead flesh, though. "Everyone all right with me taking the token?"

Everyone indicated assent. Unlike Oakway, with a token for every level, the Crypt had tokens only for levels ten and eighteen. Aubert had a token for ten, which was how we'd gotten here without wading through all the other lower levels.

"What now?" asked Cloridan. "Do we go on, or call it a day?"

"I'm good for another level or two," Janie said. "Though if I burn any more mana, I won't recover it with just one night's rest."

"My father did say he would have a job for us tomorrow," Aubert said. He'd warmed up somewhat over the course of this delve. It was hard not to, working together against the threat of death.

"I think this has been a good shakedown," I said. "It's given us a good idea of what we can all do. I say we take our profits and stay fresh for tomorrow's job."

"You're the boss," said Janie, still not above making a dig at Aubert. I rolled my eyes, and teleported us back to the entrance.

We split the loot up back at my old house. I still had the lease, so I'd decided to keep it as a base of operations for the group. The fine people of Smithy Street had expressed concern about all the non-Guild members tramping along their street, and I thought it worthwhile to placate my neighbors. Given some time, I thought I could outfit it with some useful stuff.

Like a bath. Baths, separate for men and women. God, I stink. I couldn't wait to get back home, but there were some formalities to take care of. I took my share entirely in mana crystals. I was looking forward to just having a jar of them for my experiments. That still left about half of them, but the others were fine with splitting them up and selling them themselves.

We agreed to meet here the next day, and then I was finally free to go home. The maid, Elodie, had a hot bath ready, bless her. I was quickly getting used to having a maid—if this kept up, I'd soon become dependent on her.

"Was the bath to your liking, Miss Hammond?" Elodie was a little shorter than me, and kind of stocky. It was hard to get an idea of her figure underneath the maid outfit that she'd arrived with, and despite being younger than me, she had some very definite ideas about propriety.

"It was heavenly," I said, with some feeling. "I see you've gotten the hang of using the fire gem."

"I still think it's extravagant to use that thing just to heat water," she said disapprovingly.

"Well, give me some time and I'll be able to enchant up some less extravagant amenities, and we'll be able to reuse it for central heating or something." I said. "But in the meantime, we've got all the hot water we can use."

"We, miss?" she asked.

"Yes, we," I said firmly. "Did you think I was going to have you scrub down in a cold tub in the kitchen? If you're going to live here, Elodie, you'll make full use of the facilities."

"As you say, ma'am," she replied, with some hesitation. "Does that mean you plan to put *more* enchantments on this house?"

"Oh you have no idea, Elodie," I said smugly. "No idea . . ."

EXPERIMENTS

I had the rest of the afternoon and evening to work on Enchanting, and there was a lot to do. First of all were the pieces for the Guild—swords, axes, and pikes all to be enchanted with Undead Bane. I guess it was understandable that there was a certain amount of demand for that. I only had two weapons available to do, though—it would take them a little while to ramp up production of suitable weapons.

With those out of the way, there was a lot of experimenting to do. What I wouldn't give for some sort of general text on Enchanting! There were so many questions that I had that I was sure could be answered by an introductory text.

For example, why didn't my Undead Bane weapons function properly? Perhaps that was a misleading way of putting it. They did *work*, and the Guild was perfectly happy with them. However, when I looked at them with Sense Mana I could see that, unlike my heating and cooling charms, mana did not flow through the runes. Sitting here on my desk, the runes were inactive.

However, in the Dungeon, where the undead actually were, the runes on my dagger became active. My theory was that runes relied on ambient mana to function. There wasn't enough mana to power the enchantment outside, but the higher mana levels in a Dungeon would allow it to work.

That a Dungeon had higher mana levels was just my speculation, but a quick conversation with Rhis had confirmed it. Lower levels had higher mana, which allowed for higher threat monsters.

Both my heating charms and the bane weapons used the same formation of runes; the only difference was the cost to buy the different runes. If I assumed that the buy cost was proportional to the mana cost, maybe equal to it, then it meant I could power up to five points' worth of runes with ambient mana. Since Constant Effect and Target (Touch) cost four points between them, it meant that I was limited to runes that cost one. That wasn't nothing . . .

> **[Sharpness] : Improves Damage on edge weapons (Cost 1) –**
> **Requires: Diamond.**
> **[Toughness] : Improves Durability of enchanted item (Cost 1).**
> **[Generate (Air)] : Creates an amount of air (Cost: 1).**
> **[Generate (Light)] : Creates an amount of light (Cost 1).**
> **[Warm] : Raises the temperature of target by a moderate amount**
> **(Cost 1) – Requires: Ruby.**
> **[Cool] : Lowers the temperature of target by a moderate amount**
> **(Cost 1) – Requires: Sapphire.**

. . . but it wasn't much. There were other runes that only cost one, but I don't think they were to do with spell effects. They were senses and . . . logic statements? Not sure how they would fit in. But I already had a model for a more powerful effect: Sean's amulet. That used a mana crystal and the Accept Energy rune to power a more complicated enchantment. There was another "energy" rune as well, Gather Energy.

> **[Gather Energy] : Gathers ambient mana to power enchantment**
> **(Cost 2).**
> **[Accept Energy] : Transfers mana into enchantment (Cost 1) –**
> **Requires: Jet.**

Arrrgh! These descriptions! Gather Energy sounded like exactly what I needed, but also like what enchantments did on their own anyway! The only thing to do was buy it and test it out.

> **[Gather Energy] : Purchased for 2 points.**

To test it, I decided to use Bane (Undead) again. It was an enchantment I knew didn't work without extra mana after all. I started carving Gather Energy onto a steel plate—I didn't want to waste silversteel on a test, after all. Maybe Cloridan could use an Undead Bane Shuriken.

There was a round dot as part of the rune; Accept Energy had something similar. So it wasn't a surprise when I suddenly "felt" the need for a mana crystal to go there. Wincing at the probable waste of ten gold, I picked one out of my jar and placed it on the dot. It entered the metal as if it were water, then froze in place when I let it go. The rune was complete.

I wasn't sure what rune to carve next. The obvious one was Accept Energy, but I wouldn't be able to put the dot on the crystal, unless I overlapped runes. That seemed wrong, but I tried carving it, hoping that the skill would provide some guidance.

Sure enough, the skill wanted me to just put the rune next to Gather Energy and link the two as I would normally. Then I went and carved the other runes. When I linked the final rune back to the Gather Energy . . . nothing happened.

> **You have crafted an Undead Bane Shuriken, Quality: Good. You earned 125 XP.**

I flushed with embarrassment. Good thing no one was there to see. I guess I needed to be more careful with what I was thinking when crafting things for the first time. Also surprising was the XP amount. I normally got 75 XP for a baned sword. It must be due to the greater complexity of the enchantment. Which still wasn't working. Or was it?

> **[Sense Mana] Level 3 acquired through use.**
> **For gaining a skill level, you have been awarded 1 XP.**

I could sense mana slowly building up in the crystal. Not enough to count as a point yet, but . . . I watched as it slowly grew.

> **[Identification] : Mana Crystal (1/10 charge)**

I'd been expecting it to power up once it got the one extra mana I thought it would need, but nothing happened. Then I realized that the extra runes needed to be powered as well, so the damn thing needed nine mana now. I could charge it myself, but that would probably invalidate the experiment. I had to wait almost an hour before the enchantment powered up.

There was nothing to see, as Bane (Undead) wasn't the flashiest of spells, but my Sense Mana could see clearly the moment it activated.

OK, so it worked. My sense of triumph was somewhat muted by having to wait an hour for results. *But this means I can make permanent spells.* That had been the promise of the Enchanting skill after all.

> **[Spell Store] : Casts a spell stored in the Enchantment at the time of crafting (Cost 3).**

This was the rune that would give me some real versatility with enchantments. If I could put any of my Illusion spells in a rune, or Janie's Fire Magic spells, then I wouldn't be limited by the range of effects I could buy runes for. After buying that, I had just one point left, so I purchased Sense (Touch). I had Trigger, but the only thing I could use with it was Sense (Temperature), which wasn't very useful. *Touch control . . .*

"Miss? Miss Kandis?" Elodie called out from the door. "Were you planning on staying up much later?"

"Huh? What time is it?" I asked, broken out of my train of thought.

"They just rang ninth bell, miss," she said reproachfully. "If you don't need anything else, I was going to head to bed."

"That's fine," I said, stretching. I'd really lost track of time. "I'll go as well. I left some notes on what I used on the bench; you can do the bookkeeping for the Guild in the morning."

"Of course, miss," she said, as I headed over toward her. She had both Scribe and Calculate, which was unusual for a maid but quite common, apparently, in Guild-members' daughters.

"Enjoy the bath?" I smirked, noticing her skin was flushed and her hair still damp.

"Yes, miss. It was very . . ." she trailed off.

"Decadent?" I suggested. She frowned. "Oh, wait," I said before she could object. "I forgot about the thing." I turned back to the bench and my Undead Bane Shuriken. "I should make sure this is safe in case it explodes?"

"It's going to explode?" Elodie took a step back and moved behind the doorframe.

"No. Probably not," I said. "But I'm not a hundred percent sure what will happen if the crystal charges up past full. Better safe than sorry, right?"

I used Phantasmal Object to conjure up a safe, and popped the plate inside. I didn't bother with a combination; I'd just cancel it in the morning. Actually, I had no idea how safes worked on the inside . . . had it conjured all the gears and tumblers a safe needed to work? Didn't matter.

"Um, what kind of magic is that, miss?" Elodie said, staring at the safe. I looked back. It did look a little incongruous. A modern safe sitting in a medieval house, but it wasn't that out of place. *Oh shit.* Elodie is from a metalworking household; she can probably see a dozen ways that thing is impossible to craft.

"It's special magic to keep us safe," I said. "You'll see plenty more of it when I start crafting devices for the kitchen."

I thought that would distract her, and I was right. "Oh no, miss, there's no need for such things!" she said urgently.

"Don't worry about that now," I said, "Weren't you going to go to bed?"

The next morning, I gave Elodie some funds and a list of things to buy, or order made. Some were work related, others merely "decadent." *I really hope this world has bath salts*, I thought as I headed out for my own appointment. I was the first to arrive at my old house, which was my aim, as I hadn't yet arranged for keys for the rest of the group. It also gave me a chance to plan out the modifications that I wanted.

Let's see, a partition there, table here . . . It had occurred to me to use Phantasmal Object instead of relying on my imagination, so as I planned, the house was rapidly becoming furnished. I . . . probably wouldn't keep it like this, though. Small though the upkeep was, it added up. If I was going to furnish with illusions, I'd want to use enchantments to keep them. Of course, just the cost of *one* illusion would pay for real versions of everything.

My team took the overnight appearance of furnishings in their stride. They quickly deduced they were illusions, knowing what my magic was. *Solid* illusions, though, were new to them. It took a few careful experiments before they were willing to sit on Phantasmal chairs, but eventually we were all seated around my version of a medieval conference table.

Aubert slid a letter across the table to me. "My father's . . . orders, or whatever it is that I should call them." He didn't look pleased to be his father's messenger.

The letter was sealed with old-fashioned—no, I guess I should say with a wax seal that was entirely normal for a Count's correspondence. That it was sealed, though . . .

"Did he not tell you what was in here?" I asked.

"He did not," Aubert admitted, shifting uncomfortably.

"Hmm." I broke the seal. Inside were *two* letters, both short. The first one, after all the palaver that nobility started letters with, stated:

". . . and the County Autumn Ball is in three weeks, to commemorate the start of the season. Consider this letter your invitation to attend, as Aubert's tutor. We can observe his progress and review your performance.

My face went blank, and I looked up at Aubert. "You'll want to read this," I said, and passed it across. He read it, and started grinding his teeth.

"I don't . . . He . . . What does this mean?"

"Pass it to me, Aubey, I'll read it to you," Janie said, with undisguised glee at whatever had gotten Aubert mad. He didn't dignify her taunt with a response, but his hand shook as he gripped the letter more tightly.

"It's about the Autumn Ball; apparently, I'll be attending," I told her.

"Oh, now I'm jealous. You really are a cut above us common folk," Janie said. She was half-serious, but at least I'd distracted her from her target, and given Aubert a chance to calm down.

"I'm sure I could take a guest," I told her, "but you'd have to lose the piercings, and wear something to cover up the tattoos."

"You can't touch my precious face!" Janie exclaimed. "Oh no, am I destined to languish in the lower half of society forever?"

"Lower *quarter*," Aubert said, seemingly recovered enough for banter. He was still angry, but he was controlling it. "Simple townsfolk have a level of respectability that you have yet to reach."

"All right, all right. The rest of this isn't team business, so I'll talk to you about it afterward, Aubert." I was saving "Aubey" for when he misbehaved, something I think he'd already noticed.

"And what might our team business be, gracious lady?" Cloridan said, quiet up until now, nodding at my other letter.

"Give me a second," I muttered. "Oh, while you wait, here, do you want this?" I passed my anti-undead shuriken to him. The crystal had not, in fact, exploded. It had managed to fully charge, at which point Gather Energy had stopped. It should now remain at full charge for the rest of its pointless existence.

"I shall treasure it always, my first gift from you. Um, what is it?"

That couldn't be a question that was often asked, what with Identify being a common skill. The others were equally puzzled by what the skill was telling them.

"It's enchanted with Undead Bane," I replied absently, my mind on the letter I was reading. "It's a version that will work outside a Dungeon."

"Undead Bane doesn't work outside a Dungeon?" Aubert asked, with some concern.

"Not the ones I've seen, or the ones I've made," I said, looking up. "Except for that one. Do people not know this?" Everyone shook their heads or said no.

"Undead don't spawn outside the Dungeon, around here anyway," Cloridan said. "Only in the wilderness—you need wild mana for that to happen."

"Well, they might work under those conditions as well," I said. "Out here, there's not enough mana to power the enchantment, which is the problem. I guess if there's more mana in the mountains, they might work there."

"Why didn't you put it on a weapon, though?" Janie asked. "And what's a shuriken?"

"Ah, it's a name for a really small throwing knife," I said. "Sometimes they're round, so if it had pointy bits, it would probably qualify as one. And it was just an experiment. The enchantment will degrade the metal in a week or two, at which point it will just be a piece of junk."

"It isn't balanced for throwing, though," Cloridan pointed out. "And a *round* throwing knife? How does that work?"

With a sigh of exasperation, I used Phantasmal Object to make a classic ninja shuriken and placed it on the table.

"There," I said. "Now, was anyone interested in our secret mission?" Everyone perked up, even Cloridan, though he carefully reached out to pick up the shuriken.

"*Secret* mission?" Janie asked.

"Yeah, this job requires our absolute discretion, and I'm to swear you all to secrecy before telling you about it."

"You have my oath, of course," Aubert said. "I'm not going to go against Father."

"Yeah . . . I guess so," Janie said. I raised an eyebrow.

"I'm not a huge stickler for sacred oaths," I said, "but maybe a little more commitment than 'I guess so' would be nice?"

"Fine, fine, I so swear," she said. I looked over at Cloridan.

"Yes, I swear as well. Can I keep this?" he said, indicating the shuriken.

"It will disappear after a day, or if you manage to do enough damage to it," I said. "But fine, knock yourself out—that's an expression."

With the oaths acquired, I could move to the next part.

"The mission statement is simple enough," I said. "The Count thinks there might be a Demonologist in the city. If there is, he wants us to find them and kill them. We get 200 gold for showing there's no threat, 1,000 for ending it."

There was a silence as they all looked at me. I took the moment to look up Demonologist, since I didn't recall seeing it before.

> **[Demonologist] : A forbidden class applied to those possessing the [Demonology] skill. No skill unlocks or bonuses are granted (FORBIDDEN).**
> **[Demonology] : A forbidden skill for summoning demons.**

That's a little different, I thought to myself.

Aubert was the first to speak. "Did father say *why* he thinks there might be a Demonologist in the city?"

"No," I said. "I guess he has secrecy concerns?" The rest of the note was just instructions to burn it, so I manifested a metal bin and put the note inside. "Janie, can you burn this? And I don't know much about demons; does anyone know more?"

"I don't think anyone knows more than the basics," Cloridan said, while watching Janie drop a fist full of fire into the bucket. "They start out weak, but if they aren't stopped, they get out of hand, and then . . ."

"The gods get involved and everything goes . . . whomph!" Janie exclaimed, demonstrating what she meant with a mini fireball.

Cloridan winced. "That's only happened a few times, but the smoking crater does leave an impression. For that to happen in Anchorbury—this seems like far too serious a matter to be given as a first mission."

"Perhaps it's a test," Aubert mused. "Father might want to see if we can keep his secrets."

"If that's the case, then all we have to do is keep our mouths shut to pass," I said. "But we should probably take it at face value."

"Right, but how do we do that?" Janie asked, "We've got no information on where these demons are . . . are we just supposed to patrol the streets?"

I nodded. "Yeah, Aubert—you're on that. Find out what the Count's willing to tell us. You might . . . can you be subtle? This cloak and dagger stuff might mean he suspects someone listening in on your home."

"Speak as if we're being overheard. I understand," Aubert said grimly.

"I'll . . . try to find out more about demons," I continued. "My social skills should let me make inquiries without raising too much attention. The question is where to start?"

"Bards," Cloridan said. "Though they might have social skills to match you, they tend to collect stories and lore. Short of a Sage, I'd say they would be your best bet."

"I suppose Sages are only to be found in the capital," I said glumly. Cloridan nodded.

"There's one to the south?" Janie said uncertainly. "Still a couple of days' run, and I'm not sure where exactly. Some isolated tower full of books. A Bard is still your best bet, I reckon."

"Then that's what I'll do. You two can take tomorrow off; we'll meet again the day after to go after what we've found."

"Yay!" Janie yelled. Cloridan just smiled, no doubt thinking of the taverns he would be frequenting. The two of them left, leaving me with Aubert.

"So," Aubert said. "What is it that my father feels you should be teaching me?"

I made a face. "I can tell you, but I'm not sure you'll understand if I do." I paused, but he just glared at me. I sighed. "Respect toward women." I answered.

He frowned. "You are . . . correct. I don't understand. I've always been perfectly respectful toward women."

"Like you were toward me?" I asked.

"I barely said five words to you, before you insulted me—"

"Your words were an attack," I interrupted him. Persuade coiled through my words like a snake. "Meant to put me off balance, be more receptive to your next 'suggestion.' Don't try and tell me otherwise."

He flushed with embarrassment. "I wasn't going to make you *do* anything, just—"

"Follow you? To a nice quiet tavern where I'd be surrounded by your friends? Unable to run away?"

"I wasn't—I wouldn't use skills for *that*; I just wanted to talk . . ."

I cut him off with a gesture. "If I wanted to, could I make you kneel?"

"My loyalty to my father is—" he exclaimed, but I cut him off again.

"Not that," I said. "I'm talking about a show of humiliation, making you kneel down in front of the team, or in the main street. Could I do that?"

He worked the muscles in his face for a bit, before admitting. "Yes. We may be the same level, but your Charisma . . . just how high is it?"

I ignored his question. "And if I took you to bed,"—I saw his eyes widen at the thought—"I'd be the dominant one, wouldn't I? I could make you do whatever I desired, inflict whatever indignity I wanted, and you'd just lap it up, wouldn't you?"

He didn't answer, but his breathing had deepened, and his eyes were starting to glaze over. *High Charisma is scary stuff*, I thought, but I kept on.

"You'd beg me to step on you, wouldn't you?"

[Seduction] skill unlocked.

"Yes, mistress." As he said that word, he got a shocked look on his face. It must have slipped out, and clued him in on just how deep he'd gone.

"I wonder if that's what your father's plan is," I mused. "If he expects me to show up at the ball with you as my obedient little puppy." *Puppy . . .* that word struck a chord; there was something . . .

Focus. "That's *not* going to happen," I said. I put the full weight of my Persuade behind it, and it snapped him out of it like a face full of water.

"Feeling better?" I asked. "Maybe now you have an idea of how some of those girls felt."

"You . . . you don't know anything about them," he said weakly.

"No, but I can find out," I said. Then my wayward thought finally crystallized. "And *you* are not a puppy!" I exclaimed.

He looked at me, eyes narrowed. "That's . . . true, but I still feel that I've been insulted."

"I think I've figured out the next step in your lesson plan," I explained. "It will take some research, but there should be some time before the ball."

"That doesn't explain the puppy thing," he complained.

"When you house-train a puppy, you—actually, I'm not sure if this is best practice—you have to catch them in the act of shitting and then rub their faces in it, so they know it's bad."

"And that's what you've been doing to me?" he asked. "You've certainly been rubbing my face in *something*," he muttered.

"I guess so, yeah," I said. "I'd forgotten that you are a thinking being that can remember his actions and have his errors explained to him. I'm sure you can see how I'd get confused."

"Ah, *there's* the insult. I should take my leave then, unless you have further wisdom to impart."

He got up to leave, but he hesitated before turning away.

"*Not* going to happen," I said again. He gave a peculiar shudder, and then nodded.

"Probably in my best interests," he said, and then left.

RUMORS

I need a dress," I said to my maid. "I'm to attend the Autumn Ball, and I'm guessing none of my current dresses are going to be acceptable for that."

Elodie stared at me, but not because I'd started talking like a Regency novel. I think. "That's for nobles, miss," she managed to squeak.

"Well, I've been practically commanded to attend by the Count," I said, "So I don't think that's the concern. I—"

"Wait, the ball's in three weeks!" Elodie interrupted. "You need a dress in three weeks!"

"Yes, that's what I've been saying." I kept my voice calm. Elodie was excited enough for both of us. "Now, I'm not familiar with the local dressmakers . . ." I trailed off, not sure if Elodie was listening. She had a look of furious concentration on her face.

"Madam Croquetaigne wouldn't be suitable, Master Royer wouldn't be able to do it in time . . ." Her voice lowered until she was only muttering to herself. Finally, she came to a conclusion. "Miss Kandis—you need *three* dresses, from Madam Didiane Auclair herself!"

That sounds expensive, I thought, but I kept it to myself. I was making good gold . . . hopefully enough for clothes. "Do you want to explain the logic there?"

"With only three weeks, you'll need to bribe her to drop what she's doing and make yours. By ordering three dresses, you'll get her attention. Plus, it's likely that you'll get another invitation to a noble event from this, so you want to have another dress almost ready."

"That . . . sounds like a good idea," I said cautiously. "And how much would one of Didiane's dresses cost me?"

"Well," she said with a thoughtful look, "you won't be looking for any-thing really showy, right? Maybe twenty gold each?"

Ouch. Maybe I'm not *making such good money.* "Fine. Now tell me, is it the custom here to bring an attendant? Because that would be you, and I assume it means you need a dress as well. Are you all right?"

Elodie had frozen in place and was only making squeaking sounds. She'd recover soon enough . . . I thought.

Didiane Auclair's establishment wasn't what I'd expected, at least from the outside. But then, this world didn't have plate glass windows for her to show off her wares. Instead she had shutters and bars across her shopfront, so you couldn't tell what kind of store she had until you entered. Once inside, I saw something more like what I expected—dresses arranged for show, fabric samples, and women cutting and sewing fabric. One woman seemed to be in charge, so I addressed her.

"Madam Auclair?" I had to raise my voice to cut through the hubbub. The woman let out a cry of frustration, and came to the front. She was younger than I'd expected, and had brown hair, tied up to be out of the way,

"We're busy! I don't know who you are, but—" She did a double take. "Actually, who *are* you?"

"A customer? I need a dress for the Autumn Ball."

The woman looked at me, glanced over Elodie, and then returned her attention to me. "I know all the nobles in the area . . . you're not even dressed like one."

"I'm not, but I've been invited by the Count." I shrugged. "The fact that I don't have an appropriate dress is why I'm here."

She frowned. "My dresses aren't considered 'appropriate' by those old biddies in the castle. You want Madam Croquetaigne's, three doors down the street."

"No, she doesn't!" Elodie squeaked. Both of us looked at her. "You made that dress for Lady Angellette last year! They're still talking about it in the Guild!"

"Don't remind me about last year," the woman groaned. "Angellette wanted to make a big splash for her coming of age with a dress from a new designer. It would have worked out great for both of us if she hadn't gotten dead drunk and puked all over her uncle and my dress."

"Plenty of people saw the dress before that!" Elodie insisted. "It was good! And if Miss Kandis wears one of your dresses, everyone will be looking at her."

"That does . . . seem likely," the woman agreed reluctantly. Her gaze came back to me, slowly, almost as if she was trying to resist a compulsion. "Who are you people again?"

"My name is Kandis Hammond," I said. "This is my maid, Elodie Garcia. She'll also be there as my attendant, so she'll be needing something to match me."

"Didiane Auclair," she said in return. "So you want me to make two dresses of the finest quality in three weeks."

"Actually, I'll need three, but only the first two need to be ready by then." I said. "I'm expecting some social engagements after the ball."

"And you can pay?" I gestured to Elodie, and she took a handful of gold from the money pouch and showed it to the dressmaker. I liked having Elodie carry the cash; it made me feel like a big shot. I did actually carry some money for emergencies, though.

Slowly, Didiane's face took on an expression I recognized from Guild Master Gustave. I was calling it the "I'm going to make a lot of money" face.

"Well, let's get you in back so we've got some privacy for fitting."

"What is that?" Didiane exclaimed incredulously, pointing at my breasts. I'd just been helped out of my dress by Elodie.

"It's called a bra," I said, cupping myself. "It provides support and comfort." Elodie very carefully didn't say anything as she made sure my dress was laid out properly. She'd already seen my bra and still hadn't decided if she was scandalized or wanted one of her own.

"How is it made?" Didiane asked, examining me closely. "No, how do you get it on?"

"Ah . . . this isn't a real bra; it's an illusion of one," I said, perhaps not entirely helpfully. "I just cast it on me in the morning and cancel the spell to take it off. A real bra has some clasps . . . here."

Concentrating, I used Phantasmal Object to summon a copy of the bra I had originally based mine on. It was the most comfortable one I'd ever owned, until the elastic started to go. That wasn't a problem with my new bra, though, as it got re-summoned every morning. I handed the copy to Didiane, who held it gingerly, as if it were about to explode.

"This is an illusion? But I'm holding it!"

"Touch is a sense as well," I said airily, as if it were the most obvious thing in the world. I didn't understand it myself, but I wasn't going to let her know that. "You can examine that if you like, see if you can duplicate it. It will last until sunset."

Reluctantly, Didiane began examining the bra as if it were an actual object. "This material, what kind of fabric stretches like this? And the stitching . . . it's impossible!" she said.

I shrugged. "I'm sure you can come up with something that women will find usable," I said. "It doesn't have to be an exact copy."

The dressmaker scowled. "This is a distraction," she said, putting the bra aside. "Let's get your measurements."

It was lunchtime before we were able to leave Madam Auclair's establishment. After measurements, for both me and Elodie, there had been a long discussion about styles and fabrics and colors. I let Elodie answer most of the questions, pleading an unfamiliarity with local fashions. Finally, though, we'd escaped and were headed for a tavern for lunch. Not just any tavern, though; Elodie assured me that The Baker's Downfall was the best tavern in Anchorbury.

We were going to the Baker's Downfall—despite the name—because I was looking for a Bard. With any luck, the best Bard should be found in the best tavern.

As we took our seats, I looked around at what was probably the most *pleasant* room that I'd been in since arriving in this world. Wide, high, open windows let in light and air, while white painted walls and high ceilings gave it a really modern look. Widely spaced tables, with flower arrangements and brightly covered tablecloths, were spread across the room in no particular order that I could see. It actually felt like a high-end cafe from my world, with only the lack of electric lighting to give it away.

There was music, too, as expected. Not so loud as to overpower conversations, just a single Bard with what I assumed to be a lute. I think I'd seen Sting play something similar in an interview once. This musician was . . . good, I guess? Frankly, I couldn't really get into the music they had here. It was nice, but I couldn't really lose myself in it like I could to a good Taylor Swift song.

Elodie had noticed something else. She waited until the server had left with our order and payment before speaking up. "Miss, I think we should have come to another place?"

"Why is that?" I asked. I was feeling quite positive about the place, myself. Now that I was moving in to the higher wealth stratum, I thought frequenting this sort of place might be nice to do. I'd have to wait and see what the food was like first, of course, but actually having choices for food was a promising sign.

"The Bard," Elodie whispered. "He's an elf!"

I looked over and saw that she was right. I don't know how I'd missed the long, pointed ears at first glance. I looked back at Elodie.

"Are you whispering because elves are rumored to have fantastic hearing or something?"

Elodie nodded nervously.

"And can you tell me why an elven Bard would be unsuitable?"

Elodie blushed, surprising me. "Umm, you don't know?" she asked hopefully. I shook my head, and she made a surprised sound. "Well, it's just that . . ." she stammered. "There aren't many elves and they live a long time, so they can get really high levels. They say that elves aren't allowed out of the forest until they reach level six."

"Sounds great," I said. "A long-lived, high-level Bard sounds just like who I want to speak with."

"Um, it's just that . . . because they're all so powerful, they can do whatever they like?"

"Right . . ." I said, still not seeing where this was going.

"So if they're wandering in human lands, it's because there's something there that they want . . ." Eloide trailed off, wanting me to put the pieces together, but I was still lost, so she was forced to continue. "Well, it's just that certain women, with how there can't be any issue, and the experience that an elf has . . . they have a certain reputation?"

She was babbling, but I think that I got the implication. Looking around, I could see that there were a number of well-dressed, attractive women paying particular attention to the player. Occasionally they glared at each other, and I now noticed that I was getting a few of these glares.

At this point, we were interrupted by the arrival of our meal, much to Elodie's relief. I paused for a bit to allow us both to enjoy it. It was really good . . . tender meat, cheese, and greens in a pasty-like shell. *Is this venison?* I wondered. Elodie clearly enjoyed her stew as well, though I think that was partly because she didn't have to talk while eating it.

All good things end, though, and eventually we had to continue the conversation. "So what you're trying to say," I mused, "is that he's been practicing how to sleep with human women for 400 years, and the fact that he can't get them pregnant means there's a horde of so-called ladies eager to be seduced?"

Elodie blushed again. She looked down with fixed concentration on her meal, but she nodded.

"And if I speak with him, everyone will assume that I'm one of these ladies?" Elodie nodded again.

"Well, thank you, Elodie, that's very useful information. Now finish your meal and head back to the house. It seems that I'm going to need to speak with this gentleman alone."

"Miss?" Elodie asked questioningly. Then, "Miss!" in an urgent whisper, as the implications of my statement sank in. I grinned, doing nothing to dispel her concern.

"Don't worry; it will be fine. Eat up." Elodie did so, the same preoccupation with propriety that caused her alarm preventing her from making a scene. I took my time, so I was still going when she left, leaving me with the purse.

Now that I knew the circumstances, it made more sense that I'd failed to catch the man's eye during his performance. He was either focusing on his harem or carefully avoiding the appearance of favoritism to any particular person. Well, I had no particular need of subtlety.

I waited for a pause in his set, and then cast Unseen Sound. Softly, but right up close to his ear, I sent my voice, saying, "I would like a moment of your time, Bard." His head whipped around to identify the sound, to find me looking directly at him from across the room. Our eyes locked, and he nodded.

Five minutes later, he was sitting down in front of me, while carefully placing his lute on my table.

"I suppose I should ask," I started, "If you actually heard any of the conversation I had with my maid."

He looked at me, his face giving nothing away. Then he turned to the server he'd beckoned over and ordered a goblet of wine by name. The most expensive one they served, I noted. Shrugging, I gave the server a gold piece. At the gesture, the Bard beamed and gave a little half-bow.

"My thanks, my lady. To answer your question, no. While I do have good hearing, it's more suited to hearing danger or prey in the forest than picking out one conversation among dozens."

"I see," I said. "Allow me to introduce myself, then. My name is Kandis Hammond, a Senior Master in the Ironworkers Guild."

He raised an eyebrow. "Should I call you Master Hammond?" At my grimace, he smiled and said, "Kandis, then. As you know, I am a Bard, and my name is Aesrideu. Unlike humans, there are not enough of us to require second names."

He sat back and sipped his wine, waiting for my next question. He seemed happy and relaxed, and not at all concerned with what I might ask. *An eternal seducer of women?* I wondered. He didn't seem like it.

Handsome enough, a full head of golden blond hair, tall and slender, but not weak looking . . . I blushed as I realized that he was looking me over in the same way, and seemed to like what he saw.

"You don't seem . . . like a level six," I said cautiously.

"Met so many, have you?" he said with an amused grin.

"A few."

"Well, I must confess, you've seen through me. You are looking at a lowly level four—and a criminal, at that. I paid to get smuggled out of my homewood and wander the world."

"Are you serious?"

"Oh, the Elders are quite serious about keeping the young ones in line," he said sourly. "If you should happen to encounter elves looking for me, I'll thank you send them the other way."

"I thought Elodie was telling tall tales . . ." I said incredulously.

"My story is a fascinating one and I tell it well," the elf said suavely. "But I got the impression that you wanted to talk to me for reasons other than amusement."

"No, I wanted to talk to you about . . . something that needs to stay discreet."

"I see . . ." he said, looking around. "That spell from before—are you taking precautions?"

"No," I replied, "Privacy isn't in my repertoire."

"Then allow me." He picked up his lute and strummed an . . . odd melody. Suspecting something, I activated Sense Mana, which let me see the mana coming off the strings. It swirled around and dispersed into an invisible cloud—or perhaps a shell—around us. As it did so, the sounds of the room cut off.

"Do Bards get Illusion Magic?" I asked.

"Was that what that spell was, then?" he returned. "Seems an odd skill for a Senior Ironworking Master."

"I'm a fairly unusual Master," I admitted.

"I'm sure. No," he said, returning to my original question. "Bardic Chant does draw on some of the same effects I'm told, but only for sounds. I thought you were a fellow practitioner. But in any case, we can speak freely now."

"Right. So what I want to know is, what lore do you have on the nature of demons?"

That surprised him. His reaction wasn't obvious, but I, or rather Intrigue, could tell. He took a moment to think about his answer.

"This is about the rumors, then."

Now it was my turn to be surprised. Intrigue let a little bit of that show, the better to match my response. "I don't know about any rumors."

"I imagine you'd like to hear them, then?" he said, probing.

"Rumors about demons?" I said incredulously. "Who wouldn't?"

"True," he conceded. "This particular rumor has been spreading like wildfire, despite efforts to suppress it."

"The Count?" I hazarded a guess.

"Exactly. The rumor is that one of his patrols was accosted by creatures that were solid one minute and shadows the next. They fled, and suffered no casualties, or so the story goes."

"This was in town?" I said, aghast. So much for the wild goose chase theory.

"Probably." Aesrideu grimaced. "The Count silenced his men, and all those they talked to, but not before *they* talked to others. The news that demons might be in the city . . . well."

"Everybody wants to tell those they care about, but they can't let the Count find out. Is he actually imprisoning people?"

"I'm not sure, but he's certainly capable of it," the elf said. "I have a few . . . contacts in the Castle that care deeply about me, so I'm ahead of the curve in this, but it's only a matter of time before it gets out into the city proper. A week or two, three at the most."

"At which point we'll have . . . riots? A mass exodus?"

"Trying times to be sure," Aesrideu said, taking another sip of wine.

DEMOΠS

You seem rather relaxed at the prospect of imminent riots," I said.

Aesrideu smiled and sipped more wine. "A Bard never shows fear in the face of an audience," he quipped. "But in truth, I spent far too long being coddled in a forest grove to not be . . . excited by the prospect of urban unrest."

I frowned. From what I knew of history in my world, mobs were rarely just *exciting*. I didn't think that this world's widespread superpowers would help things.

"Of course, as a Bard, I have less to fear than most from a fearful mob," Aesrideu added. He glanced significantly at his lute.

Oh. "Crowd control," I said aloud.

"Yes, support roles like you and I do have our uses," he said. "Of course, I can't influence the whole city, but I'll do what I can to help those close to me."

"That's something, at least," I said.

"Of course, it would be better to stop the riots before they start," he mused. "Perhaps you might know where to start?"

"I don't know anything about what's going on," I said bitterly. "I don't even know what demons *are*."

"Ah, yes, the original topic. Well, I can help with that, at least. Demons are creatures—or people—from outside of our world."

"How is that different from Worldwalkers?" I asked. Charm kept my voice clear and my face showing only curiosity.

Aesrideu raised an eyebrow. "Interesting that they came to mind. It's been a long time for human memory since they were last here."

"I recently happened to purchase a book on them." *Which I should really get around to reading.*

"Well, the difference is that Worldwalkers are brought here by the gods, under the auspices of the Status. They are awarded skills and abilities the same as ourselves. Demons . . . are not."

"Then how do they get here?"

"They are summoned. By Demonologists, using knowledge that is outside of the Status—or at least not available through it. Anyone who learns too much about how is marked by the Status, so no one really knows where it comes from."

"What does 'marked by the Status' mean?"

"Demonologists count as monsters. You can use Identify on them and see what they are."

"Most people don't go around using Identify on random people, though," I mused.

"Not unless there's a suspected Demonologist about," Aesrideu agreed.

Well, it's better than throwing them in a pond and seeing if they float. "So what are demons like then?" I asked aloud. "Do they come in types?"

"A wide variety of them, I'm afraid," he said sadly. "It all depends on *where* they come from, amongst the many worlds that aren't ours. Generally, in any given incursion, if there's a variety of demons, they all share certain characteristics. But between different incursions, there's rarely any similarity."

"So we can expect the demons to be all some sort of shadow-people this time . . . I don't suppose those have come up before?" I asked hopefully.

"Not to my knowledge, but I've never gone through the histories looking for such."

"Anything else that I might need to know?"

"Hmm," he pondered. "There are some commonalities, but they have to do with the summoner. For one, the summoner tends to just keep summoning demons. I don't know if they're compelled, or if they just keep escalating to gain more power, but they keep increasing the number of demons until they're taken care of."

"That . . . doesn't really describe what we have here, though, does it? A bunch of demons show up, and then no more sightings . . ."

"True, and it might indicate that the Demonologist was only passing through. Good news for Anchorbury, but it makes them harder to find. It's . . . unusual for a Demonologist to travel like that, though. There are few tales where they did, but it was because they were being chased."

"And no one's showed up saying they're chasing a Demonologist . . ."

"Exactly; it's odd. The other thing is that if you kill the Demonologist, the demons all disappear."

"That sounds ... easy?"

"Not at all, I'm afraid. The demons know of their vulnerability and will defend him ferociously. That's about all I have."

"Thanks. What do I owe you for this?"

"You've already paid enough, my lady," Aesrideu said, raising his wineglass. "After all, it's the duty of a Bard to instruct."

"If you say so . . . actually, would you be interested in some work? I need someone to track down some stories about a different matter." I put some gold down on the table. "You can tell your friends that this is what we were talking about."

He looked down at the gold and smiled. "Tell me more."

Back at home, I considered my next move. I'd done everything I said I would for our assignment; anything further could wait until our next meeting. It grated at me to just sit around with rumors of demons floating about, but realistically, I couldn't think of anything to do about them. So I decided to practice some Enchanting.

Yesterday, Elodie had bought me a locket, with one of my silversteel disks welded to the inside. I *thought* that if the runes were attached to a device, I could link the Trigger rune to a physical action taken on the device, like opening the locket. I could do the same thing with Sense (Touch), but one less rune made for a more efficient enchantment. Theoretically, with just the two runes, the mana cost would be under the ambient mana, but I decided to attach a mana crystal as well. I wasn't sure if Spell Storing would cost just three or if there was an additional cost for the spell. Having a mana crystal would let me see just how much mana the enchantment was using.

The enchantment went smoothly, though having to cast a spell while keeping the rune "hot" was a bit of a challenge. *A good thing I don't need words or gestures to cast spells,* I mused. Just maintaining concentration was hard enough, and I suspected that I could only do it because of my superhuman intelligence. Unlike Strength, I didn't *feel* five times smarter, but every now and then I noticed myself doing something I probably couldn't have done before. Using Memorize to remember a song and hold the entire thing in my mind while instilling it into Unseen Sound was one of those times.

It did take a lot of concentration, though, so it was only after I'd completed the circle of runes that I realized Elodie was trying to get my attention.

"Miss Kandis!" she called from the door in an urgent whisper. I looked over and beckoned her to come in. She wasn't banned from the workshop by any means, but she was afraid to come close when I was Enchanting.

"What is it?" I asked, still a little groggy from casting that spell.

"You have a guest!" she said. "A noble! He's waiting in the dining room. A Duvost!"

"Not Aubert, then?" After watching me use him as a beast of burden, she wouldn't be so excited to see him here.

"No, it's his cousin, Guillaume!"

Okay . . . why is this guy calling on me? And why can't they pronounce William right? I had questions, but there was only one way to get answers. I looked down at myself and sighed. I was in my work clothes, which consisted of my most worn—and most comfortable—dress. It was hardly suitable for meeting nobles.

With a sigh, I cast Disguise. My dress was replaced with the one I'd been out and about in earlier today. Elodie gasped, I think half scandalized and half jealous.

"I'd better go see him, then. Elodie, can you get word to the Guild Master that I have another enchantment to show him? At his convenience, of course."

I only had one room for receiving visitors, and it was currently set up as a dining room. The table left a lot to be desired, though, and I was thinking about turning it into a sitting room and having meals in the kitchen with Elodie. Right now, though, one of the chairs was occupied by a young gentleman who reminded me a lot of Aubert. He had the same brown hair and eyes, but his face was less round and he was broader across the shoulders.

"Mistress Hammond!" he said, quickly getting up and bowing. "Guillaume Duvost, at your service."

Since he'd bowed, I curtsied. "Please take a seat," I said. Charm told me that our respective statuses were . . . a gray area. He was a noble without a title—it would have been mentioned by now if he'd had one—while I was a senior Guild member. The least important form of noble versus a fairly important commoner. Since he was a guest in my home, though, I had the edge.

I took a seat opposite him with a warm smile. "What brings you here, sir?"

"I'm here to apologize on behalf of my cousin," he said. "I heard you'd had some trouble with him, and I wanted to assure you that the Duvost are not all so boorish."

Intrigue perked up. I was being Intrigued! Not against, but . . . with? This man was using me against . . . Aubert? His father? There weren't many other prospects.

"How gracious of you!" I said, radiating good will. "But you should know that your cousin has already apologized."

"That . . . doesn't sound like him," Guillaume said cautiously.

"He did seem somewhat upset about it," I said, leaning forward conspiratorially. "I think my Guild Master spoke with his father, who enforced his parental authority."

Intrigue flashed again, at the slight tightening of his eyes when I mentioned the Count. *So it's the father, then . . .*

I let Charm do its thing, going through the motions of polite society on automatic pilot. I was bemused both by the elaborate customs and my effortless navigation of them. Tea was offered and accepted, and we sat and exchanged flattering compliments. Intrigue had some suggestions of how to indicate that I was open to offers, but he didn't make any. It seemed he was just here to feel me out.

Naturally, I followed him when he left. It was pretty easy, once I'd gotten Elodie to go through the front door to cover for my Invisible self. Walking down the street took *some* care, but nothing too difficult. My Dodge skill needed the workout anyway.

Guillaume led me to what I assumed was his house, a richly appointed three-story building in the better part of town. I spent a little time looking for possible ways in, so I was still around when a *very* suspicious looking man left the house from the back door.

This fellow had an eyepatch—which was very unusual—and was dressed in boiled leather armor. Not a matching set, either.

[Identification] : **Reinforced Leather (Partial) – Quality: Excellent – Properties: Enchantment (Hardness)**
[Identification] : **Reinforced Leather (Partial) – Quality: Excellent – Properties: Enchantment (Empower Agility)**
[Identification] : **Darksteel Short-Sword – Quality: Great – Properties: Enchantment (Sharpness)**

That was odd. His equipment didn't *look* that great; it looked tattered and worn. My impression was that as equipment wore out, it lost quality levels . . . perhaps a disguise spell?

He seemed worth following, anyway—I wasn't getting anywhere

trying to case this joint. He led me to a much worse part of town while I pondered the eyepatch.

The reason that eyepatches were so rare was that this world had HP. Recover the HP, and the injury that caused the loss disappeared. I hadn't developed *extensive* experience with injuries—yet—but to my knowledge, losing an eye permanently shouldn't be possible.

People on the street didn't think my target was *impossible,* though. Unusual, yes—people glanced at him in surprise, but no one reacted that strongly. One-eye was able to continue on his way without interference. He let me to a large building—perhaps a warehouse—knocked, and was allowed entry.

Well, that leaves me no wiser. I hung around for five minutes, in the hope that he'd come out and lead me somewhere else, but to no avail. *I need some lackeys.* I could task one of my team with keeping an eye on this place, but it seemed a waste of their talents.

For now, I returned home to consider my options. Where did I stand in a conflict between Guillaume and Count Duvost? One of them was paying me, but Guillaume's approach had at least been courteous. For now, I determined, it was best to keep an open mind and see what developed.

To that end, it occurred to me that I didn't want Guillaume finding out that Aubert was working with me. Or *for* me, if I wanted to put it that way.

"Elodie," I said innocently, "Lord Aubert has a reputation, does he not?"

"Yes, miss." Elodie was cooking us dinner, and I was watching the process intently. I did intend to cook for myself at some point, but I wanted to get an idea of how it all worked when you didn't have an induction hot plate.

"Kandis, remember? And does his reputation go so far as to give any specific details?"

Elodie blushed. "What kind of details, miss . . . Kandis?"

"Like what tavern I can find him in tonight."

"There's no tavern in town that crew won't show up in," she complained. "But there are a few that they like best."

"Crew?" Now that I thought about it, he did have a bunch of friends behind him that time.

"He goes drinking with a bunch of lordlings—some of his cousins and the kids of the nearby barons." She thought for a moment, and then named some taverns. "The Vagabond Rose, the Ivory Chestnut, and the . . . Deep Fiddle."

I raised an eyebrow. "Isn't that last one a piece of dirty slang?"

"No!" Elodie exclaimed, blushing. "It's the name of the place."

"Are you sure?" I asked with amusement. "I'd hate for there to be some misunderstanding if I asked someone on the street where I could find a Deep Fiddle."

"*The* Deep Fiddle!" Elodie returned to the stove and repositioned pans with a little more force than seemed necessary. "There won't be a problem as long as you use *The*!"

"Well, if you say so," I said doubtfully. "To change the subject entirely, what do you know about orphans in this city?"

CATFISHING

Aubert was in the second tavern I looked in, the Vagabond Rose, which meant that I didn't need to take a chance on asking about the Deep Fiddle. He'd reverted to peacock mode, strutting in front of his friends and relatives. I was probably going to see these people again at the ball, so I made a note of their faces as I approached.

I wasn't looking like myself, of course. Blonde hair, again, but slightly darker than Katherine's. Bigger boobs. Not that I had a problem with my current set, but I was after a certain impression here. At the last minute, I remembered I'd need a new name. Probably. He might not ask. *Gwendolyn, Gwen for short*, I decided.

It really was ridiculously easy. I didn't even have to approach—the minute I wandered into his line of sight, he was all over me. Buying me a drink, bringing me over to his table, trying to impress me with his friends . . .

I lapped it all up, of course. Smiling at him, laughing at his jokes, hanging off of his arm . . . It wasn't long before he'd swept me away from the group and suggested a quick trip upstairs. I agreed, of course. I was worried he'd think I was *too* easy, but he just seemed to count himself lucky. That all changed once we had some privacy, of course.

"I thought I told you never to let me catch you wearing that again," I said, turning off the Disguise.

"Mother of a whore!" he swore, snatching his hand away from my décolletage. "Must you torment me everywhere I go?"

"I needed to meet with you secretly," I said, sitting on the bed and adjusting my clothing. I'd been pawed at rather a lot. "It's not my fault this was the quickest and easiest way."

"Was it, or was it just the most amusing?"

"Tomato, tomato," I said. Neither pronunciation was a word in their language, so it didn't really help. "Now that you've finished complaining, I need to tell you a few things."

I waited while he got himself under control. I liked this. Alone in a room with a man much stronger than me, but *I* was in control.

"First of all, did you know your cousin is plotting against your father?"

"Which one?" Aubert asked sourly.

"Guillaume," I said.

"You're wrong," he said scornfully. "We've been close since we were young—practically brothers."

"Oh? Then why isn't he downstairs?" I asked.

"He's never liked this sort of thing," he said dismissively. "He's always studying at night."

"Hmm." You couldn't learn skills from books (well, not unless you had Research), but you could pick up a lot of information that wasn't covered by a skill. "Studying what?"

"Different things. Heraldry, history, crop yields for the different duchies. I don't know."

"Things useful for a leader?" I wondered. "Is he due to inherit anything?"

"No; his father's already dead. He was . . ." Aubert hesitated for the first time. "The previous Count."

"Why didn't he inherit?" I asked, starting to see where this was going.

"It was ten years ago . . . we were . . . he was too young. There was talk of a regency, but the King stepped in, awarded the title to my father."

"Scratch a noble, find a disputed inheritance," I said wryly. "Did you know he has a townhouse in the city?"

"He doesn't; he lives in the castle. Uncle Ansel's wife and children are all being provided for by my father."

"Hmm. Well, I'm not here to convince you. It's better that you keep treating him the same way you always have."

"You can't just throw out an accusation like that!"

"Can't I?" I asked. "If you must know, he came around looking to see if I could be used against your father in an Intrigue. My own skill picked up on it; he's not very good with Intrigue."

"That's not even close to proof."

"Quite. So don't do anything about it," I said. "What you *are* going to do is make sure he doesn't find out that we're working together."

He snorted. "That's not how I'd put it."

"Regardless of how you'd put it, he can't find out," I said. "I'm going to try and see if I can get in on what he's planning, but it won't work if he knows I'm working for your father. So tell your father that, and maybe arrange to be heard around the castle saying some less than complimentary things about me."

"I *might* be able to manage that," he said sarcastically.

"I have full confidence in your acting ability," I replied. "Now, only contact me at my old house; I'll make sure to approach that in disguise from now on. Have you spoken with your father about the mission?"

"Yes, I—" he started, but I held up my hand.

"Save it for when we're all together," I said. "But tell your father this: the rumor of the demon sighting that he's been trying to suppress is all over the castle, and it's only a matter of time before it gets into the city."

"What! but that's—"

"Bad news, I know," I interrupted. "Keep your father in the loop, and if he wants us to change what we're doing, you can let us know tomorrow."

"Loop?" he asked, confused.

"Keep your father *informed*."

"Could have said that the first time," he muttered, loudly enough for me to hear.

"Right!" I said brightly. "That should be everything. I'll go down invisible; you stay up here long enough to convince everyone you're performing adequately."

"Gods, am I going to have to check if every woman I meet from now on is actually you?"

"You underestimate my ability to impersonate women you *already* know," I said, grinning. "Rest assured, if it happens again, it will be for a good reason."

The next morning, I made omelettes. Fluffy ones, stuffed with ham and cheese. I had to conjure a whisk instead of the bundle of sticks Elodie suggested, but frying pans worked much the same. Toast was a bit of a struggle, but I conjured a wire frame to hold the bread over the fire, which actually worked better than the real thing. It couldn't get hot, so Elodie didn't have to worry about being burned.

She worried about everything *else*, mostly about me doing her job.

"It's not right, you making a meal for *me*, Miss Kandis," she complained. "And . . . I'm not sure I've ever seen anyone cook eggs that way."

"It's fine, Elodie," I reassured her. "The toast is done, right?" I slid the finished omelette onto her toast. "Try this, while I finish mine."

Suspiciously, Elodie took a forkful of the eggs and put it in her mouth.

> **Competency displayed with [Cook], Level 2 awarded.**
> **For gaining skill levels, you have been awarded 2 XP.**

Ah, been a while since I got one of those, I thought, feeling smug. Omelettes were simple enough, but I'd had the feeling that the prep work involved would elevate it beyond a level one skill.

With the System's approval, I didn't really need to know what Elodie thought, but it's always nice to see someone enjoy your cooking.

"This is delicious!" she exclaimed.

"Glad you like it," I said, smiling, and returned to making my own meal. As always, having the skill made everything easier. It wasn't long before we were both seated at the kitchen table, enjoying our omelettes. They really were good—better than I remembered making. Better ingredients? Skill shenanigans? I didn't know; I just enjoyed the results.

Now I just needed coffee. Tea just wasn't the same. Still, it wasn't a bad way to finish off breakfast. I relaxed, and let Elodie remind me of what I had to do today.

"Guild Master Langelier said he was free this morning, if you wanted to show him your enchantment."

"I should be able to get to that before the team meeting," I mused. "That's all I've got scheduled, right?"

"That I know of," Elodie agreed. "Did . . . you want to go looking for orphans today?"

"No, I think you're right about the dangers of that. Put out the word around the Guild kids; see if anyone wants to sign up."

This was about getting some minions. Recruiting street urchins *did* have a long tradition behind it, going back to Sherlock Holmes, but Elodie had given me a different suggestion.

The Guild took care of its own. To my surprise, that included the children of deceased Guild members. They were raised in something like an orphanage, apprenticed to established members and generally went on to become smiths themselves. Generally. There were always some that weren't suited, or who didn't want to become smiths. They . . . were on their own. At a certain point, they were turfed out of the orphanage, and if they hadn't secured a line on a profession, then they turned to thievery or adventuring.

Elodie thought that there were at least some kids on the cusp of that transition who would be looking for a way out. She rated them as *far* more trustworthy than someone I picked off the street. That was partly Guild prejudice, sure, but it worked both ways. These kids would have been raised in the Guild, so as a Senior Member, they'd look up to me.

Elodie knew them, a little, as she was in something of the same boat. She wasn't orphaned, but she wasn't planning on becoming a smith. Her parents had arranged different educational opportunities for her, which was partly how she had ended up here.

I got ready for the day and headed off to see Gustave.

"And what have you brought me today, my dear?" he asked, once the pleasantries were out of the way. He had a hopeful look on his face.

"I was wondering if there was a market for enchantments that weren't combat related," I said, taking out my enchanted locket. I opened it and the sweet strains of Pachelbel's Canon filled the room.

Gustave sat totally still while the music played. I'd gone with classical—even though I didn't know much about it—because it didn't have singing. And I because I wasn't sure this world was ready for Taylor Swift. Even so, orchestral music was a huge step from what Gustave would be used to. I didn't know if they had orchestras in the capital, but I was fairly sure they didn't here.

"What . . . is this music?" he asked finally, as it came to an end.

"By a man called Pachelbel—it's something I heard when I was younger," I said. I wasn't lying, either; Dad had played this incessantly when I was a kid.

"Is there more by this man?"

"Not that I remember?" I said uncertainly. "I know some songs that are a similar type of music."

"It just plays this one song, correct?" he asked. He closed and opened the locket to start the song again.

"Yes, and not indefinitely. You can get two plays from a full charge, but then you have to let it recharge or fill the mana crystal manually. I can play around with those numbers, but it will change the costs." I handed over a sheet of paper with my estimates for the costs of different options. "The same goes for one that plays multiple tunes; it will almost double the cost."

"The nobles will go mad for this," he predicted, grinning with greed. "Though I don't imagine the Bards will like losing income."

"They might be interested in a deal. Get their own songs recorded and distributed to a wider audience."

"Perhaps; we'd have to cut them in, though." He frowned at the thought. "Music like this—while it may eventually fall out of favor, right now it's something new."

He looked at me suddenly. "You should show it off at the Autumn Ball."

"Where did you hear that? Does everybody know I'm attending already?"

He laughed. "Elodie has been telling anyone in the Guild who will stand still long enough. She's very excited about attending."

I made a face. "I don't want to attract that much attention at the ball," I said. "Aren't you invited?"

"I normally plead age," he said. "Balls aren't for old money-grubbers like myself."

"You're right that it would be an opportunity, but I think it would look better if you were to show it off. After all, I'll be selling through the Guild, no?"

"True . . ." he mused. "If you were to demonstrate it, they would no doubt come straight to you, try to cut us out."

"We wouldn't want that," I agreed.

"Well, I suppose I should thank you for your consideration, even though it will mean more work than I'm accustomed to," he said grumpily.

"We must all make sacrifices for profit," I said, amused.

"Very well; at least my wife will be pleased."

THIEVES GUILD

There were a lot of glum looks around the table for my second morning meeting.

"So," Cloridan said, after Aubert and I had finished talking. "It really *is* demons, and there are riots coming as well."

Janie was looking a little hunted. "I need . . ."

"You can't tell them, Janie," I said. "Oath of secrecy, remember? Even if it's going to get out eventually, it can't be us that starts it."

"My father will keep things from getting out of hand," Aubert said. "He's aware of the problem, and called in the levies."

"I suspect they might be too busy dealing with the demons," I mused.

"Unlikely," Aubert scoffed. "For all the menace, they haven't shown up since that one time."

"That's exactly why," I said. "They're biding their time, but for what? For the moment when your father is weakest."

Cloridan cleared his throat. "That's, uh, not what demons do."

"I know," I replied. "But these have been very unusual demons. Everyone says they start out small, in some out-of-the-way area, and then escalate."

I looked over at Aubert, who'd given us the report from the Count's soldiers. "Instead, we have one attack with a dozen demons, and then nothing."

"It could be a mid-stage Demonologist on the move," Cloridan suggested.

"That would be good for us if it's true, as it would mean they aren't *here* any more," I said. "But it doesn't hold up. Where did they come from, where did they go?" There haven't been any reports from the outlying areas, right?" I looked at Aubert again, who nodded. "So there's no one crying for help, no one complaining about having driven out a demon . . . they've come out of nowhere and disappeared."

"We can't go to my father with 'they're probably gone,'" Aubert countered. "He needs something more certain."

"So we assume they're still here," I said. "Where does that leave us? With demons that don't behave like demons, or who aren't demons at all."

"They weren't ordinary monsters," Aubert asserted. "The soldiers used Identify and got no results."

"Does Identify work on illusions?" I asked. Everyone looked at me.

"You're the Illusionist," Janie said.

I shrugged. "Never had to try," I said, and used Static Image to produce a dagger on the table. Everyone looked at it.

"Identify tells me it's a dagger," Cloridan said, and the others agreed.

"Let me try something else," I said, canceling the illusion. I recast it, concentrating on the result I wanted.

An identical dagger appeared, and everyone looked confused. I took a look with the skill myself.

[Identification] : (Illusion) – Call it what you want.

"Do you guys see the Illusion tag?" I asked.

"No," Janie said, "But it's called 'Call it what you want,' so I guess you can control what goes in there."

"Now, let's try something else," I said, casting Disguise. I turned my skin and clothes jet-black and made a sort of black mist come off my skin.

"Identify isn't going to give you anything on me, right?" I said. I made my voice sound like Darth Vader's for kicks, and they all jumped.

"Ugh, that's creepy," Janie said. "But yeah, that could be how they're doing it."

"Or," I said, canceling the illusion, "they could be a normal race that we don't know about."

"That seems unlikely?" Cloridan said. "We don't get much foreign traffic these days, but these guys probably would have been contacted during the Empire's era."

I shrugged. "Maybe, but it's a big world out there. The point is, there are at least two things it could be, and probably a third we haven't thought of. Oh, *and* it could be very unusual demons."

"So how does this help us?" Aubert said. "It seems to me we now know less than before."

"Well, if we assume they're acting according to a plan, then we can try to figure out what that plan is."

"Based on one attack?" Aubert asked skeptically.

"Based on the results so far," I said. "Which is your dad mobilizing, and the incipient riots."

"Given the timing, so close to the ball, should we assume that there's something planned for that date?"

"Could be," I said.

"They can't control when the riots start," Aubert objected. "That's going to depend on when the rumor gets out of control."

"Ah, but they *can* control that, by spreading it themselves," I countered. "Since the rumor is there already, you won't be able to tell unwitting rumormongering from deliberate seeding."

"Lot of foreign nobility at the ball," Janie said. "No Dukes or other Counts, but their children or representatives. An attack while they're all there would make the Count look bad, even if it doesn't succeed."

"Could be an attempt at one of the guests," Cloridan speculated. "Demons and riots to draw the guards away, leaving them free to make a targeted strike."

"Father can just increase the guards to cover either of those possibilities," Aubert said dismissively.

"Ah, but he can't ignore a riot, can he?" I countered, "Or a demon attack. Even if he thinks it's fake demons, it's still real people behind them. Our adversary can drain his troops away with feints until he's vulnerable to the real strike."

"What do you suggest then?" Aubert said, eyes narrowed.

"Fill your father in with our speculation—I'm not going to tell him what to do. What we should do is what we were paid to do—eliminate the problem before the trap is sprung."

"How?" Janie asked.

I considered. "They must have troops inside the city," I said. "Either to pretend to be demons, or to conduct the actual strike. They can't keep them *completely* hidden, right?"

"Unless they were smuggled in, they should have had their names and professions recorded as they entered," Aubert said. "I can have recent entries reviewed."

"There are actually a number of new faces in the delver taverns," Janie said. "The delver community is a good place to hide armed men in plain sight. I can check out just how many new people are around."

"Which leaves the two of us to check out a suspicious warehouse I found," I told Cloridan.

"You know I can't just break in, don't you?" Cloridan said, as we watched the warehouse in question from a safe distance. "I may have some skills that would help, but I'm not actually a criminal."

"That's disappointing," I said, only half joking. "How would you suggest we find out what's going on in there then?"

"If we can find a place to camp out, we could keep a watch on it," Cloridan said, looking around. "See who or what comes and goes . . ." he trailed off, then lightly grabbed my arm.

"Trouble," he whispered. "Don't look around; just head this way." We headed off down the street, away from the river and toward the better part of town.

"What's going on?" I said in a low tone.

"Thieves Guild was keeping a watch on the place; now they're looking at *us*."

"*Thieves* Guild?" Part of my induction into the Ironworkers Guild was a brief listing of the other guilds, informing me of which were fellow respectable tradesmen (Jewellers), and which were cut-rate swindlers (Blacksmiths). The Thieves Guild hadn't appeared on that list—but I suppose it wasn't an official one.

"I'm not a member or anything, but if you're a Rogue in Anchorbury, you need to know enough about them not to be dragged in. They're the only ones going to be following someone via the rooftops."

"So . . . we want to lose them?" I asked.

"That'd be ideal," he whispered forcefully. "But they aren't easy to lose."

"Oh, please," I said scornfully. Taking charge, I steered us into the nearest shop. It looked empty from the outside, and when we entered, I was pleased to see that there was only a single attendant and no customers. Perfect.

"My husband would like to look at your . . . hats," I said, quickly ascertaining the contents of the store. I didn't wait for the attendant to respond, though, as I was already Silent Casting Unseen Sound.

A crash of broken glass and ceramic came from the door leading to the back, and the man serving the store got a green look on his face.

"Excuse me for just one moment, gentlepeople," he said, and rushed to the back room.

Next was Greater Invisibility, cast on Cloridan. "Right, you're invisible; follow me back to the house." I cast Disguise on myself, making sure to change to a visibly different dress. We then left the store before the man came back.

"Nod if you think it worked," I said, as we got to a clear street and I could speak to the air without being overheard. He nodded, so we continued on.

"Well, it means the building is *definitely* suspicious," Cloridan said, back at our base.

"Do you think they're watching it for the same reason we were?" I asked. "Are they going to rob whatever's there?"

"No. Well, maybe, but they were interested in *us*." Cloridan said. "People interested in the building. That means it was either one of theirs, or they were paid to watch out for it."

"Eyepatch guy *was* shady-looking enough to be in a Thieves Guild," I mused. "That would mean Guillaume was working with them on something. Although . . ." I paused for thought.

"What?" Cloridan asked obligingly.

"Guillaume went right into that house, no knock or anything. I thought it was his. If I was dealing with thieves, I wouldn't leave one in my house while I made social calls. I think Eyepatch works for Guillaume . . . probably."

"Well, this puts paid to the surveillance idea."

"I was thinking of hiring some kids to do stuff like that."

"Not a bad idea," Cloridan sighed. "But the Guild has already thought of it. Any street kids you hire will probably work for them already."

"I was thinking of Ironworkers Guild orphans, actually."

"Well . . . they're probably more trustworthy. They'll run into problems going around the city, though. Street kids have territories, and those guys probably don't get to go outside their Quarter."

"What, really?"

"Yeah," he said, his eyes growing distant. "They don't bother the adults, but any kids are fair game. You need to be able to fight, or make some accommodation with whatever gang you find yourself living in the territory of."

"And do all the gangs report to the Thieves Guild?" I asked, fascinated.

"Just some. Those are the worst ones, since they have someone nasty to back them up if they get into trouble."

"So either way, we need to deal with the Thieves Guild."

"Not sure if you mean negotiate or 'deal' with them, but either one's a bad idea," Cloridan said glumly. "Best idea is not to mess with them."

"Just how tough are they?" I asked.

"Not so tough, in a stand-up fight," he admitted. "No one gets into thieving to do hard work. Mostly level threes or fours. Probably got a level five or two. They're rumored to have a level six Assassin, but I doubt that's true."

"Then—" I started, but he kept talking over me.

"Problem is, they won't give a stand-up fight. You manage to corner them, they'll surrender, but you'll never corner all of them. The rest will get you while you're sleeping, bust the ones you caught out, and they'll all go right back to crimes."

It took a long while to convince Cloridan to make the break-in. It was an exercise in not using Persuasion as well, since I didn't want to force him into it. I managed to avoid turning it into a Social Contest, at least, by keeping it light and not pressing my case.

The fact that he could go in under invisibility at night, and that he just had to see what was in there and not take anything, helped a great deal. I was close by for backup, though I wasn't sure what I'd do if something went wrong. Nothing did go wrong, as far as I could tell. He went up the wall and in through the roof, lifting up tiles away from the line of sight of the watchers.

It wasn't long before I saw the outline of his invisible form making its way back to me. I clapped him on the arm to let him know I was there, and then we headed back to base.

RECRUITMENT

I t's soldiers," Cloridan said. He was reporting to the group what he'd told me when we'd got back from breaking and entering.

"In uniform? How many?" Aubert asked.

"No, and not armed, either. But they had a . . . disciplined air about them that you don't get from adventurers sitting on their heels for a long period. They're waiting for something. About fifty, though I wasn't in a position to count them all."

"So where does this leave us?" Janie wondered.

"With needing more information," I replied. "Did you find anything among the delvers?"

She shrugged. "There *are* a bunch of new faces. They seem like adventurers, but they are a bit standoffish. Not in one group, either, more like five groups, twenty something in all?"

"What could your father do with this information, Aubert?" I asked.

He scowled. "Not much, I'm afraid. It's not illegal to house men, and while being watched over by the Thieves Guild is *concerning*, it actually makes things harder. If he wanted to arrest them, he'd need to gather a lot of men, and that would probably be noticed."

"They'd be gone by the time he got there," I speculated.

"Yes, they probably have a sewer entrance—we tend to find those after we've failed to raid a Guild establishment. Obviously, we can try and block that route . . ."

"But the Guild will have people watching for that as well."

"I can at least tell father to expect seventy men if there is an attack," Aubert said. "It's strange . . . that's too many for a surgical strike, but not enough for a more widespread attack."

"There may be other groups we don't know about," I countered, "Or they may be split up into multiple groups, either to attack separate targets or to include distractions for your father's troops."

"True . . . we really do need more information."

"Cloridan, how do you feel about keeping a watch on the place?" I asked our Rogue. He groaned.

"Gonna be up to me to play footsie with the Thieves Guild?" he complained.

"If you think Janie can help . . ." I suggested, but I wasn't surprised when he shook his head vigorously.

"Absolutely not," he said. "She gets . . . antsy, if she isn't doing something after a while."

"I do get bored easily," Janie agreed. "I thought it would be the way I always attract attention that you'd be objecting to, though."

"I can make you wear a cloak over your damn armor," Cloridan said. "And this will need to happen indoors anyway. But damned if I'm going to spend days cooped up with you and no alcohol."

"Indoors?" I asked.

"For this to work, I'll need to find a place that's either empty or doesn't mind us camping out," Cloridan explained. "We'd get noticed if we just sat out on the street, and the rooftops are taken."

"I see. Well, I'll be somewhat available for shifts, but I do have other duties. Aubert . . ." I looked over at the scowling noble. "Should be available to help."

"Much appreciated, my lord," Cloridan muttered. "I'll get on to finding a place, then."

"All right, and I'll see if I can find you some more backup," I said.

It wasn't as bad as Cloridan had said it was going to be, but it was going to be hard to make it workable.

"Yeah, it's true about territories, but I can get most places," the kid boasted. The others looked nervous, but didn't contradict him. His name was Cutter, according to him, and the others seemed OK with calling him that, so I went with that as well. He was the oldest and biggest of the kids, at age thirteen. They all looked pretty well fed, for orphans, but they certainly tucked into the pies Elodie had bought like they were starving animals.

"Is that true for the rest of you as well?" I asked the other two. Maslin and Lundy looked at each other and Lundy replied.

"Kinda?" she said. "Cutter's older and he fights, so there's not many that would mess with him. But Ironworker kids get on pretty well with most gangs."

"Why is that?"

"'Cause we've got armor, and we can get them weapons!" Cutter answered. I got the impression he would have liked to brandish his sword to make the point, but he settled for banging on his pauldron with his armored gauntlet.

Armor, well . . .

[Identification] : Plate Mail (partial) – Quality: Poor – Properties: Squeaky

---

I'd been under the impression that Poor quality equipment was melted down as a failed piece, or caused by maintenance issues. Looks like sometimes it got handed down to the brats. The other two were also wearing bits of plate.

"Is that how you show you're . . . Ironworker kids?" I asked.

"Yeah!" Cutter exclaimed, and the others nodded less enthusiastically.

"Did you do this as well, when you were younger?" I asked Elodie, who was "supervising" the kids from the corner of the room.

"I wasn't running on the streets, miss," she huffed. I looked at her skeptically, and she crumbled. "Well, sometimes when I had errands, I had a helmet that my father made."

"Fascinating," I said, and meant it. That an entire social stratum could exist that was just ignored by the adults, even though some—most?—had been a part of it? My major was economics, but I'd taken a few sociology units along the way, and this practically demanded a study.

Sadly, I had other concerns at the moment. "What can you tell me about the other gangs?" I asked and was answered with a babble of half-coherent ideas.

It seemed that the guild kids were the most numerous type of gang, but also the smallest. They weren't really what I'd call a gang, since most of them were actually fed and housed by their respective guilds—and also policed by them. They mainly focused on protecting each other and their turf. Unless there was a feud going on, guild kids could enter each other's territories without incident—as long as it was on some kind of errand. Hanging out was not generally tolerated unless the groups were friendly.

Altogether, the guild kids probably numbered about as much as the three larger gangs that Cutter knew about: the Snakes, the Rats, and the Crows. I sensed certain self-esteem issues with whoever had named those gangs.

The Snakes had territory near the Dungeon, where the adventurers tended to live. They mainly survived by running errands for adventurers (who shed money) and by robbing adventurers when they were dead drunk. They were always trying to get a slot in a delving team, or to make enough to get into the Dungeon on their own.

The Rats worked the docks, either looking for honest unskilled labor or committing crimes—pickpocketing or running lookout for grown-up thieves, for the most part.

Finally, the Crows hid out in the poor Quarter. They didn't work there, though, sneaking out at night for burglary. They were the most criminally accomplished of the gangs, and also the most violent. Cutter thought they were the most likely to be connected with the Thieves Guild.

"Everyone claims they are, but those bastards are so cutthroat, they just might be," he claimed. "Plus, they got their own line on weapons, so they won't talk to us."

Those were all the gangs they knew about, though they were dimly aware of the existence of others. The Nobles Quarter, for example, was a place they didn't go. Nobles wouldn't be a gang, exactly, but noble kids did sometimes go around in groups beating on their lessers.

"You see a noble kid, you need to give 'em a wide berth," Cutter said. "Even the young ones are level three, and they'll cut you just for the XP."

"You guys are all level two, right?" I asked, and they nodded in response. "Elodie should have told you what I'm looking for you to do, so why don't you tell me what you're looking to gain. Is it just money?"

The youngest two were somewhat reticent, but Cutter responded right away. "I heard you were a big-shot adventurer—can you get me into the Crypt?"

"The Dungeon?" I asked, surprised. "Do you want to be an adventurer?"

"Yeah!" he exclaimed. "I like to fight—that's why I'm called Cutter!"

"Uh huh. And what about you two?" I said, looking over at them.

"Um, I was- . . . we were . . ." Lundy stammered, looking nervous. "Hoping you were looking for apprentices?"

I stared blankly at them. "You want to be mages? Do you even know what kind of mage I am?"

"Doesn't matter," Maslin muttered before clamming up again. Lundy continued for him.

"Any kind of mage is a step up or three from what we're looking at. And we do know you can Enchant; that's scary big important. Everyone in the Guild is looking up to you!"

"I see. Do you have the requisite Scribe skill?" They only looked embarrassed.

I looked over at Elodie. "How did you get Scribe and Calculate?" I asked. "They're not in the Maid profession."

"My parents paid for me to study for two years, miss." I must have looked puzzled, because she continued: "Oh, my tutor didn't have Teach, miss; I had to learn it all the hard way before getting awarded them for competence." The kids seemed impressed by this admission.

"Ah. I didn't think that way was generally known."

"Most of the guilds know about it, I think. It's only really important for those two skills."

"Right." This had come up when I was researching other magic types. Most skills could be gained by simply attempting the skill until you succeeded, but Academic and Magic skills needed to be taught.

"How rare is the Teach skill, anyway?" I wondered.

"Pretty rare . . ." Elodie answered uncertainly, but I was already doing a search of the system. Professions that unlocked Teach . . . wow, there weren't many. There was Scrivener at level four, but otherwise it was all classes like Phantasmal Illusionist, advanced mage classes at level five, or above. Master Arcanist, Sage, Leymaster . . . not professions I could see teaching a Guild kid to read. Aesrideu had said the calling of a Bard was to teach, but they didn't get the skill. High Bard did, though.

"Wow, that is rare. Just Scrivener? I guess they get monopolized by the nobles."

"Yes, it's hard to get to level four just as a Scribe, and that's where Scriveners generally come from. I think most noble houses hire a Scribe and advance him to level four to serve as a personal tutor for the family."

"So assuming you can get Scribe from somewhere, do you really need a master to become an apprentice?" I hadn't, after all.

It was Elodie who answered again. "Without a master, how would you support yourself while you were an apprentice? The profession doesn't have any skills that make money."

"I guess that's true," I said thoughtfully. That hadn't been a consideration for me, since I'd been an apprentice for all of five minutes.

"And think of all the things you learned from your master about magic that weren't included in the skills!" Elodie continued. "Why, without that instruction, you'd be fumbling in the dark with only the Status for guidance!"

"Yes, that would be terrible," I said dryly. I returned my attention to the kids.

"Does that mean you *can't* teach us Scribe?" Lundy asked.

"I can do a great many things," I said evasively. "After all, am I not a great and powerful wizard?"

They nodded, impressed or afraid, I wasn't certain which. I sighed.

"It seems to me that I'm far too young to take on apprentices, but I suppose if you're going to be working for me, I should take care of your futures." They brightened at this, which only made me feel more morose.

"So this is the deal," I said. "You'll spy for me, and I'll pay you and see that you get the training you need. Assuming you can meet the requirements, I'll take you on as apprentices. And yes, Cutter, that training will include Crypt expeditions . . . for all of you."

Cutter was pleased by that last, while the other two looked nervous.

"Is that acceptable?" I asked them. "I'm not going to have you running around the city at level two." *Aubert will no doubt enjoy taking the kids on a field trip.*

They still looked nervous, but they nodded.

"Very well, then, glad to have you aboard," I said. "Did you have any other questions before we start?"

Cutter once again leaped into the breach. "Miss, is it true that you're the Guild Master's new mistress?"

I scowled. "No. And no more questions from you."

BULLYING

Cutter moved down the street swiftly and confidently. I was surprised how much his demeanor had changed. He had been the most confident of the three kids in my dining room, but now he was in his element, the street. He knew where he was going, what he was doing.

I drifted along behind him, invisible. He moved quickly, but he couldn't hope to get away from the speed and endurance that went with being a level four. Not that he was trying to get away—he didn't know I was there.

A few cuts through alleys—I was learning a few things about getting around in the city—he found what, or rather who, he was looking for.

"Toss, mate!" he called quietly. One of the kids in the group across the street looked over at him, and came over.

"What'ya want?" Toss asked once he got closer.

"Got something for ya," Cutter said. He held his hand so that Toss could see the coin inside. "Someplace more private, yeah?"

Interestingly, what the two were speaking was quite different from how Cutter had been talking before. Still quite intelligible to me, but I wondered if Elodie would be able to understand it.

The two found a back alley to talk in. Invisible, I couldn't prompt Cutter, but I'd briefed him thoroughly before he started.

"Here, this is for you," Cutter said, handing a few copper coins over.

Give them something just for talking with you, I'd said. *It shows that you value their time, that you value them. Food is good.* He'd started, recognizing as I spoke that I'd done the same to them. I'd grinned at him. *But money's better.*

"What's this for?" Toss asked, making the money disappear.

"Show that I'm serious. And so you know that this is between us, yeah?"

"I guess so," Toss said doubtfully.

Once you give them the money, get a small commitment out of them; it'll be easier then. And it helps establish the pattern—you give them money, and they do things for you.

"Now, there's more where that came from; you interested?"

"'Course." Toss tried to keep it cool, but I could tell he wanted the money.

"Got me a gent, lots of money, wants eyes in the Rats. Someone to tell us what they're doing, what's going on in their territory."

"You want me to rat on the Rats?"

"Yeah. There's good money in it, maybe even good steel if you get me the good stuff." I'd loaned him my old dagger, and he flashed it at the kid.

"Shit, that's—"

"Good quality, yeah. You in?"

"Shit, man, I can't be seeing some geezer all the time."

"Nah, mate, not how it works. You'll be working for me. Ain't nothing wrong if you have a chat with your old pal Cutter, am I right?"

"I spose . . ."

"Start by telling me about Trent Street—you guys are staying clear of that, right?"

Make sure you get something compromising out of him before you go. Maybe the warehouse—they've probably been warned off if the Guild has a long-term presence there. If you can seem like you know more than they do, it'll make you look like you have an in with the Guild, so they'll be scared of you.

"How'd you know bout that?"

"Never you mind; who was it that told you guys to keep clear?"

The kid hesitated, but he soon caved. "Mask," he admitted.

"Nice work," Cutter said, smiling. He poured five or six copper into the guy's hand. "We'll meet again tomorrow, eighth bell, right here, all right? I'll have more questions, you'll get more money." He turned and jogged off, leaving the kid looking at the money in his hand.

Once you've got something, cut it short; don't give him time to ask more questions or have second thoughts. Just get out of there.

Cutter had done his part well, and now it was my turn. I patiently watched the kid as he shook himself and then started hiding his fresh wealth in various places. Then he headed back into Rat territory.

The group he was in had moved down the street a bit, but he didn't go after them, instead heading further in. This didn't bode well, but at least it'd be over quickly. I didn't think kids would have a lot of impulse control, but if he'd sat on this overnight before making a decision, I would have been . . . majorly inconvenienced.

Sure enough, he made his way to a ruined looking building. A dozen nasty-looking kids were hanging out inside. Toss looked around and then went over to one of them.

"Mask!" he said, "You'll never guess what I heard—" Then he stopped, frozen.

Mask came over. He was an older kid, maybe as old as sixteen. "What, brat?" he asked roughly. "What did you hear?"

Toss didn't say anything. He'd frozen in fear the moment he'd felt the invisible edge of my knife across his throat. Weapon Mastery matched my intent exactly—there was no blood, just a cold sensation of sharpness.

Mask, of course, couldn't see a thing. "What, brat?" he asked again, but Toss couldn't move. Mask looked down and got a disgusted look on his face. "Damn, kid," he said and struck him with a backhanded blow. I got out of the way before it hit, allowing Toss to fall unimpeded. "Get cleaned up, and get out of my sight."

Toss didn't need to be told twice. He ran from the room, crying, and as I followed him out, I could smell that he'd pissed himself. *Good job, me, you made a kid so scared he pissed himself. Mission accomplished.* If only.

I followed the kid down to the river. Without any sort of ceremony, he jumped in, soaking his lower half, which I suppose was the best way he had of washing himself. He was still crying, but he'd found a spot away from anyone else, so this was probably my best chance.

[Unseen Sound].

"I toldja this was just between us, didn't I?" Cutter's voice whispered in his ear. Toss jerked violently, away from the voice, falling over in his panic. Now he was all the way soaked. Cutter continued on, "We're always watching, see? Next time, it won't be a warning."

You have defeated Jérôme Plante in a Tier 3 Social Contest! You have earned 5 XP.

[Intimidate] Level 2 acquired through use.

For gaining a skill level, you have been awarded 1 XP.

"I got it, Cutter," the kid stammered. He started crawling out of the river. "I swear, I won't, I promise . . ." he kept babbling, but I was already leaving. I'd put the fear of Cutter in this informant, and this was about all the suffering I could stand to watch.

I really hoped I didn't have to do this with *every* kid Cutter recruited.

"So I meant to ask before," I said, freshly out of my evening bath. "Did you have hopes of becoming my apprentice?"

"What, me?" Elodie asked, "What—what made you ask that?" She put down our food—I'd started eating in the kitchen so she didn't have an excuse not to join me—and sat down.

"I've been wondering about it since I learned you had Scribe," I said. I started eating my meal, pieces of chicken and vegetables wrapped in pastry. "Don't get me wrong, it's been very helpful to have you around for the Guild accounting, but I couldn't help wondering if Gustave wanted you to be around as a possible replacement for me."

"I don't know anything about that!" Elodie exclaimed. "Why would the Guild Master want to replace you?"

I shrugged. "I've been *very* cooperative with the Guild because I want to fit in here and keep them on our side . . . but to Gustave, I'm an unknown quantity. It makes sense that he'd want the option available."

"So you realized this, and you didn't say anything about it at the time . . . because you wanted to be cooperative?" Elodie asked, somewhat incredulously.

"Well, succession planning is an important part of any well-run business. I can't fault Gustave for a little due diligence." The business-speak tripped off my tongue with familiar ease, but I reminded myself to keep it simple. Who knew how something like 'actionable deliverables' might translate?

"The other reason I didn't say anything," I continued, "is that I didn't want to have to confirm or deny that I had the Teaching skill."

"You have? But that means . . ."

"I won't be able to hide that fact if I start teaching Scribe to the kids. But I'd prefer it if Gustave didn't find out right away." I gave her a significant look.

She blushed. "I won't tell, miss."

"Miss?"

". . . Kandis."

I smiled. "Good. So that brings us back to the start of this conversation. You were shortly going to realize that I could teach you Enchanting, so I thought I'd ask you first: what do you want?"

"I don't know," she said, getting flustered. "I never thought about this!"

"That's fine," I said. "Take all the time you need. You don't need to give me an answer tonight, or this week. And if you do give me an answer, it doesn't have to be a final one."

There was a long pause, which lasted long enough for us both to finish up our dinner. Finally, Elodie looked up from her plate.

"I mean no offense, m- . . . Kandis, but I'm not sure I'm ready for the excitement that comes from being an Enchanter."

I grinned. "I *think* that's more me than the profession. I'm sure the Guild would love to keep you well away from any excitement." I went to clear up the plates, my impropriety shocking her into action. Snatching the plates away from me, she went over to the sink to clean them.

"There are other possibilities as well," I said. "Once you complete Apprentice, you qualify for just about any mage-type profession. I'm actually poorly qualified to educate someone about magic, but you can keep doing this job while you get your skills."

"Really? Poorly qualified to educate, when you have Teach?"

"Yeah . . . my master didn't teach me much of that non-skill stuff you mentioned before. I've been pretty much feeling my own way."

"I can't believe that," she scoffed. "You've been so confident, ever since I met you."

"Well, bullshit baffles brains." Elodie gave me a funny look at the expression. "Sorry, that's a saying back home."

"If you say so . . . anyway, I'd have to get another level before I could complete Apprentice."

"Not impossible; remember, we're already committed to escorting those kids through some Dungeon levels."

She shuddered. "I went on a few Guild trips to get my third level. It's horrible in there."

"No argument there," I said. "Another possibility is that I can Teach you Teach. From what you said, you could make some good money with that."

"You can do that? Can anyone with Teach do that?"

"I actually haven't *used* Teach properly yet, but I think so."

She frowned. "Shouldn't the skill be more common then?"

"I don't know . . . maybe the Scriveners don't want competition— Teacher might be a more dangerous profession than Enchanter."

She thought about that for a moment. "Why are you willing to make competition, Kandis? Why would you do all this for me? I'm your maid, but I get paid for that. Why offer me all this?"

"Hey, I'm not saying I'll give you everything you want." Her face fell at my words. "Don't look at me like that—I'm saying I'll have conditions—maybe a price."

I got up and came round to her side of the table. "But honestly, it's not a huge cost for me. There's time to make a book, and time to use the skill, but that's easily met." I took hold of her shoulders and looked her in the eye. "It's much more important to me that you decide what you want and don't choose a path that's wrong for you."

Is there something wrong with this society? I wondered. I know schools are a mostly modern institution, but this place seems so lacking in any sort of education. Do the skills have something to do with that?

Answering that question would have to wait, much like Elodie's decision. I had a lot of more immediate problems to deal with.

SPY GAMES

> **[Illusion Magic] Level 4 acquired through use.**
> **For gaining a skill level, you have been awarded 1 XP.**

Finally, I thought, as I watched Lundy head off, following a cart. She should be back before the Greater Invisibility spell wore off. My spy network was coming along, but there was still far too much work that needed my personal touch.

I sighed, and returned to creating a Calculate text, while still keeping an eye on the house I still thought of as Guillaume's residence. We were *fairly* sure now it wasn't—he never spent the night there, but we weren't sure who *did*. Cloridan hadn't managed to find us a hideout with a good view of the warehouse, but he'd had more luck in the residential district. I'd been able to rent a room with a window, "for my writing."

So far, we'd seen Guillaume enter and leave several times, and seen a few deliveries like this one, but we hadn't seen the master of the house— unless he was actually the servant who accepted the deliveries.

Guillaume had actually paid me another social call, but I still didn't know what he wanted with me. It had been a nice distraction from all the work I had to do, though. Surveillance was deadly dull at the best of times, so it was lucky I had something to occupy myself. Now I had another distraction, spending the 45 spell points that I'd gotten from my skill increase.

I'd spent some time considering this already, but I went back over my reasoning to see if anything had changed since then. My main options were:

> [Phantasmal Entity]: **Creates an illusory creature or person that can move or act as the caster directs (25 points).**
> [Disguise Other]: **Modify target's appearance and clothing as required (20 points).**
> [Dispel Image]: **Destroys an existing illusion if caster's effect level is higher than the target's (20 points).**
> [False Emissary]: **Creates a false image of the caster that they can see and hear through (20 points).**

I'd looked, and there didn't seem to be a *detect* illusion spell, which was a shame. That seemed to be the province of Identify or Perception, with high enough effect totals. My own spellcasting total was *much* higher than my Identify, so spamming Dispel Image was a more likely way of identifying an illusion.

The next spell in the Phantasmal list was irresistible to me, to be honest. The thought of creating and controlling "real" creatures was just too crazy to say no to, regardless of the tactical uses. Phantasmal Emissary might have been even better, but then I couldn't get one of the other spells.

Satisfied with my choice, I picked Phantasmal Entity and Dispel Image. Giving in to temptation, I immediately cast Phantasmal Entity.

A mouse immediately appeared on the desk in front of me. We looked at each other for a moment, and then I willed it to turn around and walk to the other side of the desk. It did so. I attempted to get it to do a little dance, and managed it . . . somewhat. It looked a bit like dressage I'd seen horses perform.

[Dispel Image]. The mouse disappeared, so it looked like it worked on Phantasmal spells, too.

Right. Back to work.

"Honestly, I'm starting to think the man's courting me," I said to Elodie as I helped her prepare our evening meal. I'd received a request from Guillaume for him to attend on me tomorrow.

"He *might* be," Elodie mused. She'd gotten used to filling in my "foreigner's" ignorance of local nuance. "It's unusual for a noble to marry a commoner, but it's not unknown. And it's not like he's an important noble."

"Why now, though? I was expecting some attention after the ball, but I shouldn't have done anything to attract his attention yet."

"Are you joking, miss?" Elodie dropped her knife and looked at me in shock. "There's all kinds of rumors swirling around about you. You're the beautiful and rich Enchanter that charmed the Guild Master and swept into a senior Guild position. You've had a personal audience with the Count and made his son back down."

She returned to chopping as I blushed in silence. I didn't think I was *that* famous. ". . . and that's just what regular people know. If it was widely known that you had Lord Aubert eating out of your hand, and were form-ing a spy network . . ."

"Are people really talking about me that much?" I asked plaintively.

"Well . . ." Elodie considered. "That's in the Guild; I don't hear much gossip from outside it."

"He's not in the Guild, though," I said.

"He does live in the castle, though," she countered. "So he probably knew about your audience with the Count, maybe even your invitation to the ball." She thought about it for a bit longer. "Perhaps he's trying to get to know you before asking you to dance at the ball?"

"He's going to—wait." I interrupted myself. "I don't know how to dance."

"Oh, hardly anyone knows how to Dance," Elodie reassured me. "Just—"

We were interrupted by an urgent knocking at the back door. Maslin was there, almost bouncing with suppressed excitement when I opened it.

"Miss, there's a carriage left from the residence, miss!" he told me. "It just left from the south gate!"

It took me a moment to comprehend this news. Maslin must have fol-lowed the carriage from Guillaume's house to the gate, and then come back here. It was weird to think of following a carriage on foot, but Maslin's running skill was higher than mine. More importantly, it was barely an hour until sunset, and carriages didn't normally travel at night.

There *was* a village with an inn barely an hour's travel south of Anchor-bury, though.

"Was our mystery man in it?" I asked.

"I think so, miss, but I didn't get a good look. He was wearing a cloak, and had the hood up."

"All right, go find Cloridan and let him know what's going on. Tell him that I'm going to check out Bourneby on my own. Don't panic, unless I'm not back by morning."

Maslin nodded and headed out the back door. Elodie had more objections.

"Miss! Miss Kandis!" she exclaimed as I went back upstairs to change into my armor.

"I'll have to skip dinner tonight," I said, as she came into where I was changing. "Hopefully this won't take too long and I'll be back later tonight."

"You shouldn't be running off like this," she objected, but her heart wasn't in it. "It could be a trap."

I shrugged. "A trap is still a lead," I said. "As long as I avoid getting caught in it. I'll be careful."

She sighed as I completed my preparations. "Don't forget, Lord Guillaume will be here at tenth bell, so don't stay out too late."

"I won't. Help me with the door?" I asked, turning invisible. She sighed again, but went downstairs to let me out.

The sun had not yet set, so there was no problem getting through the gates. Invisibility helped me avoid questions as I slipped past the last-minute incoming traffic. The carriage had more than a half hour's start on me, so there was little chance of catching up, but I knew where it was going.

I headed out, in what I thought of as a quick jog. I was moving a bit faster than an Olympic sprinter, but I knew I should be able to keep up this pace for the whole trip. After a bit of consideration, I started adding long jumps every ten or so strides. I'm not sure if it made me faster, but I'd been neglecting my Jump skill.

[Jump] Level 2 acquired through use.
For gaining a skill level, you have been awarded 1 XP.

There, that was worth looking like an idiot for half an hour, I thought as the village came into view. It wasn't like anyone could see me, anyway. The village had a wall, like all settlements on this world, but it was low enough that I could jump right over it. I noted that the gate (now closed for the night) was manned by uniformed Duvost troops, just like the city walls.

I saw the carriage almost immediately, outside of the inn as I had expected. My target was inside the inn, no doubt. I hesitated, planning my approach. It was the end of the day and people were heading to the pub; it shouldn't be too hard to slip in behind one of them.
Or I could go and see what that's all about.

About 500 meters down the street, there was a sudden loud clanging. I could make out people shouting as well.

Um, OK . . . I dithered. That was clearly something interesting, and *probably* connected to my target, but he was probably in *there*, wasn't he? Then one of the bystanders opened the door to the inn and shouted out to the room.

"Hey, there's an attack on the Mayor's house!"

At which point nothing else would do but for them to all come pouring out. Some of them went off to help, but all of them came out to gawk. Including someone that had to be my guy. Dressed much more richly, with a hooded cloak, the middle-aged man looked as confused as anyone. Is this unconnected, then? Or is he establishing an alibi? *I didn't know what was going on, but spam costs nothing.*

[Dispel Image].

The image of the harmless rich man was replaced by a decidedly less harmless-looking thirty-year-old with a ragged beard and bad skin.
Oh, ho, ho.

"Hey, what happened to the rich guy?" One of the villagers next to him had noticed the change. He shouted and grabbed a hold of Bad Skin, attracting the attention of others.
OK. That guy doesn't look like an Illusionist, so he must be the alibi, while the real Illusionist is over there.

I started heading toward the fight. As I drew closer, I could see what all the fuss was about.

Demons.

Jet-black skin that seemed to fade into the shadows, horns, no clothes—or genitals—and nasty-looking claws about twice as long as human fingers. They were cutting a swath through the lightly armed villagers. Some fought, others fled in terror, but it didn't seem to make much difference to these inhuman monsters.

Or so it seemed. *[Dispel Image].* One of the demons was instantly replaced with a greasy black-haired man wearing chain mail and wielding twin short swords.

Amusingly, everyone else noticed before he did.

"What the fuck!" yelled one of the demons. "Bryce, what are you doing without your skin!" Until the shout, Bryce had been occupied with slashing at a villager with an axe. The villager had noticed the change immediately, of course, but demon or brigand didn't really change the situation for him. Bryce being distracted by his commander *did* change things, though. Bryce looked over to the commander and then down at himself. That was plenty of time for his victim to get a good swing at him.

The commander cursed as Bryce took an axe to his shoulder. He seemed to be in charge, so I did him next. *[Dispel Image]*.

The commander turned out to be a woman, which I wouldn't have guessed from her voice. She cursed as her true form was revealed. "Where's that damn fingerwiggler!" she yelled. "His spells are no good!"

At this point, the fight had . . . half-stopped. The demons that were engaged were still fighting, but those without an immediate opponent weren't chasing down new villagers anymore. Confused, they were standing around waiting for orders.

The villagers were less confused. Seeing the demons change had lessened the terror, but they were still fighting or fleeing for their lives. I knew that any delay favored the home side, though. The town guards were surely on their way, and they were a much more even match with these guys.

"It's not me, Commander," someone said, their voice appearing to come from the air above us. "There's another Illusionist canceling my illusions."

Two could play that game. *[Unseen Sound]*.

"I'm afraid this mission is compromised," the voice continued from above. "So I'll have to make sure you don't live to reveal anything."

One of the quirks of Unseen Sound was that you had to hold the whole sound in your head when you cast it. It made conversations a little awkward, but it wasn't too bad, unless you were trying to respond to surprising dialogue.

The other thing was that it only started making sound *after* you finished the spell. So as "fingerwiggler" responded to my spell with his own Unseen Sound, I was already casting my next spell.

"That's not me! They're trying to fool you!"

[Improved Blind].

A dark bubble went up around the commander's head even as the voice rang out. I don't think she heard any of it.

"They got the commander!" one of the demons yelled.

"Who? Wasn't it Master Archambault that did that?"

"Don't say my name, you fool!"

Tsk, tsk, wasting your spell on people who aren't going to listen. *You should silence them like this,* I thought. I grinned, even though only I could see it.

[Improved Blind]. My target was the fool who'd yelled the name.

"That was our guy that did that! Let's get him!"

"No, you idiot!"

By this time, the fighting had stopped completely, as everyone was yelling at each other, or at the sky. The commander was standing on her own, slashing out at random.

And then the guards arrived, and things got a lot worse for the bad guys.

HUNT

The guards plowed into the demons with what I guess you could call holy fervor. I don't think they knew why the demons were standing around arguing with each other, nor did they care. They charged in, screaming with either rage or terror, I couldn't tell.

No expert on battlefield tactics, I was getting a beginner's lesson in the importance of "maintaining a battle line" and "readying against a charge." The guards were actually outnumbered, but the first exchange—over in a flurry of blows—almost evened the odds.

"Retreat!" came the voice from above, and some of them heeded it. It turned out, though—another basic tactics lesson for me—that disengaging from a determined enemy isn't all that easy. It's easier when you have an Illusionist on your side, however. One by one, the demons started to disappear.

Well, this isn't good. They're going to get away!

On the other hand, did I really care about them? The Illusionist was the key, and he was always going to be much harder to catch. Would he retreat *with* the troops? The troops probably had a fallback position; how likely was it that he'd go there?

Pretty likely, I decided. His other options were the inn, which I'd kind of spoiled, or back to the city. He couldn't go back tonight via carriage, and he didn't seem like the type to walk. So I needed to follow these guys back to their extraction point. Hard to do when they're invisible . . .

But not if it's my spell!

I picked one of the still visible demons and cast Greater Invisibility on him. Now Archambault couldn't target the guy with his own spells, *and* he thought he was invisible. Well, he was, but not to me.

Soon I was following along behind as he made his escape. Over the wall, and into the night. He moved cautiously, but it wasn't long before we were out of sight of the village. About five minutes after that, I started to see others in the area appear out of nowhere. The mage must have canceled his spells, I realized, so I canceled the Invisibility on my little cat's-paw.

They greeted each other as they drew near, but they were quite subdued, falling into line as they headed for their destination. There were eight of them left, from a force of about twenty. Eventually they made their way to an organized camp. There were tents, a campfire, and lanterns, all concealed so well by the geography and carefully placed tarpaulins that I didn't see it until I was almost on top of it. There were two more guarding the camp; they looked a little shocked to see these guys come back.

"What happened?" one of the guards asked.

"Mage fucked up," replied one of the returnees.

"I did not," said a familiar voice out of nowhere. An equally familiar middle-aged man appeared in front of the soldiers. "As I said, there was another Illusionist there to counter me."

Gotcha! I crowed to myself. Although . . . was this another illusion?

One of the soldiers must have had the same thought, picking up a twig and flicking it at the mage. It bounced off of the mage's robes, much to his irritation.

"Yes, yes, greet the person who saved your lives with mistrust," he said, scowling.

"Didn't save the commander," one of the soldiers said, and the others murmured agreement.

"I couldn't lift their spell; they were simply more powerful than me," Archambault admitted. He looked around, evidently for a comfortable seat, because he slumped to the ground and leaned back against a nearby tree stump. "After disguising the lot of you, I've now almost exhausted my mana casting Invisible Other on you seven."

"Eight," one of the men interjected.

"What?" the mage asked. Even under the current circumstances, he could still manage a decent "how dare you interrupt me?" tone.

The soldier wasn't intimidated, though. "There were eight of us who escaped."

Archambault's eyes flicked around the group. "I only cast the spell seven times," he said. "And no one escaped who wasn't invisible. One of you is that Illusionist, disguised."

Hands went to weapons, and the group collectively took a step back from one another.

"Hang on," said one of the soldiers. "There's no way someone here is an imposter; we know each other too well."

"Except for the mage," another said.

"Why would I sow doubt if I was the one infiltrating, you fool!" Archambault sneered.

"Everyone say their names!" one of the soldiers called out. "He won't know his own name if he's a fake; none of us said ours."

"Except for the mage," said the same one that said it before. I think he might have been a bit upset at being called a fool.

Everyone called out their names, to no real effect except I knew their names now. They all stood around confused that their plan hadn't worked.

I should be taking action at this point, but what am I going to do? I wondered. I didn't really want to kill them, even if that was a realistic possibility. I wanted proof of who hired them, but it didn't seem like I was going to get that tonight. Eventually, Archambault would be going back to his house. I doubted any detours he took getting there would teach me anything. And these men probably didn't know who hired them. I'd be better off tracking their blinded commander. Actually, the spell must be wearing off around now . . .

"I don't understand," Archambault was muttering. "I know that . . . oh, of course!" The others looked at him. "They couldn't follow invisible people, so they made one of you invisible and tracked their own spell."

"So they're just standing around somewhere listening to us?" Royce asked. He had an angular face, a stubby nose, and now a worried expression.

"Undoubtedly. Go and wave your swords around randomly if you think it will help." The mage pondered for a moment. "I'm going back. Do not rejoin with your company. Stay here for as long as you think safe, and then split up. Our opponent can only follow one of you."

"You're not the boss of us, finger wiggler." Vaden, an unreliable looking man with a nasty burn scar on his face, snarled at the mage.

Archambault sneered. "Do you think I care if you heed my advice? I have given it, as contracted. Do as you wish." For an Illusionist, he was a real people person.

"If you're so important, won't he be following you?" Varden asked.

"They would, but I intend to make that impossible," Archambault said. "They may be the more powerful Illusionist, but that is not the only magic at my command." He gestured, and a sudden wind rose up, whirling around him and kicking up dust. Before I could react, he had flown up out of sight in the darkness.

Well, fuck.

Upon reflection, I decided that Archambault's dramatic exit *hadn't* been a win. I knew where he was going . . . probably. There were two possibilities that I knew of, and if he was going back to the nearby inn, I expected him to be unpleasantly surprised.

I was just a bit pissed that he managed to make sure I couldn't follow him. Also that he had more than one type of magic. And that *he* didn't have to walk back home. I had plenty of reasons to be pissed, but all up, I thought I could count it as a win. I just had to see how it had been wrapped up at the village after I'd left.

Slipping back in was easy, even though they'd gone on full alert. There just weren't enough guards to stop an invisible person jumping over that wall. Skulking around, I saw that the guard lieutenant seemed to have things well in hand. The attackers were either dead or arrested, and statements were being taken from the villagers and the surviving attackers. The lieutenant had a really confused look on his face, but I was confident the important details would find their way to the Count. I could fill in the rest later.

"So this is payment in full for our first job," I said, pushing two bags of gold over to my teammates.

"Job's not done though?" Cloridan objected, though he happily took his bag.

"One of the clauses was to prove there's no threat of demons. Since we've shown it was an Illusionist, we've fulfilled the conditions. That's 66 gold each, one third share of the 200 gold payment."

"One third?" Janie asked, looking around the table.

"Since the payments come from my father, it would seem churlish to take a share," Aubert declared.

"Must be nice, being so rich that you can turn down money," Janie said. "But like Cloridan said, job's not done, though? Stuff is still going on."

"True, but the Count decided that could be our second task," I said. "Ending whatever plot is going on. If we manage that, we get the other 800."

"At least we won't have to deal with riots anymore?" Cloridan said hopefully.

"Don't be too sure," I said. "I spoke with my . . . contact, and he says that while the truth is getting out, there are still some who believe the first rumor. Another "demon" attack—if not foiled—could start them up again."

I sighed and continued. "Most of our leads have dried up," I said. "The Count raided the warehouse, but the troops got away before they arrived. I'm not sure if Archambault returned to the house, and Guillaume—"

"Hasn't done anything," Aubert quickly interjected.

"Exactly. If it makes you feel better, I don't think he can be *behind* this plot," I said. Unless your father pays his wards way too much, there's too much money involved."

"True," Aubert agreed thoughtfully. "What we've seen so far would require a significant portion of the resources of a baron."

"Or a really rich adventurer," Janie said.

"Such a person would be better served to *become* a baron," Aubert said with disdain. "Qualifying for Leadership is a common preoccupation of the mid-levels," he said smugly.

The others didn't disagree, so I kept my mouth shut. *Is Leadership really that good?* I wondered. It had come up on our first Dungeon delve, but the others hadn't wanted him to use it, so I hadn't given it much thought.

[Leadership] : Provides a skill bonus to underlings in return for a share of XP.

As in-depth as always, thank you, System. An XP share did sound like it could be a bit of a cheat, though.

"Anyway," I said, returning to the conversation. "No real leads, so for now we'll keep looking. I'll keep building up my network, with your help, Cloridan."

Cloridan nodded agreeably and made a half-bow from his chair. "I always enjoy spending time with you, my lady."

I snorted. "Pressure's off, so you start with the sweet-talking?" I turned to Janie. "Lundy and Maslin haven't reached level three yet, so can you take them through the Dungeon?"

"Sure thing—I don't think they've gotten any better with explosions, though."

"If they don't want to go with you, I can get Aubert to take them."

"I'll be gentle," she promised.

"And that leaves me the only one without an assignment," Aubert noted.

"Oh, I've got a special assignment for you," I said.

"Normally, you look happier when you're about to humiliate me," Aubert told me after the others had left. "Dare I hope that you've tired of the game?"

"No," I sighed. "There's just not much to be pleased about what's coming next. I've got some clothes for you in the next room; go and change."

He narrowed his eyes, but left the room. I soon heard muffled cursing, but he knew protests weren't going to get him anywhere. Say what you like about Aubey, he didn't have a problem with authority.

He was pretty pissed when he came out. "These clothes don't fit, and this cloak scratches," he complained. Then he looked at me. "That *is* you, right?"

"Of course," I said. I'd cast Disguise and was now dressed in a similarly common manner. I had a different face, but I'd still given myself a hooded cloak. No matter what I made my face look like, I still seemed to attract attention.

"Where we're going, it wouldn't be good for you to be seen there," I explained. "It won't take long."

"Fine," he said, and stalked out after me.

It was fortunate we weren't actually trying to fool anybody, because he was rubbish at this. I started some conversation to distract him from glowering at me.

"Having an adventurer team was supposed to be cover for teaching you, but this has been getting much deeper than I anticipated," I said.

He shrugged. "Father never does anything for only one reason," he said. "You must have impressed him, for him to have . . . put you in authority over me. I'm not surprised he wants you working for him in other capacities."

"That had better not be innuendo," I said, but I wasn't really worried. The Count hadn't given any indication of that sort of interest.

"It's not; my father has been scrupulously faithful to Mother while within the County."

"Within the County?" I asked.

"I don't know what happens in Dorsay," he admitted. "The courtesans of the capital are renowned for their skills—and their discretion." He sounded wistful.

Ew. Well, at least we were at our destination, which should put an end to such thoughts.

Aubert frowned as we came up to the gate. "In all the gods' names, why have you brought me to a cemetery?"

SEWAGE

nd why a *commoner's* graveyard?" Aubert complained.

That stopped me for a second. "Are you complaining because you think I'm going to murder you and leave you in a hole that's beneath your station? And it's the *second* part that offends you?"

"That would be stupid," he said. "I just—it's not—this is not the sort of place that I would normally go to. Paying respects—" He cut himself off.

"—to commoner dead?" I finished for him. "Don't worry; you're here to learn a lesson." I turned away and started following the directions that Aesrideu had left me. A few turns, and a lot of counting, eventually found me at my destination.

"Here we are," I said, indicating the stone. "Estelle Marcheterre."

Aubert blanched. "What!" he said, turning to the stone, his eyes scouring it for every detail. There wasn't much. "It was only two years . . . she was too young!"

"Knew her, did you?" I asked, though I already knew the answer. I'd guessed I'd find something like this when I sent Aesrideu looking for stories about the lordling. *Sometimes you can get everything you want and not be very happy.*

"We were in love," he said dully.

"I don't know the full story," I said. "My informant didn't want to open up old wounds for the parents, so he relied on thirdhand reports. You were actually there for the first half, so I'd like to know your side."

"There's not much to tell," he said. "Her parents . . . didn't approve. They forbid her from seeing me; I abided by their wishes. That's where the story ends. At least my involvement in it."

"Not quite," I said. "You see, she was pregnant."

"With—" he started, but I interrupted.

"You'll feel better if you don't ask that question. But yes, as far as the neighborhood gossip goes, you were the father. She fought with her parents about it, and left home."

"She would have come to me!" Aubert insisted. "If that happened, I would have provided for her . . ."

"Like the others?" I asked. "I'm curious about how many bastards you've fathered already at your age, but don't tell me."

Aubert glowered at me. "Why didn't she come to me?"

"I don't know why she didn't," I said. "I only know that she left her family and got a job in a different tavern. It wasn't as nice, and she had to live on her own, but that's what she did."

I sighed, and pointed at the grave next door. "She died during complications in childbirth." The stone read, "Unnamed daughter of Estelle Marcheterre." "She might have lived," I continued, "if she'd been able to afford a Healer, which she would have been if she'd reached out to you. Which she didn't."

"Why?" he asked me again.

"I don't know," I said. "The only reason I can think of is that she hated you so much that she was willing to risk her life keeping you out of it."

"But she loved me!" he protested.

"That's . . . not what it looks like from where I'm standing," I told him.

"I preferred it when you were humiliating me," he said, shoulders slumped. "This . . . hurts. What lesson am I supposed to learn from this?"

"I'm hoping," I said, "that this will show you that just because you think someone likes you, it isn't necessarily so. Your wealth, your power, your skills, will make people smile and flatter you because they're too scared to do anything else."

"So all affection is false?" he said grimly. "Are you sure you're not a noble?"

"No, you idiot. People like each other for real all the time. The difference is respect."

"Respect," he repeated thoughtfully. "You're saying that I wasn't respectful toward Estelle?"

"I wasn't there," I said. "And she's dead. The only one who can answer that is you. Have a think about it."

After all that, the sewers came as almost a relief. Almost. Unlike every sewer I'd seen in a film, these sewers had a raised platform running through the middle of the stream. It meant that you were right under the highest part of the curved ceiling as you crept along, while fetid water flowed on either side.

Cloridan and I were mapping out the sewer system. Neither of us were happy about it, but if we wanted to get the jump on the Thieves Guild, we needed to know the way around their neighborhood.

I'd planned on doing this alone, as it would probably be safest for me to do this invisible, but Cloridan had pointed out, reluctantly, that the Guild probably relied on traps more than guides, and his skills would be needed. Then he'd recovered his senses and spouted a lot of nonsense about putting his body between any "fair flower" and any danger, but the first part made sense.

Once in the sewers, he was all business, insisting on silence and an excess of caution. He taught me a few hand signs, we braced ourselves against the smell, and in we went.

Progress was slow; this was the second day, and we still weren't close to mapping the full network. As Cloridan had suspected, there were traps.

This can't be good for sewer maintenance, I thought as I watched Cloridan temporarily disable a hidden mechanism so we could get past it. *Maybe they know where the traps are? Or the Guild knows where they do maintenance and disable the traps beforehand.*

Most of these traps were pretty permanent. There was the occasional trip wire, but a lot of them were dug into the walls and floor, the stones removed and replaced. We were noting the location of all them, and would be comparing the layout with the historical plans we'd gotten from the Count.

The only warning I got was a shouted "Move!" from Cloridan. Suddenly there was a massive crash all around me, pain, and darkness.

The next thing I knew, I could hear voices.

"Whoo, what a mess!"

"Good thing we don't have to clean it up."

What happened? I wondered. I was still groggy, because the box that told me was still in my face.

You have taken 200 damage!
You have been stunned from massive damage.

We must have triggered a trap.

I tried to move, and found it . . . difficult. I managed to get an arm up, dislodging some rocks.

Rocks . . . a deadfall trap, rocks coming down between Cloridan and me.

It was dark; that's why I couldn't see. My Light spell had gone . . . I went to cast it again, but then I remembered.

Voices. Oh, shit.

There was a light coming from the other side of the pile, where Cloridan was. They were probably Thieves Guild.

"Hey, you see that? We got somebody!"

Shit. First things first. I cast Greater Invisibility again, and then started freeing myself from the rockfall. Fortunately, they were all fairly small, rounded rocks. From a river, I guess. Did they use these so that they would tumble correctly? They used a lot of them, whoever they were. The pile of rocks had blocked the channel completely and formed a pile about a meter above the old water level.

I managed to clear myself, but not without attracting attention.

"You hear that? Somebody on the other side?"

"Go check it out."

I heard a clattering of rocks from the other side. Well, time to try an old classic. *[Phantasmal Entity]*.

"Fuck!" The climber reached the top of the pile, only to be greeted by foot-long rat, which hissed at him . . . and then ran away. "Just a rat!" he called, and gave the area a cursory look round. "Nothing else."

He slid back down to the other side, and I used the racket he made to cover my own climb.

"Whoo, they sure took the time to do a proper trap in the old days, hey?"

"Stop gawping and help me with this guy."

Below were five people. Three were human and two were some animal-kin that I couldn't identify in the darkness. They had pulled Cloridan out of the rubble and were tying him up. Hopefully that meant he was alive.

Speaking of alive. I pulled out a healing potion and consumed it, immediately feeling better. I could have used the other one, but I only had two and Cloridan had just lost his.

[Body Development] Level 3 acquired through use.
For gaining a skill level, you have been awarded 1 XP,

"Hey, he's got enchanted weapons!" one of the animal-kin called.

"Nice," said a human. "Undead Bane—must be one of the new ones they're selling now. I hadn't heard they were doing daggers."

They bickered over who was going to keep the blades as they headed back down the tunnel. I followed silently, and I had my rat come along too. It might come in useful later. Phantasmal animals couldn't do damage, but they could soak up a fair bit before disappearing. And they were always good for a distraction.

They only had to travel for a short distance before they stopped. Their leader banged on the ceiling with his club. To my surprise, the stonework rang with a hollow sound, instead of the dull thud that I'd expected.

There was a sharp clang, and a light shone down from the ceiling. The leader stood square in it, looking up. "Viridian Monkey," he said sourly. There were scraping sounds, and then more light shone, as the ceiling opened up and the ladder came down.

I needed to get up that ladder. If the trapdoor only opened from the other side, this was my only chance to get into the house above. Maybe I could figure out where it was from the sewer maps, but I really didn't like my chances.

Of course, my chances of getting up the ladder and into a room filled with at least six people didn't seem high, either. I watched as they efficiently got the unconscious Cloridan up the ladder with the aid of a rope. One by one, the remaining thieves headed up. When there was only one left, I made my move.

Sic em, Rex, I thought, and sent my rat in. He couldn't actually hurt them, but no one wanted a rat climbing up them. The man on the ladder cursed, and let go to take a swipe at the furry bastard. That wasn't the best idea, as he fell off the ladder and fell into the sewage below. Acting according to my will, the rat jumped off him and scampered up the ladder.

I was right behind, as I could direct him properly without eyes on him. When I poked my head above the trapdoor, I saw a scene of instant chaos. It looked as if everyone had either lunged toward the rat and collided with each other, or flinched away and tripped over one of the bodies on the floor. Cloridan had been the first of these, but now there were three thrashing bodies on the ground—someone yelling, "Get it off me!" and five fools running around chasing after the rat.

I had it move into the farthest corner of the room, and slipped into the space that made. Once I was out of the way, I had Rex run between their feet and drop back down into the sewer. He didn't even make it to the ground before I canceled the spell. When one of the cursing thieves ran to the trapdoor to take a look, there was nothing to see.

"Goddam, you idiots, falling over yourselves over just one rat!" one of the meaner looking humans yelled. The others mumbled into the ground, and didn't mention that she—I was pretty sure she was female—had been fumbling around with the rest of them.

"Get this guy to the cells and tie his fingers—he might be a mage. We're supposed to be on the lookout for an Illusionist."

They went about their business while I quietly watched, tying up Cloridan and moving him—they could be quite professional when they weren't distracted. Two of the four that ended up carrying him out were the ones that had ended up with Cloridan's knives. I had noticed that they hadn't brought those items to the boss woman's attention.

I followed them along a corridor to another room. I thought that we might be still underground, but not by much. Noises from above made me think we were at cellar level, and that this corridor had been dug out to connect the cellars of at least three buildings.

The "cells" were four closet-sized rooms arranged along the side of a larger one. It looked like it was set up for guards to watch over the cells, but no one was there when we arrived, and the porters didn't stay. They put Cloridan in one of the cells, locked the door, and put the keys back on the wall, and then left.

I sighed. This was making it *too* easy. I pulled out a piton and moved over to the exit. The piton was part of the adventurer's kit that I'd picked up on the others' advice. A few items that had multiple uses. This door opened inward, so I jammed the piton into the gap in the doorframe on the side with the hinges. Now the door couldn't open without crushing the piton—in practice, the door or the hinges would break first.

Confident that we wouldn't be surprised by visitors, I now unlocked the cell door and moved over to Cloridan. I lifted him up and poured a healing potion down his throat, then held him steady as he jerked around in shock.

"What—what's going on?" he asked, confused.

"Well," I said, taking my knife to his bonds, "the good news is that we've found the Thieves Guild's hideout."

CONFESSION

The exit to the sewers is only down the corridor a way, but it's guarded, and the trapdoor makes a lot of noise when it's opened." I finished my recap of our situation to Cloridan.

"I see. Are you thinking we should try to escape, or should we infiltrate to learn more about what's going on?" He stretched himself out as he talked, working out the kinks from being tied up.

"It would be a waste to just run away," I said, considering. "Something you should know, though, if it comes to fighting—I've never actually . . . killed another person."

Cloridan looked at me. "Really? I'm surprised; you give off an air of someone competent and ruthless enough to have made that call before."

"I've *seen* people die," I said. "And giving off that impression makes it less likely that I'll have to again. I think."

"That's probably true. Well, I suppose I should tell you I haven't killed anyone either," he said. He laughed at my look of surprise. "Why so shocked?"

"Well, I've spoken to other adventurers about this, and I got the impression that it happened a lot."

"Ah, well, you're forgetting that I'm not an adventurer," Cloridan told me. "Adventurers spend a lot of time in free Dungeons or on the frontier—places outside of the King's Law."

"Um . . ."

"The Crypt is held by the Duvost family in the King's name, so the Law applies there," he explained. "Kill a man in the Crypt, and it's the same as if you did it on the town streets."

"Oh, right. That doesn't mean it doesn't happen, though. Some have already died," I said, thinking about the village.

"All illegal deaths, and assuming this whole affair gets resolved, we can be prosecuted for any crimes we commit. So. What's the plan?" Cloridan asked. "It won't be long before someone comes along, if only to strip my armor off me."

"Right. About that . . ." I gestured for Cloridan to get out of the cell, and then cast Phantasmal Entity. It didn't work, but I got some feedback as to why, so I quickly followed up with Phantasmal Object.

"Huh, so a corpse is an object, so I need to use the other spell," I said absently. An illusory corpse of Cloridan, naked and apparently strangled to death, now lay on the floor of the cell.

"Um," said Cloridan, "for future reference . . . I'm a lot bigger than that."

"What?" I asked, not understanding. Then I did. "What."

"It's fine; you couldn't know," he said reassuringly. "Obviously now's not the time, but if you'd like, we could schedule a modelling session . . ."

"Cloridan, shut up," I groaned.

"Or if you'd rather, I can probably arrange for some testimonials . . ."

[Greater Invisibility].

"OK, I can't hear you now," I said, "but I can still make out an outline." I went over and pulled the piton out of the door. "You take the lead with sneaking; I'll follow you. You've got those hand gestures. If you need to talk to me, get us somewhere we can't be overheard and make this gesture." I made a T with my hands.

Cloridan pointed at the corpse in the open cell and turned his palms face up. A question.

"Oh, when someone comes to strip you, they'll find that you've been killed for your armor and/or to silence you. They'll be looking for a thief—and this place is full of thieves. Let's take a seat, and wait."

I cast Greater Invisibility on myself again, and we settled in.

It really wasn't long before someone showed up, but it felt like forever. I was dying for some conversation—even Cloridan talking about his size—by the time someone came in the door. He took one look at the corpse and went running out of the room.

He left the door open, so I looked over at Cloridan to see if he wanted to use the opportunity. He did. We slipped outside and went exploring.

The thief that had opened the door went right, so we went left. We passed one door, which Cloridan listened to, then the corridor took a turn and opened into the sewer entrance we'd come in from. As I'd thought, there were two guards sitting down on a table placed right on the trap-door. There'd be no sneaking past them.

Cloridan took in the scene, and then turned back. The door was still open to the cell room, we could hear voices coming from inside.

"Just found him like this, haven't touched him!"

"Where are the keys?"

"They must have taken 'em."

Cloridan kept going. We went past another closed door, and continued up the corridor to where the boss must have come from. The corridor ended in a closed door.

Just before we got to it, Cloridan stopped and pointed at the ceiling. I looked up. The ceiling was different here. Instead of slabs of rock supported by wooden pillars, there was a wooden construct. It looked like a trapdoor, but I could only see rock between the spaces in the boards. Cloridan pointed at a lever on the wall, and then brought his hands down like he was playing a waterfall in a school play.

A deadfall! I realized, like the one that got us. Not a trap this time, but something they could deliberately trigger to cut off one part of the complex. I clapped Cloridan on the shoulder and we moved up to the door.

This was also closed, but it looked like it opened inward, so there was something I could try. I clapped Cloridan on the shoulder again and cast Static Image.

Nothing changed, as I had just cast an illusion of the door overlapping itself. Taking a quick look back to make sure there was no one to see, I unlatched the door and pulled it toward us.

Cloridan was confused when the door opened to reveal another door, but I pushed him through into the room beyond. This was an armory, but the more immediate concern was the guard.

He was stationed on the other side of the room, near some stairs, and he was looking puzzledly in our direction. It was the noise, I realized. The argument coming from down the hall was now audible to him.

Oops. I closed the door as quietly as I could, and the noise ceased. I'd attracted the guard's attention, though, and he wandered over with that puzzled look on his face.

Fortunately, the armory was quite open, and there was room for Cloridan and I to get out the way. I canceled Static Image as the guard slowly moved over. We leaned back against locked racks of weapons as the guard stood in front of the door, his head cocked.

He stood there long enough that the door eventually opened, revealing the boss.

"What are you doing?" she demanded.

"I, uh, heard a noise?" he replied.

"Was it me shouting? Then get back to your post."

He scuttled back to do as she said, and the two thieves headed upstairs, the boss reeling off names and what it was she wanted them to do. It sounded as though she was going to gather a bunch of people in the meeting room. We tried to follow them out, but her assistant was a bit too zealous in quickly closing the door. And locking it, from the sound of it. I backed down the stairs to get out of Cloridan's way. He looked at the guard and then pointed at the door.

I repeated my trick from before, hoping there wasn't anyone on the other side. There was a faint click as I opened the door, but the guard resolutely ignored it. I pushed Cloridan through again, and we moved on.

This time, Cloridan went as far as the door next to our old cell. He tried it, quietly, but it didn't move, so he knelt down and started doing something to the lock. *I guess they didn't find his lock picks.*

It wasn't long before he had the door open, and we quickly slipped inside. It was dark, so I carefully cast Light at a low level. Barrels were revealed all around us, and what looked like wine bottles. Cloridan made the timeout gesture.

"This looks like a wine cellar," he said, after we'd snuck into an out of the way corner. He pointed. "And that sounds like a tavern above. That meeting room she mentioned is probably in there."

"You think we can sneak out here?"

"Maybe. I was thinking you might want to listen in on the meeting, but it will be crowded. A better option might be above the armory—they should have fewer people there when the meeting is going on, and that seems like the leader's command post. We might find evidence there."

"That does sound like the best option. Where do we hide until the meeting?"

Cloridan grinned. "Where else but the cells?"

So we waited some more. We watched as a pair of thugs came in and carried Cloridan's corpse down to the sewers. We waited some more, and a small crowd hurried along the corridor, led by the angry boss. I tapped Cloridan on the shoulder to let him know I was paying attention, and we headed back to where they'd come from.

There was still a guard on the door. Cloridan gave me the gesture for "stay" and moved forward. The guard's attention was on the door at the top of the stairs—he never had a chance.

Your party has defeated Gradasso Compagnon – your experience share is 22 XP.

This was the first time I'd seen unarmed combat in action in this world—I hadn't even known Cloridan had the skill. He'd grappled the man from behind and pinned him until his struggles ceased. Keeping the man from crying out or making too much noise must have taken some doing. We dragged him to the side, and I placed a Static Image of a crate over him—it might buy us some time.

Cloridan then turned his attention to the lock, and in a minute, he had it open. We just had to hope there was no one on the other side.

The next room held . . . leather. Lots of leather, in various cuts—it seemed as if we were in a leatherworking workshop. We could hear activity from what I guessed was the shop front, but there were stairs going up, and that's where Cloridan headed.

Through *another* locked door, we found ourselves in a room much more richly furnished than I'd expect for a leatherworker. It looked like a primitive version of a CEO's office. There was a big desk for her to sit behind, and a low couch for her underlings to sit in while she yelled at them or whatever.

More importantly than that, there were papers. Letters, ledgers—we started going through them, when we were interrupted.

"Nobody's supposed to be up here while the meeting's on—Hey!" A thug standing in the door shouted in surprise to see his boss's papers going through themselves.

Oops. [Phantom World].

I'd hoped that this spell would incapacitate the man more thoroughly than Improved Blind, but it didn't work as well as I'd hoped. Taken by surprise, I went with the first illusion that came to my head—that he was falling through the sky. It had the advantage of being easy to do, just wind, blue sky, and the sensation of falling. It certainly terrified him, but I'd forgotten about the screaming.

I should have remembered about the screaming. The other problem was that he overbalanced as he flailed around and took a tumble. It turns out that when you take a hit that isn't accounted for in the illusion, it breaks.

Shit. So all I'd managed to do was knock him over and attract everyone's attention. I cast Phantasmal Entity.

"Something I can do for you, lad?" Archambault sneered, standing between us and the thug. I started grabbing papers and stuffing them under my tunic. If they were covered, the Invisibility spell would make them disappear. I was relieved to see Cloridan following my lead.

"You're the Illusionist—no, you're the *other* Illusionist!" the thug yelled from the floor, proving he wasn't so dumb. "And this is one of your illusions!"

"Think so?" Archambault said. He reached down and brought the guy to his feet. Amusingly, he was so shocked by Archambault's touch that he let him.

"What? You're real? You can't be?"

"I'm as real as anyone," Archambault declared. We weren't going to wait around for this discussion, though. Cloridan had found an exit. He unlatched the barred shutters and jumped through.

"It seems that I must depart. Do give my regards to your boss," Archambault said, fading out as I cut the spell. I was already out the window.

Jump skill, don't fail me now! Really, though, it was an easy jump. I rushed after Cloridan. We had escaped.

I N T E R R O G A T I O N

And what fortunate happenstance has brought you to my door?" Guillaume asked, as the tea was served.

"It occurred to me," I said carefully, "that one explanation for you not saying anything of consequence in four visits was that you were waiting for me to show enough interest to come visit *you*."

Guillaume smiled as he sipped his tea. We were sitting in his private sitting room, part of his suite in the castle. Needless to say, even as a mere ward of the Count, his room was furnished much more lavishly than mine.

"It is tradition for the woman to be the one pursued," he admitted. "However, I feel that the true criteria for that distinction is that the more powerful of the two parties should be the one pursuing."

"Flattering, but do you really think a commoner holds the power here? Or, in the city more generally?" I tried one of the biscuits he offered me. Delicious, of course. I was starving, but Charm kept it from showing. This meeting was happening . . . not *right* after our sewer adventure, but I'd been too busy to eat between then and now. Or wash, for that matter. I thanked whoever was responsible for Disguise that it covered the sense of smell.

"Of course," he said easily. "I may have noble blood, but I hold no title, or office, and am merely a ward of my betters. You, on the other hand . . ." He trailed off, perhaps hoping I would say something about myself. I raised an eyebrow and he shrugged.

"You, on the other hand, have swiftly moved to solidify a position among a leading guild. They've been very closemouthed about what you've done to earn that position, but it would be quite a coincidence if you didn't have something to do with the sudden availability of enchanted weapons."

I affected an innocent look, while I had Charm give me a countdown on how I long I had to wait to take the next biscuit.

He wasn't done, though. "Enchanter has a level five requirement, and requires that you have the skill," he mused. "All the other classes with the skill have even higher level requirements."

"A profession isn't the only way to get the skill," I pointed out.

"An unknown patron is even more frightening than a curiously humble Archmage," he countered. "You, at least, can offer assurances that you mean no harm, but can you say the same about a mysterious power that uses you as a cat's-paw?"

I grimaced. Well, this was a polite conversation. I creased my brow, ever so slightly, which was the equivalent.

"I should hope that my actions speak more loudly than any speculation about my intentions," I said calmly. "I've brought nothing but prosperity to those who have taken me in."

"Speaking, again, to the power you hold. You can bring prosperity, while I have no useful skills." He bowed his head, a token submission.

"Even if I was the most powerful between us, the fact is that you have a backer of your own."

"You are referring to my uncle?" he asked, smiling. He knew that I was not.

"Of course." It wasn't yet time to bring that up.

"Then perhaps we should contend on merely our own merits," he conceded. Contending for the position of "least powerful" didn't seem very useful to *me*, but the point here was to keep him talking, so whatever. "You haven't said, but it's quite common for those with the Enchanting skill to have an additional form of magic."

"It's not a requirement," I pointed out.

"Still," he insisted. "There are rumors of a mysterious Illusionist in town."

I gave him a look. "Are you referring to the rumors of the Illusionist who magicked up a horde of bandits to terrify . . ." I paused to fake my recollecting the name of the place. "Bourneby? I hope you're not accusing me of being in league with bandits?"

"Not at all! Have you not heard that there were two Illusionists in that fight? One saved the day by dispelling the miscreant's illusions."

"Unlikely," I scoffed. "If there was such a person, wouldn't they have shown up to be rewarded? Far more likely that the Illusionist turned on his companions, and invented the other one in case he failed."

He laughed. "That is an amusing thought. Bandits are a suspicious lot, so I'm sure they gave him a hard time. However." He sobered up suddenly. "If that were the case, the man would have also shown up for his reward from my uncle."

One of the . . . dozen knots of tension in my spine slowly released. He didn't mention the Thieves Guild. *He didn't know yet.*

> **[Conversation] Level 4 acquired through use.**
> **For gaining a skill level, you have been awarded 1 XP.**

I *thought* that we'd moved fast enough for word not to have reached him yet, but I hadn't been sure.

Time to give him something. "I suppose," I said idly, "that it might be possible a second Illusionist was in the village on their own business when it was attacked."

"How unfortunate . . . for the bandits."

"Were they really bandits, though?" I asked. "They must have been quite organized to have obtained help from a caster."

"You think they were part of some scheme?" he asked, his eyes narrowing. The conversation had gotten a bit dangerous for him, as—of course—they *were a* part of *his* scheme.

"Who can say?" I shrugged, releasing the pressure a bit. "But if they were, then this Illusionist might have spoiled it just because they didn't know what was going on."

"Two ships . . . colliding in the night." He looked at me doubtfully. "And what do you think that second Illusionist's goals might have been?"

"Well, I'm sure *I* don't know," I admonished him. He flushed with embarrassment at his gaffe. *That had practically been a direct question. Foul!*

"It seems likely, though . . ." I said, letting him off the hook. Or maybe this was giving him line? "That if they were new in town, and had just stumbled on to a scheme involving major players, they would take steps to make sure they didn't step on any toes again."

"That would only be natural," he said. I could practically see his mind racing. "And would they—" He cut himself off before he asked a second direct question. "I'm sure that the major players would be interested in any input or direct aid he could give."

We looked at each other, not saying anything, each of us knowing what the other wanted. I smiled. Persuasion was starting to kick in. You couldn't just hit someone with the skill; you actually had to have *persuasive* reasons.

If you framed it right, they identified the pressure they felt as their own feelings. Guillaume wasn't bad at the skill either, which made it harder. But I was better.

I changed the subject, the better to keep him from realizing what had happened. "I'm surprised that you're willing to have this discussion here. Aren't you worried about eavesdropping servants?" *Spies of your target, your uncle,* I didn't say. Nor did I say: *This is a dangerous conversation.* Both messages were received clearly, though.

"I've lived all my life in this castle," he said smiling. This was solid conversational ground for him, and it put him at ease. "I know where all the hiding holes are."

"Then tell me, what are you offering?" Sudden directness. We were conspirators now, in a safe place.

"I can't offer anything right now . . ." he said helplessly. I suspect if I was the mercenary I was pretending to be, I would have walked out of there. Instead, I just gave a slight frown. "But I don't need you to take any action! Just don't interfere in anything until the Autumn Ball."

"That's when it's going down?" I asked, and he nodded. "I'm *attending* the ball, did you forget?"

"You'll be fine! The guests are witnesses," he assured me. "None of them are going to be hurt. And afterward, well, I'll have need of people. I'll be able to pay, grant titles even, to the right people."
Because I'll be the Count, *he didn't say.*

"Are you sure it will still work?" I asked. "The Count surely knows there are no demons by now."

"That part was only a distraction anyway." He shrugged. "It will be less effective, but the townsfolk will still believe what they see rather than what Uncle tells them."

"I heard the story," I said. I needed to deepen the emotional connection. "How your father used to be the Count."

His eyes narrowed. "Uncle Lowell should have been my regent, ruling only until I came of age. But that wasn't enough for him."

"You've been planning all this since then?"

"There was nothing I could do as a child," he said bitterly. "Nothing that I could do even now, without . . . help."

Not quite time yet.

"He has heirs, though. Are you really going to . . ."

"It's the only way." He looked away, ashamed. These were his family members he was talking about. People he'd grown up with. I was pretty sure there were a few younger children in that family as well. "To restore me . . . to restore justice. Someone else will . . . be taking care of that part."

"Your backer. The one behind this. What are *they* getting out of it?" I tightened the screws ever so slightly on Persuasion.

"My loyalty. I'll swear to Duke Victor, but my loyalties will lie elsewhere," he said. "That's why I can't offer anything now. I could take this to him, but we're so close to the event, I'm not sure he'd even give me an answer before the day."

"Hmm," I said, pretending to think about it. "Fine, but I need reassurance. Who is he?"

"Duke Finley," he said. Immediately, he knew he'd made a mistake.

> **You have defeated Guillaume Duvost in a Tier 2 Social Contest! You have earned 40 XP.**

Conversation was the art of getting information without asking questions, and without getting answers. Persuasion was rarely so subtle.

I sighed, and canceled Greater Invisibility. Guillaume jumped as Count Duvost appeared in the room. He'd been here all along, of course.

"What—what's going on? Sir." Guillaume tried to look innocent, but he knew the game was up.

"We raided the Thieves Guild," I said. "Found out you were their contact for the money they'd been receiving to smuggle in and hide the mercenaries."

I looked over at the Count. "I didn't get an Intrigue notification or anything."

"Nor will you," he said, looking sternly at his nephew. "The Intrigue is between myself and the Duke of Arryen. And it is not yet over."

He looked at me. "Your part is, though. You can go."

I curtsied, took one last look at Guillaume, and left. The guards were just outside.

DANCING

Aubert put the three bags of money on the table.

"This feels familiar," Cloridan said, sweeping up his bag and checking inside. "Once again we're getting paid before the job is complete."

"My father feels we've done enough," Aubert said without expression.

"Your dad hasn't tracked down half of those mercenaries that were supposed to be hidden around the place," Janie said. She also didn't let her concerns stop her from grabbing a bag.

"Nevertheless, with their main contact gone, and their headquarters compromised, Father doesn't think they'll be in a position to make a move during the ball."

"What's going to happen to him?" I asked.

Aubert's controlled expression got a bit gloomier. "Father is going to ask the King for his judgment. He has the right to do it himself, but it looks better for him, and he can accuse Duke Finley of being the one who caused it."

The three of us looked at each other. "Will that go anywhere?" I asked.

"Probably not," Aubert said sourly. "The testimony of a traitor isn't enough to hang a Duke. But it will cost him at Court. I should mention that if any premature mention of the Duke's involvement should get out, it would hurt both my family's plans and the Duke's reputation. It's not likely to go well for anyone spreading rumors."

"We're all sworn to keep our mouths shut on this subject anyway," I murmured, and the others nodded. Aubert sighed and changed the subject.

"I would request of you, Mistress Kandis, leave from my training until after the ball. My father wants me to devote my attention to securing the guests."

"You don't want us to help?" I asked. "We've been the ones chasing up leads so far."

"You've done enough," Aubert said. "Truly, we're grateful, and Father will keep you on retainer, but he'd like you to take a break."

"He's the boss," I said. "I guess I'll see you at the ball."

Aubert nodded, bowed, and took his leave.

"He doesn't seem all that happy, for all the help we gave," Janie said. With Aubert gone, her grin came out.

"That's his cousin we put away," I said.

Cloridan shrugged. "The gratitude of nobles isn't worth much at the best of times. Are we actually going to stop working on this?"

"Spy rings don't exactly take a break," I said. "But on the other hand, I don't fancy chasing down humans in town without legal protection. Best leave that to the guards."

"Spy stuff, boo," Janie said without heat. "What about delving?"

"We won't have a frontline without Aubert—and we won't be getting his free entry, either," I pointed out. "It's only for a week or so; can you hold out that long?"

"I suppose so." Janie pouted. "It's not like I'm skint." She hefted her new money pouch.

Elodie got out of the carriage before me, a necessary precaution to ensure I got out safely. It wasn't that I was fragile, but my dress was another matter. It wasn't as ridiculously ornate or expansive as some that I'd seen in period dramas—society had not yet gotten to that stage yet, it seemed. There were petticoats involved, but no wires. I had convinced Didiane that my bra was superior to a corset, so I also didn't have to deal with any breathing problems.

I did have to deal with not seeing my feet, though. That was what Elodie was for, to hold my hand and warn me if my feet were going off the steps. At least I didn't have to worry about heels.

Elodie had our letter inviting us, but the guards seemed aware of who we were and waved us through. It was a short walk to the main hall, where the ball was being held.

It was . . . a somewhat glittering assembly. My standards were a bit spoiled from the few times I'd attended a company party put on by the partners, but seeing as this world hadn't invented disco lighting and glitter body paint, they were putting on a good show.

The lights were . . .

> **[Identification] : Brilliant Sconce – Quality: Great – Properties: Enchantment (Generate Light)**

OK, so they were actually enchanted. They must have been heirlooms, because they hadn't come through me. I did a quick count and calculation and was appalled at the amount they'd spent just on lighting the place. It did look good, though. There was a lot of silver in the decorations, which took the brilliance and reflected it back at us.

I took my place in line, Elodie going ahead to scout out the drink situation. She'd be shuttling back and forth keeping me hydrated and generally taking care of me. In the line ahead of me were what were clearly a noble couple. From the amount of gems sewn into the lady's dress, I guessed their rank at baron.

I curtsied as soon as they noticed me, but etiquette demanded that they got to speak first—if they decided to acknowledge me at all.

"Why, aren't you the loveliest thing!" That was the lady, exclaiming with delight. "Isaac, can you believe this? She puts us ladies all to shame!"

"She doesn't hold a candle to you, my dear," he replied, shooting me a scornful look. I wasn't sure if it was actual disdain, or if he was just pandering to his wife. He was older than her, with a bit of gray in her hair, but he was still in good shape.

"Oh, what do you know, you flatterer," she said, but she was clearly pleased by the compliment. "Do tell us who you are, my dear," she said to me.

"I'm Kandis Hammond, a Senior Member in the Ironworkers Guild," I said, curtsying again. "I'm very pleased to make your acquaintance."

"You're an ironworker? But you don't look a thing like a blacksmith!"

"I'm pleased you phrased it that way, my lady. Our feud with the Blacksmith Guild is long running, and I would have been quite insulted if you'd said I *did* look like a blacksmith."

She laughed delightedly. "I'm sure you would have been! Allow me to introduce my husband here. He is Baron Isaac Harper, and I am his lovely wife Rachel."

I curtsied again, to be curtly acknowledged by the Baron. Rachel took my arm as I rose. "Now, you *must* tell me how a delightful girl like yourself became such an important member of your guild."

"I'm afraid it's not that interesting. I just had a certain set of skills that the Guild Master determined to be of value to the Guild. Are you and the Baron in service to Count Duvost?"

"Oh no, dear," she said. "We're from north of here, under Earl Rankin."

"You've come a long way for a party, then."

"Well, it's all part of being a noble. You've got to keep up relations with all the other nobles. In this case, we're representing our Earl and his friendly intentions to the dear Count."

At this point, another noble couple joined at the end of the line. I curtsied but they chose to ignore me, which was fortunate, because Lady Rachel was intent on bending my ear all the way to the Count.

Ahead of us, I could see Gustave exchanging greetings with the Count. Strains of Pachelbel floated down the line, catching the attention of just about everyone.

So the sales pitch has begun, I thought. *Good—Undead Bane sales were starting to dry up.* Even if they were a great weapon for this Dungeon, there were only so many people in the town that needed one.

It wasn't long before I had my turn in front of the Count.

"My lord," I said, curtsying.

"Mistress Hammond," he nodded. "Have you found the tutoring profession to your liking?"

"It's been a challenge, my lord, and I'm not sure about the results." I hesitated, worrying about what to say before listeners. "Some of what occurred was outside of my intended curriculum."

"That's life," the Count said bleakly. "Things never go as planned. We'll talk later about this, but for now—enjoy the party."

I curtsied again and moved along. Respects paid, I was now free to mingle. Where and with whom was the problem. Gustave was one of the few here that I knew, and he was rapidly gathering a crowd of music lovers to show off my device to. I wanted to stay far away from there, but if I moved too close to the musicians, I'd surely get pestered for a dance.

That wasn't the worst of fates, but most of my potential dance partners were young nobles. Younger than me, arrogant, with nothing to lose and everything to prove. Aubert was enough to have put me off the breed.

Aubert was one solution. I could presumably just order him to keep the wolves off me, but while I was looking for him, I saw another potential safe port. A man stood on his own in a small bubble of space. The other guests seemed to be avoiding coming near enough to be forced to interact with him.

At first, I thought he was a guard, or a servant, but he stood with a drink in hand, and was far too richly dressed. All in black silk, he cut an elegant, if intimidating figure. The old me might have been intimidated, but that me hadn't gone up against a vampire.

His attention was on me as soon as I made to cross the invisible line keeping the other guests away, but he made no move to stop me as I approached.

"Doesn't it defeat the purpose of cut silk, if it's all in black?" I asked.

"I'm sorry, but I'm not sure I take your meaning," he replied.

"Your jacket." I gestured. "The point of cut silk is to have it in different colors so that you can show how many layers you can afford. There's no point if it's all in black."

His lips twitched, and he turned his head to carefully consider his jacket arms.

"I assure you, dear lady," he said, turning back to me, "that the layers are in slightly *different* shades of black."

I giggled, surprising myself. Charm at work. "That's not exactly *showing*," I protested.

He shrugged. "In truth, dear lady, my clothes are chosen and provided by my master. I believe that he put priority on the theme, instead of impressing others with the wealth of his servants."

"Your master?" I asked, confused.

"Permit me to introduce myself," he took a step back and bowed. "Tom Parkes, of the Ebon Order."

"Then your master . . ."

"Is Aghen Shadthe, the Ice Arcanist," he said easily. He watched for my reaction.

So that was why he was all alone, I thought. I'd heard of Shadthe and his Order. Shadthe was a powerful magician, at level eight in the book that I'd read about him. The Ebon Order was a fancy name for "Shadthe's minions"—his solution to not being able to be everywhere at once. They sought out things he wanted and spoke with his voice. A chill ran through me, as I realized that Shadthe was exactly the kind of person that Milly had warned me about. Charm came to my rescue and kept my reaction under control.

"How intriguing! I'm Kandis Hammond, Senior Member in the Ironworkers Guild."

That didn't mean I had no reaction. I understood now why he had a bubble around him. *Anyone* would have some sort of reaction to finding out who his master was. So I let a little shock show, along with some excitement and . . . interest?

I needed a reason to keep talking with him, after all. It was better he thought that I was attracted to dangerous men than realize that I was pumping him for information on his master. That was a job for Seduction, a skill I didn't have, but the Socialite bonus gave me a decent effect total.

"I didn't think that High Mages interacted with the nobility," I said.

"It's in the interest of both sides to keep up friendly, if distant, relations," he replied. He gave me a speculative look, curious that I hadn't immediately made an excuse to leave. "My master is usually invited to events like these, with the understanding he probably won't show. When one of his agents is in the area, we attend in his name and make a polite showing."

"And what brings you to the Duchy of Bargougne?" I asked.

"Actually, my business was to the north. In Arryen," he said, watching me closely. A small free-town called Oakway."

FENCİNG

Oakway? I don't believe I've heard of it," I said, my voice steady.

"It's a little soon for news to be widespread," Parkes replied, "but they've recently had their Dungeon core stolen."

"That's what you were doing there?" I asked incredulously. "Am I standing next to a criminal?"

"No, your respectability remains intact," he reassured me. "I arrived after the crime."

"Rumors do say that wizards like your master have a habit of taking cores," I mused. "And you say you showed up before news of the crime had spread?"

"It would be more accurate to say that wizards who *want* to be like my master hunt for cores. I was looking for someone."

"Why? What do they do with them?" I asked. I'd much rather hear about cores than who he was hunting for.

"I'm afraid you'll have to ask them," he said. "I can't comment."

I made a moue. "If you're not going to spill the secrets of the wise, then what am I doing here?" I said jokingly.

He chuckled indulgently. "Well, I suppose I can let a few things slip."

"Oh?"

"This will be common knowledge soon anyway," he said, leaning in. "The gods have chosen Champions again."

I made myself pause, as if I had to think about what he was talking about. The Champions were well known, but it had been 200 years since they last appeared.

"The Champions?" I asked. "Is that who you were looking for?"

He nodded.

"Why?"

"Champions are only summoned when the gods have some change they want to make in the world," he said. "The powers in this world have a vested interest in finding out what that change is going to be—or shaping it."

"Not stopping it?" I asked. "I'd have thought they'd want to keep things as they are."

"No one is ever *entirely* happy with the status quo," he told me. "There's always something they think could be improved."

"So you were there to . . ."

"Make contact, and invite them to meet with my master."

"Is that all?" I asked doubtfully, "And how did that go?"

"Alas, by the time I got there, she was already gone, along with the Dungeon core. Half the town is blaming the guilds, half some mystery ranked wizard—they're probably still arguing."

"She?" I said idly, but there was a metallic taste in my mouth. Turns out playing cat and mouse with the hunters isn't as fun as they make it seem in the movies.

"If the reports are to be trusted," he said. "Which they can't, because they also suggest that they're an Illusionist."

"How interesting," I said. "Do you know, there's supposed to be an Illusionist causing trouble in *this* town."

"I had heard that when I arrived here," he said. "Quite a coincidence, no?"

"I suppose one of your duties is to keep an ear out for local rumors."

"Indeed. I've been here a few days, and there's a lot to be heard. Can I assume that you're the mysterious Enchantress that everyone is talking about?"

"Oh, for . . . what are people saying about me now?" I protested.

"Nothing bad," he assured me. "Some are calling you the Enchantress because they believe you're the source of the Guild's new product, while others assume that you've enchanted the Guild Master, but all of them agree about your beauty."

I blushed, and wished that I had a fan to hide behind. Why didn't I? An oversight. I thought about correcting it, and then blushed harder. *Yes, Kandis, go ahead and cast Illusion Magic in front of the guy looking for an Illusionist!*

"Incidentally," Parkes said, "may I commend your on your Odierian? You speak it like a native."

Fuck, what? As soon as he said it, I realized he'd switched languages on me three sentences ago. Gift of Tongues had compensated so smoothly that I hadn't even noticed.

This must be like *Finding Worldwalker Tricks 101*, and I fell for it. Wait, were there any other language tricks in our conversation? *I invoked Memorize—no, this was the only other language, but . . .*

"Thank you, but I've never heard it called that," I said. "When I learned it, it was called Lyran."

"Ah, my mistake, I always get those two mixed up," he said. In *Odierian.* I kept my face blank.

"I'm sorry, but you have the advantage of me there," I said. "Was that Odierian?"

"Yes," he said, giving me a speculative look. I needed to change the subject before he started asking me questions about . . . Lyrar. I knew the names because that was part of the language, but I didn't have the faintest idea of where the country was or what the language was . . .

"Do you think this local Illusionist is your Worldwalker, then?"

"It's unlikely. This has the feel of a plot more than a few weeks in the making."

"Then why did you come here? Weren't you hunting the Illusionist?"

"Ha! No. Unless you're a priest of Tondeni, hunting an Illusionist is asking to go on a never-ending series of wild goose chases. Making friendly overtures to nobles is a much better use of my time."

"So . . . Lord Shadthe has just given up?"

"He prefers *Arcanist* Shadthe," he corrected me. "And no, but learning what magic they've chosen has changed our approach."

"Oh?"

"An Illusionist works through people," he explained. "It's a little reassuring, we don't have to worry about them descending on Master's Ice Tower riding a dragon and flinging fireballs. Instead of watching for the Champion, you watch for changes in the people."

"And so you're maintaining your contacts with the nobles."

"Exactly. Of course, being the sort of person that works with people, the Champion may well decide to contact us on their own. My master has considerable resources, both material and arcane."

He paused briefly. "Speaking of which, I understand you're in the market for magical texts?"

"How did you know that?" I managed to not raise my voice, but Charm struggled to contain my alarm.

"My apologies; I made inquiries after I heard about the Enchantress. Booksellers aren't priests; they're happy to talk for a few silvers."

"It's starting to feel like you're stalking me," I said uneasily.

"That wasn't my intent," he said. "If I hadn't encountered you here, I was planning on making a social call. I just wanted to offer my assistance." He held out a small black card.

"What is this?" I asked, taking and examining it. As far as Identify and Sense Mana could tell me, it was just an ordinary card. Embossed in silver was an address in Dorsay.

"My master's mail drop in this country. If you wish to contact him, you can send a letter to this address."

"Why would I—why would your master want to correspond with me?" I asked.

"As I said, he has the magical texts you're looking for. He won't part with them, but access can be negotiated."

"What would the price be?" I asked suspiciously.

"Obviously, money isn't a concern for him. I suspect someone with as many interesting rumors about her as you do will be able to find something to interest him."

I made the card disappear into one of the dress's hidden pockets. One of the good things about having your dress made from scratch for an exorbitant rate was that you can insist on a few customizations.

"I'm starting to think you might deserve the wide berth everyone's giving you."

"I apologize again; I was just gathering information to find out what might interest you. I'll take my leave." He bowed and slowly backed away. I didn't have the courage to stop him, even if it meant he was making an opening for my erstwhile suitors.

Surely he just *suspected—he can't know.* For my part, I didn't know if he was serious about not hunting me.

Elodie arrived at my side then, with a drink and a look of shock and awe.

"That was Dark Winter's man!" she hissed. "Do you know him? Was Dark Winter your . . . teacher?"

Oh, God. This was going to be another rumor, wasn't it?

"No, and feel free to tell *anyone* who asks that," I insisted. "He's just another person who is *far more interested* in me than I would like."

Elodie blinked, and then handed me my drink. "Maybe you should try to be less interesting, then?"

I laughed, almost spilling my drink. "Well, you have me there," I admitted. "Have you seen Aubert?"

"No, and I've been looking. He should have been standing behind his father for the greetings." She saw someone coming from behind me, curtsied, and faded away.

I turned to greet the newcomer as he confidently approached. He was dark and somewhat handsome, lacking only tall from the trifecta.

"I'm Marcel d'Marleau, the son of the Baron there," he said. "You're very pretty, for a commoner. I'll allow you to dance with me."

It wasn't a question. I felt the wave of pressure coming off his skill—and felt it crash against my Charisma.

"Intimidation?" I asked scornfully. "Really?"

Since he'd started it, I fired up my own skill. My total wasn't *that* much greater than his own—I think his skill was higher—but close counts for nothing.

"Do you have *any* idea of who you're insulting?" I asked. Just a random statement, but it had the weight of my own Intimidate behind it. It shocked him, set him back, and then the notification came.

> **You have defeated Marcel d'Marleau in a Tier 3 Social Contest! You have earned 20 XP.**

Level four, then, the same as me. I smirked at him and neglected to waive the penalty. Going down so easily, he must have had no willpower at all. Odd that willpower wasn't an Ability.

Fuck it, I thought, and stuck my hand in my pocket.

[Phantasmal Object]. I pulled the fan out and covered my face. Fans weren't in fashion, so I had embraced the anachronism and summoned an exquisite Japanese fan I'd seen in a museum. I used it to cover my shit-eating grin as I stared Marcel down. He'd lost the contest, so there was nothing for him to do but retreat, which he managed with a modicum of grace.

What a maroon, I thought as he backed away. Tom had made my heart beat faster without needing to resort to any skills . . . wait.

Tom? Why am I on a first name basis with a guy who might want to kidnap or kill me? Did he use Seduction on me?

I tried to think about this calmly. I hadn't got a notification, so I was in the clear, right? Only . . . I wasn't sure if Seduction *did* give a notification. Bargain didn't. It seemed like it would be a bit of a buzzkill to get a notification of your loss right before you went to bed with someone.

Another thought struck me. You only got a notification when the Social Contest was over . . . so there might not be one if he hadn't given up.

Or, my heart might have been thumping because I was as scared as hell during half of that conversation, and because he was tall, mature, self-confident without being arrogant . . . *Arrggh!*

I needed to seduce someone to see how this worked. No. I needed to ask someone about it. I couldn't ask a guy . . . I couldn't see myself asking a girl, either. Books were no use. I needed to talk to . . . Mr. Parkes again and see if I ended up in bed? . . . No. That was definitely a dumb idea.

Priests were supposed to give advice, right? The Nature goddess had an . . . earthy reputation. Maybe I could talk with one of her priests? Of course, I'd been avoiding the gods and their followers for a reason . . .

It was then that I heard Aubert's voice call out. "Ladies and gentlemen, your attention, please."

I looked over to the musicians' platform, where Aubert was standing, trying to look relaxed. "We've had word from the walls that the city is under attack."

Oh, thank God, I thought.

POÏSOΠ

◆

I'd ask everyone to keep calm," Aubert called out over the sudden increase in noise. "We have intelligence on the attackers, and everything we know suggests that this hall is not the target. Despite that, we have extra protection for you all, and this hall is the safest place that we can arrange. That is all."

As he stepped down, there was a further increase in the hubbub, and quite a few people sought more personal reassurance. Not from Aubert, but from the Count, who was still holding court at one end of the room. Between his relative unimportance and his sullen glare, Aubert discouraged most of the guests from questioning him further.

That didn't apply to me, of course. "Did you manage to get the plan out of him?" I asked. He must have really enjoyed his week of freedom from me, because I could see the resignation settling over him as I spoke.

"Some of it, at least," he admitted in a low voice. "There were to be two attacks on the walls, and further incidents inside, with the intent of driving the citizens to riot from fear of demons."

"That's pretty much what we knew already," I said.

He nodded. "Guillaume was supposed to . . ." he took a breath. "Was supposed to open a gate to a third force that would enter the fortress and kill my family."

"How much of it have we spoiled?"

"Not enough," he said bitterly. "We think we've captured most of the forces inside the city from the notes you extracted from the Thieves Guild. They weren't involved in hiding the forces out of town, and we failed to find them. The Illusionist hasn't been seen since the village attack, though, so those attackers are just normal men."

"Wait, that means—"

"There's no chance of them breaching the wall—or of being the distraction that the plotters hoped."

"Then why are they even attacking?"

"We don't know," he said, making a sour face. "It could be that they just haven't been told to stop. Or the plan may have been adjusted."

"The Illusionist," I realized. "If he's not with the attackers . . ."

"He's somewhere," he agreed. "If we're lucky, he's gone, but I'm not that lucky." He had to excuse himself at that point, to reassure a noble who had come up asking for more details.

"The worst place for him to be would be right here," I mused softly to myself. "Helping hide an assassination attempt on those two." I idly cast Dispel Image on the noble to no effect. I didn't have the mana to cast it on everyone here, but I could probably manage everyone who came close to Aubert.

Invisibility would be harder to deal with, but I knew that moving around a crowded hall would be hell if you were invisible. Better to be disguised as a guest. Or a servant. I cast Dispel Image again, this time on a servant who happened to be wandering by.

"Stay here," Aubert said, apparently forgetting who was in charge. "I'm going to get further updates from the wall."

I nodded agreeably, but ignored what he said and followed after him. The nobles had mostly gathered in a protective huddle in the middle of the hall, with the men on the outside, guarding. All of the men, and a few of the women, were armed with a small-sword—a kind of short rapier. Commoners like myself weren't permitted to carry arms openly, but no one had searched me. I doubted Tom Parkes was as defenseless as he appeared. No one was wearing armor, of course, so I'm sure everyone was feeling a little vulnerable.

Really, Aubert had been right when he said this was the safest place. I'm sure there was such a thing as a lazy noble who relied on his guards, but most of them were deadly fighters. I still wasn't sure how Leadership worked, but it gave them a levelling edge. Not to mention their own private Dungeons to grind.

Aubert skirted that main group, moving along the edge of the hall, through the servants and the few commoners who were attending. Most of them gave him a wide berth. I followed at a discreet distance and cast Dispel Image on those who didn't.

[Dispel Image]. A noble who had separated from the pack and wanted to go see the fighting.

[Dispel Image]. A Guild Master (not mine) who wanted word of what was happening in the city.

[Dispel Image]. A serving girl—apparently well known to Aubert—who wanted reassurance.

[Dispel Image]. A servant whose face just changed. *What?*

Aubert actually reacted first. His attention must have been drawn by the sudden face change, but his gaze flicked down to the knives that had also appeared, no longer covered by the disguise spell.

"Assassin!" Aubert screamed, backing away from the false servant and drawing his sword. The assassin, realizing his cover was blown, cursed and lunged at Aubert, a dagger appearing in his hand. I cast another spell. It had a short range, but Aubert had backed up—right on top of me.

[Phantasmal Object]. In an instant, a cuirass of steel appeared around the lordling's torso. Just in time to block the assassin's dagger.

The way my Phantasmal Objects worked was a little weird when it came to armor. The way armor worked was that it took off a flat amount of damage from hits. If that wasn't enough to negate the blow, then the weapon would find its way through a gap, or just go *through* the armor. Which sounds impossible, I know, but things were different here. I'd watched Cloridan stab my darksteel dagger straight through a steel *ingot*, so I think it was fair to say regular Earth rules didn't apply.

With Phantasmal armor like this, what happened was that the attacker did full damage to the *object*. He still had to overcome the defender's total to hit, but as long as he managed that, he got to do full damage to it, without any reduction from the defender's efforts. If the damage was more than my spell effect total, the spell ended and the object disappeared. But that was it. There was no knock-back or follow-through. The weapon just stopped at the edge of where the armor had been, and physics could just take a running jump.

That's what happened this time. It was quite disconcerting to experience. The assassin froze; the uncanny grace that he'd used to avoid Aubert's defense deserted him for a second as he tried to work out what had just happened.

Aubert wasn't fazed. He'd been around when we were working out the rules and took the opportunity to deliver a nasty thrust to his would-be killer. It felt to me as though that should have killed the man, but . . . hit points. He probably still had more than half. Around us were a lot of people screaming or drawing swords, but for the moment, no one was approaching.

My turn now. *[Blind]*. The bubble of darkness that appeared around his head was enough to turn the tables. To judge from that first blow, the assassin had been the better fighter, but losing his sight gave the edge to Aubert. His blade flicked out again, sliding past the feeble attempts at parries by the assassin. Without sight, the assassin's return strikes were just as ineffective. It wasn't long before I got the notification.

> **Your party has killed Burrell Allaire – your experience share is 125 XP.**

Level five, I thought. Aubert looked down at his fallen opponent. Then he looked up again, a sudden realization coming to him.

"Father!" He took off running toward the dais. The dais where, I now realized, another fight was going on. I took a moment to look at the daggers.

> **[Identification] : Gray Hand Athame (2) – Quality: Excellent – Properties: Darksteel, Poisoned**

Maybe I'll just take these, make sure they don't fall into the wrong hands. Not that I'm an assassin or anything. I took the time to gather the scabbards. I had the feeling that it was too late to intervene in the Count's fight.

Sure enough, it was all over when I got there. I joined the crowd and worked my way through to the front of the ring. No one—except for Aubert and a few nobles who'd joined in the fight—was coming close. The assassin was clearly dead, but Count Duvost had taken a wound. Given that these guys were fighting with poisoned blades, that didn't bode well.

I went to speak up about the poison, but they already knew. Healers were being called for, and Aubert was cradling his father, as if to hear his last words. I didn't want to watch this. I wanted to leave, but there was an attack and a potential riot outside. Leaving would have looked suspicious at best.

I could back away at least, so I did so. A number of others had the same idea, and the ring of onlookers thinned as the Healers arrived and tried to save the Count. They quickly decided to move him, and they soon left, Aubert and his mother going with them.

That left the rest of the party hanging. Unable to leave, unwilling to have a good time. It was two long hours before word came that the Count had succumbed to poison. With that, the party was definitively over.

"You saved me last night," Aubert said flatly. It was the next day, and I'd been summoned to the County Court. That sounds like I was getting a traffic fine, but it was really a cut-rate throne room, where the Count sat and dispensed his judgments. Aubert was sitting on the throne. We weren't alone, but it was just a few functionaries—no official audience.

"You don't sound too pleased about that," I said warily. Obviously, he was upset about his father, but you'd think he'd be a tiny bit pleased.

"You should have saved my father."

I shrugged. "I was *near* you. There were too many people around him—there was no way I could have cast the spell enough times."

"Perhaps," he said. "I can't deny you've done a great service for the House of Duvost. Some sort of reward must be given. I'll think on it."

"If you must," I said. "I'm not such a mercenary to require a reward from stopping a f- . . . someone I know from being murdered in front of me."

"Honor demands it," he said, his mouth twisted as if he was eating a lemon. He paused. He didn't look happy, but that was understandable. "I'm only acting as Count until my status is confirmed by the King. That means I must make a trip to the capital. I won't be able to leave for a fortnight, and it will probably be another four weeks before I can return."

He took a deep breath. "When I return, I don't want you to be in my city. You've got that long to settle your affairs and move on."

"You're kicking me out?" I exclaimed, outraged. "After saving your life?"

"I don't like you, Mistress Hammond," he said. "Not since the first time you humiliated me, and not when my father made me listen to you. Every time I've seen you, it's been either personally humiliating . . . or worse."

"Your father thought you needed that," I said. "It wasn't my idea."

"Well, he's not here anymore," he said through gritted teeth. "And now I don't want you here, either. Don't let me see you again."

You have been defeated in a Tier 2 Social Contest. You may not act against the winner for one day.

ABOUT THE AUTHOR

Christopher Hall, also known as Maxlex, is the author of the Phantasm series. Hall started writing his first novel while sailing the Tyrrhenian Sea one summer, the salty night air flavoring and enriching his worldbuilding. Since then, he has continued to hone his craft while holding down diverse jobs in metalworking, marketing, perfume sales, and briefly, modeling. In addition to writing, Hall's interests include illuminated lettering and artisanal brewing. He endeavors to convey a sense of l'esprit in all his creative pursuits.

Podium
DISCOVER
STORIES UNBOUND
PodiumAudio.com

www.ingramcontent.com/pod-product-compliance
Lightning Source LLC
Chambersburg PA
CBHW021812110726
47902CB00006B/1751